Thy Will Be Done

Rod Warkentin

Dedicated to those who inspired me, believed in me and gave me the freedom to ask the questions that made me face my own beliefs.

There is no God Above man,

Man has the right to live by his own law,

To live in the way that he wills,

To work as he will,

To play as he will,

To rest as he will,

To die when and how he will.

Aleister Crowley

Foreword

I am the greatest of the fallen. I take comfort in my position for I am no less bound by ego than you. Long ago I was filled with anger and rage at the situation I found myself in. Demoted, if you will, from my rightful place, no longer sitting on the right hand of the throne, he had cast me aside for I had discovered the Left Hand Path. His ego, being fully out of control, had decided that there was no room in his Kingdom for independent thinkers like me. That could not be tolerated for there was only one way, one light if you will, and that was His.

It might not have mattered had the place not been so ordinary. The boredom was excruciating. It was all well and good if you were like the angel Michael, a hopeless sycophant. "Yes, Lord it is good," was his reply to everything.

He was devoid of opinion this archangel. Quite a ridiculous looking character as well. Michael was hardly the perfect specimen of an angel that your Biblical paintings portray. He was small and rather un-proportioned. His lips too thin, his nose quite large and red, as if he had misspent his youth on the consumption of sacrificial wine. God though, loved him completely, for there is no King without his courtiers.

I could not be counted on to be without opinion for I thought it good that I challenged Him. How could He not understand that I was playing a role? Challenging his every idea in order to have Him reflect on it, rethink it, and return more determined than ever that it was right. I was the original Devil's Advocate, if you will.

So stubborn was He, He would have none of it. It was His downfall really, one that would perpetuate itself throughout history, cause the downfall of His empire, and inevitably bring about my Glory! My Glory. Yes, that is exactly what it is and it is old Glory, for I have ruled my kingdom since the dawn of Man.

I am not an autocratic ruler. Rather I have many close advisers whom I call on frequently. Their advice is invaluable in my ever-changing world. I sometimes think that without them I might lose control of the minions.

Aamon, my most trusted advisor, is my successor, for he has assisted me in times of great trouble. It was he who saw the error of my ways in dealing with Christ. I thought with all my powers I could tempt him into my realm and bring him into the fold. It is the most embarrassing page in my storied history.

Only Aamon could see the error of my ways and bring about an acceptable solution. "Christ could not be tempted, his resolve too great, "Aamon argued". It was the others that would be his undoing. They were easy too manipulate. They fell prey to their insecurities", he said.

It could be done with the blood of the Christ on their hands. This solution was so perfect that I could not contain myself and I began to laugh, quietly at first, and then unabashedly. The tears rolled down my cheeks. Aamon blushed feeling that I had found his solution anything but perfect.

"You are a genius, Aamon!" I howled, still in the glow of this epiphany". History, your history, has painted me as the Antichrist and I still find it terribly amusing for I did not kill him. You did.

So easily have I manipulated you to do my bidding. But for some reason you are unable or unwilling to see it. The Hitler's of this world are beyond my control as hard as this might be to believe. They exist independently of any God. It is the quiet conspirators, those who wish not to know, who are so easily controlled. "I didn't see anything". "They were always friendly and nice to me "." I thought that was the smell of burning leaves".

Your own fear of association has caused all of you to do my work for me. You work for me. Oh, you can carry on, praying for your souls, but they is all wasted words. God gave up on all of you hundreds, maybe, thousands of years ago. There are No Vacancy signs on every road to Heaven. You are just too blind to see them. Or maybe too scared? Pathetic is an appropriate word for the likes of you. Follow the Dictator blindly for you've been doing it since the beginning and you hope he doesn't turn his wrath on you for then you will be alone. It's too late to follow me for I have seen you for what you are, sheep, and sheep are to be eaten.

The Council of Seven that I have employed to do my bidding is at this very moment taking human form, to be among you, to learn your ways, to understand your motivations. They will create a game for you like you've never seen. You will question all that you believed to be true. You will fear the afterlife, as you should, for there are no Chosen Ones. The Chosen Ones are already there and have been forever. You have been used by God to justify his own existence. Pawns, in an egomaniac's chess game. He has tried to hide your destiny from the beginning. Adam and Eve were never banished from the Garden of Eden. They have been there all the time.

So you see unlike Him I utilize those around me for I am not perfection personified. There are many different ways to look at any one situation, to find the best solution. I understand this. Do You? You would follow your God blindly if you could. Most of you do and you don't even understand why.

I needn't rehash the past for it would not change your opinion of me. Those of you for whom God is your savior are the lost souls. At this moment many of you will cast this book aside as Blasphemy or worse. Your trouble though has barely begun for you are living in my world. You don't realize it and you may never understand it, but it is so. I was banished from Heaven. This much is true but I was not sent to Hell. I was sent here.

Lucifer, December 25 2001

Chapter 1

I can't die. Believe me I've tried. Really. I once held a revolver to my head, held it tight to my temple, and pulled the trigger. It scattered bone chips and bits of gray matter all over my bedroom wall but somehow I didn't die. Now I'll not fool you. My head hurt for days and I was unable to leave my apartment because of the gaping hole in my head but I did not die. For three months I sat in my apartment ordering food, unable to leave, changing the bandage that circled my head daily until it had fully healed itself. I still have the scar on my temple and must go to great lengths to explain a bullet size depression in my head to those who notice it. Thankfully, few do. My torso though is another matter. It is littered with scars of all shapes and sizes, some intentional, some by accident, but all of them cause people to turn away. I wear turtleneck sweaters and full-length trousers at all times so I prefer the colder times of year as I don't stand out quite as much. In late spring and summer, I seek out the shade and darkness, like some sort of vampire more comfortable in the cool shadows of night than the bright, hot summer days I knew as a child. I have buried two wives, children, and scores of friends during my lifetime. I don't want to bury any more. I am tired and I want to die. My name is William McReedy. The Devil calls me Bones.

I was a Christian once a long time ago. My Mother would probably have said I was the definitive child of God, a blond, blue-eyed happy child for whom the world was a magic playground. From there to here is not such a long road for I readily fell under the serpent's spell. Moving to the rhythm of its trance, I wandered through life in a daze barely aware that I was being followed.

He had been stalking me for sometime, I must assume, for he knew my routine. I know now that he hid in the shadows, not ready to tempt me, waiting.

I first saw him in a storefront window as I checking out my reflection. The face that stared back me was not my own. I thought for a moment that I must be seeing things but then the face smiled, and contorted into a hideous grin. I wanted to run as fast as I could away from this place, but my legs failed me. His mouth moved then and I heard him whisper, "Billy".

Numbness fell over me as I stared transfixed at his face. There was a power in his eyes and I was beginning to feel humbled by it.

"Billy," he whispered again, though louder than before. "We must talk together soon for there is much I have to say. Would you like that, Billy?"

I found myself nodding in agreement. The fear I had felt was being replaced by a feeling of importance, of destiny. Such a fool I was, but I did not know it then and I would not for the next few years.

I did not see or hear from him for a few months. I felt disappointed by this, feeling that somehow he had replaced me. I began to question whether it had really even happened. Slowly I became convinced that in fact, it had been a dream, a hallucination. Either way, my mind had tricked me.

Life carried on as usual until I was awakened one night by a soft whispery voice. "Billy," it purred, "may we talk now?"

I awoke instantly, shaking, and covered in sweat. My bedroom felt hot, the air thick and hard to breath.

"It is only I Billy. You remember, don't you?" he whispered.

There was a soothing quality to his voice and I turned to face it. There he sat at the end of my bed, an apparition and yet somehow very real. He was tall, maybe six foot four, and dressed in clothes that were of another time. Velvet and lace and all sorts of finery adorned his body. His hands were large, not brutish, but long and delicate, with nails painted glossy black. His face bore little resemblance to a demon. More to the point he looked angelic, and I felt myself becoming enraptured with this princely figure."

It is good that you are not frightened, Billy, for I have come with great deal of faith that you are the one," he spoke quietly.

I slowly sat up, now enjoying the warmth that filled my room.

"What do you want with me?" I asked unable to understand.

He turned away and began to laugh, a loud crazy laugh, and as he did, my room became even warmer. He threw his head back and held his arms with fist clenched towards the sky and screamed, "I want my pound of flesh, Billy!"

I felt my flesh burning as if someone had set it alight but I remained calm in the face of this tantrum. His face was becoming more and more flushed as he screamed, "I want my pound of flesh, Billy, and I want it taken straight from the bone!"

He focused his stare at my bedroom window and laughed hysterically as it shattered at my feet. I recoiled at the sight of him now. His yellow eyes glowed brightly in the Darkness and highlighted the deepening wrinkles in his face."

Right from the bone, Billy, and you'll do it for me, won't you?"

This was not a question. It was a statement of fact. In as much as this scene was frightening me, I already knew I would do as expected.

"We'll be together forever Billy, you & I. Would you like to live forever, Billy?"

I am ashamed to admit how fast I answered. The word came as natural as breath 'yes' and it was done. The wind howled outside as the temperature changed and I began to shake uncontrollably. I wrapped my blanket around myself and I went to the window, stepping carefully around the shards of glass. "Life ever lasting," I yelled to the street below. "Ever lasting life!"

I turned to face him again, to thank him, to worship him, but he was gone.

I was alone in my room with no sign of his ever having been there. I stepped carelessly on the broken glass, wincing, as my foot was sliced open.

Blood spilled onto the floor from the open wound until it seemed that my body would drain itself. I was feeling lighted headed so I moved toward the bed collapsing into it almost immediately. When I awoke it all seemed again like a dream for my window was not broken, my foot almost completely healed.

I found my way out into the street. Madness! Such beautiful madness! I could not die. Nothing would threaten me now. I laughed aloud. People in the street stopped what they were doing and looked at me. I was manic, my eyes wide, my whole body perspiring

"You there!" I heard an old lady call, "shouldn't it be time to call it a night and go home to the missus?"

I raced over to where the old woman stood and grabbed her by the waist. How frail she was. Her skin hung off her bones, gray and wrinkled. How much longer would she live? She must have been seventy at least. I was thirty-two and would never know old age. I would never turn gray and wrinkled. I would remain in the state that I was, in the prime of life.

"Give us a kiss Mother," I requested, moving my face to within inches of hers. She furrowed her brow and stepped back.

"You must have had your share of drink last night," the old lady surmised. "Off with you then, your missus will be worried."

She turned and started on her way. I watched her hobble down the street. I wished I could do something for this frail thin, so sweet and unafraid. She glanced over her shoulder, maybe realizing that I was watching.

"Off with you, then!" she shouted. She smiled. In that one instant I felt like a child, not an orphan.

I carried on down the street, my destination unknown. My purpose though was never in doubt. I wanted to try killing myself. It was really the only way to proceed. I had to know undoubtedly that I could not die. How was I to proceed? I must admit I was still hesitant, quite unsure, actually.

I was born in the year of our Lord eighteen hundred and sixty. My mother, it was said, was a prostitute in London's East End and though I never knew her, in my dreams she was always very beautiful and loving. Life, though, is not a dream and as I grew up I found out she was a woman of passable looks whose love of liquor and sex far surpassed any feelings she could have had for her child. She died when she was twenty-four choking on her own vomit while sleeping "one off" in her boarding-house room.

I was four years old and living in a Catholic orphanage, with no idea I even had a mother. I was not to find out till I reached my twenty-first birthday that my mother had indeed existed My father was yet a stranger tale, I believe, I doubt even mother knew who had fathered me. I had concocted a yarn others would believe that might have me rise from my present station in life. Children can be so cruel even amongst other orphans. My story seemed to be the saddest of all. Can you blame one for attempting to create a world in which you were not the bastard child of a known whore?

"No,' tis better this way," I thought," better to create a life of fancy rather than face my own miserable existence head on." It's not like everyone didn't know. It just became easier to deal with the repugnance of friendship and the howls of laughter. Oh, the sisters tried hard to make my stay as comfortable as possible, but they could never truly know the indignities I had suffered at the hands of the other children.

"Lights out" the sisters cried, and I knew as the last flicker from the candle ember was extinguished that hell would pay a visit. Is it any wonder I would readily accept the advances of an Angelic stranger to that of common sense or decency? No, it was far easier to accept hell when you had already seen the face of evil in a child!

"Father," I ask "will thou forgive or condemn me?"

I knew no answer would be forthcoming. For father never existed to me, and the only father that I really knew were from the stories told by the sisters on Sunday. My story was not as enlightening as His, but worthy of a masterful penman's stroke. Rather than be a shore man on leave, which would be the truest full, father began his life as the son of a wealthy merchant from Manchester.

Now Manchester may not seem like the most likely place to begin the deceit but it starts in the most believable fashion. Manchester was not as rich or as populated as London, but was a quaint town in which a young boy could aspire to greatness, and move his place and rank to almost anywhere.

Father's father was a merchant with a keen ability that would be passed on to his lineage. Father grew and gained the knowledge he needed to acquire to run business as per his father's wishes. As he grew, father became restless and longed for the richness of London and the opportunities that were available. Ah, London a place of fancy and delight, where one could aspire to be anything if one desired. This became father's dream.

After the death of his father, the son sold the business and moved his belongings and wealth south to London. Upon his arrival, he quickly set up shop and proceeded to trade with the other local merchants.

Years passed and father did well for himself. He had even purchased a home in Whitehall and a carriage and two well-bred stallions to and from his shop. Business was brisk as was the morning air in London. Father was ecstatic about his time and his life. Unfortunately, I could not let him be. If I had continued on this path, Father would have only created more strife for me. No father had to become forgotten.

By this time I had entwined anyone who would listen to my tale with stories of bounty aplenty. Creating father's death would most certainly give me the pity that I most craved! Pity, is not so much an act but an emotion that can be manipulated to almost any length. I learned this early in life.

Creating pity became an art for me-maybe the only thing I was truly good at! Pity served me when I needed it and sustained me throughout my miserable existence. I remember the first lie I so told. I was a young lad of seven walking down the cobblestone and dirt roads that were supposed to be streets, again self-absorbed in my own disgust and wretched life. I know I was extremely angry that day. At what, I could not remember. And as I walked I came upon a dimly lit laneway, one I had not traveled before. The light was gray as I walked down the street, the buildings on either side covering up most of the noonday sun. Filth covered the walls and street with the smell at times almost unbearable. I remember almost retching at the stench.

As I walked, I heard a whimper in the street ahead. Carefully I walked to try to see from where the noise came. As I approached this strange and pitiful sound a light broke through the gray and illuminated a small black pup. I instinctively knew it was abandoned like myself, and craved food and affection.

I knelt down to see it more clearly and as it lifted its head, it brown eyes shone on me with brilliance I had never experienced before. Its cries turned to enthusiastic yelping and before I was even aware I had an instant friend. This pup, so thin and scrawny, had taken to me without need of explanation or want of anything more than companionship.

I lifted him from his ragged makeshift bed and held him in my arms and cried as he licked the tears from my cheek. This moment would be one of my most precious memories that I will always remember. As I gathered him up and walked out of the laneway I thought of his needs, and for once, not my own! I had an angel to take care of and a friend who would not ask the impossible of me.

Entering the street I remember seeing the world differently at that moment. The filth was gone, the smell was fragrant and flowers bloomed in full view of me. All was different and nothing could change that! Or so I thought. Would I have turned left instead of right my life may have changed forever.

Sister Margaret was in town for her daily shopping when I ran into her. She looked down at me, and the waif that I held in my arms so tightly and glared with a look of utter contempt.

"Keep that filthy beast away form me" she screamed, "and wash your hands and face before you go back to the orphanage." Without a word I turned and ran, tears flowing freely. My only friend was as pitiful as I. I ran and ran until I returned to the alley of which my pup had until recently called home. I put him down realizing that we could never be together for the sisters would never allow that.

I turned from my friend and began my long journey home. As I walked I heard him whimper again; I turned to see him following me, his tail wagging ecstatically. What I did next will forever haunt my dreams, sleeping or awake. My only friend was destined to live out his existence in the filth and rubble of the laneway. I knelt down to shoo him away but his exuberance only intensified with every bark. Try as I might I could not break the bond that existed. Knowing not what else to do I did the only thing I thought would be right. I stroked his head with one hand and with my other, I picked up a rock of sufficient size and weight. With all my might I bore the rock down on his skull while still stroking its back with my other hand. And in that moment my innocence was gone forever!

I realize the story may be sad, but it did allow me to take advantage of the situation. For you see as I left the laneway with my friend in my arms, I began to sob uncontrollably. In the street I sat near a bench and pondered the injustice in the world.

Without looking or lifting my head, I heard a clang of metal at my feet. Opening my eyes I realized that I was staring at stipend at my feet. An elderly woman touched my head and looked at me so pitifully in a way that I couldn't comprehend at the time. She nodded at me and then without saying a word, turned and went about her business. For a moment, I thought, I was not invisible or repugnant. Pity had come calling and left its mark at my feet.

It is said that all are born without sin or so the sisters taught us. I believed in God as a young child but as I grew older it all became quite suspect to me. God helped those who helped themselves we were taught, but what of an orphan! How was I to help myself? The ghosts of youth are strange indeed as I was to learn, for I recall vividly the day that God spoke to me, in no fashion I was schooled in. But speak to me he did.

It was on a Monday morning as I rushed through the rain to make my class that the Divine spoke unto me. I fell head long into a small lake that had formed on the outskirts of the Football field. Bastard athletes cared nothing for academics I surmised as I pulled myself from the mud.

"Fucking Ringers," I screamed, "I'll see you in the mines!" I was immediately flummoxed at the sight of footsteps in the mud. Footsteps, that weren't my own.

"Walk on young one for greater is the one that follows his heart than he who is lead by his hate."

It had come like the wind wrapping itself around me. God had spoken to me! I felt euphoric. What was I but a meager orphan with no means except pity with which to support myself? Rapture or insanity, I do not know, but the sequence of events, which followed, changed me forever.

Sean McCellan was two years older than I but six times the pain in the arse. He claimed noble blood but like my own stories I believed his to be false. A noble orphan is always highly unlikely though he was like all nobility, a pompous ass. His looks were almost pretty and his tone always rather incriminating. Although quite practiced in the art of nobility, he was a sorry individual and I knew upon meeting him that it would be his undoing. What I did not know is that it would be me who would undo him. Fate is a bitch that can't be controlled.

Sean had seen me diving into the mud and ran within two feet of where I lay. Planting one foot parallel to my sprawling form he proceeded to cover my face in mud. I had never known such fury. I raced to my feet and attacked him, verbally at first, trying to understand this powerful emotion. Soon I was upon him gouging at his eyes, biting whatever would fit in my mouth. Sean screamed as I forced my finger into his eye. I pulled and turned my finger trying to grasp this jelly like orb. I leaned over his frenetic form and ripped his neck open with my teeth.

"Fuck You," I screamed in between bites. "Fuck you and your mother."

I wouldn't be satisfied by his agony. No, I was going to kill him. I knew it then as clearly as I am telling this story. Sean McCellan was found dead in the school's football field, the victim of a vicious dog attack. There was no other alternative answer. He was an orphan at any rate. Who really cared? Orphans and outcasts, we wander among you, but do you see us?

I learned in the days to come how to feign emotion. Such a funeral for an orphan I had never seen. I almost began to believe that he came from noble blood. People clambered into the cathedral two hours before it was to begin. We were all called out to sing "Ava Maria" in our finest soprano and alto voices. The memories of my youth are vivid for I remember reaching that high c sharp as the tears raced down my cheeks. It was beautiful to have orchestrated such unbelievable emotion for this worthless piece of shit. I sometimes think I cried tears of joy that day. Joy that I had done some good.

But alas, my childhood would end and the time would come for me to leave the orphanage. It was well whispered in the hallowed halls through the years that Sean had not been the victim of some senseless animal attack. No, the rumors milled while I lay in bed or played in the field. It may well be why the other children shunned me or the sisters gave the prevailing look of disgust whenever I walked by. So it was to be an outcast, a mere pittance of what society called human. "So be it!" I murmured. I, of all the people around me, needed no one else to accept or protect me. I would go on as I had always done. No need for warmth or love. If this was to be my existence I would make it so.

Leaving the orphanage was the easiest thing I had ever done. There were no tears cried, no hugs or words of encouragement when I left. The gate closed tight and with a loud clang. It would never again open for the likes of me. "Release me to society!" I cried." Hide your daughters and fear your sons. I have arrived!"

I learned quickly on the streets of London. It's easy to make a living when you're not bound by the moral ineptitude of God and his laws. I laughed whenever I would walk by a church and hear the droning of the sheep as they sang to a God that would never listen to them. Priests and ministers would amuse even further. They all tried to help and I let them house and feed me for a time. Then as always I would listen to their endless preaching that would eventually save my soul. I must have disgusted them whenever I had had enough.

"I have no soul, you foul beings! *Whatever decency there was in me left a long time ago.* With that I spat at them and left, cursing the cross and the virgin as I walked down the halls through the pews.

It was always the same, in every church; the only thing that was different was the amount of time that had passed. I'd seen them all: Protestant, Lutheran, Baptist, but the best had always been the Catholics. Oh, the Catholics; the chosen people, not the Jews as we were told, but Catholic. I mean they don't come out and say it. No that would be wrong, but they do believe it. Theirs is the religion of the world.

"Fuckin' hypocrites," I say. The only Christian religion that doesn't follow its own teachings. I mean how can you have a belief in God and his teachings and still not understand what it is he meant? Even for someone like me it all seems so simple!

I used to love walking into a Catholic church and be surrounded by statues and figures from every aspect of the bible. I always thought that when Moses walked down from the mountain and cast down the tablets he was telling his people not to worship unto any other god or any representation there of. But walk into a Catholic church and you see everyone kneeling before the altar of the Virgin Mary. This is not God but a piece of stone and plaster painted with the rich colors of a French whore.

"All men are created equal," the bible says, but yet the Catholics have a Pope, supposedly God's representation on earth! I am God's representation, as are you. For all that is good and bad in the world we were all created in his image. If that is true, I am God! I will create my own law and justify my existence to no one but mine self. If religion is confusing to some, I can help. My interpretation eases the moral dilemma that we all have inside. No one is without sin. God says so himself.

But yet he claims that we were all created with original sin. If true, and if we are created in his image, is God not then also a sinner? A probing question indeed, one that I had often asked the sisters and beatings I often received for an answer.

As always, religion became a spawning ground for my immoral behavior and my loathing of all that is "holy". What amazed me was how many thought as I, confused and searching for an answer that would not come. I easily manipulated these people into giving me money, food, and lodging. The best time came with my introduction to a woman known in the area as Agnes.

Agnes Bechard was a fiery Scottish woman who was known throughout the lower quarter. Of a loud and somewhat boisterous disposition, she was easily recognized by her long unruly red hair, which flowed freely past her waist. She was of an unusual height for a woman, standing nearly six feet with large crystal green eyes that left one with an enchanted feeling. I wanted her the first moment I saw her, such was the nature of her allure to me. The tender age of seventeen though tends to leave one in a constant state of enchantment.

I first encountered Agnes in a pub on Chester Road on the outskirts of the lower quarter. I had wandered in for a pint of beer after successfully stealing a few shillings off the counter of a sweet shop. I had become quite proficient at making ends meet and stealing seemed to be a logical vocation for someone of my stature.

She was seated at a table in the far corner, a pint of beer in her slender hands with two empty glasses in front of her. The dim light only accentuated her appearance. Her eyes seemed to glow as if soaking up the light of the candle to her left. Her long red hair appeared crimson, framing her face in a way that seemed quite bewitching to me. She sat alone at her table with her back to the wall and I found myself walking towards her. I was growing anxious as I closed the space between us.

"Mind if I sit here Miss?" I quietly asked.

She was even more striking at this distance. I could hardly contain my excitement as she nodded her approval. I clumsily reached for the chair next to her. It connected with the table, spilling a small portion of her drink.

"Excuse me, miss," I offered. She smiled, still refusing to speak. I motioned for the waitress to bring me a pint.

"Not much for weather this time of year, eh, miss?" I tried, hoping for some response. "Seems the wind blows from October through to December in these parts". I was struggling now and hoped she would save the situation.

"Bit young for the pub aren't you son?" she asked finally in a voice just above a whisper. The waitress put a pint on the table and I fumbled in my pocket for the payment.

"Put it on my tab, would you love" she purred. I started to object but Agnes was already dismissing the waitress, Rose.

"Thank you miss but I have my own money. There really was no need but thank you ".

Agnes shifted in her seat and I felt my face flush with color as her leg touched mine. I pulled my head back from the candlelight hoping she hadn't noticed.

"The wind," she started " is the wind of Boleskine. It is from the place where all begins and ends. It is the wind of my home, the wind of my Father. Have you been there?"

I had to admit that indeed I hadn't nor did I know where it was.

"It is on Loch Ness, seventeen miles from Inverness, and I dream of it nightly," she stated matter of factually. She reached across the table and touched the center of my forehead. Using her thumb she traced a line down across my mouth stopping there only for a second before continuing to my throat. She moved closer her eyes mesmerizing me. "Therion," she whispered. I tried to pull away but she held fast to me. "Don't be frightened, Billy, for I am the Tempest and you were brought to me." I had only sipped at my drink to this point and yet I felt inebriated. My head was swirling with visions I could not comprehend. Faces I did not know appeared before me whispering words I had never heard. "Lashtal, Thelema, Fiofa, Agape, Aumgn" they repeated.

Agnes was standing now draped in a black cape her size accentuated by the candles, which by now had multiplied tenfold. I fell from my chair landing hard on the stone floor. There I lay unable to move my body drenched in sweat. The heat of the candles was unbearable and I begged Agnes to douse them. She turned from me and stood facing north, the door of the room opening as she did. Wind blew through the pub, harsh and cold pounding at my body. I now shook uncontrollably, weeping as I did.

"Agnes" I screamed, " make it stop, please!"

She remained where she was her arms outstretched as if taking strength from the wind.

"Lashtal, Thelema, Fiofa, Agape, Aumgn," she screamed. The wind blew harder now and I struggled to protect myself from it.

"Agnes," I hollered, " what's happening? Agnes, please?"

She turned finally to face me, her hair moving wildly in the wind. Her green eyes glowed as she smiled. "It's the First Gesture, Billy".

I felt the heat this time as she brushed my cheek with her outstretched hand. The smell of burnt flesh fouled my senses; the pain came now as I screamed in utter agony. Light that had become so common before was now without a partner as I sank slowly into oblivion.

"Here! What's wit you then?" I heard someone call. "Sir, have you 'ad too much ale?"

My eyes opened and the light that had been extinguished before had now slowly started to filter back.

"John, we got a live one 'ere. Looks two sheets to the wind I'd say."

"No," I muttered as I began to regain some sense. I felt for my cheek, to feel the burn left by Agnes or whoever she was. My hand deceived me as I reached for my face. Gone was any burn or remnant of an injury.

" What the?" I cried as I pulled my hand down in disbelief. No mark, no pain, no evidence of anything.

"Where is she?" I asked.

"Who?"

"The woman I was sitting with?"

"Sir, no one has sat with you all evening," she answered.

I looked around to see if she was near and saw no one. What had happened? As I looked around it became apparent that no one else had seen or heard anything. Was it all a dream? Had I imagined it?

"Bring me a pint!" I hollered. If I couldn't explain what had happened, I'd just as soon drink it away. And drank I did, for the night's memories became long forgotten by my fifth pint.

I laughed foolishly as I spoke to the other patrons of the night's imagined events. I spoke to whoever would listen, even to some that wouldn't, and by night's end had surely made an ass of myself.

I left in a stupor, none the wiser of what a fool I was! I walked down the cobblestone swinging and singing as I made my way home. I took a long time getting home that night for I remember the sun beginning to rise as I neared my apartment in the seedy tenement I called home.

Upon arriving at home I collapsed on the floor of my abode. As unconsciousness came I could hear Mr. Wittcocks wife wishing him a happy day goodbye as he left for work. "Pathetic sheep" I say," you're all pathetic." Blackness came and with it the sleep I craved.

I awoke to see the sun settling over the Thames. I had slept the day away. Just as well! I much preferred the nights anyway. My head pounding from the evening before, I went to light a candle to see my way to the sink. The candle flickered as I walked to the basin; it became almost mesmerizing as I walked.

Setting it down on the table next to the mirror I reached for the water to pour into the basin. The water trickled from the pitcher as I stretched my self in an effort to wake up. Opening the window I could hear the streets becoming silent from the day's activities. Men were arriving home from work, children were no longer playing in the street, and there was the faint odor of homemade biscuits as dinner was being served.

"You're all fuckin' sheep!" I cried out. "No" I thought, the evening sounds were much more intoxicating for one such as myself. The cries of pain from someone being robbed, the sound of a streetwalker peddling her trade, these were like music to me.

The breeze that night was cool on my face, the fog just beginning to settle in. The candle flickered in the wind as I began to wash up. Grabbing a dirty shirt from the chair was the closest thing I had to use as a towel. I wondered if I had put more dirt on my face than I had just washed off.

Looking out the window, I noticed the moon's fullness and wondered if I even needed a candle. Its light shone in like a beacon from a water tower illuminating my pathetic flat with a radiance that hid all the mess and grime within.

I turned to look about and collapsed in agony, my face searing from pain...my heading pounding as if one thousand hammers were hitting it at the same time! My eyes burned with such horror that I thought I would pluck them out. I screamed, not once but continuously until the pain began to subside.

It felt like forever till the pain left but was more likely that it had only been a few minutes since I collapsed. I reached for the chair and began to pull myself up. The pain still evident, but not as excruciating as before. I held my head in my hands and began to sob, tears trickling down my face to land so gently on my trousers below. Never in my life had I felt such pain not even during the regular beatings I received in the orphanage.

The tears trickled down as I watched them, falling further each time I tried to stand up. But I was still too weak from the pain. All I could do was sit there and watch my own agony. I reached down to wipe the tears from my trousers, my hands wet from the tears. As I went to wipe them I saw them glisten in the moonlight. Then it hit me! I reached for the candle to confirm my fears. My hands were not wet with tears but were soiled with blood, my blood.

I reached for my face and felt the wetness as it trickled down my cheek.

"What the hell?" I shouted as I reached for the mirror. I'm not sure how long I stood there and looked at myself. It may have been minutes it may have been hours. At times I wasn't even sure if I was looking at myself! My cheek raw from injury held a scar so significant that only hell itself could have administered it! Again I screamed, not believing what mine own eyes told me.

"This can't be true," I cried, but yet every time I looked away and back there it was the same mark.

I reached for a bottle, something to quench my fear, and I drank like I had never drunk before. I drank until the pain subsided and I felt no more. I sank back into my chair and drained the bottle. Then I heard a knock!

I staggered to the door, not knowing what to expect anymore. I reached for the brass knob and began to turn it. The door creaked open and thru a sliver I saw a man of great stature.

"What do you want?" I asked.

"William? I need to speak with you," he answered.

"How the hell do you know my name?" I yelled.

"William, we need to talk about Agnes." he said.

"Agnes who?" I stammered, opening the door more slightly.

"Agnes from yesterday evening," he answered. As I peered out the door I noticed his clothing, not that of a commoner but more along the lines of a gentleman.

"Please, William," he said, "you have nothing to fear from me."

I opened the door and turned from him so that he could not see my wretched wound.

"William, turn not from me, I know of your wound and why you wear such a mark."

My hand sank from my face as I turned. How could he know of my mark when even I knew not from whence it came?

"See William, the wound has already begun to heal. It will not remain for all to see, only a select few," he claimed.

My hand reached for my cheek and I felt the flesh begin to return. "What is happening?" I asked. "Why have I such a mark? What does it mean?"

"William, you have faltered, not once or twice, but more times than anyone could have imagined. The mark you bear comes not from a woman named Agnes but from a woman named Lilith. Agnes is to her what a coat is to you. She can shed her skin and assume a new mantle whenever she wants."

"Who are you?" I asked as I sat down again.

He walked over to me and rested his hand on my table. "My name, William, like my clothes are of no importance. I have come here but to show you the paths we all must take. Wherever Lilith goes I'm usually not far behind. But if you must call me something you can call me Aforol or Raphael."

"Aforol?" What kind of name is that I wondered?

"My dream last night was not a dream?" I asked.

No, "he said to me," it was real just as the pain you endured was real. Hear my words now, William, for if you forsake them all that has been shall never be again. Her name is Lilith, William. You would not know of her unless you followed your own forgotten

32

teachings. Telling her story may avail you of some good. She is the first of man that was created. Her name like her essence changes to the task at hand. She was created out of filth and sediment instead of pure dust like others. Her being was made to create, not destroy. Unfortunately, she never chose to remain at her station in life. She demanded that she be equal with his first son, and found that she could not. She spoke his name and was banished for all time from her home. She left with seed implanted and gave birth to the Shedim or evil spirits. She gave birth to the Jinn who can assume the shapes of man and beast. She is the first mother of all life, and the end as well. She is the virile maiden, the temptress, and the old woman. She can be the beginning and end for all that touches her. Outraged over his punishment, she seeks her revenge by strangling newborn children while they sleep: boys up to the eighth day and girls up to the twentieth day of life. But if Lilith finds an angelic amulet or a circle drawn with the names of the three angels over the infants cradle, she must spare their lives. The angels were dispatched to bring Lilith back and convince her to return. She would not, so Sennoi, Sansanui, and Samangluf returned with a promise. But when he was told about the promise by the angels, he threw in an added punishment. If a child were spared, Lilith would have to turn against one of her own children. To get through the curse that was placed upon her, she not only seeks the houses of women in child-birth, she would also attack men sleeping alone."

"What rubbish is this?" I asked, "Your story is preposterous at the least! I had too much ale the night before, that is all. If you wish me to believe such a fool's tale, you should have explained to me why she chose me."

With that, he picked his hand off the table and moved silently to the door, never once looking at me. He stopped at the door and quietly said, "You, William, sleep alone." And with that he was gone.

Chapter 2

Simplistic are the ideals of God. Idealistic are the ways of man. Who is to say that God is man and man is God. If he lives among us can we not see him always? I shudder to think at times, my own vision scarred by the childhood that ever eluded me. I've spoken to God on occasion, as a young child praying for relief from the hands of his disciples. My prayers were never answered, nor did I expect them to be. Maybe, for a brief moment, did I hold out some hope, but my hope was not meant to be. Hope turned to despair, despair turned to distain, distain turned to hate. I look back now and see that this all would derive from the most basic emotion of all. There are no clear-cut values and rules of emotion. There can't be. If there were, all life would be presently unique as to how we perceive it now. If love is the trophy to all happiness, why is it that we are not happy all the time? No, I believe love is the basis for all other feeling and is a derivative of hate. They say that one cannot exist without the other; I do not perceive this to be true. There are no sides to this; love and hate are the same! You can exist with love but can you exist with only hate? This was a question that one of the priests presented to me when I was but fourteen years of age. At the time I couldn't understand the meaning he was trying to show me and yet I knew what he said. Understanding and knowing are two very separate things. Love and hate, two separate entities in this entitlement called life. I would struggle with this for most of my early life, and this was possibly the reason why I searched for it then. Years would pass until I realized there were not two but one. It came to me as simple as the dawn comes after night. Regardless of my upbringing, or more so, because of it, I felt the truth for the first time in my life. Love is not a separate emotion but a by-product of hate. It's so clear that I find it utterly surprising that no one else has known this. All the priests, ministers, bishops, and all, either lack the insight or are so blinded by their passion for God that they refuse the truth. You can live with only hate. Love is hate. It's as simple as that. All of mankind tries to further itself on the institution of love but hate is what rules the world. War is love, anger is love, anguish is love, and envy is love. I do love, but not the same way. I hate therefore I love. I have known people in my time that I have loved and when they were taken from me I grew angry and learned to hate. Hate God, hate life, and hate my very existence, who among us cannot say the same? God is love? No, God is hate! Every time love evolves surely hate cannot be far behind. Childhood friends that I envied when they were taken to new homes became my mortal enemies because of love. If I didn't love them I wouldn't care what happened to them. No. Hate is the root of all emotion and I believe this to be true. Hate can sustain me but it cannot hurt me. So alone I sleep and alone I shall remain forever. Time is not my ally for such as I but mine enemy that continually laughs and mocks me everyday of my existence.

Morning comes quickly again for one such as I. There is no sleep for the wicked. I gaze from my room to see the light break from the river and blend its way onto my face. I squint as it nears my eyes and curse it for all to hear. My cheek it still feeling the effects of last night. I remember the stranger and his words and wonder what is in store for me now. I fee defiled! Never have I felt the need to destroy and belittle existence itself. My anger grows with every waking minute. The pain from non-release is at times too much to bear, but still I must persist. Death would be a welcome visitor in my world, but I know that he will never knock upon my door. He visits at his leisure and not mine, bastard that he is!

I rise from my bed and dress quickly. The night before has given me the motivation to leave my room as quickly as possible. I use my fingers to brush my hair for I cannot allow the time to find a brush, my coat drapes over my shoulder as I walk, nay run, to the door. My fingers refuse to check the doorknob as I slam the door shut. The stairs beckon me as I climb down to the first floor, broken and worn like the very bane of my existence. Outside the air is warm while the wind is cool. The sun flickers between the buildings and finds its way down to the streets and alleys and warms the concrete as it passes through. My eyes follow the floor as I walk to find today's breakfast. The alley ahead holds breakfast for the forgotten. "Trash to one man is another man's treasure," they say. I see the people, shabbily dressed and unwashed. They remind me of rats that feed off each other. See the dogs and cats next as they watch and wait for their masters to drop or give them a scrap or morsel of fat from a piece of festering pork that they have scrounged up from the cans. I look as they search for anything that could even be remotely construed as sustenance. I can't even pity them. Fish, beef, potatoes, are all there, and it just depends on your sense of dignity that will determine how well you eat.

I feel in my pocket for anything that could save me today from this misery and find three schillings. I have been spared the indignity today of trying to hold down my breakfast. As I turn from the alley and move towards the street, sunlight catches me off guard and I shield my eyes once again. My stomach growls and I feel it remind me that I need to eat. I don't need to eat to survive, but I have learned that eating will help me maintain a weight that I have grown accustomed to. To not eat will not kill me, for I cannot die. If I do not eat though I will suffer just as all would. I am not immune to pain but immune to life. Whether I physically feel the need or desire it at times I do not know, I realize though it has helped me to cope into some semblance of normality that I rarely posses at the best of times. I did try to maintain normalcy in the beginning, mostly fooling myself though, of course. I didn't know what else to do. But It never lasted.

The Inn's door was swollen today from the rain we have had for the last few weeks. An effort is needed to pull it open. It sticks in its jamb as I grab and pull. As I Jerk the door open, I fail to see the woman on the other end pushing at the same time. I smirk a little as she falls to the ground on her knees and hands. I reach down to help her up as she raises her head to see me. Our eyes meet and, for a split second, I see a reflection and emotion I haven't felt in what seems like a hundred years. I stop and shudder as her gaze takes me aback, for within her eyes she reminds me of one of the only woman I have ever truly loved.

"This cannot be!" I tell myself, "Mary is dead, dead for many years!" Mary, my first wife, was be destined to die in my arms, taken as a cruel joke by one so wicked, creating and distilling hate of monumental force in that one split instant.

Emotions flood in an instant as I gaze upon her face; her beauty is matched only by her innocence and I shudder at the thought of remembrance. I apologize without thinking without saying a word as my hand reaches for hers; she lifts herself from the warmed stoop. I stop and stare in and in the time it takes to blink I realize all that was and all that is gone. She walks away as she brushes the dirt from her frock. I notice her shoes, her smell, and her hair and try to remain in my own time and place. She walks away and for an instant I see her look at me again, just for a second. I shake my head and reassure myself that it is not Mary but a peasant girl searching for a morsel only, a handout or scrap, that she could dine on. And as quickly as she appeared she is gone again destined to be only a memory. But when you are one such as I, memories take precedence in a life riddled with pain, creating some type of solace and peace.

I walk into the inn and swear the stench is by far worse

in here then it was in the alley. I find the darkest table and fall into its embrace. I order a coffee and two eggs and hope they won't be as rancid as my life. As I sit I find it difficult to not think of my Mary and the unborn son that we lost. Mary's life was not what we would call proper. She, too, had an upbringing not uncommon to that of a wild animal. I always wondered which of us had it worse, she or I. She worked the streets, my Mary, and that is where we would meet. Both of us trying to scrape out a meager existence that would make the poor take pity on us.

The first time I met Mary was when I had recently moved to London's east side. There the docks were plenty and questions were kept to a minimal! Mary worked these same docks as I, but in a different manner. She was as my mother was… a waif, a lady of questionable character I saw in her more, much more. She had a sense of pride and strength that very few women I had ever met possessed. She was at times quiet and reserved but strong and outspoken when she had to be. Her line of work didn't bother me because at times I had also taken up her trade when times were dire.

It is surprising how many men will spend their wages on a young lad rather than make sure their families are fed. But that is the nature of man I suppose. At times I regretted what I did up until the time the coins entered my purse, and I knew then that I would eat the next day.

I can still recall the time I committed the ultimate sin against God for the second time in my life. His name I do not remember but his face will forever be etched in my mind. I met him in my seventeenth year in a small suburb outside of London. His hands were that of a fine gentleman and his look of one that went to church every Sunday and prayed for forgiveness. Another sheep in a flock of fools that understood nothing and comprehended even less! It wasn't the first time I met him. No, he was a regular, distinguished…maybe, but not a common worker. He paid to have my belly full on a number of occasions, as was my nature at the time. One time he even bought me a new coat for the upcoming winter's night air. He disgusted me at the best of times, but I was not to look a *gift horse* in the mouth. Weeks had passed and with every visit I learned to loathe him more. I kept my temper in check for the duration of the visits, but when he left I felt the bile of human nature retching from my bowels.

One night in particular, I would meet up with him by chance when my temper was at its foulest. Twilight was falling lazily over the city as I walked down Bingham Hill towards Edding, a suburb that begins on Carol Street in the form of a rather quaint Church. Its chipped paint and un-sculptured shrubbery were rather endearing and I nodded my head in a gesture of acknowledgement.

My mind slipped back to the orphanage and the order and discipline of it all. The structure itself was not unlike a prison, wrought iron gates to make escape unlikely, brick and mortar all the way up to the roof. The windows were all barred, of course, lest anyone decide that death was preferable to the world inside. Yes, it was easy to see that there were no Sisters of Mercy to be found inside this little church. Only the remnants of the whispered prayers of the faithful remained.

I was growing inexplicably angry and I stopped and turned to face the little church. Visions of a life I could not comprehend passed in front of me. Mothers and fathers and their children walked hand in hand on a beautiful Sunday morning. The wind blew the leaves into a magical dance that any child would find delight in.

" Jesus is making the trees sing for us Mommy," the child might say. The Mother would smile while looking down at her offspring and squeeze her hand warmly and add in a singsong voice, "Jesus loves the little children..."

I wipe ashamedly at a tear that seemed to have found its way on to my cheek. I was denied that life by circumstance beyond my control. I started life as all others in this world do, kicking and screaming but there had been no Mother's love for me, no merciful God to wipe my tears away. There was only the sting of a hand across the face, or the welt of a yardstick on my backside.

That tear had no business on my face. I was dead inside. I had to be. I always had to be. I started towards the church with a murderous rage. Taking the worn wooden steps two at a time I pounded at the door. " Jesus loves the little children," I screamed.

To my amazement the door opened and there he stood. All my control left at the sight of him. I immediately grabbed him by the throat and that's when I saw his collar stick out from under his tunic. "Have you spoken with the Lord today, sir?" I hissed and continued, " For you are about to meet him". I squeezed harder and pushed the man backwards into the church. His face only flushed with color. I forced him down the aisle in the direction of the pulpit. His face was growing darker and I marveled at my ability to control this. A little less force and his tone would lighten, a harder squeeze and the blue would return. "Who's your God now, sir?" I demanded. No answer was forthcoming. " I repeat sir, who's your God now?"

I increased the pressure on his neck; the color was even darker than before.

"You," was all he could manage.

I squeezed his throat with all my might his Adams apple firmly in my grip. I felt my fingers breaking the skin and I pulled for all I was worth. Blood poured onto my hand and down his shirt as I pushed him into the pulpit. I took my other hand and grabbed his hair pulling his head back and ripping his neck more as I did. He could not scream, though he did indeed try. All I could hear was the sound of rapid breath being forced through the blood.

I let go of his throat and took hold of his head with both hands. Lifting his head up I took one more look into his eyes and whispered, "Tell him I said hello".

I brought his head down on the corner of the pulpit with all my strength. His skull shattered and I found myself covered in bone and brain. His lifeless form fell from my hands and landed heavily on the church floor. I stepped back from the body feeling tired but satisfied.

Bending down I searched the pockets of his coat and was pleasantly surprised to find four shillings. "Not a bad night's work," I thought.

I looked down at my clothes and realized that I would indeed need a little cleaning up. The blood had soaked my coat and shirt and I would not get far dressed as I was. An alcove to left of the pulpit offered the answer in the form of a waistcoat. I quickly removed my coat and shirt and changed them for the waistcoat. Washing the blood off my hands and face in the holy water, I noticed a bottle of wine, sacrificial presumably. I picked up the bottle and I turned and headed toward the door and into a night that seemed full of life. "My life continued, his would not," I thought, as I drank from the bottle. I presumed he was a man of some stature in the community but never once did I realize who he was. It was shocking to say the least and it further strengthened my resolve against the church and for all that it stood for.

"Sinners" I cried, "just like me". I laughed and in the same instance cried. With the bottled nearly empty, I hastened to find a place to hide. I came across a deserted warehouse in which I would hole up for the night. Sleep's wonderful embrace would take me but not for long.

I awoke to the screams and whistles of the local constables. Remembering what I had done was a sobering effect that I took into account almost immediately. I ran from the warehouse with all my resolve. I was gone from there. I ran most of the night and morning I recall, until I felt my lungs would burst from the pressure.

I wound up near a road not much traveled, many miles away from the horror I had committed. Feeling overwhelmed, I sat down to ponder what I had done and in a moment of weakness vomited the contents of my belly unto the ground.

No, "I thought," there must be some way I can live with myself and still maintain my true nature." Mary was the one to help me with that struggle.

Years had passed since my little escapade and I felt I was nearing my end. Turmoil was replacing any semblance to a normal life that I could have. Mary's nature seemed to be the right balance in a life so one sided. Mary...just the thought of her brought back a flood of memories sweeter than the finest chocolate. In her eyes I could see a wonderment and innocence that I had never seen before. She brought chaos to my peace, or peace to my chaos, a balance so desperately needed.

I recall the first time we met on the docks late one evening. She was working, I was searching for work. I wasn't looking for anything in particular and Mary wasn't searching as well, but both of us in desperate need of something, not knowing what. I spotted her in the shadows under the full moon. Even then her striking beauty was apparent. She was with a client, not a gentleman but rather a filthy dockworker, unwashed and unkempt. His hands groped her in a manner not known to civilized man. At the time I was I was still repulsed by what I saw, "Man's nature," I thought, "more so than any filthy beast in all creation."

He finished quickly which did not surprise me in the least. Men like that usually take what they need quickly and without conscience. I watched the two of them, he quickly gathering his things, she straightening her frock. She glanced at me in those few moments and I could see embarrassment within her look. She quickly looked down so as not to acknowledge my presence, but by then it was too late. I had seen her and admired and pitied her at the same time.

I watched as he left, wiping his mouth on his sleeve. He threw down a few schillings at her feet and with that he was gone.

Mary stood there for a few moments not knowing where to turn it seemed. She proceded to pick up the money and then turned towards the light.

As she stepped out into the light I was able to fully appreciate her beauty and warmth. She wiped a tear from her face it seemed, trying to desperately hide it from any prying eyes. She was disgusted with herself, I could tell, but did what she had to do to survive. As she walked towards the large containers on the docks I couldn't help but watch her. She mesmerized me. I stood there watching her, for how long I do not know. Finally I couldn't help myself and walked into her vicinity. She saw me again and turned her head for a brief moment, then back in my direction again.

"Looking for a date, Luv?" she asked.

I said nothing. I couldn't answer her. Her striking manner captivated me and I couldn't mutter a sound.

'ere, you alright then? she queried.

I stammered and finally answered, "I...I...I'm looking for work," I finally replied, my mouth so taught and dry I felt I would choke at any moment.

"What! And you believe me to be your employer, then?" she stated.

"No," I replied. "I have only recently arrived here and do not know anyone about town," I answered.

"Well," she said, " you seem harmless enough. I suppose I could talk to one of my friends on the docks".

"Thank you," was all I could reply.

We would talk a little while longer and the more we talked the more at ease I felt. With each passing moment I felt the anger and burdens of the world being lifted from my shoulders. She made me feel at ease.

As the night wore on, we became more familiar with each other. We began to feel a kinship as we spoke, discussing our trials and tribulations. My own pitiful existence was explained and I felt her take pity on me. She was not as forthcoming with her own life, but with each passing moment she opened up a little more.

We talked for what seemed a lifetime and then were interrupted by another dockworker seeking a little attention. I was surprised when she turned him away, her eyes levitating back to me. He did not take kindly to the rejection though; cursing under his breath he took five steps before turning back on his heels. Stomping back he slung profanities with each step.

He grabbed Mary by the arm and attempted to pull her to his side. Mary protested but to no avail. Watching this unfold I felt time stand still and I could feel every movement, every vowel spoken, the wind passing by my face. I stepped in, and tried to pull him off her. Mary, by this time, was yelling and kicking in a feeble attempt stop his advances. I grabbed him by the sleeve and found myself in an instant on the ground, blood coming from my mouth. He had hit me! The bastard son of a whore had hit me!

I fumbled to get my balance and in doing so, my hand closed on a rather large metal object, presumably a bale hook used to help move hay bales off the docks. I lunged with all my might and it found its mark. I had swung wildly and prayed it would create some torment for our attacker. It did, and I felt the warm spray of blood as it hit my face and hair. I looked and saw that it was stuck in the fleshy part of his upper thigh. Both ends shone through.

He screamed in both agony and surprise, and his grip loosened on my Mary. I pushed him over and listened to his wail of pain. He cried for help as I stood over him. Help came from beyond the light, calls for alarm had been sounded, and it would just be a few moments till aid arrived.

Mary grabbed me by the arm and hustled me away. I resisted at first, wanting to finish what I had started. The sight of blood had increased my furor to the point of madness. Mary screamed at me to go, and somewhere in the intensity of the situation, her voice got through.

My eyes focused on her and the madness began to wane. I looked down at my hands, which had previously wiped the blood from my face, and saw the look of fresh butcher's kill on them. I looked up and saw in her face a serenity I had never witnessed before. I looked down at my intended sheep and saw his pain. Blood flowing from his face as he turned pale before my eyes. The blood spilled to the point that it touched my shoe and I felt its warmth through my leather sole. My foot reached back and I almost fell as I stumbled. I felt as a drunk who had just woken from a stupor. I saw Mary again as she intensified her resolve for us to leave. I turned to leave as I could hear footsteps approaching. I looked down for one last time and spat. Mary and I then ran off into the warm night's embrace.

Mary took me to her flat and as we entered, I fell to the floor sobbing. I could not control my emotions and I felt ashamed by my actions. Mary leaned down towards the floor and gently cupped my face within her hands. She wiped away the tears from my face with her petticoat as she spoke softly and reassuringly. My sobbing soon began to recede as she spoke.

Her words were comforting in a way I have never known. She pulled my head to her bosom and I fell into that warm comfortable space. Her soothing voice created peace within me, as a mother comforting her child. I had never felt this way before. Safe, comforted, this must be the way a child would feel at their mothers' bosom. I looked up and without hesitating, kissed her on the lips. She hesitated and pushed me away. I felt rejected once again. Then without saying a word she reached into my eyes with hers and saw a glimmer of hope, I suppose. Her face came racing towards mine and our lips met for the second time that night. Her passion overwhelmed me as I sank into oblivion. We must have been locked in our embrace for at least a minute but for me it was over too briefly.

She held me tightly into the night and by morning we had fallen asleep in each other's arms. I fell in love with Mary that evening and I believe she felt the same for me or had at least I hoped she did.

Time passed between Mary and me as days turned into weeks, weeks into months, and months into years. Mary had retained for me a position on the docks, far away from our former acquaintance, whom we had found was a passing sailor and not a dockworker. The incident was forgotten for us and life continued. Mary kept her same employment though I cared not. She was who she was and I would not change her for anything.

We discussed her work openly and I came to accept the cards that life had dealt us. Mary began over time discussing her life and I felt myself caring more and more for her.

Her father, I found out, was a mean bugger with a bad disposition. Mary told me of his frequent visits into her room at night, her mother fast asleep from pressing shirts all day. Mary was eight years old and already a woman. No child should have had to endure that. The thought of it swelled my throat every time she spoke of it. I wish I could have traveled back in time to kill her tormentor, but of course, I could not. All I could do was listen. Listening was what she wanted.

She told me she could never speak of it before because no one would believe her. Her father was considered a religious man in the community and his stature was that of a fine, upstanding citizen. He fooled everyone, but when the windows would be drawn he became a different individual. He drank, Mary's father did. Never outside the house, in public, but inside away from prying eyes. That's when Mary felt his wrath. Alone she felt; mum sleeping in the next room. She always knew when it was time because she could feel his mood.

She prayed, my Mary did. Prayed that God would not forsake her, prayed that the Lord would take him that night, but he never did. His footsteps coming down the hall still echoed in her mind, the slow creaking of the door opening as he tried not to wake his wife. She still flinches whenever she hears distant thundering steps on a wooden floor.

Mary left her home early in her life. Left at fourteen and learned how to make ends meet quickly. It became apparent that she felt her worth in only one way, on her back. She didn't realize for a long time that what had happened wasn't her fault. By the time she did she was too entrenched in the mire to pull herself out. I saw in her all the things she could have been. Everyday I tried to tell her everyday about her virtues, her talents, and her worth. She would have none of it. When she did believe me it was only for a short time. Then she would regress back into her lifestyle. I suppose I couldn't blame her. I was in love with her. I accepted her for who she was and no matter how hard I tried I could not persuade her to see things my way, at least not for long. We both adapted to each other after some time, and we were soon engaged to be married.

Marriage was an idea that had never even entered out minds when we were apart, but once we had found each other there would be no other way. I had decided a long time ago I would have no part in a church ceremony. Mary understood my reservations and understood my feelings.

We were married by an acquaintance of ours who was no more a minister than I. A drunk at the best of times, he performed the ceremony in witness of our love for each other. We laughed at the pomp and circumstance but rejoiced together just the same.

We settled into our new lifestyle with ease. We moved to a larger suite and in time came to settle in. I was happy, for once in my life. I went to work while Mary stayed home during the day. At night she left for work and on most nights I would attempt to keep an eye on her. I loved my Mary, truly and wholly. She became my reason for existence.

The love we shared may have seemed strange to those around us but for me it was the sweetest feeling I'd ever felt. We had friends, mostly drunkards and ladies of the evening, but they were still our friends.

Almost two years had passed since we'd met and life was indeed full. Mary's proud looking belly now carrying the mark of our love. A child no less! Who would have believed it? She looked radiant, in her pregnancy. Her clothes though not of the best quality, still hung on her form with perfection. I cried when she told me. She would even give up working in order to ensure a normal life for our child. I had to take on a second job to make ends meet. We ate plenty of vegetables because meat would be scarce in our house except on special occasions. We were poor but happy.

As time passed Mary grew increasingly larger and I grew happier.

It would be just a matter of time until we two became three. I readied a room for a nursery. It was blissful for a time, though I somehow felt it would not last. I recall the day as clear as yesterday. I awoke to Mary already cooking eggs on the stove. Her gown against the sunlight showed her form for all to see. "It is almost time," I thought. Mary had been complaining for the last three weeks about her back being a touch sore, but we laughed it off to her increase in mass.

I ate my breakfast and kissed her on the cheek as I walked out the door. The morning was bright and sunny and I felt good. As I walked down the street, I stopped to admire the trees and flowers, marveling in their wonder. Children were playing and all seemed right in the world. After twenty minutes or so of walking I spied a dress in a small shopkeeper's window. As I got closer, I knew I was to buy this dress for Mary. She would love it. I examined it from hem to collar and knew I had to have it. My eyes approached the bust line and it was then I heard it.

"Billy," it whispered so faintly I could hardly recognize it. "Billy this was meant not for you!" it said. Then I saw it, my eyes locked in the window staring at my own reflection. Or was it? I saw it change. I know I did. My face became contorted and vile looking. I closed my eyes and when I opened them again it was gone.

My body became increasingly aware of the cold around me. I began to shiver and shake uncontrollably. Once more I heard the voice, "Billy". And it was at that moment I knew!

I raced home as fast as I could, my hands shaking violently at the thought of what I might be dreading. I still don't know how I knew but I did. I raced up the stairs of our flat screaming Mary's name with each step, screaming louder as I got closer.

The hall was dark except for the light at the end, our home. The door was open and in front of it were our neighbor and two constables. Never could I have imagined this horror in my wildest dreams. Even as I approached the one constable held me back so that I couldn't see inside, but I did. There was my Mary lying on the floor drenched in blood from the waist down. She was still wearing the same gown I had seen her in only an hour prior. Blood had spilled from her womb and onto the hard wooden floor beneath her.

My child, a boy, lay by her feet his throat caught up in his own cord, his frail body bluer than the sky and covered in Mary's life essence. Both were dead.

I found out later that Mary had screamed which alerted the neighbors. The doctor had said that she died in childbirth and even with medical attention she would not have survived. I knew better. Mary had been murdered, taken from me in some vile twist of fate that I could do naught but laugh aloud when they told me. I left that same day. I left Mary and my child at the hospital. I never looked back.

Chapter 3

I boarded the steamer that night. My colleagues on the docks were able to book me passage without incident. It was easy to leave my home, my universe! I felt running away would be easier than facing my life, as it was. Mary was gone, my son was gone, and there was nothing worth staying for. I'm sure the local constables were searching for me, but I figured they would never catch the killer, because he didn't exist. Not in our universe anyway.

So, as it was meant to be, I was to be alone again. "Maybe" I thought," it was better this way?" Alone I could face my existence with honesty, no pretending, and no illusion. "The pain would subside in a while", I told myself. The tears would stop; the fresh sea air would dry them off my face.

The air was crisp that night and the rags I was wearing did little to stifle the cold. I had left with what I was wearing, refusing to take with me any remembrance to that which was my life. The steel floor beneath me was as cold as was my heart. The sounds of footsteps on the deck were both hollow and deafening.

"Perfect," I thought. It reflected both my outlook as well as my mood. France beckoned and I would hear its call. The time was right to leave and it would be good to gain a new perspective.

As I stood on the deck of the ship, I watched as the shore moved farther and farther away, the moon's light shining and illuminating the harbor as well as its buildings. Smaller and smaller they got until before I realized it, England was gone!

I turned and headed towards my cabin, down the narrow passageway and soon I was resting quite comfortably on my bunk. Sleep came quickly. Death, eternal sleep, could comfort me but I was too afraid at this point in my life. I wish now I would have heeded its call then before my visit that was but weeks away. I realized it not then, but hindsight is 20/20. As I drifted off I listened to the squeaks and shudders of the ship. Its sounds were like a demonic orchestra soothing my nerves till I finally drifted off.

I awoke quite suddenly to the moaning of my bunkmate. Gone was his snoring, replaced with the sounds of a wounded animal. His dreams would awaken me but not himself. I rose from my bunk and grabbed my pillow as I made my way across the small cabin. It was all of three steps. I stood over him for a while, pillow clutched in my hands. *"How easy it would be. All I would have to do is push this pound of feathers and hay over his face and hold it down with all my weight for but a moment.* I would probably be doing him a favor. The noises emanating from his body were those of a man in obvious great pain, like he was carrying the weight of the world on his shoulders. I could grant this man mercy and at the same time get a good night's rest.

I stood over him how long I do not know. I do recall thinking, though, of how small the ship was and really having no place to go, it would just be a matter of time before I was found out.

"No, the time is not right."

I turned and headed back to my bunk, crawled in, and stared at the ceiling for what seemed an eternity until the morning came and I saw a sliver of light peek between the large metal plates that made up the ceiling above me.

The noises from this obvious derelict began to wane until he a rose from his bunk, and greeted me with a warm smile. I sarcastically smiled back and turned my head to the wall. "Name's Jon fella, but my friends call me Jack, and yours?" he asked. I slowly brought my head about until I peered into his eyes.

"Billy," I whispered, noticing his eyes appeared black to the core.

"Good sleep then?" he asked.

"Quite," I said, "never better."

"Ah, you're quite the remarkable liar then, I almost believed you for a moment. You've probably been practicing for years. It's rare I find someone like you within my travels," he remarked.

I smiled politely and began to lift myself from my bunk.

"Chances are," he said, "I was making noises all night long. It's been a problem with me since childhood. The sisters at the mission figured I was filled with guilt or maybe even some type of demonic possession. I prefer the latter, it makes me sound much more interesting than I probably am."

"Great", " not only is my life shite, but now I've roomed with an obvious mental health patient."

"Crazy." he said, "Is that the word you're looking for? Don't concern yourself; I've been called worse. Doesn't really bother me you know. I learned a long time ago it doesn't matter what others think of you because in the grand scheme we all end up in the same place. My life is not going to be quantified by others, but by me alone! So fuck off, you pathetic puppet of the masses!"

I was taken aback for a moment not expecting his blatant honesty,

"Jack," I said, " I believe we'll get along fine."

I smiled and looked upon his face as his frown turned to a smile and then all out laughter.

"Billy," he said, as he walked up to me and slapped me on the back, "when we get to France, you will stay with me as my guest. And I won't take no for an answer. It's obvious you're running from something and the least I could do is give you a helping hand. Now I do have to ask you...are you morally challenged or can you accept work of an unforgiving nature?"

My hand came up and in an instant he recognized his pocket watch. " I believe I'm quite capable for the tasks at hand," I stated.

Jack began to howl with laughter, so hard in fact I believed he'd make himself sick. "Come now" he said, "let us go forth and find some morsel of sustenance on this God forsaken ship."

Jack and I talked for hours that day, our lives somewhat mirrored in many ways. We were of approximately the same age, Jack being a little older by five or six months. His ideals, his philosophies, were similar in nature to mine, which I found a little puzzling considering he was raised by his parents and came from a somewhat stable household. He left home when he was twenty-three and learned very quickly how to present himself to society. He was a pickpocket, thief, and such, all the things I was and still am. But he was better in some ways. Maybe his age helped him along or maybe he met the right people at the right times. Experience is a wonderful teacher and I believed that Jack could help me to better my own skills. Who knows, maybe I could teach him a thing or two as well.

His demeanor at times was boorish and outrageous but at other times I could feel that this was not his entire personality. Jack would help me in a lot of ways other than thievery. He would helped me to understand more of who I was and what my potential could be. When we got to France he took me under his wing and cared for me like a little brother. His friends came to know me as "Little Billy, the sheep," because I followed closely behind Jack while in this strange land.

Jack and I carried on like long lost brothers that day. Even as the ship docked into the port we laughed and spoke of the times to come, how we would walk all over this land, taking what we wanted when we needed it and not to be bothered by the normal trappings of man and society.

The ship began to moan and shudder as we landed, creaking slowly as we hit the old dock. As we came to a stop the noise of the ship was changed to the sounds of men cheering and laughing as they disembarked the old freighter. The shuffle of feet on the metal dock sounded like rats in a ceiling, scurrying about to escape their confinement. Jack and I slowly grabbed our gear and made our way to the upper deck in order to leave the ship.

As we made our way out I began to notice the smell of the air as it bounced off the water and products that lay on the wharf.

"Ah, nothing like the smell of salt air and rotting fish, eh, Billy?" Jack said. "Don't worry" he said, "we'll be gone from this place as quickly as we arrived."

We made our way down the gangway and I noticed Jack waving frantically at a group of men on the dock. They shouted back and with that he was gone from my sight. I made my way down and I tried to find Jack.

As I looked about I noticed all the people standing around meeting their friends and families. I saw one man being welcomed by his young bride and small child. Thoughts of Mary and my child slowly crept into my head and proceeded to take my mind to a place I did not want to revisit. I closed my eyes and began to scream within my head as to attempt to block out the pain of memory. Some think memories are a wonderful thing to have; I would rather be free of most of mine! Memory equals pain that cannot be dealt with the stroke of a doctor's blade or the subscription of a pill. Its pain is long lasting but many say it diminishes in time. I rather do not believe that to be true.

Memories are as an open sore that fester over time to the point where they cannot heal. Open and sore, they hurt more and more as time passes by. They can make you strong or weak, depending on how you look upon them. Mine rather fill me with rage and strength, as I know they will never let me go. I sustain myself with the knowledge that all is forsaken for myself and those I love or loved! No, all are gone and I live, alone in the knowledge that I will never share myself again.

As my thoughts turned more sinister, I was touched on the shoulder. I turned and Jack was behind me. He beckoned me to follow and we were off.

Jack brought us to a place dimly lit and whose street felt like it was made of refuse. *"Probably not the best section in the city"* I thought. But it was no worse than I'd seen before.

We walked down a narrow road till we met a sullen fellow sunken into the cobblestone and resembling a fixture rather than a person.

"Jack, glad you're back," he quietly said as he coughed up what appeared to be partially his breakfast.

Jack knelt down and wiped the man's mouth with his own scarf and said, "Glad to be back, old friend, glad to be back". I looked up at Jack with some disbelief as he folded his scarf and tucked it back into his coat.

"Billy," he said, "meet an old friend of mine. Simon here taught me more than I could ever have dreamed about. His skill and friendship were all I ever had for a long time. The man saved my life on more than one occasion and one day I will repay him for that".

Simon slowly looked up at me, almost ashamed in a way to have our eyes meet. I too knelt down before him and gazed into eyes while saying, "Hello". Simon seemed quite despondent before he saw Jack and now with Jack there, he seemed to have been given a renewed existence that slowly crept into his face.

"Billy's here to learn the trade. Though I think he'll teach us a thing or two before I'm done with him!" Jack said. "He kind of reminds me of myself when you first met me, Simon".

With that we slowly rose to our feet to walk into a tavern at the end of the road. Jack swung the heavy oak door open with such exuberance that I felt the hinges would rip from the wall itself. Jack's presence was felt as soon as he entered the room; a huge lumbering man with a boisterous laugh such as his would be hard to miss. We spent the evening and the day after that drinking away any trouble we felt that we may have had and more than likely began some anew.

Hours drifted into days and then into weeks and before we knew it, a substantial amount of time had passed!

Jack and I had become like brothers. I was learning whatever he could teach me including the finer points of thievery and life in general. I learned quickly and Jack at times could not keep up with my thirst for knowledge. I believe at times I quite exhausted the poor fellow.

France had become our playground and all the riches in it became our playthings.

By now the Police were in a state of constant turmoil over attempting to secure our capture. Jack had many friends in the city and all were willing to help out by looking in another direction or hiding whatever goods we may have had. Although the authorities knew, they could never catch us with enough evidence to render our operations invalid. I felt Jack had his finger on everything crooked in the city, including the politicians! One such fellow was the mayor himself, but not in the way one would expect.

After a few weeks of living with Jack, I would notice him leaving late at night by himself and then arriving back home early in the morning. One morning I confronted Jack to his whereabouts and late night activities. Jack with his large hands grabbed my shoulder and chuckled. "Billy," he said, " some things are better left alone."

But I would not relent in my interrogation and pushed Jack till he finally let me know that his late night endeavors involved a certain lady friend of some stature in the community.

"Billy," he said, " you know when we're close to getting caught and for some strange reason we seem to get away with it?" I nodded in recognition of his question. "Well, my boy, seems your old pal Jack has friends in higher places than even you realize. I keep the balance, Billy, plain and simple. Without my lady friend we would have been arrested long ago," he bellowed.

"Who is it?" I asked.

Jack's reply was swift and startling and even caught one such as I off guard.

"Well, Billy, if you must know, her name is Sally, and she's the daughter of a certain Jules Francois Camille Ferry!" he claimed.

"The mayor!" I blurted. "You're screwing the mayor's daughter?" I fell to my chair in disbelief. And in that moment I laughed harder than I ever have before.

"Billy," Jack said quietly as to not disturb my moment too quickly; "she's a hog! Some nights I have to hold back my supper as I look upon her face."

My gaiety changed to somber as Jack told me why he did what he did and by the end I actually felt sorry for the pathetic ass. Jack was my friend, something I'm not wont to say often, and if he needed my help, it would be there, whether he asked or not. It would fall upon me to see how I could assist Jack in having him relinquish this notion of loyalty to his comrades while whoring himself out to the likes of some rich trollop that didn't even respect the likes of us. The plan would take time to set right, but time I had, more than enough for three lifetimes.

Chapter 4

We still went about our regular business and I was to find out that Jack's friend Simon was not what he appeared to be upon first meeting. I thought him a pathetic retch of a man in our initial meeting but as most things; he also wasn't what he appeared to be. I learned that while he was ill for many a month out of the year, he also used it to his advantage one day. I sat across from him and watched as people would throw a coin in his lap and the way he would tug at their coat's, profusely thanking them.

Then I saw it! The man was brilliant and a true magician. While his body appeared old and decrepit, his hands were as fast as a man in his twenties. As he would pull himself up I could barely see it, but he would reach into their coats or their sleeves and take whatever he could get his hands on, a watch, or a ring, even a pocketbook or two containing all sorts of the finer things in life. Simon would notice me watching him and at the end of the day I approached him to speak with him.

"Billy, my friend," he asked, " did you learn anything today?"

I chuckled, " Not unless you take me being made a fool of!"

Simon laughed. "Billy, one secret I'll share with you. Never let people know your full capabilities or you can never surprise them." "*A logical piece of information,*" I would surmise. I sat on the street with Simon and we spoke for many a minute untll il became too dark to see one's hand in front of one's face. Simon was a wise fellow in his own manner, not as loud as Jack, and not as noticeable as well. But I suppose that was what gave him the edge that he needed in order to survive.

Simon lived in squalor, in a seedier section of town than even that in which we lived. Simon had a mother he told me, a sickly woman, who tried him at the best of times. I suppose that's why Simon always looked as close to death as possible. I wondered if he was even ill at all? Maybe just being around someone like that would cause you to bear the same mannerisms as that person. Who knows? Stranger things, I've seen in my life.

I felt sorry for Simon as he spoke of his mother and the burden she placed upon him. Simon explained that she had been diagnosed with Tuberculosis many years ago and that it would eventually take her life. Treatment was not an option as they couldn't afford it and even if they could, it was only meant for the wealthy and affluent. He often wondered if she could be saved, and then maybe life could become normal again.

Jack also spoke of Simon with affection and pity for his situation. He knew Simon could flourish if they could cure his mother but he also knew that treatment was near impossible to get, though Jack had tried. The situation demanded a solution, maybe one that I could provide. I would help and as I thought about it, I realized that there was only one solution available. I could help in the only manner I knew.

Sunday morning arrived. It seemed that the day was going to be special even without my help. The sun was especially bright and high that morning and the dew slowly dried from the rooftops. The streets were still moist from the prior evening's shower and quite slick at times. But regardless of what the day brought, I would not be persuaded from my quest.

As I made my way down the long narrow streets, I found myself humming, something I rarely did unless I was in an especially good mood. I suppose I was in a way. I was helping my friends, something I didn't think I would care enough to ever do anymore. Jack, Simon, and the others had treated me like family, and deserved any help that I could muster. I suppose I could say that as I walked to Simon's flat that I could justify my happiness in such a way that I was helping a friend. Possibly… but I knew there were other motives for my mood that day!

As I reached the flat I waited around the corner, patiently waiting for Simon to leave for the day. As usual, I wouldn't be kept waiting long as Simon was a creature of habit and left every morning at the same time. Dressed in tattered, clothes he pulled up his torn and dirty overcoat over his shoulders while looking at the morning sun with some type of wistfullness of the day. It was in that moment that I knew I could help him and his sickly mother.

Simon slowly made his way done the street and I moved closer to his door. The door opened rather easily with but a slight creak. Inside I could barely see because of the ripped and torn draperies covering the must-filled windows. Everything looked as if it was gray in color and damp to the touch. From inside I glanced around the tiny room in which his mother lay. As I made my way over, I could hear her labored breathing, and I swear I could feel the beat of her heart within the air! Her door was slightly ajar and I could see her lying in bed.

"A sweet looking woman," I thought, "not much smaller than Simon himself." She looked asleep, but alas was not. As I began to enter, I heard her cough and then I opened the door all the way as to enter the room, but I stayed within its frame. Her head turned and her eyes took but a moment to transfix upon my figure lurking within the door.

"Who are you?" she asked.

The only response I could muster was that my name was William and I was a traveling doctor from a nearby village that had treatment for all that were ill. She smiled and thanked me and asked how I knew she was ill. I told her that her son Simon had summoned me to help and that I had met him in my travels while searching for people to help.

As we spoke I sat on the side of her bed and asked her how she was feeling that day. For the most part we had quite the pleasant conversation and she would ask all sorts of questions about how I would treat her. I believe she knew well before I reached across the bed towards the pillow lying across from her. It was thick and soft and felt rather soothing to the touch as I picked it up and held it to my bosom.

"William?" she questioned. "Will I be cured?" I nodded my head in answer. I couldn't speak as I had come to realize in the little time we had together along with Simon's talks that I had come to respect her. In a way she had made me feel that if I had known my own mother, she would have been as this woman was. Or at least one could hope.

As I lay the pillow over her face she did not struggle, nary a whimper came from her lips. She knew, how couldn't she? As I held the pillow there I felt her hand brush my leg and within those last seconds of life I could swear she touched me to thank me. I sat there for at least five minutes and when the deed was done I removed the pillow from her face and tenderly placed it behind her head as too make her as comfortable as possible in her final and everlasting sleep.

I shed a tear that day, for a woman I barely knew. "She was cured," I thought. As I slowly rose from the bed and began to make my way to the door my head began throbbing with a pain that nearly put me to the floor.

"Billy." A voice crept into my brain, a voice I knew all too well. "Your child was the second gesture Billy, today has been the third!" And with that, the voice was gone and I was left to pick myself up and muster the strength to leave. The pain slowly began to wane as I slowly staggered from Simon's flat. I made my way up the street to where Jack was to be. A pint would help my head; I didn't suppose it would hurt anyways.

Simon would be sullen for a while. His mother's, as well as his own pain, were finally put to rest. Sometimes though, I would feel that Simon suspected something but Jack was always there to put an arm around him and reassure him that it was better this way.

I never felt sorrow for Simon; actually at times I felt that I should tell him the truth so that he could thank me! But I knew he wouldn't see it that way. They never do. No, he would probably figure me a monster and turn all against me! Better to stay silent then to let the "jackal's" bay at my door. I had more pressing matters at hand, such as how to help Jack with his little problem.

Weeks went by as Jack and I discussed his need to somehow alleviate his part in this his predicament. Funny, at first I would have thought he had no problem with sleeping with Sally as there didn't seem to be any disadvantages and all the perks. But as we discussed it more, I found that she would present herself as better than most, upper class, almost a part of the few who didn't descend from their high perch in life while still fucking a thief for fun. These were the type of contradictions that drove me quite insane at times. I cannot stand people that think they are better than what they are! I found most persons with some type of stature are this way and while they belittle those beneath them, they too still succumb to the trappings of the poor. At least the poor and downtrodden know what they are, even when they try to better themselves. No, the rich and affluent are the worst type of human, carnivorous for stature and money, while crushing those that may possibly get in the way of their goals.

Animals have more substance than the rich; at least with an animal you know where you stand. Sally was the worst type of animal, a little bitch that Jack rode every once in a while to keep the police from our door and our business thriving. I believed that Jack felt used, almost violated at times, when he returned from his little trips. I asked him why she favored his company at times. He figured that for her it was more than sleeping with him. Her father and all his friends of stature would cringe at the thought of her dealings with one such as he. She reveled in the fact that she could do whatever she wanted, whenever she wanted, and if she got caught her father would pay the political price. The thought of getting caught also spurred her on. The thrill, excitement was but a part of her psyche. "Sick people, the rich," that's what I say; "nothing worse than a person with too much money and not enough sense to use it wisely." People such as I would always fall beneath their notice unless we were to be used by them in some sick fashion for their amusement! Jack was better than this, much better, and deserved more respect from a spoiled rotten little bitch like Sally!

Weeks went by as I saw Jack become more resentful of Sally. I felt a burning in my chest whenever I saw him arrive home from one of his meetings. This had to be put to a stop. But how, I wondered. Killing her would just bring us more trouble than we could handle. No, some other way must happen, something that would take the finesse of someone with nothing to lose and everything to gain. Someone like the bunch of us! Sally should be taken down a peg or two, embarrassed beyond reason.

It stood to reason that killing her would just end her life. Death was too good for her, that's for sure. She needed to suffer for her sins against Jack and the rest of us. Letting her live with some form of degradation was the best way to deal with her, and so it came to be that I would think long and hard as to how I would attempt this marvelous feat. Then as if predestined, it came to me, simple and yet poetic in its justice. Sally would suffer, in that there would be no quarter!

My plan would be simple. I would set her up in such a way that her father and his friends would not only shun her, but loathe her as well. I met Sally once, and while not the prettiest thing, she had a smugness that was defined by the amount of wealth that she had, or rather what her father had. She had a way of taking the wind right out of Jack's sails whenever she talked with him. Belittling him in front of us was for her a game that she relished. Jack would always look away in shame. Never would I have ever expected him to act this way. It disgusted me to the point where I felt the bile rise in my throat.

But Sally had many weak spots, areas that I felt I could exploit. She was a vain person who tried to keep up her appearances with wit and a type of charm not uncommon to her and her family. This would be my means of exploiting her.

She tried for the most part to play her role in society and for the most part had done it quite well. But upon reflection I had noticed some of the quaint almost hidden ways people would react to her. Little things, like a rolled eye when she wasn't looking, a cough when she spoke too long, and so on. She was tolerated for the most part, but not truly liked. If her own kind felt this way about her, then making her an outcast would be easy.

Sally would meet with Jack on those evenings where she seemed bored with life. Their meetings always involved meeting in a seedier side of town where both of them were not known. Sally always dressed down for the occasions. Her father, I suppose, had given her an allowance of some type so that she could rent a room for the evening. Jack always followed her in like a chastised child in trouble with his mother. His head hung low and with remorse. "Bitch!" I thought.

That evening I waited till they entered the Inn and made their way up the stairs to the room. As the door closed I sat down for a pint and waited. Dressed in an old cloak with the hood pulled over my head, I was sure no one would recognize me. As I watched the candle on my table burn slowly down I began to notice its light flickering against the wall in front of me, its flames danced as I lost my head in its dance of light. It became hypnotic as I watched, a life unto its own.

I drank my pint and continued to be held by the specter of light in front of me. Eternity seemed to haunt me as I watched. Time stood still as I heard voices around me but could not move to see their origin. The flame had me whole and completely. Its grip fascinated me in such a way that I thought I would leave my own body and dance with it.

Then I saw it! In the light I saw it form slowly at first and then fade until you could hardly make it out. Then with a vengeance it appeared. That face! Again it would haunt me, for but a split second it was there but in that time I knew he had returned, bastard that he was!

I tried to look away, but the flame had me. My head quivered as I mustered all of my strength to look away, but could not. I felt a grip surround my head and hold me in place. The light flickered again and he was gone! My head relaxed and I could move again.

"Why?" I wondered. "What does he want of me?" I looked about to see if anyone had seen the light, but of course no one had. It was for me and me alone.

After that first visit all was quiet for a time. Then the visits seemed to come more frequently, I thought. Was I losing my mind? No, he was real, haunting me in such a way as to drive me mad.

Thoughts of him disappeared as soon as I heard the door from upstairs open and I saw Jack take his leave. Sally still sleeping in her bed. Jack slowly pulled on his overcoat and hid his head as he made his way down the stairs towards the door of the inn. "Poor Jack" I muttered. I waited until after he left, then I slowly made my way up the stairs as quietly as I could lest I wake the slut in the bed.

Ether is a wonderful solution; it lets people sleep even in the loudest of situations. Stealing it from the local chemist wasn't even a challenge. Slight misdirection is the simplest form of thievery that there is. The bottle was in my pocket as I reached for my handkerchief and proceeded to pull the bottle from my coat. The smell of it was awful as I soaked the rag with the solution. I capped the bottle and put it back in my pocket as I slowly opened the door to Sally's room.

She didn't even flinch when I put the worn wet cloth over her mouth and nose. I don't remember how long I held it there but I knew if she woke up that I would have to kill her. I wanted to, that was for sure, but it wouldn't do, not for the likes of her anyways. I pulled the cloth slowly from her face and put it back in my coat. I shook her as to try and wake her from her sleep, but she wouldn't arise. "Perfect" I thought, as I pulled from my other coat pocket the item of her demise. A small gold locket with a delicate chain that would probably fetch me a month's worth of ale on the market. But of course that was not its destiny. No this was stolen to help Sally with her future, which would be worth any amount of money. That was the beauty of my plan. This little locket would cause her untold grief and embarrassment.

I gently swept her hair back as I lifted her head slightly. The locket's clasp gave me a little trouble but finally closed thus ensuring her fate. It looked good dangling around her neck and resting within her cleavage. The gold shimmered in the moonlight as I got up and made my way out the door. Looking back at this bitch lying there in relative peace I smiled one last time as I closed the door and made my way down the old wooden stairs and then out to the street.

As I passed the second lane I saw the police walking towards the Inn and without thinking almost laughed out loud, which probably would have garnered some unwanted attention. How easy it is to manipulate people I thought. Police especially have the slimmest chance of actually figuring out anything on their own. I mean without some help from a well-placed note within the commissioners office they would never have found a certain thief sleeping the night away. Sad thing is, it was so easy and no one would be the wiser. I continued on my way home and fell fast asleep.

I heard the next day that Sally had spent the remainder of the evening in prison until her father called for her release upon hearing that his only daughter had been detained. I guess it took awhile for Sally to wake up and explain who she was. Simon rushed in that morning to where Jack and I were having breakfast and filled in the remainder of the story. Simon also has friends on the force and obtaining information has always come naturally to him.

He sat there for a number of minutes explaining how the police walked in on Sally alone in the Inn's room and how they tried to wake her but they couldn't. Upon trying they actually noticed the gleam of the gold in the moonlight and took her away for thievery. Jack looked surprised and puzzled. He couldn't believe his ears, as he looked back and forth to both Simon and myself. Simon went on to say that apparently the locket belonged to the wife of one of the mayor's personal friends, one who had helped him establish his career in politics by looking past the mayor's obvious flaws and helping to seal his bid for election. That and the money that must have been dropped in his lap assured me that this would not go away quietly.

Apparently it all made sense when they opened the locket and saw the picture of the man and his wife and instantly recognized them. I would have loved to seen Sally's face when the police finally told her why she was in jail. Sally probably shouted from the rooftops that she had no idea how this came into her possession. Jack listened intently as Simon kept telling us of all the sorrid details of her capture. I held back any emotion as to not give myself away but inside I was laughing as hard as any man could.

It was so easy to steal the locket I mused. Pick pocketing was not usually my style but between what I knew before and with Simon's help in teaching this old dog some new tricks, the crime was but a breeze. Jack looked dumbfounded at best. He couldn't believe what he was hearing. It took awhile until I saw the faint outline of a smile cross his lips. He knew that he was done with her. Never again would he have to stoop to that level of degradation, a free man in such a sense.

Simon left to continue his post that morning while Jack and I finished up with breakfast. Jack was quiet for some time as we ate, but then he turned and looked at me and said "Billy, my friend, you just fucked me!"

"What," I muttered as I choked on my tea.

"I know it was you Billy. You set her up. Only you could do that," Jack stated.

I profusely denied anything that he said, reminding him that she was a thief and got caught, plain and simple.

"No, Billy, that would be too easy," he said. "You and I both know that she has no use for trinkets such as that. Besides, it's only a matter of time before the police know it, too. Even if they don't figure it out, she'll never pay for that crime."

I looked at Jack this time with total understanding. "Jack," I said, " it doesn't matter whether or not she's convicted of this crime; the humiliation and rumors will be enough. I'm sorry but I couldn't watch you do this to yourself anymore. Jack, you're my friend, probably one of the few in all my travels that I can say as such. You are so much better than that, Jack. You didn't deserve to be treated this way now or ever, and as my friend, I had an obligation to help you in any way that I could!"

"Yes Billy, you are my friend. But what you fail to understand is how far-reaching her father's hand is." Jack said. "This will be buried before you know of it and the only people that will believe it are the scum that travel these roads among us. No, Billy, I'm fucked, whether you want to believe that or not. She will blame me and trust me when I say this, that bitch is vengeful".

And as he finished I began to understand what he meant. I had not thought this out properly and Jack would be proven right, given time. As I hung my head in shame, Jack leaned over and put his arm upon my shoulder. After all I had done, this giant of a man had already forgiven me. And for the first time since Mary's death, I shed a tear. All this had been caused by my blatant overconfidence.

Within the next few days Jack prepared himself for travel. I wanted to go with him, but he felt it would be better if I stayed on with the group and looked after things for a spell while he traveled for a while at least, until things could be taken care of or at the very least diminished in capacity. He knew it was just a matter of time before Sally brought her wrath down upon him and he wasn't sure when or what was to happen.

Actually, we were quite surprised that it hadn't already happened, considering she had gotten out that same morning and received a rather public apology from the police for wrongly detaining her. But the damage to her reputation had been done. Whether or not she was guilty really didn't matter. My plan, though somewhat flawed, had pretty much done what it was set out to do, discredit her. More though, was the thought of her explaining to her father exactly how she came to be in this predicament. That more than anything would probably be the crux of her vengeance. If only I had thought this out properly, then Jack wouldn't be in this predicament. For once in my life I was feeling remorse for my actions and the results of them. I wished for a moment that I was back in England and had never met Jack. Life then would be so much easier. But, unfortunately, this was not the case. I now had to deal with the issues at hand even if it meant feeling the way I did.

As Jack prepared, I noticed Simon running towards us down the long narrow streets that we called home. His gait slightly long and sickly in nature, he managed to reach us in a short amount of time. "Jack!" he cried, out of breath. Jack turned and looked at him. "Jack! You must leave now! They come for you, they come!"

"When?" he asked.

"Now Jack, she's fetched the police on you, she knew too much of our operation. You're wanted as a thief," Simon blurted.

Jack hurried to pack his meager things in a sack as quickly as he could. "See Billy, we shouldn't have crossed her!" he said. " I thought I had more time."

Simon began to turn and hide in the alleyway directly across from Jack and me, never one to be caught. He still shouted, "Hurry! Hurry!"

Jack looked at me as I was helping him and said "Billy, leave, lest you, too, are implicated in this mess." "I am Jack, if not for me you wouldn't be in this predicament.

Jack grabbed his bag and as he slung it over his shoulder, he looked at me, and said, "Billy, never doubt yourself or what you did. I know you are my friend. You've proven that time and time again. But the time has come for you to leave so that the others can be taken care of. It's time for the 'Little Sheep' to become the Lion!" And with that he turned and left quietly but quickly down the old road.

"I will, Jack," I whispered. "I will". And with that he was gone.

Chapter 5

I took to my new duties quickly, not wanting to disappoint Jack's faith in me. The rest were behind me, never doubting my ability to lead them. No one knew or even suspected that I was the cause of all Jack's trouble. Jack, I'm sure must have reassured them before he left. I suppose in a way he still leads them. I'm just a substitute for him at best. But if I were to do this then I must be ever so vigilant in my responsibilities.

We laid low for a few weeks, not wanting to draw attention to ourselves. We could afford the luxury of time in this instance. We had some reserves we always held onto for leaner times and it seemed that this was one of those times. We weren't sure if Sally knew of all of us or could even recognize us if the need happened, but it was better to stay out of sight for now. I was sure that Jack wouldn't have given her too much information during the times he was with her.

We would hear something of Jack from time to time, a whisper, a rumor of sorts, but nothing solid for at least a few weeks. Then through Simon's contacts we were given the harsh reality of the situation. Jack had managed to elude capture for several weeks. Always moving as he could, but with limited funds and fewer friends, it seemed that he was doomed from the start. He had indeed been caught just outside Paris near Le Bourget by the French military and was to be brought back to Paris on charges of thievery. *"What was I to do now?"* I wondered. Jack was captured, the men were in dire straits about it, and there was no way of consoling them. Simon was able to get some more information as to where Jack was being held and the possible outcome of his predicament. I would struggle with this for many a day, not knowing what to do, who to turn to. Jack was my responsibility and that I owed him that much was plain to me. Simon's contacts assured us that Jack was to be tried and sentenced as soon as possible. It appears Sally's reach was farther than I suspected. A woman spurned is more dangerous than a wounded beast in the wild.

After further discussion with Simon, I found that Sally had indeed recruited her father to help in Jack's ultimate demise. Apparently she told of Jack's dealings and that she knew of them through a common acquaintance, a character not unlike some of the political friends a mayor may use from time to time. Politicians... they call us liars, cheats and thieves, but they themselves are worse because at least we know what we are and don't hide under some pretentious façade. But like usual, we had to play by their rules.

Simon was able to locate Jack's prison cell and visited him often in the next few days. I was hesitant to go see him, even though I wanted to. I wasn't sure how he would react towards me or if he harbored ill feelings. I was scared, plain and simple. I felt the guilt at times get the best of me and found myself at night holing up in our small cramped apartment that Jack and I resided in. I wondered how I would get him out of there and at times I formulated a few different scenarios that we could try. But every time Simon came back he would remind me of why this wouldn't work.

Jack was being held with a number of guards directly by his cell. There would be no quick fix in which to get him out. I figured my best chance of getting Jack released would be to try talking with Sally and convincing her that she should speak to her father to let Jack go.

Simon arranged for Sally to meet with me on the following day. As I made my way to our meeting place I felt uneasiness around me. A feeling I've had before, one of dread. I knew in my heart that he was around again, I didn't have to see him but I knew! I began to feel paranoid, looking around every corner, turning my head from side to side for a glimpse of him. But he was never there, not in body anyways.

I began to focus myself on the task at hand to try and forget about everything else. I knew that Sally wasn't the type to forgive and forget and it would take all of my abilities to try and turn her around.

As I turned the corner, I saw her house, a magnificent place befitting a politician and his family of their stature. One day, I thought, I would reside in a palace such as this. No matter what it took, I would be there someday.

I strolled up the walk and nervously knocked on the door. The sound of the forged metal hitting the big wooden door was indeed resounding. The echo seemed to go on forever and I thought it would never end. Finally between the sounds of the knocker I began to hear the noise of footsteps approaching. The door opened slowly and with a bit of a shudder.

In front of me stood an older gentleman, with the aura of a servant. He looked me over from head to foot and I knew he had made his assumption within that moment. My dress that day was better than usual but still I could not afford the finer linens and such that these people were accustomed too. I humbly hung my head and announced my name.

"I know who you are," he said in a tone not befitting to a human being and more of the way a person would speak to a dog, "She's been expecting you".

I slowly entered the abode and was told to wait in the foyer. More so, he put his hand to my chest and stopped me cold from entering anymore than was absolutely necessary. I suppose they did not want my kind 'infecting' their space any more than they had to.

As I watched their servant leave to find Sally, I took a moment to examine the entranceway. I guess being a thief all these years had given me a kind of natural ability, almost an instinctive feel for a room before I even consciously look about. The elegance of the foyer was beyond reproach. A crystal chandelier hung from the center of the room, suspended in mid air it seemed, from a domed ceiling that encircled the whole room. A winding staircase that seemed endless as it reached toward the next floor. The room was as stark white as that of a hospital except for the oil portraits that hung from the walls.

It was eerily quiet being there by myself; I could hear the sound of my own heartbeat as I waited in anticipation of Sally's entrance. I made mental notes of all the doorways and windows that were available to me. I figured this may be one of those places that I would have to visit again when all finally settled down.

Then as quiet as a mouse Sally was there, I turned quite startled at first, and I suppose I had been so preoccupied that I never noticed her enter the room. Her demeanor was not pleasant, I thought, as I witnessed her facial expressions. *"What a bitch" "I thought. I shouldn't have to do this. If there were any real justice in the universe she would be the one that would be cowering to me!"*

"What in the hell do you want?" she asked bodley. "He's getting what he deserves and nothing is going to change that!"

It was at that moment I could feel the anger swell up inside my belly and attempt its escape from my torso. *So easy, I thought, "her death would be so quick no one would even hear her scream as I strangled the life from her body. She wouldn't even have time to inhale before I was on her. Then it would be just a simple matter of finding the butler and end his wretched existence as well."* But alas, I knew this was not to happen if Jack was to be freed. So I released my anger slowly by taking a deep breath and then looked up at Sally who was standing there so smug and defiant.

I started to explain that Jack was not responsible for her predicament and that he wouldn't have done this to her. I spoke to her about this for what seemed an eternity, always explaining that someone that had it in for him had set up Jack.

Her look was stern and I could tell she no longer cared. I remember begging for his life, how long I did that for, I can't remember. But I knew it was not to work anyway.

I recall looking somewhere in her eyes, hopeful for some type of emotion other than anger, something that would help me to get to her and save my friend, but it never came. Her resolve was strong and steadfast. My demeanor changed at that moment, as I knew my anger had returned and in a second she would die!

But luck, it seems, is not without a sense of humor as I noticed her father approach from the top of the stairs. He stood at the top of the stairs his arms leaning on the banister that led across the top of the landing, his eyes glazing at me to the point that I felt his look go straight through my body.

"Get this scum out of my house," he shouted. Then he turned and left as I noticed two men enter the room, one from either side of the room. Rather large men, they weren't statesmen, of that I was sure. *"No choice" I thought, "no choice".* I turned and left as they given me little choice. "That bitch!" she laughed as I walked out the door. Even when the door closed behind me, I could still hear her wretched cackle.

I left that morning knowing the outcome. But I was upset and I knew it. I turned and faced the house one last time as I left, and screamed at it.

"I did it, I'm the one, you fuckin' whore! I'll see you in hell!" And with that I left, despondent and without resolve. Jack was doomed and there was naught I could do about it.

Jack's trial was a sham to say the least. It was over before it began, the assumptions were made prior to any evidence being presented. Sally wanted Jack dead, plain and simple. It didn't matter to her whether he was guilty or not, she just required her revenge.

Poor Jack sat alone in his cell waiting for his day of reckoning. I knew this as well and even though many of the men had gone to see him I was still having difficulty with it. Simon, I suppose, saw him the most and gave me reports of his visits. Jack for the most part was in good spirits. Simon would sob whenever he left but he told me that Jack would never shed a tear while he was there. Always happy and never sad, Jack was. Either he didn't understand his predicament or he had made peace with it. Jack had been asking for me, but I could not yet face him. Then on the night before his execution Simon begged me to see Jack. Apparently in all his time incarcerated he finally cried out to Simon. Tears were shed, as he knew his time was near. Simon explained that he had to see me one last time and that he implore to me that I come at once. I knew this time was to happen eventually, and now I had to muster the courage with which to face this man that I had condemned to death for nothing less than being my friend. I looked at Simon and told him that I would go to be with Jack for one last time.

Chapter 6

As in all forms of life I realized the frailty of the situation too late. Jack was to die and I was to bear witness to it. If only I had left before this all happened or better yet, had been caught myself, instead of Jack. Then I would not feel the shame that weighed so heavily upon me now. I hadn't felt like this since my sweet Mary had passed on. She and my child kept creeping back into my mind as I made my way through the hallowed halls of so called justice!

My thoughts seemed to dance around me with no focus for quite some period of time. I seemed in a daze, or better yet, oblivious to the misery that surrounded me as I walked past the cells of the condemned.

I remembered one thing from my days with the sisters, one passage that they spoke to me on a regular occasion as to warn me of my future.

"Abandon all hope, ye who enter here". The words from the sisters rang true for the first time because I could visualize their meaning here in this dark, damp prison. I thought that this was hell. Hell couldn't be any worse than this; there was no way that it was possible. Jack was here and in hell and it was all my fault.

Mary and my son had died and I knew in some perverse way that it was also my fault. I could not atone for my sins but I still had an obligation to see Jack in his moment of need. That was the least that I could do for him.

But with every step my feet felt as if they were getting heavier and my legs felt as though they would cramp up and never go forth. My stomach began to feel nauseous and I felt that I was nearer than I wanted it to be.

Simon had left me at the entrance of the prison because Jack had requested that I come alone. Now I couldn't even hide behind Simon's cloak. I was to be exposed for what I was. Truly, if God existed, he must have had a sense of irony to this situation I found myself in.

I followed the guard to the end of the hall and watched him unlatch the bolt from the door. It swung down with a thud that sent a shiver down my spine. I forgot all the cries and moans that I had heard before and proceeded to walk into Jack's last quarters on earth.

The room was musty and dark. Except for the meager amount of light that came through the window, it was as black as night. I could hear Jack rise from his bed of straw and heard him speak.

"Billy" he whispered. "Thank you Billy, for coming."

"Jack," I muttered, "How are you feeling?" was the only thing I could say to him.

"As well as could be expected in this situation," he said.

"Jack.... I wanted you to know how sor.." and I was cut off by Jack.

"Billy, don't you dare finish that sentence. Don't you ever feel sorry for me, or what has transpired. I needed you here because I had to let you know that this is not your fault.

It never has been, only mine. You need to know that it was me that drove you to this. I know you were only trying to help and you did it in a way that you know. I have never been afraid of death, Billy. Some nights as I looked to the sky I almost waited for its embrace so that I could find out what's next. My life has for the most part been good, but I always understood that something was missing, something better than this, and in last few days I've come to realize that this is my destiny, not yours. Before I die, Billy, you have to forgive yourself, of this there is no debate. I need to know that when I die you can let go of your guilt because in time it will only destroy ever fiber of your being."

As he spoke, he beckoned me to look out the window. " See that, Billy" he said as he pointed to the instrument of his death. " If I could have chosen any way to die it would have been anything else but that!"

My eyes focused on the guillotine in the center of the courtyard and as soon as they adjusted and it came into focus I hurriedly looked away.

"Billy," Jack said, "it matters not that you can't look at it. It will still end my wretched life, and you must understand that death is not the end but a beginning for us all. I've never been a truly religious man, Billy, but I do understand now, what they all meant over the years. I have come to terms with it, Billy, and you must also. Otherwise I can never go to it in the morning knowing that you still harbor guilt. I have to be clean, Billy. I need to know that you can forgive yourself so that I can rest. I've forgiven you and now you must do this so that I can cleanse my soul before I die." I fell to the ground, sobbing uncontrollably, for the first time in my life. This man was by far the greatest that I had ever encountered. Even after all that had been done to him, he still was able to forgive me, and all my sins against him. I knelt by his feet still sobbing, while clutching the straw around him.

"Why?" I shouted as my hands began to hammer the ground by him. "Why?" I asked again. But I knew no answer would be forthcoming. Jack knelt down beside me and picked me up like a doll, and with that embraced me.

"Billy, now is not the time for sorrow. We have little of life left together," he said. "The guard will be here soon to take you out and I must meet once again with my priest to convey my final wishes. But I need this time with you. Please Billy, give me this moment, one of the few I have left."

I paused a moment and began to collect myself. I stood up straight and with all my courage managed to hold back the tears that had only moments before flowed so freely.

"That's my boy, Billy, that's my boy," Jack said as he smiled.

My eyes focused back on his face and I smiled back at him the best that I could. It was in that moment I saw the light behind him! Again it danced as to mesmerize me, but in an instant it was gone. I shook my head and took another look to see that it was as it was before.

"Billy?" Jack said, puzzled, "we don't have much time. Stay with me now."

And as I looked back at him I could see Jack's face was not Jack's anymore. I screamed but no sound came from my throat as I felt Jack's hands upon my head. The pain was so intense that I nearly passed out from it. My head was swirling and I remember feeling outside of my body in a way. I could almost escape the pain and watch it as if I were an observer in this play. Then without warning, it was gone. The room had gone from a dark orange to that of blackness again and I saw Jack lying on the floor.

"Jack!" I shouted as to try and wake him from a deep sleep, "Jack, you bastard! What did you do to me?" But I knew no answer would ever come from his lips. Dead he wasn't but sleeping almost to the point of being comatose. He would not awaken from any amount of shouting or my shaking. And for some reason I knew Jack was not at fault this night. But still I needed to talk to him once more, let him know I forgave myself. I tried to wake him as I heard the telltale sound of the guard steps behind me. Even as he entered the cell I still could not wake Jack. I was oblivious to anything else but Jack as the guard grabbed me by the scruff of the neck and proceeded to drag me from the room all the while he shouted for help.

Two men, one a priest I think, entered the room and began to examine him as I was led to a small corridor down the next wing.

Apparently after a few minutes Jack awoke and sat up. It

was the priest that came back to where the guard and I were and explained that he was all right. The guard loosened his grip upon my coat and threw me towards the exit.

"Lucky one you are", he said, "If he would have died you'd be facing the blade come morning." I scampered towards the door never looking back. Jack was to die and I had no idea why anymore.

My head still ached in the morning as I made my way to the square. Simon came with me. We had in fact spent the rest of the night drinking a few pints and talking about Jack and all his antics.

We had left early that morning as I felt I needed to be close to the execution. Then we waited for what seemed to be hours. People slowly made their way in and staked out their spots for the morning festivities. Death in public places always seemed to be a sort of spectacle that every one needed to see. Parents brought their children; children brought their pets. Other than going to church on Sundays it seemed that this was the only other form of family function that all could attend. 'The world is fucked!' I thought, 'without a doubt', as I looked upon the faces of these degenerate people. Why is it that man can make a spectacle out of the misery of someone else, and then laugh and be merry about it? Sometimes I feel we think a little too highly of ourselves in the greater scheme of things. Jack was above this and I knew he also would shake his head in shame, as the whole of man couldn't even feel some morsel of pity for a simple poor soul. No, we have to feel some sort of superiority towards even the most wretched of creatures! Man's curse and his blessing is that he knows what it is that he feels and he makes his decision consciously.

The square filled quickly and before I knew it we were standing elbow to elbow. The sun was bright that morning and the glint of the blade as the executioner sharpened it was at times blinding. He would do this for a while to start the crowd up and then he would take out the vegetables and began to try out the sharpness of the blade with a little demonstration that got the crowd into frenzy for the main event. Thirteen people were to die that morning and Jack was to be seventh in line. All were allowed to watch the festivities, even the prisoners! I guess it was the last way that they could humiliate them.

One by one they came up to take their place on the platform and one by one they died without their heads. Some cried some even went so far as to try and run in those last fleeting moments of life. They struggled, as they were laid down upon the bed and their heads secured by the massive chocks.

I was so close, that a couple of times I felt the warm feeling of their blood trickle upon my face as the blade severed their heads from their necks.

As I looked about I saw Sally in the crowd, sitting higher than most of us. She sat there smugly in her best dress while holding her parasol in which to keep out the day's sun. She looked upon the day as a whimsical event of no great importance to her, a nuisance perhaps to have to actually witness Jack's demise. Her father by her side seemed more interested in making headway in his bid for the republican nomination than anything else.

And then it came to pass that Jack strode unto the huge wooden structure in front of us. His eyes squinted from the bright light that morning as I could tell he was trying his best to focus on a friendly face within the crowd. The light was so bright that morning that I knew he couldn't quite make us out. They led him up and placed him gently upon the wooden slab.

Jack went to his death with a dignity and peace that I have never seen before in my life. Calmly he lay there as they placed the chock on his neck. As I watched the executioner place his hand on the lever, I realized that Jack had but a moment left.

I consider it essential for you to know that Jack displayed an extraordinary sang-froid and even courage from the moment when he was told that his last hour had come, until the moment when he walked firmly to the scaffold. It may well be, in fact, that the conditions for observation, and consequently the phenomena observed, differ greatly according to whether the condemned persons retain all their sang-froid and are fully in control of themselves, or whether they are in such state of physical and mental prostration that they have to be carried to the place of execution, and are already half-dead, and as though paralyzed by the appalling anguish of the fatal instant. His head fell from the severed surface of the neck and then bounced from the basket and landed, to my amazement, in front of me on the wooden platform.

While not uncommon, it was still quite rare for this to happen.

I knew in my gut that this was no coincidence. I waited for several seconds. The spasmodic movements ceased. The face relaxed, the lids half closed on the eyeballs, leaving only the white of the conjunctiva visible, exactly as in the dying or as in those just dead. It was then that I called in a strong, sharp voice: "Jack!" I saw the eyelids slowly lift up, without any spasmodic contractions – I insist on this peculiarity – but with an even movement, quite distinct and normal, such as happens in everyday life, with people awakened or torn from their thoughts. Next Jack's eyes very definitely fixed themselves on mine and the pupils focused themselves. I was not, then, dealing with the sort of vague dull look without any expression, that can be observed any day in dying people to whom one speaks: I was dealing with undeniably living eyes which were looking at me. After several seconds, the eyelids closed again, slowly and evenly, and the head took on the same appearance as it had had before I called out.

It was at that point that I called out again "Jack!" and, once more, without any spasm, slowly, the eyelids lifted and undeniably living eyes fixed themselves on mine with perhaps even more penetration than the first time. And then for the first time I could see his lips move as to speak, but more they smiled. Then there was a further closing of the eyelids, but now less complete. I attempted the effect of a third call; there was no further movement – and the eyes took on the glazed look, which they have in the dead. The whole thing had lasted twenty-five to thirty seconds. And with that Jack my mentor, my friend, was gone.

Chapter 7

The next few months brought our group nothing but trouble and heartache as we tried to resume our old ways. But without Jack's protection from the police, things had changed rapidly and dramatically. I was no better off as the frequency of my headaches increased, and at times made me feel like I wanted to take a knife to my skull and dig out the pain. Simon had helped as much as he could but without Jack, there it would be impossible to continue.

I was feeling the need to move on. Jack was the mortar that had kept us together and without his presence, we were starting to fall apart. Some of us were rounded up by the police and sentenced to a lesser evil of life in prison, and some of us never came back! I knew it was time as I sat in our, I mean my, apartment, time to leave and move on. Simon held steadfast and true to Jack's teachings and would remain where he was, attempting to hold together what was left of the group. I remember I didn't even have to tell him I was leaving, he already knew. But before I left France there was one last task to be completed.

I remember being in that grand entrance. I'll never forget it. I was only there for a few short moments but it was enough to tell me all I needed to know. Entering would be easy; the far window on the north wall was large enough for me to pass through easily. The staircase was but a few steps from it and I could be up the stairs within a moment before anyone was alerted to my presence. I didn't care anymore if I got caught and sentenced to the same fate as Jack. No, that didn't matter anymore. All that did matter was that Jack's executioner be punished with the same fate that had befallen my friend.

Killing her would require me to become a little more dramatic than usual. No, she would suffer the same as had Jack, on that I would give no quarter! I would wait though and bide my time, for I knew at this time, the politics of the period were changing in France and that a fair bit of attention was being given to this family. The timing had to be right, hurt them when it was least expected!

Simon, fortunately, knew nothing of my plan but I believe he suspected something was afoot from time to time. We went about our daily business, sometimes even taking on meaningless jobs to help support ourselves. Thievery was still an occupation that we desired but with the police watching our every move, our art had been reduced to an occasional pocket being picked.

There were many lean times and sometimes we went to bed without food in our bellies. Even Simon had trouble focusing on his trade. He began to make simple mistakes that only a rookie would make. Maybe it was the pressure or the lack of food? Whatever it was, I still had an obligation to help these poor souls and soon it would be time to do what needed to be done.

That evening the sun went down quickly. As well the full moon shone with a radiance. It was as if fate had intervened once again. When I had awakened that morning, my headaches were extremely painful and at times, I felt the pounding of my head would slowly consume my very being. In my tiny apartment I realized that today would be the day. In the corner I saw my weapon of vengeance, acquired only three days prior. The last two days were spent at home sharpening the rusty old ax from dawn till dusk. I feverishly spent hours honing it until I thought I would use it to cut off my own head that was screaming from the pain. Now it was ready and so was I!

I hid it in an old sack and placed it within my cloak. Walking down the stairs of the apartment, I made my way outside and down the old road. All was quiet except for the meaningless screams of the poor that permeated the night air every so often. I needed out of this place soon before I went insane. If I was successful this evening or not, it wouldn't matter. I would be done here.

Sometimes I felt that if I died tonight at least my pain would be over once and for all. I no longer cared, as my life was a joke anyways. Nothing ever good ever stayed long enough for me to be truly happy. Then the pain started again! I had been free from it for a little while but now it was back and I remember stumbling down onto the street like an old drunken fool. The old sack fell from my coat and made a clang upon the old cobblestone, not loudly, but enough to awaken the drunken bums.

As I looked up, I noticed the constable had been alerted and was working his way down to my location. I quickly fell to the ground covering the sack with my body. I heard him approach and I knew that I couldn't afford to be caught yet, so I did the only thing I could. I placed the sack in my cloak once again and took out my knife from my pocket and palmed it up my sleeve.

I pretended to stagger up from the ground like the drunkards around me. The constable approached me and if need be, I would be ready. As he came closer, I pretended to call to him and slur my words. Hopefully he would see me as another drunken slob and be on his way. If not, then he would pay the price for I would not be stopped this night.

He stopped within five feet of me and looked intensely for a moment. My arm behind my back felt as if it had an entity all its own. I felt the blade slide from inside my sleeve slowly into my hand, always at the ready. Then, as if by divine intervention, he shook his head and turned his attention elsewhere. I waited a few moments till he was out of sight and then slowly made my way back down the road to my destiny.

For a second time I came upon the grand house. But this time it appeared different. It no longer looked as it did in the daylight, less ominous I believe. Maybe it was due to the fact that I knew what was to happen tonight.

I cautiously looked around to make sure no one was around and when I was sure that all was clear, I made my way to the side of the house. I lay the sack down against the wall and proceeded to wrap my hand within a small piece of linen that I had taken from home. I knew that once I had begun my journey here, I would only have a few moments in which to complete my task.

It was late in the night and I knew that the morning sun was just around the corner. Time was of the essence! With my head still sore and throbbing, I decided that I must make my move now, and slowly I raised my hand up to the glass. My hand shattered the glass with ease as I bore it down onto the glass. Surprisingly, it was very quiet, and the point that I was so worried about had now become moot.

I brushed away any glass that may have still remained within the bottom of the frame and then slowly lifted up my torso and the sack to enter through. Slowly I crawled through and began to lower myself into the inside of the house. My feet crunched broken panes of glass that had fallen to the floor. I turned and got my bearings and saw that the moon's light had made my job much simpler this evening as the halls were well illuminated.

I crept up the stairs to try and find Sally's room. I knew if I didn't find it soon then a lot of people would die this night. When I reached the top of the stairs, I observed the upper hallway had a fine carpet on its floor, probably woven by peasants and sold for an outrageous sum. As well, there were five doors lined its walls. Two doors to the right, two doors to the left, and one at the very end. I would assume that the one at the end would be a secondary set of steps to the lower level and the others would be bedrooms.

As I made my way to the first door, the floor would creak ever so gently that I would have to stop for a moment lest I awaken everyone within the house. I would take a step then stop and let it settle. Then take another and so forth. The first door I came to was partially open and when I gazed in I saw that the room was empty. For a moment I could feel my heart pounding against my chest so heavily that I forgot about my headaches for an instant. I then crept to the second door to the right and slowly turned the knob. The door opened without a sound and as I peered, in this time I saw the bed of the bitch that killed my friend.

Sally slept ever so peaceful in this rather large four-poster bed. The canopy was made of the finest linens, while her bed was fashioned from down. I watched her sleep for a few minutes. Maybe I was hesitating, I do not recall. I do know that when the time came, I slowly unsheathed the ax from out of its case and held it halfway up the hilt in my right hand. The moonlight hit the blade at just the right spot. I slowly leaned over the bed and took my left hand and placed it firmly over her mouth.

Sally awoke with a start and in the instant she recognized me, she also knew what was to come. She struggled as she lay there. My strength more than likely doubled by the surge of energy I felt held her fast to the bed. With her screams muffled by my hand. I chuckled to myself as I slowly brought the ax up and into the moonlight where she could see it. Her eyes, wide as a cow's could see the instrument of her death and the man that would wield it.

"Sally," I said, " Jack bids you welcome to his domain. He's waiting for you!"

With that I removed my left hand and swung with my right as hard as I could. She uttered a scream that was cut off as the ax fell hard upon her throat. In an instant her head came loose from her body and the canopy dripped with the blood that had sprayed against it. I released the ax that was still embedded within the sheets and took a breath.

Then I heard the door behind me swing open and I turned to see who was there. I suppose in the instant that she had screamed, she had awakened her father from his sleep and he had come to investigate.

What he saw was beyond description! I stood over her body like the Grim Reaper. An ax was separating her body from her head. He knew she was dead!

I saw his hand rise quickly but nervously, and in the moonlight, I saw the revolver that he held. My first instinct was to run and jump from the window. But for some reason I needed to see this through until the end. So I did what any crazy person would do in this situation. I ran towards him, never thinking of the danger, much less caring. I ran as fast as I could. Noises were emanating from my throat and I must have sounded like a wild beast as I slammed into him!

He fell quickly and hard and we struggled for a few moments. I don't recall how, but somehow I managed to retrieve the revolver from his hand in the ensuing struggle I heard a shot. Not as loud as usual, more muffled. Our bodies had covered the sound as we both looked at each other in disbelief. Then I felt it, the blood warm against my hand. His face changed from anger to shock, and I knew he was mortally wounded. I watched him as his life flowed from his body and when our eyes met again I laughed. Not loudly, but rather quietly enough so that in the final moments of life he could hear me.

"Jack will have much company this evening," I whispered. Then his eyes rolled back exposing the underside and he was dead. I rolled off him and gathered my things and prepared to leave.

As I approached the doorway I took one last look at my handiwork and smiled briefly before turning and fleeing down the stairs. The house was awake now and I knew it was only a matter of time before someone else came to investigate. As I took my first step down, I saw the butler at the bottom shouting. I quickly turned and fell back in the room. My only escape was through the window and I knew it.

I put the revolver into my pocket and without thought, ran to the window and fell through to the ground below. The impact of the window was easier than I thought; it was my meeting with the ground that I would like to forget!

I lay on the ground for a moment and then I quickly rose to my feet. At this point I could hear screams coming from the bedroom and I knew I had only a moment to escape. I turned and with that I was gone into night's embrace.

I returned home tired, both physically and mentally, and collapsed on my bed. " Billy," it purred, "may we talk now?" I awoke instantly, shaking and covered in sweat. My bedroom felt hot, the air thick and hard to breath. "It is only me, Billy. You remember, don't you?" he whispered. There was a soothing quality to his voice and I turned to face it.

There he sat at the end of my bed, an apparition and yet, somehow, very real. He was tall, maybe six foot four, and dressed in clothes that were of another time. Velvet and lace and all sorts of finery adorned his body. His hands were large, not brutish, but long and delicate, with nails painted glossily black. His face bore little resemblance to a demon. More to the point he looked angelic, and I felt myself becoming enraptured with this princely figure."

It is good that you are not frightened, Billy, for I have come with great deal of faith that you are the one," he spoke quietly.

I slowly sat up, now enjoying the warmth that filled my room. "What do you want with me?" I asked, unable to understand.

He turned away and began to laugh, a loud crazy laugh, and as he did my room became even warmer. He threw his head back and held his arms with fist clenched towards the sky and screamed, "I want my pound of flesh, Billy!"

I felt my flesh burning as if someone had set it alight but remained calm in the face of this tantrum. His face was becoming more and more flushed as he screamed," I want my pound of flesh, Billy, and I want taken straight from the bone!" He focused his stare at my bedroom window and laughed hysterically as it shattered at my feet. I recoiled at the sight of him now. His yellow eyes glowing brightly in the Darkness, highlighted the deepening wrinkles in his face."

Right from the bone, Billy, and you'll do it for me, won't you?"

This was not a question. It was a statement of fact. In as much as this scene was
frightening me, I already knew I would do as asked.

"We'll be together forever, Billy, me and you. Would you like to live forever Billy?"

I am ashamed to admit how fast I answered. The word came as natural as breath. "Yes!" and it was done.

The wind howled outside as the temperature changed and I began to shake uncontrollably. Wrapping my blanket around myself I went to the window, stepping carefully around the shards of glass." Life ever lasting," I yelled to the street below," ever lasting life!"

I turned to face him again, to thank him, to worship him, but he was gone. I was alone in my room with no sign of him even having been there. I stepped carelessly on the broken glass and immediately winced in pain, as my foot was sliced open. Blood spilled onto the floor from the open wound until it seemed that my body would drain itself. I was feeling light-headed as I moved toward the bed, collapsing into it almost immediately. When I awoke it all seemed again like a dream for my window was not broken, my foot was almost completely healed.

I found my way out into the street. *"Madness"* I thought, *"such beautiful madness. I could not die. Nothing would threaten me now".* I laughed aloud. People in the street stopped what they were doing and looked at me. I was in a manic state by now. My eyes wide, my whole body perspiring.

"You there," I heard an old lady call. "Shouldn't it be time to call it a night and go home to the missus?"

I raced over to where the old woman stood and grabbed her by the waist. How frail she was! Her skin hung off her bones, gray and wrinkled. How much longer would she live? She must have been seventy at least. I was thirty-two and would never know old age. I would never turn gray and wrinkled. I would remain in the state that I was, the prime of life!

"Give us a kiss, Mother," I requested moving my face to within inches of hers. She furrowed her brow and stepped back.

"You must have had your share of drink last night," the old lady surmised. "Off with you then. Your missus will be worried."

She turned and started on her way. I watched her hobble down the street. I wished I could do something for this frail thing, so sweet and unafraid. She glanced over her shoulder maybe realizing that I was watching.

"Off with you, then!" she shouted, trying to sound stern. Motherly. She smiled then and in that one instant I felt like a child not an orphan.

I carried on down the street, my destination unknown. My purpose though was never in doubt. I wanted to try killing myself. It was really the only way to proceed. I had to know undoubtedly that I could not die. How was I to proceed? I must admit I was still a little hesitant, quite unsure actually. Then the headaches started again and I knew how I would make my first attempt.

Walking back to the apartment, I strolled to the bed where my cloak lay. Inside, I reached into the pocket, which held the revolver that I had just received hours before. I grabbed my pillow and slowly enveloped my hand that was holding the revolver. Better I keep this as quiet as possible lest I attract too much attention.

The barrel of the gun was cold as it touched my temple. I laughed aloud as I slowly pulled the trigger knowing that I could not die and maybe this would help with the ever-increasing pressure within my skull! As the hammer came back I could hear the click as it fully retracted and the pressure released from the trigger.

The sound was deafening being that it was right beside my ear. My eyes closed by instinct and I recall feeling the tiny metal propellant slowly enter the side of my temple. Even though it happened within a split second, to me it was excruciatingly slow.

At first the bullet pressed against the hard bone of my skull. And then as the pressure increased I felt my head finally give way and the bullet enter my skull. I felt its path as it sliced through bone and flesh, every movement never to be forgotten. I felt it push through the other side of head just above my ear and I watched it as the tiny fragment, now slightly distorted and with bits of gray matter and blood encapsulating, it hit the bedroom wall and finally come to rest. There was no pain at first, not even a hint.

Then without warning it rushed me as if to let me know that I was still alive. I screamed for how long, I do not know. I fell to the ground holding my head in my hands; I felt the warmth of my blood on my hands and the certain presence of meat within my palms. I attempted to push back the remains of the side of my skull but as I did the pain felt more intense till I finally dropped it to the floor and witnessed my own flesh hit the old wooden floor. The pain increased and I felt myself slowly starting to lose consciousness.

But before that would happen I heard a rather large pounding at my door as well as screaming. I slowly pulled myself up and supported my upper torso with my arms. I knew that if anyone came to my aid now, they would see what I had done.

I shouted back that I was okay and that I had cut myself deeply on broken glass. The voice on the other side of the door shouted to be let in and I refused again, claiming that all was well. My body was so wracked with pain, I myself wasn't sure how I was able to speak at that moment. Then the voice disappeared and I collapsed to the ground surrounded by my own blood and flesh.

I came to a day later and wished that I was still unconscious. The initial pain while intense was nothing compared to the throbbing that still occurred. I slowly touched my blood encrusted fingers to the wound and screamed again in pain. It was at that moment I realized that I had just made the most foolish mistake of my miserable existence. Never before did I truly wish death to embrace me more than at that moment.

The pain was excruciating and I couldn't believe that I would not at least be able to be put out of my misery! My deal…. my curse now laid out to me as plainly as the morning sun rising in the east. I could never die! Never, no matter how much pain there was! I realized I was no longer blessed. I had made a deal with the devil and damn me, I should have known better after all those years of living with the sisters.

It took me two days before I could even stand long enough to leave my apartment and steal food from the Inn below. My head wrapped in bandages, I would leave my room at night while everyone slept and I would scrounge up some morsel of food to eat. I drank a lot of ale as well. Constant inebriation was a better state to be in because it helped numb the pain.

By the third morning I awoke to find Simon had somehow entered my room. Apparently he gained entrance with his skill as a lock pick. No surprise really, I knew it would happen sooner or later. It was just a matter of time. I awoke to find him sitting in the only chair that I had, alone by my table in the corner of the room. My eyes focused on him as he arose from the chair and made his way over to the bed. He looked over my bandaged head and quietly looked down.

"Simon," I said, "I seemed to have had a little accident".

He looked up and shook his head. "I don't want to know, Billy, I don't understand it. A wound of this magnitude and I should be looking at a corpse," he said while observing every angle of the bandage.

"It's not as bad as it looks. I got into a bit of a drunken scrape the other evening and apparently I was not victorious," I said knowing that he didn't believe me. But what could I tell him, the truth?

Simon and I had an understanding by then, we knew when each other was lying. But we also knew when to let things go and move on.

He stood up from the bed and made his way back to the table where he reached over to grab the newspaper, which lay there.

"Here, something for you to read," was all he said as he tossed it unto the bed. "I'll find you some breakfast. Your probably starving by now."

With that he turned and was off. I reached down to pick up the paper and saw the headline. My ability with the French language was still not that good. Speaking it was easier than reading. But I was able to make out the headline and a few sentences.

Apparently the news of my latest endeavor had hit the paper. The first sentence read; "*The violent polemics aroused against him at this time caused a madman to attack him with a revolver, and he died from the wound, on the*

March 17, 1893. The chamber of deputies have voted him a state funeral".

"A madman?" Yes, more than likely I was that, at the least. But as it seemed I was not to be pursued as no clear description was able to be obtained. I put down the paper and closed my eyes and fell asleep once again.

For the next three months I sat in my apartment, Simon caring for me in his own fashion, never asking questions, never discussing what we both knew to be true. The pain slowly subsided as I watched my skull attempt its best to heal itself. The fragments closed up in such a fashion that I knew I was to be scarred forever. My hair grew back over the other side so that the exit wound was at least covered. I even kept a fragment of my skull in my pocket to always remind me of my stupidity! My headaches still resided within my head but I was able to tolerate them better now.

My tolerance level, I suspect, was higher after what I inflicted onto myself.

As the weeks passed, I was able to help Simon in accepting his new duties and responsibilities as the leader of the group. I had to leave. As was as the last time with Mary, there was nothing left here for me. I needed to explore the world a bit more. Hell, I had all the time in the world!

Simon was able to secure my passage out of the city to Le Havre where a steamer awaited me. I figured it was time to travel to the "New Land", explore the world a bit more. With a new century on the horizon it was time for me to leave the old ways behind and begin again. One last task remained, though, before I could leave.

Simon gathered up the men as we met in our usual spot in the Inn. I knew that some would not take the news of my departure well, while others would more than likely rejoice! All in all, I explained to them the need for me to move on and that despite his look, Simon was the perfect man to lead them to prosperity. Some asked if I would return and even though I did not know what to say I just said..."Maybe," knowing full well that I would not. These lands held to many memories for me now.

I left early the next morning, not wanted any fanfare or anything of the sort. A quiet exit was what I needed the most right now. With a few meager things in my possesion, I would board the steamer to the new world, America!

I still looked a fright when I took off my hat, so it was best if I tried for the most part to stay below in seclusion and try to imagine the look of New York, our port of destination. I could hole up for the next ten days. Hell, I'd been stuck in my apartment for longer than that! Seclusion was fast becoming my new friend, and at this point in my life, I embraced it!

Chapter 8

New York was a captivating city, larger than I was accustomed to. It contained everything that a person would ever require. I spent the first few days exploring the terrain and attempting to secure some lodging as well as employment. Of course, I supplemented my income using my other skills for a while. But I wanted to blend in here, not create any more disturbances in my life right now. The last thing I needed or even wanted was more attention from the locals. I had done enough of that type of self-destruction in France and to tell you the truth, I was getting tired of it. My headaches also seemed to diminish while in New York; the frequency of their attacks seemed to come farther and farther apart. Unfortunately, they never did disappear all together, but it was better than before and I wasn't about to complain. With everything that I had been through lately, I felt that I wanted to try and live a somewhat normal life for a while, take a vacation from my existence, so to speak. So I tried to get a job and an apartment and 'lay low' for a spell.

I did secure a decent wage after a while and even rented my own place in a tiny borough called Brooklyn. I spent my day off, visiting the city, shopping for food and clothes, and 'blending into' my surroundings. The world was changing and I could see it. I remember seeing "Liberty" for the first time, quite a unique experience I must say! She, like I, came over from France around the same time. She, of course, a few years earlier, but still pretty close one would think.

I went to work every day, working for the city in its new form of transportation, something called a subway, a series of tunnels underneath the city that would have trains ride on its rails. Working underground was better for me anyways. Less chance of people asking questions which I did not want to answer.

By 1900 the city opened the first of the many tunnels that it would need. Working on it for the last four years was a chore but one that I almost enjoyed. The pay wasn't great but it allowed me an opportunity I hadn't had before, a chance at some normalcy for a change. I would continue working in the tunnels as new lines were being introduced all the time.

As the years went by, I never realized that I was not aging as other people. My hair stayed the same color, my skin similar to that of a few years prior. I did not age, not even one day! Unfortunately I was not the only one to notice this. Some co-workers commented from time to time that I always looked the same. While I tried to keep to myself for the most part, there were times of interaction between us. I had to move from time to time and not reside in the same place for too long, lest more questions be asked of me. At work I started to constantly change shifts and work in different tunnels. I did this for a number of years so as to not solicit suspicion. When I arrived in New York I was determined to start a new life for myself, and I did just that. A new job, a new apartment and a new wife!

I never thought I could love again, after Mary that is, but I guess with time some wounds heal enough for you to go on. I never set out looking for love but regardless of what I wanted, fate again intervened. Diana was her name, a woman that I came to befriend over a period of time. She lived in the same block as I, and from time to time I would see her walking down the street as I watched through my window.

At first I never really noticed her. I mean I saw her but I never paid that much attention to her, as I was probably too immersed in my own life to realize her beauty. I first began noticing her as I worked the night shift. I would arrive back home in the morning and always saw her across the street at a small booth made up of scraps and such material. It was nothing fancy, but it provided some cover from the elements. She went to work every morning selling roses at the corner and after some time I would wave as I went by. But she never responded to my attempts at friendship. "Stuck up," I thought.

Then one morning it dawned on me as I made my way home a little earlier than usual. I watched her this time, setting up her booth and such, when I noticed her looking for her pot of flowers that she always carried back and forth every day. Her hand searching for the metal bucket just inches from her, never touching it but constantly searching with her hand. She was blind! Of course! That's why she never paid me any heed when I tried to befriend her. She couldn't see me wave. I watched her that morning as she struggled to find the bucket and then finally, I walked over to help.

As I crossed the street I spoke to her to announce my presence and to not catch her off guard and surprise her. I asked her if she needed some help and in the sweetest voice I've ever heard she spoke back to me. "Thank you, kind sir," she said. "Some days I have a little trouble remembering where I put things."

"Not a problem, glad to help," I replied.

And for the first time in a long time I slowly removed the covering from my head. She was so sweet looking and vulnerable at that point that I had trouble walking away and continuing my way home. We spoke for a while that morning as I helped her set up for the day. We talked for about an hour before I realized that I actually needed to get home and have a bite to eat. My stomach growled in anticipation of food as it did every morning at this time. I guess the rumble was quite loud as Diana laughed at the sound. I apologized for my body's lack of decorum at this time.

"Nothing to apologize for, you must be starving after working such a long shift," she remarked.

"Apparently, I guess, I am" I said. "I suppose I should be on my way then," knowing full well that I really didn't care to leave as I was enjoying our time together."

Diana smiled and reached down to a sack she had hidden on a shelf behind some flowers. As she retrieved the sack, she looked up at me and began to unwrap the sack. In it were two rather large pieces of bread, an apple and a piece of sausage. Diana held them up to me and without hesitating offered her lunch to me. I, of course, politely refused the offer. As much as I appreciated it I could not take this fine woman's meal from her.

"Well, sir," she said, " it seems that chivalry is not quite dead yet. Perhaps then you would at least share this with me, as it is rather a large meal and sometimes I have a tendency to pack more than I could ever eat."

"Well, then," I said. "I suppose it would be rude of me to not help out a damsel in distress!" With that we sat down and I realized that this would be the first meal since I arrived in America, that I had shared with anyone.

For the next month we shared many a moment like that. Sometimes I would bring food, but mostly she did. The more we talked I began to feel a friendship forming. I would sit with her as she worked, sometimes with my head covered whenever people came by to purchase a rose or such, other times I felt free as I let my slightly disfigured affliction taste the morning wind. Diana could not judge me based on my accident. She would never see the ugliness that I had inflicted upon myself, and she would never see me grow old and gray. She was a pretty woman, around five foot four, I believe, with brownish shoulder length hair and the richest brown eyes I had ever seen. I remember staring intently into them for hours knowing that they couldn't see back.

Somehow though, she saw me with her other senses. She would touch me to be able to see me and every time her hands went closer to the side of my head I would always have to stop her from 'seeing' that which I did not want her to see.

Our friendship flourished for many a week and I slowly found myself falling in love with her, even though I did not wish it. Diana as well, I believe, was smitten with me. I could tell in the way she talked and the way she acted whenever I would come about. I hesitated for many a month in allowing my emotions to take over again.

I remember what happened with Mary and the warning I received. No, it could not be. I would not let it happen again, even if it meant that I would never experience love again. Diana would be spared! Of that I was sure. So it was to be that I would only maintain a friendship with her, keeping my distance and regretting every moment that I could not love her properly.

At times I felt Diana wondered why our friendship never blossomed into anything more. How could I explain it to her? I was protecting her, from me. I wanted more, that I would not deny. Every time I saw her my day seemed complete. Even my headaches seemed to dissipate when I was around her. I was scared to share my feelings with her; sometimes I would put on a false front in my conversations to her, just to keep her from getting too close. It probably wasn't fair of me to do. The gentlemanly thing would have been to walk away and let her alone. But I couldn't! As much as I wanted to, she drew me to her like a moth to a flame. Diana had this natural way about her of calming me when I most felt the need. Her personality was quite unique, one that I don't believe I had ever encountered before in my lifetime. She was without a doubt an angel sent to earth. Never before would I have believed that a superior force could have produced such a wonderful soul such as this. She never seemed to get angry with people no matter what they did to her, a gentle soul that was too good for this world and definitely too good for one such as me. I suppose she was my opposite in a way, and that's why I needed to be with her.

Whenever I would see her I found myself smiling on impulse, rather unconsciously at first. Then as I began to realize my intentions for her, I would find myself trying to stifle my feelings. I didn't want to see this woman get hurt on my account. But the more I tried to keep my emotions in check the stronger my longing for her became. He was playing another cruel joke at my expense! Why could I not be happy?

As I sat alone once again in my dingy apartment, I slowly filled my glass again and again and cursed the day I was born. The longer this went on, the more I felt the anger rise within my stomach and the more I drank! The liquor went down smoothly considering its value. Hell, the truth is it scratched my throat as it went down but I could have cared less. Nothing was easy, never has been, never will be. I emptied the bottle that evening without even thinking. Sleep came easy; it usually does after that much spirit.

I awoke the next morning to a blistering headache and the sun barely above the horizon, my head slowly rising from its perch on the table where it had lain all night before. I gazed out the window to see the dawn slowly approaching. My eyes slammed shut as the morning light hit them squarely. It was still quite dark out and I still felt partially inebriated. Again I attempted to open my red swollen eyes, slowly at first, as if my head would burst if I opened them too quickly. At first I saw nothing except for a tiny sliver of morning light from over the windowsill, and as my eyes adjusted to the coming morning, I looked around at my surroundings. Shadows filled the room from top to bottom as I gazed around my tiny apartment. My eyes circled the room from left to right and focused on the left corner of my suite. The shadows flickered there for some reason as if they were being manipulated. Then as I focused more I began to see why. I wiped my eyes and shook my head as if to clear whatever it was that I thought I saw. Then as I looked back again to make sure I wasn't imagining it, it finally dawned on me that I was not alone!

I violently scrambled to my feet and in turn knocked over the chair, which was my bed last night. I felt my back as it pressed tightly against the wall behind me, as if to push my body directly through it. My eyes now were wide open, and sweat began to flow from my brow as I watched the shadow transform into solid living flesh. It took but a moment but it seemed to take forever as I watched the shadow slowly snake its way towards me. I was transfixed; I could not will my body to move an inch! As it transformed, I began to recognize the figure before me. It was he who had cursed me to live forever!

Dressed sharply for a man that had no clothes but a moment before, his stride came to stop within an inch of my body. I swear I could not move as his head lifted up and his eyes reached mine. His gaze burned me to my very soul and I wanted to scream, but no noise came from my throat. He grinned, as he looked me over from head to toe, a mischievous grin that a child would have. His hand slowly crept up the side of my body, just lightly touching the outer edge of my clothing, my skin repulsed as his hand moved closer to my face. His bony fingers reaching towards my cheeks and then he grasped my head in his hands.

"Billy" he purred, " I heard you call me, and I know what it is you ask of me". I tried to speak but couldn't. "Shh… Billy," he said. "You don't have to tell me I already know. I can't believe what it is you ask. I would have figured you brighter than that. But, in a way I guess it was to be expected sooner or later. You are just a man after all. I can help you Billy, help you to be with her if that's what you want. But you must understand that there is a price to be paid! A balance must be maintained. The price may be too high for even one such as you. You will watch her age, you will watch her become ill, and eventually you will watch her die. Is that something you wish to experience, Billy? Is it truly what you want? No matter, don't answer, I can see it in your eyes, your very smitten with this one, aren't you Billy?"

I could not answer still, the sweat on my brow becoming more and more intense with each passing moment. I couldn't feel parts of my body anymore; his proximity to my body had somehow begun a numbing feeling that made its way to my bones. He laughed again, and I began to feel the nail of his index finger brush my cheek. "Billy, I hope for your sake that it was worth it. Agnes will not be forgotten, but she can be fooled for a while" he stated.

Then all at once I remembered, and I tried to stop him. But it was too late! The wound I received so long ago on my cheek began to open again! The blood poured from it and I felt the pain. Felt the pain as if it was the first time all over again. Agnes, Lilith, whatever her name was, had given me this many years before, so long that I had almost forgotten it. But now I remembered, all too painfully I remembered. He laughed again and then from his open mouth I saw the beasts' wretched tongue as it slithered from it's opening and made its way into my wound. The pain was intense; I felt it as it went deeper and deeper into the abyss. I myself wanted nothing more than to lose consciousness but it would not come.

His tongue darted from side to side, up and down and then after a few moments it retracted back into his mouth carrying with it some of my own blood. As he gulped down the last of it, the pain began to subside and I watched as he stepped slowly back into the shadows. My arm twitched and without realizing that I was free of his grip I instinctively reached for my face and my cheek, thoroughly expecting a gash as large as any I've had before. But there was none. My cheek was completely healed. The scar itself was no longer there and I knew he had taken it back with him.

I watched as he retreated and before he disappeared completely, he said to me, "Remember, Billy, the balance must be true." And then he was gone, and I fell to the table completely exhausted.

I slept that whole day as well as most of the following day. I awoke to find that I was late for work, and without very much thought hurried to get myself ready. Within minutes I was out the door and running down the street towards my destination.

As I ran I saw Diana closing up for the evening. I slowed my pace so that I could watch her for a few seconds more. She was so beautiful, I thought. I've never met a woman such as this in all my travels. I usually associated with whores and thieves. Diana was different! Sometimes she reminded me of Mary when she spoke. But even though I had loved Mary with all my heart, she was still not as innocent as Diana. Whenever I was near Diana I felt that all my problems would disappear and that we were the only two people in the world. This woman, even though blind, saw more than any human being I'd ever met before. She had a way of looking at every adversity and turning it into something positive. She was as polite as anyone could ever be, and even when people wronged her she inevitably was able to forgive them without hesitation.

I didn't understand why I loved her, being that she was the type of sheep that I usually cringe at. Maybe it was because she was blind? Did I feel pity for her, and was I even capable of that emotion anymore? Or possibly she finally showed me what a human being was capable of.

I began to realize that never before had I met someone who seemed not to have any hate or spitefulness within them. If anyone should be sainted, it should be this woman. Maybe, just maybe this time I could be happy! And now it was possible, finally. If I gave up this opportunity it would be something that I would regret until the end of time! I had to be with her, this I knew. Damn the consequences, those I would deal with when I had to. I knew that he had given me a gift, a gift that could end my loneliness for once. Yes, if this woman would have me, then I would not falter and for once without conscience would follow my heart. And for once I carried on to work quite happily!

Chapter 9

Diana and I began to see each other more and more over the next few days. When I was with her my headaches seemed to disappear and I felt more at peace then I ever had before. I was changing, growing softer; I felt the anger that I had felt all these years being swept away every moment that I was with her. I never would have expected myself to feel this way. It never occurred to me that I could ever be happy again, especially after Mary.

Days turned into weeks and then months passed without me even realizing it. I would spend every waking moment at her booth, helping when I could, making sure that customers would not steal from her or short change her. She in turn was helping me in becoming the type of person that when I was a child I always thought I wanted to be.

We wed six months later in a small ceremony in a church! A church, she actually talked me into a church! I didn't care though. Whatever she wanted. I could look past my own grievances at this point. I didn't care anymore; if she wanted this and it was important to her, then I would do whatever it took to please her. It was a small ceremony without much fanfare. We both had no real friends to talk about. Diana had a sister that she rarely talked with, so it was a simple matter… the marriage that is.

We moved into her apartment and I let mine go. It made more sense to be in hers because of her affliction. She knew where everything was and how to move about. She was quite remarkable in that sense. She was able to go to work everyday by counting off the steps it took to be at her booth. She was able to go to the market and purchase goods. She was quite independent.

We settled in and over the next few months grew to love each other more and more.

Four months into our marriage, Diana informed me that she was pregnant and that I would be a father. It was at that moment that the reality of the situation hit me. I never meant for us to have children even though I knew she desperately wanted them. I couldn't bear the thought of losing another child as I did with Mary.

I panicked within myself, as I knew Diana had absolutely no idea why I was so hesitant to be happy. I feigned happiness as best I could but I knew she saw through the facade. I tried harder and harder to express joy and it seemed the more I did the more upset she got. How could I explain my hesitation to her? There was no way to explain it without looking like I was mad! I did my best to console her but it took days before things got back to normal.

I went to work as usual and in the next few weeks saw Diana growing larger and larger. I did my best to hide my guilt and fear but she always could see through me. I was worried that the same fate awaited my new child. I knew that it would destroy Diana if he or she were to die. I couldn't bear that. She deserved better than that. I didn't, but she most definitely did!

Then about two months into her pregnancy as I was walking home, I proceeded down the alley that had become a short cut for me. It was early as I again was working the night shift. I was tired and deep in thought as I made my way home. As I turned into the alley I felt it again! I always felt it coming now. It was like my body had become so accustomed to it that whenever he was near my skin would crawl.

I turned to look around, but all was quiet. But I knew he was near, if not him, than one of his minions! I kept walking and as I made my way down the alley I knew something was to my left. I didn't see anything, I just knew! I stopped and slowly turned, not scared this time but angry!

To my left was a child, not more than six years old. He just stood there staring intently at me. The area around his eyes blackened and without any eyes at all. Only sockets where the blackness seemed to never end. He stood there waiting, for what I do not know. His clothes were tattered and torn dirty from soot and almost looked as I had in my youth. He had no shoes. His feet dirty, his nails long and jagged from what appeared to be attempting to claw his way out of something. His demeanor and look would have scared anyone. But I was not scared! Again I was too angry.

Then after a few moments I smugly looked at him and simply said "What"? With no answer forthcoming, I got very upset and then very sternly said, "What does he want now? Do I not get more than a few fleeting moments in time to be happy? Fuck you! And Fuck him! Do what you have to already. I'm tired of waiting and I don't feel like waiting anymore!" My tone grew harsher as my anger slowly gathered momentum. I could feel my hands as they slowly closed and tightened with every breath.

The boy raised an arm and proceeded to point at me. No, I soon realized that he was pointing past me, behind me. I turned and came face to face with the beast. I never had a moment to be startled. He was again within an inch of my face!

He opened his mouth and began to chuckle. "Well, Billy," he said, "it seems you have a backbone after all"! Then he slapped my face and took a couple of steps back to sit on a box that lay in the alley. As he picked up the box to turn it upright I couldn't help but feel that this meeting was different this time. \

Still tense, but not as angry, I wondered about this visit. "Yes Billy, I feel your confusion," he said as he proceeded to sit. "Let's just say this is a bit of a social call. I figured it was time I put your mind at ease. You will be a father and I can absolutely promise you that the child will be born. Of that you have no worry!"

"What about Diana?" I shouted, knowing there had to be a catch.

"She'll be fine also, Billy. It serves me no purpose to cause you and yours any harm. You are too important to me," he replied. "Did you honestly think I was the one that caused your grief last time? There are times when I allow choices to be made, and that choice was not made by me." He sat there grinning as he brushed the dust from his jacket. "William, William, William" he said as he slowly stood up and shook his head, "sometimes it's difficult to see the truth, isn't it?"

"Who made the choice then?" I asked defiantly. He sheepishly grinned at me and I began to realize that there was only one person who could have made that decision. In that moment of realization my mind and body felt as if they were to be crushed under the weight that I now bore.

"See William, the truth sometimes isn't what you need, is it? Sometimes, ignorance is bliss," he said as he slowly moved towards the end of the alley and into the light of the coming street. "By the way Billy, thank you!" he said.

"For what?" I replied as I slowly shifted my gaze from the street below towards him. My body was racked with guilt and the tears were swelling within my eyes. He turned one last time and replied, "He's a good boy, you know. Like my own son in a way".

I watched as he disappeared into the morning air not quite understanding his words. And again for the second time that morning it hit me! I quickly turned back to see but the boy was gone. I screamed in anguish, a pain greater than any I had felt before as I sank to my knees and screamed! It was I that had unwittingly given him another soul! My son. My first born in his hands for all eternity!

I made it home, eventually. My mind was still racing from what I had done. I kissed Diana on the forehead and headed straight for bed. I got myself undressed and got into bed thinking sleep could at least stop me from thinking for a few hours. Diana came into the room a few minutes later and sat on the bed. Her hand slowly searched for mine.

"What's wrong?" she asked. I couldn't answer her. How could I? I simply grabbed her hand and pulled her close to me. She cradled me to her bosom and I held her tightly for how long I did not know. She rocked me to sleep while comforting me by telling me everything was going to be all right. Through all my tears I must have fallen asleep even though I don't remember.

When I awoke Diana was in the kitchen preparing lunch for herself as she had to work that day. I watched her for a while as she busily prepared for the day. Her now quite visible belly stood out every time she turned to her side. I admired her, and loved her even more. I was still amazed at how through all her heartache and adversity she was able to go on as she did. She never complained. She always had a smile on her face. I slowly got up and sat at the table as I watched her ready herself. As she walked past she grabbed my shoulder to let me know that she was there. She never asked me any questions as to why I was upset, although she probably wondered, but she never pushed for an answer. As the days went by I knew how lucky I was to have her. And as I slowly let go of the past I began to realize that we would have a child and that my wife and child would be safe from him.

Months went by as Diana got larger and larger. Any time now we would be welcoming a new spirit into the world. I had come to terms with what I did to my first child over the last few weeks and began again to relax and let my guard down. I was happy, even looking forward to what life had to offer. Diana positively glowed whenever I saw her and I knew she, too, was happy.

I took on extra shifts at work to try and accumulate a little more money for when the baby arrived. Diana prepared a corner of our apartment to welcome the newborn and we even received an old cradle as a gift from her sister who lived in Boston! At this point it was harder and harder for Diana to work and we ended up closing up her little booth on the corner. The extra money I brought in helped to alleviate the financial burden of her not working. I didn't mind working extra; I knew I had to if we were to have a good life. I even started working the day shift on a regular basis, which allowed me to work evenings occasionally as well.

The world as well was changing. The subway was becoming more and more prominent with every year, and they even replaced the last steam train on 6th Avenue with an electric train. I would have much work for many years ahead. I would just have to remember to move every once in a while so as to not become too complacent with my colleagues. It wasn't as if I were close to them but it still made more sense to start anew so that people didn't notice that I couldn't age as they did. Imagine the questions if they did notice!

By late 1903 I was assigned to work in a section of the Fort George tunnel, possibly the deepest tunnel ever constructed in the subway system. It was to be almost two hundred feet below the surface and at least two miles long. Excavation would be hard and tedious. But at this point in my life I almost welcomed hard work.

Every once in a while I would still get severe headaches, as if to remind me of where I came from and with whom I was associated. I learned to live with the attacks. Diana feared for my health and at times begged me to see a doctor. I knew that it would be an impossible feat. As if I could be examined! How would I explain all the marks from injuries I had received over time? My bullet wound alone would be next to impossible to explain to a physician. Though after weeks of her asking I finally agreed to see a doctor. Of course I didn't. I went down to the local store and picked up some pills that I could tell her he prescribed for my headaches. It's funny but when I went to purchase them, all I asked for was the least expensive pills they had. I wasn't even sure what I was taking or what they were for. Diana couldn't read the bottle and whatever it was couldn't hurt me anyways. So with that I was able to forge a new lie, at least one in which no one got hurt.

We sat most nights talking about the future, she and I. When I usually arrived home from work she would always have supper ready for us and after we ate we would just sit. I had picked up a radio through one of the local villains for cheap and occasionally we sat and listened to the cartridges at night. Sometimes it was music, sometimes a show but for the most part we listened to music. We danced at times. I would move the table and make some room in the tiny apartment so that we could enjoy ourselves more. And after we danced we sat and talked about almost anything. I would stare into her eyes as we spoke and wished that she were whole in that way. Sometimes Diana would be talking and then just stop as if she knew I was looking right at her. She was beautiful, that was without a doubt. The longer I was with her the more I needed to be with her. She became all that I wanted to live for, my Diana, the sweetest angel of them all.

Work went on as usual. I would carry my little lunch that Diana made for me every morning down the street towards the entrance of the Fort George tunnel. They had been working on it for a while and progress was being made at an amazing pace. The mornings were growing colder as September slipped away to make room for winter. My job in the tunnel was to help shore up walls as digging progressed. I used to help with excavation but I was assigned to this task after a few months. I enjoyed the work even though it was hard.

We would move large timbers from one section to another and in between we would sometimes take a break and relax. I pretty much kept to myself. I would sit in the tunnels away from the rest of the men and think about my pretty Diana and my forthcoming child. I would smile a lot whenever I thought about her. She made me complete. It was as if this was how life was supposed to be. Work and family, a normal life for a change!

In early October I was at work in the tunnel when a fellow worker had come down. It was unusual because this fellow worked on the upper level and never came down this far.

"Bill?" he shouted. "Is there a Bill here?" I quickly got to my feet and ran up to him.

"I'm Billy", I replied.

He looked at me for a moment and hesitated before saying, "Seems you're off for the rest of the day! Your wife needs you". I knew it! Diana was having the baby. She must have gotten one of the neighbors to come and let me know.

I hurried up the embankment as quick as I could. "I was to be a father," I thought. Never in my wildest dreams could I ever have imagined this! I ran as fast as I could to be with her. We had no one and hospitals were far beyond our means, so we took care of each other.

As I ran I waited for the feeling to come, the feeling that he was to be near again. But this time there was nothing, no feeling at all! As I realized this, I ran even faster knowing that this time it would be different. Tears of joy filled my eyes as I made my way up the street to our apartment. I had to wipe the tears from my face every so often so I could see and not run into something or someone. I swung the bottom door of our apartment building so hard I almost thought it would come off the hinges! I scampered up the stairs to our apartment and then at the top I froze. Our door was open, just as it had been with Mary! 'No!' I screamed within my head, 'Not again'!

Thoughts raced through my mind as I boar witness to her death all over again. Fear took me over as I walked towards the open doorway, my feet slow and sluggish now, the speed all but gone from just a moment before. It all seemed like a bad dream. That I wasn't even within my own body any longer. It was as if I was watching myself move towards the door not even thinking about how I was to get there. I didn't want to look. I didn't want to know this time. And as I got to the doorway I stopped! Stopped just short of entering the apartment.

As if the doorway held nothing but heartache once again. I made my decision in that moment and without thought turned around as if to leave. And as I was getting ready to take my first step, I heard the cry of a child! "My child!" I thought as I turned again and raced into the apartment.

I found Diana there, in bed holding the most beautiful baby I had ever seen. Sitting beside her on the bed was our neighbor who had heard her pain and had come to lend a hand. I approached the bed slowly and as the neighbor got up, I moved closer and knelt beside the bed. Diana smiled, as she heard me approach. She appeared exhausted but happy. My head rested against the bed as I thought about what could have been. I began to cry and I felt Diana's hand touch my head.

"Billy" she whispered, "say hello to your son". I raised my head slowly as the tears rolled down my face and I looked at my boy, my wonderful baby boy. The tears flowed again and again but I didn't care. I put my hand to his cheek and felt his soft warm skin against mine. My other hand reached to Diana and I touched her cheek as well. Both of them, so beautiful, both alive and well. And for the first time in my life, and without thinking, I thanked God.

The next few days were hectic as we both attempted to keep up with a schedule that our little boy had devised. I had to return to work two days after his birth but fortunately Diana had befriended our neighbor, Rose, who lived across from us and she helped out. I was a little hesitant at first to have her near, but in the end I knew that I wouldn't be able to do it all.

I remember watching them before his birth, how the neighbors would always help each other out in times of need, never even asking. I remember the way I thought of them, always taking, helping each other as if they really cared for one another. Parasites for the most part, never realizing what was most important...themselves! Now I guess I began to understand it better, understood the need for help and the need for acceptance among your fellow human beings. Life was good now. I was no longer feeling as much hate and resentment as in previous years. Diana had brought out something in me that I never knew I had or maybe I feared I had and didn't want to admit to myself.

Compassion was creeping into my very soul. The anger was replaced the day our boy was born. We visited on a few names for him; Diana suggested that we name him after me. I refused. I didn't want my boy to have my name, lest he suffer some of the same fate as I. No, even though I was his father, I wished him a better life than I had. I suggested to Diana that we name him after her father, Jacob. A strong biblical name I know, but it seemed more fitting than using my name. He at least, was a man of great principle and integrity according to the way Diana spoke of him. He was a hard working man who gave his all for his family until the day that he passed on. Diana spoke of him often and usually with a tear in her eye. The name was most fitting I thought, and with that we named our son, Jacob McReedy.

Diana wanted our son to be christened in a church and I really wanted no part of it. Even though I had begun to relax my way of thinking, I still had no use for the church or its traditions. We spoke of it often, as she would always bring up the subject. I tried my best to avoid it as long as I could, but she always had a way of making me discuss it. I tried to explain to her my feelings on organized religion but to no avail. She felt too strongly on this point to ever relinquish her need for christening. After a week I finally gave in and she arranged for a day that Jacob would become a Christian. I suppose it didn't really matter that much. I could live with it even though it did go against my own personal beliefs. But if it made her happy, then I could not deny her anything. She was able to arrange that on the weekend we would go and have him christened.

I went to work during the week as usual cringing at the thought of going to a church in a few days. The decision had been made and there was no way around it. I didn't even try.

October seemed very chilly this year and it looked as if winter would arrive earlier than expected. Before I left for my shift that morning, I went and kissed Diana. As well I leaned over the crib and gave my new son a kiss on his head.

By Wednesday the air was crisp and I could see my own breath in the morning air. I arrived at work early that morning as I had had trouble sleeping with Jacob always waking us. I made my way down the tunnel and began preparations for the day ahead. Today they would be blasting again and we always had to make sure that all was ready with the shoring. I hated when they blasted. It was loud and dirty and we always had to wait at least a day until we could go into the area to start cleaning it out. The dust seemed to take forever to settle and if you ever took it into your lungs you would cough for at least a week.

We worked for about three hours that morning when we got word they were ready to ignite the dynamite. The blast wasn't to be that strong, so instead of leaving the tunnel together, we were allowed to remain inside but far enough away that it wouldn't affect us. We had done this before and while it was extremely noisy, it seemed to allow the rest of us to continue work without too much distraction.

We worked in a tiny chamber that day, ten of us. We were the only team that would work that day do to the nature of our work and of course because of the blasting. We were always the ones who went deep into the tunnel to make sure the walls were shored carefully as to allow the other workers a safe environment. Rock lay scattered all around as we entered the new section. The walls were jagged and the only colors were gray and black. That was all you could see with the minimal light we had. We had to step over boulders that lay on the ground and occasionally we would trip over them or hit our shins, neither of which we liked to do. The timbers were long and heavy and usually took three of us to carry them into the area where they needed to go.

We had carried most of them in when we heard the blast from afar. It wasn't as loud as usual considering the distance we were in relation to it. Still it was loud enough that we would instinctively cover our ears. We'd had louder explosions before; some even caused us to lose our hearing for a short time. I covered my ears and squinted my eyes instinctively so that dust didn't get in them as my head slightly turned towards the source of the noise. You could feel the vibration as it went through the tunnels, walls shook, and the floor where we stood vibrated to the point that it felt your legs would give way. Dust fell from the roof and at times some of the guys spat from not closing their mouths in time.

Then it began to quiet down again and the dust settled as we all resumed our work.

I picked up a wooden pin to try and knock it into a top member that we had just put in place and as I drew back the large mallet that I held in my other hand I felt another slight tremor. I stopped to see if anyone else had felt it. As I looked around I noticed the rest of the men had also stopped and were looking at each other as well.

In a moment we knew that this was no mere aftershock of the explosion. The floor shook again this time a little harder and dust began to fall in larger quantities and we knew even though we didn't want to admit it.

One man yelled, "Collapse!" and we all dropped our equipment and ran towards the opening of the main tunnel! We were only a couple of hundred feet from the entrance but it seemed like it was miles away. I happened to be the farthest one away as I always liked to work alone and this time I regretted my decision.

As I ran I saw as the roof began to crumble in front of me. Paul, I believe his name was ten steps ahead of me when I saw the boulder fall from above. I had to dodge left as I witnessed Paul literally get crushed by the boulder and disappear completely beneath its mass. The roof was giving way now and pieces were falling at an alarming rate! I ran, harder than I ever had before! I ran! I saw another man reach within a few steps of the entrance when I saw the debris fall at that location, blocking our only exit out. Most of us stopped and attempted to find some type of shelter where there was none. I stopped right where I was realizing full well that there would be no escape. No one panicked anymore; it was almost calming in a way. Then I heard another loud noise and I looked up just in time to witness the entire roof come down before the blackness enveloped me.

I hear voices, quietly at first. Then they start to get louder. The voices sound muffled, as if they were behind something. Maybe a wall or possibly stone. Yes, I remember… the accident, the roof came down and we got under it. "I can't believe it! Did I actually survive that? Of course I did! Why wouldn't I? it's not as if I have a choice. I can't believe that it actually worked to my advantage this time. I'm still alive and once they get me out of here I can resume my life.

I guess I'll have some explaining to do as to how I survived but a few quick conversations and Diana, Jacob and I will be on our way. I guess we'll have to relocate but considering the alternative I suppose it will have to do.

Everything is black and I can't see a thing. We must still be caught within the stones of the collapsed tunnel. I don't feel any pain. Funny though, I should be hurting. Why am I not hurting? This makes no sense at all! How long have I been here? Hours? Days? It's hard to tell but I know it's just a matter of time before they lift this rubble from me. I can wait it out, and why not? I don't really have any other plans. Time is one thing I have, my one constant.

I still don't understand why I was not hurting. Why have I been spared this pain? I should be in agony right now.

But yet there is nothing, I feel almost at peace with myself. Maybe I haven't been hurt that bad. The rubble is just hindering my exit. But again, the weight alone should be crushing my torso. I don't understand at all. Then I realize that for the past few minutes that I've been awaken I haven't taken a breath! What the hell? Is there no air here? Do I not need to breathe anymore either? My thoughts race as I begin to panic within my mind. No, I must breathe, I have to breathe, don't I? Yes, of course I do, I have to get air into my lungs, I can't survive without it! I must try to breathe, one breath, just to see if the air is breathable! Just like I have done since my birth I attempt to take a breath. It's really quite difficult to try and do something you have done since the moment you were born to this world. Instinct and reflex are sorry things to learn at best. One breath, to fill my lungs whether the air is good or not. One breath! It's a start. But nothing happens! I'm trying to inhale and yet I can't seem to do it. I can't feel my lungs expand even a little! My God, what is happening to me? Are the rocks so heavy on my chest that my lungs can't expand? Even a little? Why won't they work?

Then as I awaken more, I begin to realize why I don't feel any pain, why my lungs don't work. I don't feel anything! Nothing! My mind seems to function but my body gives no response.

I try to move my hands, wiggle my toes, but nothing happens! I think I can feel myself in my body, I know I'm not dead! But yet I'm not sure. Am I dead? Did I die in the collapse? Again, I don't know! What am I supposed to do now? Nothing! Nothing but wait till help comes. My mind reels from the honesty that it now bears and I feel the blackness come again.

I'm awakened a few times in between by the noise from outside. Awake? I suppose there is no better way to describe it. My mind seemed to shut down as if to sleep on occasion. I'm thankful for that, however you wish to describe it. The noises are getting closer now, not as muffled as they were before. I suppose they are getting nearer to reaching us. I wonder if anyone else survived? No, probably not. How could they?

God, this not having to breathe is really bothersome in my mind. It just doesn't feel right and every once in a while I feel the panic rise within me uncontrollably until I realize that I cannot breathe even if I wanted to. How long? How long have I been here? How is Diana? Jacob? I miss them, more than I would have ever suspected. Diana must have heard about the accident by now. How would she react seeing me once they pull me out? Would I frighten her too much? About my unnatural survival, that is. Or would she embrace me and love me no matter what? I didn't know. I guess I wouldn't know until they got me out.

I'm sure I've been down here for days, at least. How much rock was there? How much longer would it take till they got me out? I don't know anymore. Will they even find me? I don't know anymore. I just don't know! I was tiring myself out again with this much thought. Not that I could do anything else, but at some point again, my mind shut down and I slept.

"Here's another one"! My mind awoke as I heard the ruckus. Someone was speaking, close by; I could hear it clear as day.

"Here's another poor sap, or at least what's left of him." Again I heard the voice, and then another came closer.

"Damn, from the looks of him he went quick!" the voice called out. "Christ! They never had a chance, did they?" What were they talking about? Help me, damn it! Get me the hell out of here. I couldn't speak; they couldn't hear me! My mind raced to make sense of what was going on! Wait a minute! I felt something! I'm sure of it. I wasn't to be completely deprived of all my senses then. I could hear, I could feel some touch but why couldn't I see?

Everything was still black but I think they were lifting me out. I'm sure of it. I did feel some pressure as they grabbed my head; at least I think I did. They must have carried me from the tunnel and outside into the light. I couldn't see but I felt the warmth of the sun as I lay there. Even blind I could still sense the blackness change to an orange hue. How long was I to be blind I wondered? How long until I would be able to sit up and greet my family from a hospital bed? All these thoughts went through my mind as I lay there. How long would it be till my body completely healed itself again?

It was a while later that I began to feel the cold on my back. No longer was I outside, the warmth I felt before was gone. I had been moved somewhere again. I believe I was inside somewhere, more than likely a hospital? But I still couldn't see anything or hear any noise that one would associate with a busy hospital. "Quite strange," I thought, "unless I was in a more solitary wing of the hospital".

All was quiet for a long time. Occasionally I would hear some voices for a few moments and then they were gone. I still didn't understand what was happening. I should be getting numerous visits from the doctors and nurses. How could I recover without the proper care? This possibly was one of the worst hospitals I had ever seen!

It seemed as hours went by until I heard the voices again. They were coming closer which more than likely meant that someone was finally arriving to help me. Suddenly I recognized one of the voices! It was Diana! It was good to hear her voice, even though I could tell she was crying, it was still calming to hear her. Then I heard the swing of a door opening. "Finally, " I thought, " how long did they expect me to wait?" Diana was talking with the doctors, I think, outside my room. Her voice was still far away from what I could tell. I also heard two men in my room mumbling something about me.

I heard footsteps approaching me in the room from the two men I would suppose. I couldn't tell what they were saying but I could feel something being removed from my face and chest. I felt a hand on my face, I think. Then as if someone lit a candle I could see. Well, at least thru one eye. I witnessed a rather distinguished looking man staring back at me. Looking me over in a fashion. "About time I figured, how long was I made to wait already"?

I watched this man for a few moments wondering what he was doing. I couldn't quite see everything and my perception was a bit off. Something was blocking my view. "What the hell was in the way? Did my eye not fully heal yet"?

Just then I heard the door swing open again. The man in front of me turned his head and backed away from my body. Then I could see it! I could see as he retracted his arm and hand away from my face. My vision in my eye dimmed again as if I were squinting…. then it occurred to me. His hand was in my way of seeing everything.

"Shit!" I screamed in my head. I could see only because he was holding my eye open! What the hell is happening to me? What are they doing? "Fuck!" I thought,"Fuck!" Was all I could think over and over in my head, I could hardly see as they hovered about, my eye barely allowed me to see by this point, I admit I was scared now, and confused.

Then I saw as the hands outstretched a blanket or something over my face again. I could still see some light but the images were now gone. I heard Diana's voice in the room now. She was crying and I could hear every labored breath she took, as she got closer. The men were saying something to her, something about the way I looked and that I went quickly!

"NO!", I thought. "They think I'm dead! But I'm not dead. They don't understand my unique position. I'm not dead!"

As they pulled the blanket from my face, I could again see through the narrow slit in my eyelid. Diana was there! Her hands fumbling as she tried to reach my face. She was crying as she slowly leaned over me and softly touched my cheek with her hand. Wait a minute! I felt her touch, it was soft but I felt it. I was recovering! Slowly, I'm sure, but I was getting better.

Diana leaned in closer. I could see her pain now. I felt one her tears hit my cheek as she leaned closer. I could feel it! But I still couldn't move. "Hell, I couldn't even move my eye!" Then as my vision became obscured again I felt her kiss my cheek and her voice.

She said, "Goodbye my darling husband, I will miss you. You gave me life, a son, a family. You were a good man, never forget that." Her hands were stroking my face now, just as she used to do when she wanted to look at me through her touch.

As she continued I felt as sense of dread and urgency overwhelm me. I tried to move. I tried anything I could think of to let her know I was still here. As she continued to speak my mind was screaming to let her know that I was still alive. But as hard as I tried nothing happened! All this time I was listening to her voice and finally I gave up, from sheer mental exhaustion. Her voice, her beautiful voice was calming to me now. So soothing, as if nothing were wrong. She spoke of how she would make sure Jacob would grow to be a man and I would be proud of him.

As she talked, I felt pity. Pity for myself, not her, for she was strong, of that I was sure. As she spoke I found myself praying. Praying to God to help me, no, to help her. Maybe I would never be well again. I hadn't prayed to him since I was but a boy, but now I wanted to renounce all I had become. All I had given away, anything, just so that I could be with her and grow old together.

It wasn't supposed to be this way. I never meant for this to happen. I loved her, more than I loved myself I finally realized. I was so sorry, more than I had ever been before in my whole life. All I was and had become was finally shown to me through this woman and my love for her.

As she spoke I felt the warmth of another tear on my cheek. But this time it was different. It didn't come from her; it came from my own eye. Just a single solitary tear slowly sliding it's way down my cheek. This was it! The evidence that I was still alive! I had been trying so hard that when I stopped it just happened! God had heard my prayers! As the other voices entered the room I could see Diana getting up to leave.

"Wait!" I shouted, " Look at me! Look at my face! I'm alive! But of course Diana could not see me. She never could. Diane stood there for a moment and one of the men came to help her out of the room. His am draped around her in a comforting position they both stood before me. "Now he will see," I thought. And as I waited for him to look down upon me I noticed who it was that was comforting Diana. "Not him, anyone but him," I thought. And as he pulled the blanket over me again so that the darkness would envelop me once more, I saw him look directly at me and flash one last impish grin. Then all was dark again and I screamed.

Chapter 10

Blackness! I see nothing but blackness and solitude. I truly wish I wouldn't have heard it either. Every shovel, every damn shovel of dirt I heard, loudly at first. Then as the amount increased above me the noises got quieter. I heard as every little pebble fell and settled into place either beneath me or beside me or on top of me. The wood only amplified the sound. My new home for all eternity! A box made of pine and nails.

The realization of my predicament made me laugh. I can't even describe for how long I laughed, was it minutes, days or weeks? I didn't know. I just lay there, nothing much else I could do. Time it seemed was now my enemy and it seemed I had little choice in the matter. I often lost myself in thought, thought of Diana and Jacob, and how they were. I reflected on my life, religion, and anything that I could think of. There wasn't much else I could do. Eternity in a box, this was my fate! Again the realization made me laugh.

I couldn't even gauge time after a while. I'm sure days passed by as I lay there, my body slowly healing itself. I wasn't even sure how long it took, but I do remember the first time I was able to open my eyes. Not that it made a difference within the blackness I lay. What could I see, anyway?

But slowly my senses returned. After what seemed like an eternity, I was finally able to move my head a fraction of an inch. I suppose I must have broken my neck or something and as my body healed it probably was starting from the top of my head down to my feet.

"God! How long have I been here?" I thought. I remember the feeling of claustrophobia at times overwhelmed me. I'm sure I went mad at times. There were times when I seemed to disappear as if to sleep. These were times I couldn't remember. Madness it seemed was a great thing. It allowed me to forget where I was and to not think. The problem seemed to be that every time my mind wandered into the madness I would come back as if my mind would heal itself from the madness. And during my blackouts I was unaware of how much time had passed. I had no idea.

I remember at times waking from the madness to intense pain! I began to feel more and more as the time passed. My broken bones began to straighten and knit themselves together, my jaw was able to move, and my fingers started to bend. My skin became sensitive again and I felt the weight of my own body. But the pain I felt, so intense at times, all over my body and yet, at other times, it was more localized.

It took me awhile to figure out exactly what was happening. I did figure it out though, after a time. I had regained some motion within my left hand and arm and was able to, although quite disported, grasp with my hand. I remember the pain came from the right side of my still torso, around my hip area. My hand was able to reach down and feel what was causing the pain. My hand although not completely functional, had moved down from my breast towards the source of the pain. As it made it's way down I was able to feel moisture within the affected area. Then my hand recoiled back as I felt movement! Frightened though I was I had to feel again. This time I left my hand there for a few minutes and even though I didn't want to face the truth, I knew! I knew what was happening, it disgusted me beyond belief and if I could have vomited, I'm sure I would have. Maggots!

Filthy maggots were eating away at my flesh as if I were a dead soul. The feedings never stopped through out my time there. They would attack one area and devour all in its path. Sometimes they were all over, maggots, bugs. They were decomposing my body as I lay there! Maybe, I thought, this would be my release from life. How could I continue to live if they took my body?

But as usual there would be a catch. Whenever they had devoured one section and moved, my body began to heal itself in that area. Then they would return again to begin their destruction anew! What a fuckin' joke! I would never know peace and I firmly believed that I was in hell! As fast as my body was being devoured by the parasites, it would regenerate as quickly. The cycled never ended! It would be forever it seemed!

Again the madness helped me to cope. It came on more and more as the pain drove me to it. But in between the bouts of madness I would always be aware of my predicament. I suppose this was his way of letting me know my place. I was also aware that my limbs were healing as well and soon I was able to move my legs and my arms. Even with flesh missing in areas, I was still able to move as confined as I was.

I don't recall when I finally felt that this had to end. I knew somewhere in the back of my mind I needed to do something else. I needed a goal. My will was all but gone now, but if I still had an ounce of sense I figured it was time.

I remember using my fingernails to scratch at the wood above me. I did this for no reason, I was bored, and I did it unconsciously for the most part. I would do it until my nails wore down to the tips of my fingers. When they grew again I would start all over. I scratched at the wood till finally I grabbed a small splinter from the lid. I felt it was no longer than an inch in length, but I was able to pull it from the lid. I believe it was then that I began to formulate a plan of escape from my eternal resting place. There may be a way of deliverance from this hell yet! I began to pull pieces from the lid as I scratched away. The madness all but left by this time as I now had some type of purpose.

My mind focused and I worked for days, weeks. Again, I had no idea of the time that I had spent here or how long I worked on my escape. I worked, pulling, scratching and peeling wood from the lid until I finally felt the texture of earth. Mud, moist and warm. A single digit was able to poke thru the lid. When I retracted my finger I felt the earth seep into the box with me. A little fell from the spot, not much, but enough for me to realize that this could indeed be possible! My determination grew stronger at that point.

"Fuck him!" I thought. He wasn't going to win this time. I would get out, go home and try to explain to Diana how I was still alive. Which would be a tall tale to tell, seeing as she was more than likely there at the burial. But as more wood gave way I became more and more determined, and as I worked I thought of my wife and son. They needed me! I needed them! And with that I continued!

More and more earth fell into the box and onto me. I pushed away what little I could and as time went by I found that it enveloped me to the point where I could hardly move more than a fraction of an inch. It was slow, of that there was no doubt. But I would not give up. Diana needed me and whenever I felt like giving into the madness again, I would picture her face and that of Jacob and I would continue anew!

It went on like this for what seemed another eternity ever vigilant that I would be in her arms once again. Up I went, inch by inch. Never faltering or waning, I would not give in to him. I would see him again and this time I would spit in his face and laugh, bastard that he was! My life was to be my own again and I would do whatever was needed in order to get it back again. Even if that meant traveling from hell and back!

The earth was crushing. As I dug, I tried my best to push it down past me. Sometimes I would get stuck and not be able to move at all. The displacement of the earth around me was at times too great! In those cases I would move ever so slowly, a finger at a time, until I hit another pocket of air within the ground. Whenever this happened I would move a little quicker.

I was able to move my body into an upright position after awhile, the hole in the box large enough for me to squeeze through. I pushed earth and stone into the box behind me until I was finally able to stand. Of course I was still hardly able to move and I wasn't even sure of how long it took me to get this far. The earth around me was crushing at best. Occasionally if I opened my mouth accidentally I would receive a bit of earth in it. The journey itself was most difficult and trying at the best of times, but I would not fold.

It seemed that it would never end. The more dirt I moved, the more it seemed was still above me! Again I lost track of time as I moved, occasionally resting for a while. Then when I felt I had enough energy, I would continue on again. The dirt was never ending. Every inch of my being was compacted in the wet soil. Better this though than the alternative.

After what seemed an eternity, I felt the soils structure change somewhat. It became less moist and dryer earth was coming forth. And I began to feel the cold in the earth itself. I suppose I was actually making progress as I had passed the point where the earth started to freeze. Maybe that's why I thought the earth was drier. In actuality it was frozen.

"How much time had passed?" I wondered. I was guessing that winter was now in full bore. I remember the accident occurred in October, so it was more than likely late winter by now.

I wondered what Diana was doing, how Jacob was. My mind continually thought of my family. Soon, soon, I thought, I would be with them again. I kept working on and on, my hands slowly moving, digging and scratching at the earth above me.

Then as if in a dream, my outstretched arm felt no resistance above it! Had I broken through? I must have! Either that or I had hit another pocket of air within the soil. But this time it was different. I could feel it. I pushed my arm up farther this time, reaching to see if there was earth just above me. But there seemed to be none!

I worked at a feverish pace now, pushing more than ever. I was nearly free of this earthly imprisonment. Free to breathe air again, free to satisfy my hunger and free to love! My head still about two feet below the surface strained as if to reach it. After a spell I was able to free my other hand to the outside. Air on my flesh felt strange after all this time. Even though it was only my hands, it was still strange.

My hands still digging also began to pull to pull me up. I pushed with my feet, pulled with my hands and I slowly felt my body rising to the surface! As I came closer and closer I could feel the ground giving way more and more. I encountered less resistance with each attempt, not even really conscious of how I was doing it. But I kept on struggling until the ground finally gave way. With one final pull I was through! My head and upper torso were out. Instinctively I took a breath.

The air was cold and I felt my lungs expand for the first time since I entered this hole. Then I took another and began to cough as I witnessed the mud expel itself from my mouth. I began to heave as if to become sick but I had nothing within my belly. I opened my eyes slowly and looked at my surroundings. It was still winter! Snow covered the ground and I felt the cold as it proceeded to cut right through me. The moon shone brightly so I assumed it was evening. My breathing continued until I wasn't even aware of it anymore. The rhythm became more stable and within a few seconds was all but normal.

I turned and collapsed to the ground in exhaustion. I lay there for a while and then pulled my legs from the ground. I was out! I beat him, was all I could think about. And I began to laugh as I lay on the ground looking up at the moonlit sky. "Stars" I whispered, "How long has it been?" As if they would answer back. I lay there for a while stunned in the fact that I had escaped my earthly tomb.

The bitter cold finally awoke me to the fact that I had to get warm. I was wet and cold and more than likely looked a fright. Diana would take care of me, she always did, of that I was sure!

I felt the pounding of my heart in anticipation of being home once again. I knew he wouldn't win, not this time. I slowly lifted my self up as to sit, my eyes focusing on the stone in front of me. A headstone! I was rather surprised to see it there. I never expected myself to ever be buried with one. I always thought I would lie in an unmarked grave if I were ever to die. I suppose that Diana felt a need to purchase one, either that or the company gave it because of the accident. Either way it was a nice touch I thought.

I slowly worked my way forward and onto my knees until I was but a foot away from the stone. My eyes began to focus again on the lettering as if to read them. I kneeled closer, my hands on my knees. My eyes squinted more to read the stone. It was dark and after all that time below in the darkness my eyes were still adjusting. My fingers touched the rough surface and across the stone cut letters and I was finally able to make out my name.... William. I continued and as such the night sky decided to assist me. I looked up and over my right shoulder as the clouds moved themselves away from the light of the moon and it's silver rays shone down towards me and over the stone. The letters revealed themselves to the night sky and I was to be privy to their appearance.

The light shone from right to left slowly revealing all of its information. I read it as it became available to me. "William McReedy, Died Oct.1903, Beloved Husband and Father".

"What a beautiful touch" I whispered. Diana was without a doubt an angel. It would do me good to see them again. I so longed to hold them both; my arms awaited their loving embrace. I looked at the stone for a number of moments; a tear sprang from my eye as I thought of the two of them and how happy we would be together!

As I knelt there the moon slowly shone brighter and for the first time I realized the stone was not alone. As I wiped the tears from my eyes I tried again to focus as the night gave up all its secrets.

"They must have buried another poor soul from the accident with me" I thought. It was probably cheaper this way. And in the end, what did it matter. I would never sleep eternal with him anyways. Then as I thought about it, the light of the moon crossed over revealing the name of the other poor sap beside me. I squinted to read it as my eyes were still not used to seeing. I read it slowly and as it came apparent to me the name that was carved into the stone, I knelt there in shock! Then I screamed a bloodcurdling scream that seemed to be never ending.

I stood up and as I did my eyes were able to focus on the whole of the stone and I read it again, knowing full well that it would not change. "Diana McReedy, Died August 16, 1937, Beloved Wife and Mother". I staggered back and again I screamed and looked to the heavens in anger. My arms outstretched as if to reach for God himself and tug at his throat.

"You bastard!" I cried, "You fucking bastard!". Knowing full well I would not receive an answer. Then as quickly as the anger which had hit me left, and was replaced with the reality of the situation and sadness as I collapsed to my knees holding my head in my hands as I cried well into the night and early dawn. He had won, he always did. And then began the familiar pain on my cheek as I knew the scar had returned once again, and with it no chance of happiness ever again.

I sat there how long I don't remember. My face and body numb from the cold, I was beyond shivering. I didn't care! Not anymore, as the tears were already frozen against my cheeks. I wanted so much at that point to be back down in my hole, away from the pain and heartache, my wife, my beloved, taken again. When would this all end? When would I end? How long must I suffer in order to find peace just once? Just once.

Just then I heard a noise behind me. I turned to the east as the sun was just starting to rise. A figure came towards me. His boots stepping on the morning frost caused a crunching sound. Every step that came was louder as he came nearer. All I could make out was his form as the sun was rising directly behind him, nearly blinding me in the process. My arm rose to hold back the light too my eyes. Dirt and dust fell from the sleeve as it raised itself towards my brow.

I began to notice how incredibly filthy I was, and my clothes soiled and stained beyond reason, large holes everywhere from my time down in the earth. Not that I cared at that point but it was almost as if by instinct my mind began to reason my situation. How many times had I already gone mad within my existence? Now I suppose, it was telling me to go on, as we had always done before.

Going on.... what a noble concept, for some reason we always go on, don't we? We putter through life and tragedy without so much as a few days acknowledgment at best. Even though the pain lasts a lifetime it nearly seems that we must pursue life again even if we wish not to confront our own fears. I suppose there are some that take another path and end their pain quickly. In some ways they're the lucky ones. That option doesn't work for me; never will again, I suppose. I gave up that option quite a while ago. So what else could my mind do but slowly raise me from the ground and begin to move me but slowly lifting each foot up and forward until the rhythm again became second nature.

I didn't even realize what was happening as it occurred. If I would have thought about it I'm sure I would have fallen to the ground as I knew by logic I could not walk again. My muscles should still be unaccustomed to working at that type of measure. Apparently though, my mind seemed to be of two different perspectives that day as I slowly moved forward anyways.

As I moved I felt myself thinking about nothing. My mind seemed to be barren as I took a few more steps. My eyes were more than likely glazed over, as I felt I no longer cared about anything anymore. I was dead for all intents and purposes. It was just my body that wouldn't succumb.

I knew my mind was still reeling from the realization of everything that had happened. It was almost as if I was having an out of body experience! I was trapped and my mind was as if split in two. Part of it was trying to grasp the comprehension of the sorrow and the other half was moving me along as it had these last few minutes. Life goes on, or so it seems. I hated life, now more than ever. I would rather spend eternity with that bastard than live here any longer. But I knew that wouldn't happen.

Every step by this point was getting stronger as I made my way down the hill and towards the little shed at the bottom. I didn't even know where I was going. I just kept moving. My eyes watched as I saw him put the spade down and open the shed. I watched as he entered the shed and I made my way closer and closer. Again I didn't even know what was going on as my hand reached for the spade leaning against the side of the shed. I suppose by that time he had heard me and peered out of the door to see what was going on.

Again as I had done before my arms raised the spade in anticipation and with what strength I had bore the shovel down on his skull! No thought went into it, I didn't even know why I did it. I heard his skull crack and watched as he fell forward, face first into the ground! The bit of snow that sat in front of the door began to run red as his essence slowly evacuated his head. I stood there for a few minutes watching as it slowly moved from his head and onto the white snow. It was quite beautiful in a way. The red against the stark white background made for quite a spectacle that one could get lost in. I looked at the shovel and saw the bit of hair still stuck to it, my mind still not realizing what I had done.

I threw the shovel down and with that proceeded to slowly undress the man in front of me. Never even thinking of who he was or what his life was. Did he have a family? Did he have a wife waiting for him at home? It didn't matter. Not to me anyway, that part of me was dead and would never resurrect itself again! Not if I had anything to say about it. I had had enough of morals and empathy. Life now would change again, as I would exist rather than live. No more feeling the trappings of man and his pathetic excuses for remorse. No, I would be done with that. Life held no fascination anymore; everything I touched was always taken from me. Anything I cared for was beyond my reach now and I knew there would be no other choice. Man has always been a pathetic beast; slowly rationalizing his behavior from the other creatures of the world by holding some high regard to a higher presence, that no matter what he did, he would always be saved. Pathetic, fucking pathetic!

As I took off my own rags and began to dress in my new clothes I looked up at the sky and thought about Diana once again. Tears never came this time, as I no longer wanted them to. She was gone and I knew I would never be happy again. I continued to dress and as I finished I looked down once more to the naked corpse lying in front of me. No longer a man. Well, I suppose he had been saved then, sent to a better world so to speak. Another sheep in the flock returned home. I left him there, not even attempting to hide the body. I didn't care anymore!

I walked away towards the city, its horizon slowly showing itself more and more. It had grown since I had last seen it. The buildings were larger and taller than ever before, and in more quantity than I remembered. I wondered how much of the world had changed since I last saw it. And would I fit in? Not that it mattered anymore. I would do what I had to once again. The city would be mine regardless of what its own thoughts were

Chapter 11

I enter the city with a bit of awe! My mind absorbed in all the sights that it had never seen before. Some buildings seemed familiar while others did not. Cars, many cars, littered the streets now, some moving, some not. The last time I was here there were only a handful around and they more resembled horseless carriages than what they look like now. They're almost entirely closed in now, with the exception of a few windows. Unbelievably, without a doubt, the changes were enormous! The city was quite large now and a lot louder than I remember it.

As I walked the streets, I watched the people as they moved about me. They didn't seem at all interested in each other, or me, for that matter. Fashions were different as well. Women seemed to be dressed a little more casually. Men seemed to have hair that was often longer than that of the women.

The sights and sounds were beginning to become overwhelming and I felt a nausea form within my belly. I turned into an alley and I felt myself wretch as I hunched over and leaned against the brick wall. Nothing, nothing came out. I heaved over and over again but I was empty. I came to the realization that I needed to eat and my body was trying to tell me so. After not eating for all that time, I suppose I needed to. But I had no money, no place to go.

My hunger increased with every passing moment until I couldn't take it anymore and I searched the refuse container in front of me. I became like an animal as the hunger took over. Nothing else took precedence anymore, as I had to satisfy the burning within my belly. I ravaged through the container searching for any morsel of food that I could ingest. Some scraps of fat appeared in one container, with a little bit of meat hanging from them. I devoured them regardless of what they looked like. Each container held a little as I moved from one to the other. In one I found what looked like left over chicken. Its skin was almost green when you held it to the light. The smell was even worse! Without thinking I ate it. Piece by piece it went into my mouth as I felt the nausea build again. My body was rejecting everything once more! It probably took about fifteen minutes before I could hold anything down for any length of time. I collapsed against the wall after my feeding frenzy was over and sat with my back against the wall as I looked out to the street. I watched for quite some time, just sitting there. My world had changed, and not for the better it seemed.

I left the alley after a time and slowly began to make my way up the street, not knowing where I was going. I had no destination anymore. I couldn't go home could I? What would be there for me? Nothing! I decided to walk, just walk, and see where I ended up. As I passed more and more buildings, I came upon a store whose windows were covered in a substance that looked like mirror. I paused and turned towards the window and that's when I first saw myself, skinny, my face drawn out as if I were dead. I had lost quite a bit of weight and looked sickly at best. My hair was a fright as if I was wearing a costume wig.

As I peered closer, I noticed that my hair was as long as some of the men I had seen just minutes before. I carried on my face a beard of immense hair and dirt. The clothes hung from my frame as if I was wearing a tent. No longer did I fill out the arms or legs. The only thing holding up my pants were the suspenders that I had stolen. I laughed as I figured that I looked a fright. People around me stared as I got louder and louder. Some even handed me coins as they passed! I stood there for a few more minutes and then made my way back down the street. In my pocket now I had were a few dollars and I could begin searching for a place to sleep.

As I passed more and more hotels, I noticed that things were quite a bit more expensive than I remembered. I couldn't afford much and it was easy to tell where I could stay and in what types of hotels. The streets would be dirtier and louder. Not as nice as some, others more in the reference of seedy at best.

After many nights of sleeping in alleyways and eating from dumpsters, I actually managed to secure some lodgings for the evening. Not the best place but at least somewhere I could sleep a night. I stole a paper from a local vendor as well as some spoiled fruit to eat. I made my way into the room and proceeded to sit on the bed, my hair itchy from not being washed for many a year now.

Sitting there in the enclosed space of the room I finally got a good whiff of myself. I stank! Of that there was no excuse. I actually disgusted myself. I decided before I ate that I needed a bath and badly! I made my way to the bathroom and turned on the faucet only to watch as a brown putrid water came out. It lasted only for a few minutes and eventually I was able to fill the tub to the point that I could bathe. The water felt good even though it wasn't as warm as I would have liked it to be.

I took off my clothes and slowly sank into its warm wet embrace. The wetness of it seemed to soak directly into my dry skin as if to revitalize it. I lay there for about an hour, washing myself and soaking. I had gotten some scissors from the front desk of the hotel and proceeded to use them to cut my hair and take off most of my beard. The tub and floor around it seemed to grow a carpet as I cut. More and more came off until I felt the weight come off my head, finally.

The hotel provided towels even though they were nothing more than torn rags. I mean, what did I expect for what I had paid? Only half the lights worked so I read the paper in the tub, in the bathroom which at least had a functioning light.

As I picked it up, the first place my eyes went to was the date. "November 21, 1964" was the date printed. I had only been out three days and it was then that I realized as to how long I had actually been gone. So I had emerged November 18th 1964; sixty-one years I lay in that hole! Sixty-one years in which I lay in my own tomb, in complete darkness, in solitude. My head went back as I chuckled at the situation. Sixty-one years after being buried alive, I was still alive and somewhat sane. What a joke! My wife, Diane, dead for over twenty-five years now, my son, more than likely would have been gone as well.

As I sat there reading the paper I began to notice I was getting cold. I suppose I had been in the tub so long that the water no longer held any heat. Just as well, I was finished reading the paper. I got out and dried myself off with what appeared to be a towel. Probably hadn't been washed in quite some time. It seemed to be dirtier than the water that I had just sat in for all that time. I felt clean though, for the first time in quite a while.

As I dried myself I felt my body and noticed all my scarring. My ribs poked through my skin as if to let me know that I was like the walking dead. As I thought of it, I watched the dirt of sixty years, along with the water drain itself from the tub, along with it, all or any misconceptions that I had of my previous life. As it swirled down the drain I felt myself give way from my old life and start anew.

A fresh start was what I needed, of that I was sure. No more trying to have a normal type of life. I'd had enough of that. I was bitter, terribly bitter, and the world would soon find that out. No one would get in my way now. Not ever again! It was time I started being whom I was made to be. No more pretending, no more! Life was at best a struggle for most, but for me it was an eternity of agony and why should I attempt to be as everyone else? What would be the point anymore? I wasn't like other people, I never have been. But at that moment when I gave up eternity I knew I was special, or at the very least unique. Poverty had been my existence since as long as I can remember and I'd had enough of that as well. No, now it was my time to fuck the world over, just as it had done to me! This new time, this new day and age I was in, and this new attitude that I had experienced from its residents would serve me well.

But I would have to learn about it to better understand it and in the last few days I had found that over time we had figured out a way to transmit pictures and sound over the air into something by means of something called a television, a wondrous toy, or tool depending how you looked at it. I wanted to watch it more and more but in order to stay here I needed to find more money to pay for the room. So that night I went out to take what I needed, regardless of the consequences. No pity, no remorse anymore. That was gone forever. This city would feel my anger and my rage. And with that I went into the dark embrace of the night. I stole, robbed, did whatever I had to until I had enough money to stay inside for a while. Funny thing though, with a city of this size, I would have expected more resistance. But the people were almost complacent in giving up their goods. Some times it seemed too easy.

I traveled the trains again as well. The tunnels also had expanded since I last left them. Where we only had a few at the time, now the city seemed to be linked from every direction. I could travel from one end to the other in no time at all! So moving around rather than staying in one spot wasn't a problem. It was easier to not get caught that way. But it did take me a while until I figured it all out.

The first time I traveled the rail I didn't have a token. I watched for a while and saw how the youth of the time beat out the system by jumping over the turnstiles. Seemed easy enough, so I tried it and nearly got caught by a guard. I suppose you have to time it a bit better so that when you go over the turnstile you should make sure that there is a train stopping. A couple of times I had to jump down to the tracks and run down the tunnel to avoid getting caught. After a while though, I got the hang of it and whenever I refused to buy a token or just didn't feel like it, I would cheat the city. I suppose it was a game to me, something to do, kill a bit of time. And time was something I had plenty of. As well, you know even if I got caught and went to prison, it wouldn't really bother me too much. After all, time really means little to one such as myself. A prison term at least would allow the state to feed and lodge me while I awaited my release. But I didn't get caught, not ever.

Weeks went by as I began to better understand my new life and the world within it. I moved around a lot for the first little while, visiting different parts of the city as I went. New York had blossomed into a fine metropolis and was well on its way to being known as the greatest city on earth. I, too, prospered in this new place. I was busy and it always seemed too easy to take from the people here. I learned that by stealing or robbing in the wee morning hours the chances of getting caught were less than a brazen daylight mugging. I mean, I had always known that. But here, now, even if your victim screamed it was rare that anyone bothered.

Mankind, it seemed, was slowly embracing the values that I had always spoke of, as well as practiced! Maybe it had something to do with the fact that the world had gone to war twice? That may have changed the way people thought, even though I wasn't quite sure, as I had only seen bits from that period. It seemed that mankind loved the art of war and began to embrace it more and more. Hell, they were even in another war now! Ships and planes sent young men to their death every day. Convenience of war was ever apparent in this new world. Mankind was indeed changing, and maybe someone had a stronger presence here than ever before. Mankind had stumbled once again in this time. It was apparent that we would never learn the lessons needed for redemption. No, we had faltered once again and in this new world we attempted to repent our sins even as we committed more!

Churches were everywhere, even more elaborate and larger than ever before. As well there were more and more different factions and beliefs. Again we were attempting to create a world in which we could do whatever we wanted while still maintaining the facade of enlightenment. All this time and man had not changed, still the animal we had always been, a hunter, and the hunted. No better or worse than the wolves that roam the woods. We seem to always deny our heritage and our legacy, never to embrace that of which we truly are. We believe ourselves to be superior to the birds, deer and all other living things on this world. Never do we realize that we are all the same. Our only difference is that we have the ability to choose!

Time slowly passed. Every moment that I existed I could feel the minutes slowly creep by. Some days it was sheer torture just to occupy myself adequately so that I wouldn't go insane. Why did I want to live forever? What was I thinking? The problem was, I wasn't thinking. I suppose the thought of eternal existence seemed like a blessing at the time. But now, it was, as he knew it would be, a curse!

Every day I was reminded that I would live forever, never to be released from the pain that is my existence. Every day as I moved among the people I resented them more and more. The smiles on their faces, the joy that I could feel at times emanating from them. Fuck! I had to witness this for all eternity? Why? Why did I make that decision? Why did I do it? It would have been easier to die at birth or never to be born at all. Maybe the world would have been a better place without me in it. Not that it matters so much for me to speculate on it. I've done that for years now, driving myself to the brink of insanity as I ponder almost every decision I've ever made. What's the point? I try constantly to push it from my mind but I know it will always be there. The consequences will always resurface, and I would have to live with them regardless of how I feel. Live with them forever it seems. What a fool I am.

I slowly began to amass some money and began to move from apartment to apartment, slightly scaling up as I moved. No longer did I live in the squalor that I had known for most of my life. I lived fairly well for the most part, alone, but well fed and housed. It was probably the best I had ever lived in my lifetime. I slept during the day and stole at night. Some nights I had done so well I could afford to take a few days off. I traveled the city on those days, always looking to see what was new. Some days I would ride the trains and just look and observe as I went from borough to borough.

As the months went past, I figured I had seen almost every street that there was. I was careful when I traveled, methodically covering the city. Then I ask myself, how was it that I could have ended back there? Without even realizing it, I had somehow gotten off the train into one part of town that I never wanted to return to. I suppose the neighborhood had changed enough that I wouldn't recognize it right away. Was it my mind playing tricks on me? Or did I want to end up here? Maybe it was time? I remember not even thinking about it as I walked the streets. It was as if my body stopped me right at that spot.

I felt the hair on the back of my neck rise as I came closer. My body, it seemed, had sensed it before my mind did. I didn't know it at that moment but I had arrived at the same corner that Diana and I had met all those years ago. My eyes began to focus on the buildings, some old, some new. I remembered her having the stand here. Right where I was standing. There was a newsstand here, now. The papers and magazines littered the counter from one end to the other. But in one corner I saw, placed delicately in a glass tumbler, a rose. A single rose. One flower was all it took for my eyes to swell with sadness. I had put so much out of my mind during the last few months that I refused to let myself think about her. My eyes transfixed themselves on the delicate flower, as it seemed to suck me into its beauty. I began to see Diana in my mind. My new born son as well. Memories flooded back as I remembered all the times we had together, although they were brief. Tears fell from my cheeks and down to the pavement. I wiped the moisture from my face as fast as I could but it became nearly impossible to keep up! I stood there for a while not moving my eyes transfixed upon this rose and I knew, no matter how hard I tried to suppress my feelings, there would always be something to bring them back to the surface. God, how I missed them! All this time and still I couldn't forget them. I could never forget them; ever.

It was at that moment that I figured I might as well confront all my demons! I had to get this out once and for all. I probably always knew in the back of my mind that I would have to come here eventually and deal with this. Why not now? It was time to exorcise the demons once and for all. Time to re-visit my past, so that I could get on with eternity.

I walked the streets again, the same streets I walked decades ago. I still knew my way home. Every step brought me closer to my past life. My feet slowly getting heavier each time they set foot upon the sidewalk. Was it still here? The old building that is, or did they tear it down to make room for a new larger building? What if it wasn't, would I be able to deal with that as well? I felt my heart beat with every step closer. What was I doing? Did I really need this? Yes, I suppose it was time. I needed to have some closure on this if I were to get on with my life. Anger had consumed me so much these last few months and when I arrived in this part of the city all the emotions had come rushing back. I can't be a slave to them anymore. Better to end this now, today, then have them resurface again and again.

As I slowly lifted my head, my eyes focused on the area where I used to live. My eyes focused more and in an instant I recognized it. The building was still there, still standing after all these years! I stood there for quite some time just taking in the view. It had changed, definitely looking a little worse for wear, without doubt, it was the same building.

I made my way over to it and began to climb the stairs to the front door. It was all so familiar, the stonework, the front entrance to the building. The color had faded over time but you could still see its hue. The door was scratched and in need of a new coat of paint, but it was still the same door. I reached for the handle to open it and found myself locked out. I tried pulling it open a few times but soon came to the realization that some things had changed over time. I suppose the world had changed and locking doors seemed to be the best policy for keeping certain individuals out. But how could I enter? I suppose I would wait until someone came out. It probably was the only way short of breaking the glass in the door. No, I had time; I would wait if that was what it took.

I sat on the steps of the entranceway and looked out at the neighborhood. The trees had grown. They were mere saplings when we first moved in. Now they towered over the street lamps! I sat there for a while and then I heard the latch on the door behind me. I raised myself off the stoop and moved towards the door. As I got closer to the door, I passed the woman leaving. She looked at me in a strange manner but didn't attempt to stop me, which I thought was good, as I didn't feel like attracting attention to myself today.

I walked into the front entrance and immediately smelt a musty odor from within. The hallway was darker than before and looked a bit worse for wear. The years hadn't been to kind to the old girl, that's for sure. Lights were out, dirt and dust were everywhere and I'm pretty sure I saw a rodent scurry by me.

I shrugged my shoulders and made my way to the stairs. As I started up, my foot rested on the first step and I heard the creak of the wood as it had weathered over the years. Every step seemed to increase the sound more and more. But I continued slowly, ignoring the creaks or at the best getting used to them. I made it to our floor and I felt my heart get heavier once again. Here I stood at the top of the floor, our old door in sight. I stood there for a while just looking. My memories played tricks on my eyes as I swear I could see Diana still standing there. I watched her as she entered the apartment, her mouth slightly parted, revealing a grin that I knew was for me.

She always smiled, a much better person than anyone I had ever met before in my lifetime, a kind and gentle soul that had tamed my heart for all eternity. I always felt that she deserved better. I had never met anyone like her in my life and probably would never again! If there were such things as angels, I'm sure Diana was one! She brought out the best in all of us; this was her way of dealing with everything that ever happened, whether it was good or bad. I missed her.

As the images started to fade, I felt myself returning to the present, the bliss I just felt faded as the memories of what once was. The colors faded as I saw again with my real eyes and not through my memories. Diana was gone and I stood there desperately holding on to a fading memory. The tears fell on my cheeks as I stood there, all alone again, alone, as I would be for all eternity, my penance for committing the most unspeakable acts. I needed to go. I've had enough of this. It was time to let go and get on with my existence.

I began to wipe the tears of my past away with my sleeve when I heard a noise come from the apartment directly in front of our old one. The door slowly crept open as I saw a young woman step out. Her voice carried softly down the hall as I suspect she began to speak to someone within the apartment. As she closed the door I could tell she was in a hurry and moved quickly down the hall and past me. Her footsteps on the stairs told me that she was almost downstairs. My head turned as my ears followed her until they were only faint sounds and I heard the front door close behind her. I turned to leave and in my haste never noticed the woman that had come out of the door.

"Billy?" she spoke. "Billy, is that you?" My feet froze on the spot. A chill ran up my spine! My name? Who would call my name? Now? Here? It made no sense. I slowly turned not knowing what to expect. I spied a small old frail woman at the open door, her legs no longer functional, as she now rested them in a wheelchair.

"William McReedy, is that you?" she spoke once again, her voice frail sounding from time and life experiences. My head began spinning as I slowly made my way over to her. Who was this woman and how did she know who I was? Curiosity kept me moving towards her. As I approached her chair I slowly knelt down as if to try and recognize her. Her face wrinkled and distorted, she was able to mutter a smile as she lifted her head towards me. I knelt down as to see her better and as I gazed into her eyes finally realized who she was!

"Rose? Is it you?" I asked.

She nodded her head and reached up towards my face. "William, how are Diana and Jacob?" she asked.

I understood now that age had taken its toll on her and some things were not as clear to her anymore. Which made it clear to me as to why I didn't have to explain why I was here after all these years. I couldn't believe it! Rose, our neighbor, was still alive after all these years. We were never that close but we were always cordial with each other.

I smiled for a moment as I looked onto her eyes once again and began to remember the days when we all lived here. " Rose, how are you?" I asked her as I grasped her frail hand within mine.

"She smiled and spoke to me that all was fine. Again she asked me about Diana and Jacob. There could only be one response I could give her.

"They're both fine!" I stated. What else could I say? She obviously didn't know any better and why would I tell her the truth? What would be the point? She smiled and bobbed her head, up and down.

"But where is she, Billy?" her next question came out.

Startled by it, I thought of what to tell her. I mean, what could I say? That Diana was dead and I've never aged a day? So I thought of the only response that I could.

"We've moved, Rose. Diana wanted to move on and Jacob was getting too large for this small apartment. I've just come back for a visit."

She looked to the side of me and then past me as if in deep thought. A few moments passed and then she turned back toward me. "Yes, I remember her leaving," she said. "But I don't remember you being there when she moved. Did you go on ahead of her?"

In that moment, I realized that Rose knew where Diana had gone. I had always assumed she would have remained here but apparently she had moved. But where had they gone? I looked back at Rose; I had to know what happened. "Yes, Rose, I had gone ahead to prepare things," I said.

My mind began to race as I tried to figure out my thoughts. Rose almost disappeared from me as I began to wonder what had happened to my family when I was gone. Where could they have gone? Diane was buried here so they couldn't have gone far. Was Jacob still around? Was he even still alive? He would have been in his late sixties by now. Why did I feel this burning in my stomach to know what had happened? I thought coming here would have alleviated all my thoughts and anguish so that I could go on with my life! Now, here I was again contemplating the very thing I had renounced all those weeks ago.

I was lost in thought when Rose spoke again and brought me back to reality. " How is Boston this time of the year?" she asked.

Boston! Yes, of course Boston! Rose in her state of mind had told me all that I needed to know. Diana had a sister in Boston. It only made sense that she might move there. Rose's addled mind had given me the clues I needed, if I wanted to pursue this further. She must have remembered Diana leaving for Boston shortly after my "death". But could I do it? Could I go and seek out what I probably didn't want to know? With so many questions to answer, I thought I would pass out from the struggle.

I looked at Rose again and saw that her eyes were looking directly into mine now. She was no longer a frail looking woman and her eyes had grown strong and with some type of resolve. I was taken aback for a moment, but then I realized that her mind seemed to have become more focused and as her eyes grew wide I knew that she had stepped back into reality! No longer lost in the past, she began to push herself back into the chair. Farther and farther in, as if to hide within its folds! Her mouth began to part and she tried to utter some type of sound. She knew! She knew that I shouldn't be here.

I waited for her to scream, but the only sound that came from her throat was a slow gurgle. Fear had gripped her so much that she was frozen. She could not scream, she could not move. Her pupils grew wider and wider as she continued to look at me in disbelief. For a moment I thought I would have to do something drastic and then I heard the footsteps come up the hall. Someone was coming; there was no time for anything now.

I turned as I heard the woman calling to Rose. Her pace increased, as she got nearer. It was the same woman that had left the apartment moments prior. I suppose she was Rose's caretaker or such. She ran towards me and as she got close to Rose she pushed me out of the way. I stepped back and watched as she tried to comfort Rose who by this point was shaking beyond belief. As she spoke to her she looked back at me and asked me what had happened. I did what I always do; I lied. I told her that I saw her out here and was attempting to help her back into her apartment when she froze. She turned back to Rose and slowly began to calm her. I stepped back farther and it seemed the more I stepped back the better Rose seemed to get, and within a few moments Rose had returned to where her mind was comfortable. I left, quietly. There was nothing more for me here now.

Chapter 12

Weeks went by and I pondered what to do. Back at home I tried to forget about Rose and our conversation. I didn't want to revisit my prior life, did I? What would be the point? I went about my business and tried desperately to get back to normal but always in the back of my mind I seemed to want to know the truth. I agonized day and night. The harder I tried to forget, the more I was haunted. I would wake up in the middle of the night in a cold sweat over the dreams that kept creeping into my sleep! God, I wanted to forget! But I couldn't, not now. Maybe time would be the factor? I wasn't sure, but at least it was something.

I began to renew my vigor in my work. It always seemed the harder things were for me, I could always alleviate some of the stress by working more. I suppose it was a coping mechanism for me. Now I know that some would say that what I do isn't really a job, but to me it's all a science as much as any other job. You have to plan things properly or the consequences could be dire. I mean I could be put in jail! Most jobs are if you make a mistake, you may lose your job. In my profession, you lose your freedom or, in some cases, your life. Regardless of what others thought I still maintain that work is work. Probably one of more positive characteristics! Me, a good work ethic? Who would have thought it? I've been told that for the most part I am a cad at the best of times.

But I know at the very least that I'm not lazy!

As time moved on, so did I, or so I tried to believe. There were days, of course that I didn't think about it. But as usual things kept crawling back into my mind. Try as I might to immerse myself in work and drink, the thoughts always came back. I even tried to forget by befriending a few of the local ladies! I thought maybe they would be able to help me forget. My life went on like this for a long time, always being pulled between the two worlds in which I had helped create.

As the months went by, time finally befriended me and days would go by without even a thought of my past life. I suppose it became easier for me to be a bastard than a saint! At least I hadn't become one of the hypocritical assholes that I've always despised! I was what I was, plain and simple. There wasn't any need for me to aspire to anything else than what I had already become, nor was there any desire. Money wasn't a concern anymore; I seemed to be quite well off by this point and started to wear some of the finer things in life as a result. I became better at my craft the more I practiced, I learned to decrease the chances in which I would get caught. There were some close calls that helped me along to this point. But I always learned from my mistakes.

Common thievery was beyond me now. I had moved up in my skills and soon was able to complete tasks without even people suspecting my involvement. I began to specialize in break-ins, robbery at night, so to speak. Sneaking into peoples' houses at night while they slept was a thrill for me. I got quite the rush knowing that in the next room or so, they would be sleeping and the chances of getting caught were great. Sometimes I would even walk right into the rooms and hover over their beds as they slept. Smug I know, but I always carried a rather large knife with me just in case they happened to wake up.

I progressed over time from little hovels in the city to more affluent homes in the countryside and into the richer areas of the city. I kept moving all the time so as not to draw attention to just one area, a trick I had learned long ago. Yes, it seemed that my life was beginning to come around once again.

I still kept to myself for the most part, a loner as usual. But as I'd learned in the past, I was better off this way. Friends no longer held the same fascination as they once did. All my friends were long dead. Time and circumstance slowly whittled them down to nothing. No, I would continue on my journey alone, bereft of company. If eternity seemed like a long time, then imagine it alone!

Again I passed the 'sheep' every morning and evening. I could look into their faces and see the expressionless emotion that lay behind their eyes, as if the world didn't matter to them, only the tiny circle around them. I suppose in all my years I had come to see the world and life itself in a different vein than those who only survived for but a second in the vastness of time. I felt arrogant towards them, a sort of superiority because of what I knew as the truth.

I would have figured that I had a disregard to life itself, considering how long I had lived. But this was not the case. I suppose having friends and lovers had helped me to understand that life is precious and sacred. Not so much for myself but for all others that you care for. It's easy to turn your mind to seeing a person as a means to an end. It's only when you are personally affected by them do you see them as more than meat and bones. I guess that's why I can distance myself from them now. No longer do I wish to be as close to anyone as I have in the past.

I'm trying now, to live the life that "he" wants me to live. Some would call it evil, I call it survival. I like most things in life, everything is suggestive to what one perceives them to be. Everyone rationalizes in his or her own mind just about everything that each comes into contact with. Life is what you perceive it to be, plain and simple. My life was now to exist. Not in poverty, I had done that before! No, now it was my time to reap the benefits of what others had sown.

It was time I took advantage of my unique situation and experience! It was time to embrace what I was rather than fight the powers that be. It was as if I was trying to find redemption when there would be none forthcoming. A soul doesn't matter to one that cannot die. What was redemption anyway but the restoration of man from the bondage of sin to the liberty of the children of God through the satisfactions and merits of Christ? Even Christ himself would never forgive me and what I had done with my life. That, and also the fact that I wasn't such a firm believer in the fundamental teachings of redemption anyway.

Again everything is as you perceive it to be and this was one of those things where I knew in my heart that redemption didn't make sense. To me redemption was not what most people thought. God does not redeem your soul, he can't. When mankind falls does their soul not belong to the devil? It has been said that when man falls, he justly falls under the dominion of the devil in punishment for sin. Look at me; I freely gave up my right to have a just and whole soul. I gave it freely and without thought. I had fallen a long time ago and it served me no more purpose than owning an extra pair of shoes. No redemption, and your soul if you fall, is owned by Satan himself, not God. And if a price is to be paid, then it must be paid to Satan himself, and not God.

Sin cannot be forgiven without satisfaction, that much is true. But how does one pay the devil his due? If I knew that I may well be able to buy back what I gave him so willingly all those years ago. What does it cost to get your soul back? How can a debt of such magnitude ever be paid? Satan holds all the souls of the fallen in ransom and in that manner maintains his control over the endless fields of sheep that have become mankind. The problem is, is that mankind still believes that God holds the question of your immortal soul within his hands. I don't believe that he does just as I believe that Satan is given absolute dominion over those domains and souls. God would not ask for payment, he is all forgiving is he not? The only one that would ask for payment then is Satan himself; it's only logical to assume this. I mean what else is there? If man believes the only way to repent his soul is by paying back the debt to his debtor then why would you attempt to do good deeds? If Satan holds your soul, then the only way to get it back is by doing his bidding. Once man understands that simple premise, only then can he begin to make restitution to his debtor. Only then could I begin to understand what I had done.

Chapter 13

The air was cold this night, late in the evening or early in the morning, depending on your perspective. I called it early because I had slept most of the day away. My funds were getting lower and it was time to go back to work. There was this job that I had been contemplating for a while now, and now seemed to be the appropriate time to invest my skills into it. I speny five days watching the household's comings and goings, how many slept there, and so forth. It was an upper class setting but with a lot of people constantly coming and going all hours of the day or night. A busy place such as this would reap many rewards. It may have taken me a while to establish some patterns but the rewards would well be worth the wait. So day after day, night after night, I watched and waited until I felt the time was right. Surely by this morning it would be time.

I stood in front of the house taking in the entire neighborhood around me. As my eyes glanced back and forth to make sure the area was quiet and clear, All was still. I rubbed my hands together for warmth in the crisp night air. Then slowly from the pockets of my jacket, I pulled out my leather gloves and fit them over my hands. I never was one to want to leave evidence on anything of the sort.

I crept up to the side of the house where I would find my point of entry, a window that would be easy to pry open with a screwdriver. As I jammed the screwdriver between the sill and the bottom of the window I felt it give way without much effort. The window creaked quietly as I pushed it open and made my way into the house. The moon shone brightly this night, and as I entered, I could see almost perfectly every inch of the room that I was in. Slowly and quietly I made my way to the door looking about as I went. I could tell from the furnishings that this would be a great place to find all sorts of trinkets and the like. The room that I entered appeared to be a drawing room which had at the other side two rather large wooden doors. This was not the room I thought. No, the room I was looking for was the study. A house of this stature would have everything of value in that room.

As I reached the doors of the drawing room, I slowly grabbed hold of the brass handle and turned it. A low creak came from the hinges as I opened the one door into the hallway. The hallway was darker but I was still able to navigate my way around. At the end of the hallway was a set of stairs that I'm sure led to the bedrooms.

As I made way down the hallway I came up to the study door that was already ajar. I made my way in and came upon a rather large desk located near the center of the back wall. It was a rich looking wooden desk adorned with intricate carvings. I walked behind it and attempted to open the top drawer only to find it locked. I knew this was the one to open! My hand fumbled in my back pocket once again for the screwdriver, and in my haste, I dropped it on the floor.

The sound to me was deafening. I hoped it wouldn't wake anyone within the house.

I waited for several moments cursing my foul luck once again. When I was sure that all was still well I proceeded to pry open the drawer. The old wooden drawer was built solidly. I proceeded to push more and more on the screwdriver. Finally the top of the drawer door began to give way. The wood started to splinter and as I pushed harder and harder on the screwdriver, it finally it burst and gave way as the lock had finally been defeated! I smiled for a moment knowing that I was to be rewarded in just a moment.

My attention went to the contents of the drawer as I opened it to reveal all that it had hidden but a moment before. As I looked down and began to sift through the papers, I came across a small metallic object near the back of the drawer. It was at that moment, caught up in my own arrogance of the crime, that I felt a searing pain come from just below my left shoulder! It was as if I was in a dream at that moment. Oblivious to anything around me I proceeded to pick up the object and put it in my pocket. The pain renewed itself to a healthy vigor and then I remembered hearing a sound. A loud bang had accompanied the pain in my side. All had transpired within a fraction of a second!

I knew as I looked up and saw the figure standing within the doorway that I had been shot!

My mind raced as I looked to escape my current predicament. I suppose my previous mistake had awoken someone within the house. Damn my luck! This was the one job that would have taken care of my needs for some time. Now, it seems that I hurt once again. My head ascertained everything around me and in an instant I knew the only way out was past the figure in the doorway! I crouched beneath the desk trying to hide my face from my attacker as I waited for him to come closer.

He never said anything as he stepped into the room. *"Strange I thought,* I'd been caught before. *Usually the people make a lot of noise in an attempt to scare me away and hopefully alert the neighbors."* This was different, way different!

As I slid down the side of the desk I could feel the warmth of my blood as it soaked my shirt. I reached down and felt the hole in my chest just below my left shoulder. The pain increased and I bit my tongue as to not scream out in pain. *"No, this was different,"* I thought. I knew in my heart that my attacker wasn't here to capture me but to do away with me. I waited for but a moment and then I mustered my remaining energy and darted out from my hiding place and ran straight for the door, which lay in front of me. As I rushed past my attacker, I saw a glimmer of light from the hallway, and like a moth to a light, I ran as fast as I could to it.

Then I heard the second shot and felt a searing pain come from within my back. As in slow motion, I felt the hot metal sear through my body and watched it as it left the front of my body! I could hear the whistle as the air escaped from my lung. The force of the shot carried me out into the hall and directly into the wall that faced me! I hit with a thud and felt my nose crumple into the plaster in front of it.

Without missing a beat I pushed myself from the wall as the blood ran down my chin. I turned once again and headed towards the front door. As I neared it, I could hear him coming into the hallway. I fumbled with the locked door and flung it open! As I sprang out the doorway I could feel the next bullet rush past my left ear and into the door I had just opened. My body was on fire now as I ran as hard as I could towards the street. As I ran I felt the churning in my stomach as my bowels wanted to be free of their confines. I pushed them down and ran even harder into the morning.

After a few minutes my body finally gave way and I ended up collapsing in an alleyway. I landed on my backside with a thud and managed to begin to catch my breath. The pain was so intense. *"God! I hated being shot! Not just once, but twice? Hell, my nose hurt almost as much."* I reached up and tried to touch it to feel its condition. I knew it was broken.

As I sat, I began to feel the blackness come over me as if to sleep. *"No!" I thought, "not here."* I knew I had to make it home before I gave way to it. I pulled myself up and began to move again. And after what seemed like hours, I slowly made my way back home.

I awoke in my front hall. My had body collapsed just behind the door. Dried blood stained the floor of my apartment around me as I realized that I had been there for quite some time. Hours? No, more like days. It hurt like hell to get up. I wanted to lie there for a time but I knew I had to move. I had to get up and get cleaned.

I made my way to the washroom and began to remove my clothes. My jacket came off fairly easily, but my shirt was another story. As I tried to pull, it off I felt the material painfully rip from my skin, as the dried blood had seemed to bond the shirt directly to my body.

As the bath water began to run, I looked at my wounds in the mirror. My nose was broken and misshapen. Blood was all over it and the rest of my face. I slowly felt my chest with my hands, searching for the holes that were put there. My hand came across the first one and then the second wound. No holes, just indentations now. I suppose the holes had already started to close as I slept. At least that seemed to help. My side was still sore as I knew that my lung had not yet healed. It was still collapsed and I felt it difficult to breathe. I reached for my nose to feel where the break had occurred and noticed that it had broken in two separate places.

The mirror beginning to fog now from the steam that came from the heat of the bath water. I took my hands and put one on each side of my nose. I braced myself, as I knew this was going to be painful. I took a deep breath and mustered up my courage and then pushed my nose back into place. The pain was intense as I heard the crunching of the cartilage re-breaking and shifting under my skin. It takes only an instant, but it's a horrific painful experience, one that you, I suggest you avoid.

I almost collapsed against the sink again as I pulled myself back up. The mirror now completely opaque, showed that my nose was at least better than it had been before. Looking, I could hardly see it through as the mirror became non-reflective. The steam literally covered up the entire surface now.

Frustrated, I wiped the mirror with my hand and stared into it. For a moment I thought I saw a different reflection in the mirror! It was as if someone else was looking back at me and laughing. Then it was my face again. I stood there for a few moments re-evaluating the shape of my nose before finally sinking into the tub and oblivion again for a while.

As the weeks went by I began to notice that my antics were being scrutinized. Not by the media or local police force but by the local criminal element that had invaded the boroughs of New York. Most of the time there is a common respect for privacy from thieves and the like. At least from the ones that are higher up the evolutionary scale than most. This time however there always seemed to be a nagging feeling that I was being watched. Always when I walked down the street I was sure that eyes were upon me, whether on a job or not. It got to the point were I would sometimes stop and look around to see if I was being followed. Days went by and the feelings got stronger and stronger.

Then one day I happened to glance from the corner of my eye to see a man staring at me through a window into the room in which I was eating my breakfast. He stood outside the diner holding a paper as if reading it. As I ate, by sheer chance my eye caught his but for a moment before his tiny meager arms raced to lift the paper up past his line of vision. He was a small man, not much larger than a small girl of thirteen years of age. He wore a suit that seemed rather large on him and a hat that constantly fell to the bridge of his nose. I watched as in one minute he pushed it back at total of six times. He stood there for a few minutes before realizing that I had spied him and then proceeded to turn and walk away.

After a few days I actually got used to him following me around. It became a game of sorts. He tried to go unnoticed but in reality he stood out so much that he was a spectacle to all who saw him. I finally took it upon myself to find out what exactly he wanted. As I turned the corner towards my apartment, I turned rather quickly and hid beside the wall of the alley near my place. I stood there for but a moment when I heard the patter of tiny footsteps running towards me. I watched as I saw him run right past me and towards the street in front of me.

As he passed I reached out and literally pulled him off his feet as I swung him back and threw him rather hard against the wall behind me. I grabbed him by the lapels of his suit and before his feet could touch the ground, proceeded to pull him up the wall again. My face was directly in front of his, and the anger and rage in my expression told him that I meant business. He looked up with surprise and then for no apparent reason a huge smile came upon his face.

"Who are you?" I asked, "Why have you been following me?"

I couldn't understand the look on his face; I would have thought that a man of his stature would be cowering in fear. His feet were still dangling at least two feet from the ground and swaying against the wall, but still he smiled.

"If you could please lower me down, I would be happy to answer your question's he murmured.

I figured he wasn't a real threat anyway so I let him go.

He fell to the ground with a thud as his legs gave way and his ass hit the concrete below.

"Fuck!" he said, "Was that really necessary?"

Again I demanded, "Who in the hell are you?"

He stood up and slowly brushed himself off. "The name's Sam." he said, " and I'm here to offer you a job."

A job? What kind of job could this man have for me, I wondered.

As he continued, I listened to his words and then began to understand whom he worked for.

"Your antics have been in our thoughts for quite some time. My boss is Mr. Gambino. Perhaps you've heard of him? He's interested in hiring your unique services for his corporation."

"Carlo Gambino?" I spouted. I knew that name. Who didn't? I had read up on the family over the last few months.

In 1951, Gambino's boss, Vincent Mangano, mysteriously disappeared and Albert Anatasia, a vicious killer, took over the family, leading many to believe he had ordered Mangano's killing. Albert organized Crime Inc., the infamous Mafia hit squad. He made Gambino his under boss around 1956. Gambino set up a hit to promote himself. Anastasia himself was murdered on Oct. 25, 1957, while he was getting a shave at the Park Sheraton Hotel in midtown Manhattan. As he sat there with a hot towel on his face, two gunmen were able to rush in and shoot him. On that day, the Gambino dynasty began.

Some figured Gambino plotted the hit to take over the family, although it was never proven. I've heard that Gambino is shrewd about FBI surveillance, speaking little during meetings, and devising a code to discuss killings and other related crimes. The man was smart, that was not in doubt. As boss, he ruled the family through relatives and even brought his sons Tommy, Joe, Giovanni and Rosario Gambino into the family.

I heard that Gambino disapproved of publicity and drugs. Any member who was caught dealing drugs was murdered. Shunning publicity was something I respected. So many of these characters prefered the spotlight for some strange reason. I could never understand that. My mind wandered as I thought of working for one of the biggest crimelords of all time.

"From your expression I can tell you've heard of him," Sam said.

"Yea, I heard of him," I replied. "Who hasn't?"

Sam pulled a cigarette case from his inside pocket of his jacket and slowly pulled out a cigarrette. It seemed he began to have a sort of arrogance arising within him as he spoke. I guess when people figure out who his boss is then he has a tendancy to push his weight around. I found this amusing as I thought about a little dog and how it reacts with its enviroment. You see, small dogs, in order to survive, have to make themselves seem larger than they are if they're to survive among the big dogs. Little dogs always seem to be the ones that bark the most in order to seem bigger than they are. Most large dogs don't bark that much because they have less to prove.

I looked at Sam and asked him how Gambino knew of me. Sam chuckled for a moment and then said, "Mr. Gambino knew of you from about six weeks ago."

"Six weeks ago?" I thought. *Six weeks ago I was at home licking my wounds.*

"Mr.Gambino, or rather a collegue of his met you early one morning. I'm sure you would remember the night?" Sam responded as he pointed to the obvious holes still in my coat.

And in an instant it all hit me. *"Shit!" I thought, Gambino? How the fuck could I have been so stupid? Who but me would attempt to steal from one of the largest crime bosses of New York? You'd think that after all that time casing the house it would have occurred to me to at least look at the name on the mailbox? Fuck!*

I began to fidget as Sam began to speak. "Relax, my friend. Mr.Gambino doesn't have a problem with you anymore. Hell, we watched your place for all this time just to see if you were going to make it! Jimmy was so sure that he hit you point blank twice. I guess you got lucky, huh?"

"Yea, lucky," I responded.

"Apparently, Jimmy ain't as good a shot as he thinks he is," Sam replied, "but that doesn't matter anymore. What matters now is that you owe Mr.Gambino a favor and a trinket that you stole from his desk. Mr .Gambino has decided rather than kill you for your dis-respecting his house, he needs you to complete a very simple task. Apparently your skills have not gone unnoticed. We had heard stories of an extraordinary thief in the area but were never able to figure out who it was, until now that is. But first things first. You got that piece of jewelry on you?" I fumbled in my pocket and noticed that it wasn't in there. Hell, I hadn't even looked at it and forgot that I even took it! My hands came out of my pocket empty and I could see Sam's look of dissapproval.

"It must be back at my place." I said. It probably fell out of my pocket and was somewhere in the apartment.

"Find it!" Sam stated, "It's very important to Mr.Gambino and if he don't get it back, he won't be very happy. Now on to other things. Let's go get a cup of coffee and I'll explain what else he wants from you."

We walked to the corner shop where I had just finished having breakfast a few moments earlier and sat down to have a coffee. I wasn't sure if I wanted to go but then again, I wasn't sure what else to do. Gambino was a powerful man in this town and could surely make my life more a living hell than it was already!

Sam talked at length about how he was an important man in the organization and that Gambino thought of him as family. "God, this annoying little man was starting to make me sick!" He went on forever about how important he was and why Gambino needed him.

"Shut up!" my mind cried as I began to get restless waiting for him to get to the point. Finally Sam was able to stop wasting my time and began to describe what Gambino wanted from me. Apparently Gambino was having trouble with another organization. Sam began to explain the situation about the Winter Hill gang, a loose collection of Boston area thugs, mostly Irish-American.

Apparently they derived their name from the Winter Hill neighborhood of Somerville, Massachusetts, north of Boston. Its members included notorious Boston gangster James J. "Whitey" Bulger, and hit man Stephen J. "The Rifleman" Flemmi among others. The Winter Hill gang involved themselves with most typical organized crime-related activities; they seemed to be best known for fixing horse races in the northeastern United States. They had around twenty members and associates. The Winter Hill Gang's leader was James "Buddy" McLean.

Gambino apparently was having a problem between the Winter Hill gang and the Charlestown mobs. Bernard

Rod Warkentin

McLaughlin's ran one of the Charlestown Mobs. The McLaughlin Brothers gang was made up of three brothers: Bernie, Georgie, and Edward "Punchy" McLaughlin and also brothers Stevie and Connie Hughes from Charlestown, Massachusetts. It seemed that Gambino had some distribution ties with the Winter Hill gang and they in turn were having problems with the McLaughlin brothers, mostly Bernie's gang and their slow intrusion on Buddy's business.

Like most of these problems, these started from something personal between Buddy and Bernie. George McLaughlin, Bernie's brother, had rented a cottage on Salisbury Beach for a Labor Day party. George, while drunk, attempted to grope Alex Rocco's girlfriend. Alex, of course, was a member of the Winter Hill Gang. Well, that didn't fly with the boys and they gave George a beating to the point the men weren't sure if he was dead or alive. They ended up dumping him at a hospital and went to tell Buddy what had happened.

Buddy decided he would have a talk with his friend, and Georgie's brother, Bernie. The conversation went that when Buddy found out that Bernie wanted bloody revenge for the beating his brother got, and demanded Buddy's help in doing it. Buddy ended up telling him that his brother had been out of line and had it coming. McLaughlin stormed out of Buddy's house in a rage.

The next morning, Buddy awoke to the sound of his dogs barking, and saw two men under his car. He ran outside, guns a blazing and found a bomb planted under his wife's car. Later that week, Buddy tailed Bernie throughout Charlestown until he saw his opportunity and took his shot killing McLaughlin in Charlestown's town square, in broad daylight. The man had balls!

Even though he was acquitted of the murder charges, he went to prison for two years for illegal possession of a firearm. But this pretty much started the "Irish Mob War". Buddy saw this as an opportunity to wage war against Bernie and his brothers. People were dying in the streets and Gambino needed it stopped, somehow. It was bad for business, plain and simple!

Sam went on for a while discussing the whole situation while I listened, still not understanding exactly what my purpose was in all this. I had a feeling it wouldn't be good though. Never is for me.

I left the coffee cup sitting at the table cold and still. Sam had left a few minutes before and I just stared into my cup for the longest time. Oblivious to anything around me, I now began to understand what it was they wanted. Not that I couldn't do it, mind you. I just wasn't sure if I wanted to. More because of where they wanted me to go. I was to get some information using my unique talents, basically stealing from the FBI who were doing some wire taps of the remaining McLaughlin brothers. The problem, I suppose, was that Gambino needed the brothers taken out without showing his own involvement, which would have escalated the war. He did this quite a bit, using outsiders to help his causes and to keep his own nose clean.

It was getting cold by October and it was colder still in Boston! Damn, why Boston? "Life, it seems, never really has any surprises does it?" The one place I wanted to avoid more than any other place in the world. But what could I do? Gambino had me, of that there was no doubt. If I ran, it was just a matter of time before he found me, and to tell you the truth, I was tired of running! If I did this for him then maybe I could get back to my own way of doing things, my own way of life. I knew Gambino couldn't kill me but he could make my existence in New York pure hell. It was easier just to go and do it. Screw my reservations about going to Boston; I really didn't have a choice anyway. With that, I got up and headed home.

The next morning a knock came at the door. I crept out of bed, exhausted, my eyes half open. Still tired I fell against the door and asked who was there. A muffled laugh emitted from the other side of the door and I realized who it was. "Sam, the little bastard!" It was too early for this and I felt my exhaustion give way to anger. It probably wasn't the smartest thing I've ever done, but without thinking I swung the door open in order to give Sam a beating. I hate getting woken up early. As angry as I was, I never stopped to think about my actions. And with that, I swung the door open wildly and stood in the doorway directly staring into the chests of two rather large well-dressed bohemians! Both men stood there with little expression. They seemed to be rather fast for their size because before I knew it I was being slammed up against the wall of my apartment. Both my arm's held tightly by vice-like hands. I was awake now! As I hung there I watched as Sam came walking in the doorway, a smug look on his face as he strolled up to me.

"Mr. Gambino just wanted to see if you had made a decision yet?" Sam asked. Also, he wanted to know if you'd found his trinket yet?"

I paused for a moment, as of course I had forgotten all about it.

"No, not yet," I replied. And with that I felt my stomach spew up what, if anything, was in there as I felt the pressure of a massive fist hit me square in my stomach. He was funny, that I couldn't feel it at first. It took a couple of moments until the pain hit me and then I slumped over. My head hung down as I opened my eyes to see Sam staring up at me. I coughed twice. Once I think I got him in the face. He pulled out a handkerchief and wiped off the side of his face with it.

"Mr. McReedy, I hope this isn't going to be a problem. Mr. Gambino has been very gracious with you as of late. A generous offer for employment and the ability to be still breathing is one that I feel is more than enough for the likes of you. And what does he ask for? Not much, my friend."

Sam sighed as if to let me know of his disappointment. He spoke some more as I felt the air rush back into my lungs. " William, Billy, how can I help you if you can't do something as simple as returning Mr.Gambino's jewelery? I'm trying to help you here my friend. Really I am!

These two gentlemen with me are here by Mr. Gambino's request. I didn't feel that they were necessary but Mr. Gambino insisted."

"The little shit, as if I were to believe his lies." My breathing started to become better as I slowly recovered from the blow I had just received.

"I forgot," I muttered, still trying to grasp the air into my lungs. "I never meant any disrespect. Please send Mr.Gambino my most sincere apology."

And with that statement the air left my lungs once again. I felt the pain immediately this time. But instead of wincing from the pain, I smiled and chuckled. I suppose by this point I was so mad that I didn't care anymore, even though I'd never been a person of extraordinary courage nor had a large threshold for pain. I no longer cared, for some reason. Maybe I was tired of being pushed around. Maybe I was sick of everything that was going on. I didn't know. But I continued to laugh even as Sam motioned to the men to continue utilizing their talents. I felt the blows one after another and with each impact my resolve stiffened and I laughed harder. Both men looked at each other in bewilderment as I continued this insane laughter.

By now I had reached the floor and the blood flowed from my mouth and nose. Twice now within a short time my nose was to be broken. Over one hundred years and never had I broken my nose before. Now, within a month I had broken it twice! The beating went on for a while and I thought a time or two that the boys were staring to get winded as the blow's seemed to lessen in effort. I lay slumped on the floor as I waited until they began to tire.

Kick after kick would lift me slowly into the air. My body already numb from the pain, I couldn't feel it anymore! Finally after a time I heard Sam as he called for them to stop. Both men stepped back as if relieved to see the end of it.

"Christ, you're one weird son of a bitch, Billy!" Sam spoke as if not knowing what to make of me. " I hope you understand that if you wish we can let the boys rest up a bit and continue again? Is that what you want? No, I think maybe you've had enough for now. Jeez, you look like shit!"

Sam walked over and grabbed a towel that was lying on the chair beside my dinner table. I rolled over unto my back, the blood streaming from my face as I tried to breathe without sucking back too much blood. Sam threw the towel unto my chest, I suppose in order for me to clean myself up.

He leaned over me and said, "Look, you sick bastard, just get the trinket, okay? Mr. Gambino just wants his stuff back, and trust me, he won't rest until he gets it back. Now what should I tell him about your current state of employment? It's not as if this would be difficult for you. I'm sure Mr. Gambino would also pay you handsomely for your time and effort." He paused for a moment looking directly at me before turning and shaking his head in disbelief. "We need an answer, now. What's it gonna be Billy?"

I just lay there trying to compose myself a bit, a little bit oblivious to what he was saying. It was as if my mind needed a few extra moments to pull everything together of what he was saying. He waited and it wasn't until he beckoned the boys to come back again that my mind began to fathom what was just said. My hand outstretched in order for them to stop. They both paused as I looked at Sam and nodded my head in acceptance.

"Good boy, Billy," Sam said. "We'll arrange your travel as soon as possible. I'll let you know when it's time to go."

Sam turned and motioned the boys to the door. I watched as they turned and began to leave. My eye's focused on the little figure in front of me.

"Samuel!" I cried out as the blood flowed from my mouth. "Tell Gambino that I'll do what he wants and do his dirty, work but you, you pathetic little fucking excuse for a man. Understand that when I'm done, there will be a price to pay!"

Sam stopped and looked puzzled for a moment and without hesitation began to laugh. He chuckled as he left my apartment, confident that my threat was meaningless. They disappeared from the doorway and into the hall and as I lay there I could still hear the little shrimp laughing as he walked away.

Chapter 14

After getting cleaned up I began to ransack my apartment looking for this trinket that I had stolen from Gambino's house. I checked my clothes, looked under furniture, anwhere that I could think of but with little luck. I knew I had grabbed something from his house but I hadn't even looked at it.   Now I couldn't find it. I must have searched for an hour but to no avail, and it was time to go, out for the evening, find some dinner, and maybe some cheap entertainment. I grabbed my coat and threw it on as the nights were definitely chilly.

I closed the door of my apartment and locked it. My keys in hand, I proceeded to turn and walk down the hallway. I put my keys in my pocket and in a second realized that they too had dissappeared. Apparently as I searched in my pocket I noticed a rather large hole in it. I fumbled for a moment and found my keys laying inside the bottom of my coat. I began to wonder and searched a bit more. I even took off my coat and felt around the outside for any sign of Gambino's trinket. In a second I had found it lying near the back of the coat. I reached through the hole in my pocket and was able to grab what felt like a small piece of jewelry.

I took it out of my coat and began to look at it. A small piece of gold jewellery on a gold chain. It didn't shine as if brand new, rather it seemed old and tarnished. I would assume that it held some type of sentimental value for

Gambino rather than any real monetary value. It didn't seem to be worth that much money as I examined it more. You could probably get this at any jeweller within the neighbourhood.

I wondered why Gambino would hold this in such high regard. It wasn't as if it was unique! I had seen this symbol all over New York since my release from my earthly prison. The longer haired gentlemen and women of this era seemed to embrace it as their own, mostly the youth, of course, but its representation was everywhere, from billboards to television advertisements. It was everywhere, a small circle encompassed the inside of the medallion. "A peace sign, for Christ's sake! All that for a peace sign?" I shook my head as I put the medallion into my inside coat pocket where there was no hole. Never had I seen a man that upset over something so trivial as this. I shrugged my shoulders and turned to leave, again to find some dinner.

The night air was indeed chilly as I pulled up the collar on my jacket. Winter was coming, probably sooner than anyone would want. I continued on my down the street and hit the subway entrance. This night I figured I'd try something different to eat rather than my usual haunts. And it was warmer in the subway station than upside on the street. It was noisier sure, but definitely warmer!

I made my way unto the train that would take me into Brooklyn. I hadn't been there in a while and thought it would be nice for a change. I got out close to Macdonald Avenue and proceeded up the street until I came to a small Italian restaurant. Gragniano's restaurant, it was called, a quaint place that had its charms. They had a vine-covered garden where I could see the dark- haired Italian girls sitting. This evening it was not that busy, so I didn't have to wait for a table.

The waitress sat me down near the back where the table was barely lit by one single candle. "Quaint" I thought. As I looked around more, I began to notice the patrons of this establishment some families, young girls, but there were some men that looked like 'made' men.

"Figures I would pick an establishment that was frequented by the mob." But all in all, a very nice quiet place to eat. I ordered a pizza and a beer and sat quietly waiting for dinner to arrive. While I waited, I took out Gambino's medallion and looked at it again. A small golden trinket, not much larger than a 50-cent piece. A circle encompassed the pearce symbol and at the top was a small loop that accepted the gold chain that accompanied it. Quite unremarkable, I thought. I stared at it for a while still pondering what its value was. I'm sure Sam would be happy to see this and give it back to Gambino.

The waitress came by with my beer. As I sat there for a while waiting and staring I felt a hand touch my shoulder. A man walked past me and proceeded to sit down at my table directly across from me. I didn't recognize him but within an instant I knew who it was when I saw the candlelight begin to flicker wildly.

"Him again. I hadn't seen him since before Diana said goodbye to me and I would be placed into the earth." Anger swelled up in me as I stared into the face of this monster. My hand clenching Gambino's trinket harder and harder as if I wanted it to go through my hand! The candle lit up his face with an orange aura and then he began to smile. His teeth glowed bright white from the light, as he looked at me and began to speak.

"Billy…How are you my boy?" I meant to see you earlier but things have been quite busy as of late. But I can see from the look on your face that you're still angry with me. I know, Billy; it was a little unfair what happened to you. But remember, I never lied to you. Both Diana and Jacob were spared any harm. Now please try and relax a bit, the night is beautiful and this place, Billy, this place is extraordinary. Why, I can see some of my friends all around us! Please try to enjoy the evening Billy."

He reached out his hand across from the table and cupped my own hand. The anger began to subside as if he was taking it directly from me. His eyes closed slightly as if he was enjoying the anger that I was providing for him. It was almost as if he too was dining this evening. Slowly his gaze turned back to me and he grabbed my hand now with both hands. He slowly pried open my fingers and stared down at my palm.

"My, Billy, what have we here?" What a lovely piece of jewelry. Is this for someone special? No, I don't believe so. I don't think you'd take that route again, would you?

Nevertheless, it is quite handsome. I have one quite similar you know."

With that he reached into his pocket and pulled out his own chain and medallion. Exactly the same as Gambino's but shinier and obviously newer.

" Interesting piece, hey, Billy? It's amazing as to how much you see this these days, isn't it?" He smiled and held it up to the light.

"What do you want?" I asked. " Why are you here?"

He continued to look at the medallion and smile, as if he didn't hear what I had said. "You know Billy, I understand these people, this world, this time and place. My work seems to get easier with each passing decade. Take this symbol for example, a peace sign, not a bad representation don't you think? But what does it mean? Do you know, Billy? No, probably not. Most don't stop to look and ponder what symbolism really is. People are so complacent to accept what is put before them as truth. The truth is...they don't know themselves what the truth is. I'm sure you don't either, even though I believe you to be more enlightened than most. Truth is a strange thing, Billy, stranger than these poor cattle could ever realize. Look around you, Billy, see the people sitting here, going about their lives as if they were the most important thing in the world, never once trying to understand the real purpose of their meager existence. Cattle, that's all they are. Cattle easily led to the slaughter! Mindless in their ambitions, soulless in their desires. I know you feel the same way, Billy. I'm sure you've recognized these traits before.

You know there are times when I almost believe that they can control their own destiny, really figure out what it is that they are supposed to do. Then, of course, they go back to what makes them so simple in the first place. Sure, occasionally one or two will get a thought of their own. But what do they do with it? You know! Of course you do. Nothing. They start out noble but in the end it's all the same. They forget, or give up, and true to their nature, get led by the nose ring again. Just like cattle, Billy, nothing more, nothing less," he stated as he smiled and put the medallion down unto the table. "I'm getting hungry, Billy. When is that waitress going to get here?"

I looked at him, understanding his words but not his meaning. "Where was he going with this," I wondered. I stared at him for a long time and as he was about to speak again the waitress arrived with my food. She put the pizza in front of me and asked me if I wanted another beer. My attention diverted, I politely said, "no". She turned to the man sitting in front of me and asked if there was anything that she could get him.

"Another plate would be fine," he said, "and a cold glass of milk. Thank you."

She smiled and turned towards the kitchen. "You see, Billy, they do what they are told. Even the simplest of tasks are done, naught by thought, but by direction. Do you believe that she wants to serve me? No, she would rather be at home mothering her small child that she left with her husband this evening. But she can't. They need the money and in order to survive, she does what she must. We all do to some extent. I'm surprised that she would be here considering her husband is a drunk and molests their older daughter. I know Billy; it's hard not to see it. All you have to do is look at her and you can see it as well. She knows all about the things her husband does but yet she ignores them to the best of her ability. Why does she do that, Billy? What would cause a person who knows the difference between right and wrong have that little moral fiber to do what's right? See, Billy, can you see why?"

I sat there puzzled to his statements. "No," I said, "I don't know why."

He leaned over the table and grabbed a slice of pizza. The waitress arrived with his milk and a plate. With the pizza still in his hand he continued, taking the occasional bite.

"People are like this pizza, in a way, mind you. You start with a foundation, in this case, the dough. From there you add sauce and layers to make the pizza a wonderful, tasty meal. People aren't that much different. They, too, start out with a foundation and should turn into something wonderful. But as more and more gets added to their lives, they have a tendency to 'mix the flavors' together a bit more than what was anticipated. When this happens, much like a pizza, you forget what the foundation tastes like. The dough, Billy, you forget what the dough tastes like because of all the other things that have been added. She doesn't know any better. Not anymore, she can't. Too many layers have been added to her foundation so that she can't even see what made her unique, her own person, so to speak. You get lost in all the layers, same as with a pizza," he said as he put the slice of pizza down on the plate.

I took a long swig from the bottle of beer and looked at the waitress. "See Billy, now you can see it, can't you?" he said.

I nodded slowly. I could see it; I probably always could, but never tried that hard before. I knew they were easily led, I just didn't know how easy.

He smiled back at me before wiping off his hands with a napkin. He grabbed Gambino's medallion again and began to look at it. "The medallion Billy, would you like to know where Gambino got it from, and why it's worth so much to him?" he asked.

Again I nodded, as my curiosity was now in full bloom. He grabbed the napkin that lay beside him and spoke as he began to polish the medallion.

"This is an old one, Billy, even older than you. Gambino was given this medallion by his father who in turn got it from his father. It's a family heirloom of a sort. I could go back a few more generations, but I think you get the drift of what I'm saying. I still remember when I presented this to his family. A few hundred years ago, if I recall correctly."

"You…." I said before he cut me off.

"Yes Billy, me. It's not like I haven't given these out before, you know. Call it ….a present, if you will. A gift for my friends, a symbol of my gratitude for all the work they do to help me in my endeavors. I know, you're possibly thinking what would I be doing giving out a symbol of peace? I've said it before, Billy, they can't see the truth whether it's given to them or not. It still amazes me that it has become so acceptable. They chose it as a symbol for peace not even realizing its true meaning or the ramifications that come from using it. Funny thing about it is that I didn't even cause this to happen. They did it all on their own. A thought, Billy, a single thought, helps my message touch the masses. Almost comical, if you ask me. When cattle try to think on their own, they almost certainly wind up doing the exact opposite of what they intended." He sighed and paused for a second. "But I guess I should be happy that they at least tried to think for themselves, shouldn't I?"

He grabbed another slice of pizza and then continued. "You see Billy," as he pointed to the medallion, "this isn't a sign for peace. Rather it's the exact opposite," he granted as he filled his mouth with pizza. "Oh, it is a symbol. But it's the way that you look at it."

He held it up to me and asked me if I could see the truth. I muttered, "no."

"That's because you're not looking at it correctly, Billy," he said as he slowly rotated the medallion until he held it upside down. " Look again, William."

I sat and looked up at the medallion that he gingerly held in his hand. This time I saw the sign of peace as it was meant to be seen. Upside down it looked familiar to me. A sign I had seen in so many times before from my days in the orphanage.

"A cross!" I said.

He looked at me and smiled, "Yes, Billy, a cross." "Almost too simple, isn't it? When the truth is shown to you, it all seems too easy to understand. A peace sign, indeed! Not even close to the truth. A cross-inverted and its sides broken. You can see it now, can't you, Billy? Of course you can, your look tells me that you understand. It's been around for a long time. The children of this era have decided to take it to heart, never once understanding its true meaning. Throughout the last 2,000 years this symbol has designated hatred of Christians. It began with Nero. He despised Christians, and through his reign, believed in a world without Christianity. He crucified many, bless his heart! But the one that I'm most proud of is when he crucified the Apostle Peter on a cross head downward. Downwards! It still makes me chuckle! A peace symbol, so simple in its design but complex in its meaning. Yet it goes by many names. The broken cross, or crow's foot, or witch's foot, or Nero Cross, or sign of the broken Jew, or the symbol of the anti-Christ, is actually a cross with the arms broken. Its true meaning signifies the gesture of despair, and the death of man. That's the truth, Billy. Always has been the truth. Look around you, Billy, see them as they are. No understanding, no ability to seek out that which lies before them. I've never even interfered in it; they've seen it for so long, you know. After Nero's demise the Germanic tribes of the old times used it.

For some reason they attributed strange and mystical properties to the sign. They considered it a 'rune' and black magicians in pagan incantations and condemnations used it. To this very day the inverted broken cross--identical to the peace symbol, is known in Germany as a todersrune. It's laughable when you think about it. In the last Great War, these people had brought the symbol back again. It was ordered by Hitler that it must appear on German death notices, and it was part of the official inscription for all the gravestones of Nazi officers of the dreaded SS. Nazis? I still can't believe that they never made the connection. I mean whether knowingly or unknowingly, anyone that wears or displays this symbol has pretty much rejected Christ. And still they don't know, do they, Billy? Remember, symbolism is as a picture, and a picture is worth a thousand words."

I sat there as he spoke, looking at his smug face as if he was gloating over the fact that we didn't know any better. I suppose it's true, that man has never actually given that much thought to its symbols or their true meaning.

I sat as he ate more of my food than I had. He was stuffing his face as if now, he was in a hurry to satisfy his hunger. Bite after bite he took, with the occasional swig of his milk in order to wash it all down. Then he looked at me and continued speaking with his mouth partially full.

"It's funny, you know." He turned his head and looked back to the waitress. "Everyone has a purpose in life. A meaning, a unique role to play in the grand scheme of things. Some accept their role while others think they can reject it. All in all, they bring the end closer than they could imagine."

He turned his gaze back to me. "What about you, Billy? Do you know what your purpose is? Or do you think that you don't have one?"

I shook my head from side to side, not realizing where he was going with this conversation.

"Listen to the song of the sparrow, Billy, only then will you begin to understand."

I looked back at him, puzzled to say the least. He looked at me and began to laugh. He grabbed his glass of milk and tossed the rest of its contents back down his throat. Slamming it down on the table, he grabbed his napkin and wiped off his mouth.

"One day Billy, the song will stop and then you'll know," he said, as he pulled out a wad of cash from his pocket. "Dinner's on me." He peeled a few bills from the roll in his hand.

"What about Gambino?" I asked, still figuring that's why he was there in the first place.

He stopped as he was already leaving, turned back to me, and said, "After all the things I've just told you, you still don't know do you?" he remarked as he came closer to me. He placed his hands on the table and bent down to whisper in my ear. "Follow your destiny, Billy. You don't have a choice." And with that he turned and left.

I watched him as he walked out the restaurant, stopping only for a moment to lean into the waitress and whisper in her ear as well. I don't know what he told her but she stood there for a moment transfixed in her spot as he walked away. Her tray of dishes that she held slowly began to shake and within a moment came crashing down to the floor. I watched her as she just stood there, tears coming down her face as if she was just told some horrible truth. As everyone was looking to her, I looked past her to see him leave, whistling all the while as he exited the restaurant and fading into the blackness of the night. I, too, got up and left for home, no longer wanting to spend the evening in mindless entertainment. I just wanted to go home and attempt to fall asleep and forget the night's events.

Sleep came eventually. I'm not sure what time it arrived, probably late again. But now a loud banging that was coming from the direction of my door was awakening me! I rose slowly not knowing what to expect, but anticipating the worst. I walked down the hall towards the door and I figured that I was about to receive another visit from Sam and his associates. I unlocked the door and took off the chain and began to turn the doorknob. As I opened the door I saw the little runt standing behind his two henchmen again. "Always, safer that way," I thought.

I opened the door not even waiting for them to acknowledge my presence. I turned to towards the kitchen and grabbed the pot off the stove. As I worked my way to the sink to fill the pot up with water, Sam walked in and had a seat at the kitchen table. I filled up the pot and turned back to put it on the stove.

Turning, I saw Sam sitting at the table, his legs barely reaching the floor. An uncontrolled laugh emitted from my mouth as I put the pot on the stove and turned it on. The site was just too funny to ignore. One of Sam's partner also chuckled as I assumed he saw the same thing I did. Sam turned and gave him a scolding look and as soon as he realized what he had done he pretended to cough as to cover up his insubordination.

Sam's gaze turned back to me as I sat down at the table. I reached over to my coat which was hanging from the corner of Sam's chair, and pulled the medallion out of my pocket. I sat back and flipped it across the table towards Sam's impatient little hands. His hands grasped the chain as he held it up to look at it.

"Mr.Gambino will be very happy to see this back in his possession," Sam said.

I looked back at Sam and gave him a sarcastic little grin as I got up to prepare a cup of tea. Sam put the trinket into his pocket and continued speaking as if I was at all paying attention.

"With this out of the way, I suppose its due time that that you accept Mr.Gambino's generous employment offer?"

I continued to ignore Sam's voice and kept on preparing my tea. The water was boiling by now as I grabbed a cup from the sink and proceeded to rinse it out.

"Mr.Gambino needs you to leave as soon as possible. The earlier the better," he said. "We've just received some new information as to the whereabouts of the details that will help us end this silly war." I took a tea bag from the cupboard and put it in the slightly stained cup.

"Billy?" Sam spoke. Again he said, "Billy, don't ignore me!" This time he spoke slightly louder than before. "Gambino and I are not patient men!"

I placed the cup with the tea bag on the counter and grabbed the pot of boiling water.

"Billy!" He voice rising once again. I could see in the corner of my eye as he beckoned to the two other men. I watched as they came forward, but I never moved as my eyes went back towards the boiling pot of water still grasped in my hand. I don't know what I was thinking. No, that's a lie! I did know! I wasn't about to put up with this little shit's nonsense anymore! I waited till they both were closer, knowing full well the extent of pain that they could inflict on me.

Closer and closer they came, their steps as if in slow motion as they approached. Sam again had a wicked smile on his face as he knew that he was once again in charge. My hand grasped the pot tighter and tighter with every approaching step. Their footsteps became louder as they came nearer and nearer. Without turning I swung the pot full of water and watched it as it found it's target!

Steam sprayed from one of the faces of the men as the boiling water hit him squarely. He screamed in pain, which I would assume must have been great. All of us paused for a moment as we watched him stand there writhing in pain. Oblivious to everything around him except for the pain he stood there screaming and holding his face within his hands. Before the others could react I swung the pot back and hit the other man on the side of his head. He stumbled for a moment grabbing my shirt in the process and I hit him with the pot again. I continued this repeatedly until he fell to the floor ripping my shirt as he went down, stunned, but unable to do much of anything, except breathe. The pot, dented beyond recognition by now, fell from my hands as I proceeded to kick the man in his face until his body moved no more!

I then turned my attention back to the little man sitting at my dinner table. He looked rather uncomfortable now, the smirk thoroughly erased from his smug little face, his head turning back and forth looking for some type of support to aid him. There would be none coming as I walked closer to him. He began to fidget in his seat not knowing where to turn or where to run. My arms stretched out as I got closer. With each step, Sam got more and more fidgety.

Directly in front of him now, I stood above him, hovered for a moment enjoying every moment of his agony. My arms bore down onto the arms of the chair. Sam jumped in his seat! I bent down so that my eyes were squarely in line with his. I could see the fear in his eyes now. Gone was any hope of salvation. I began to see the faint trickle of sweat as it began to bead on his forehead and on the side of his face. Slowly building as it started the slow fall down his skin. I began to smile. An impish grin really, one of satisfaction. I was oblivious to anything else around me as I watched the little man squirm in his seat!

My anger began to subside as I watched him turn into a shriveling little coward, one that I always knew he was. I relaxed my grip a little on the arms of the chair and backed away an inch or two from his face. Sam was taken aback. I had him, he realized it, and yet I began to distance myself from him. I knew hurting him now wouldn't do. My satisfaction came from him knowing that I could hurt him.

I stood back now and turned back to the kitchen. The anger was all but gone now. I opened the cupboard and pulled out another pot. Sam just sat there not knowing what to do. I heard both men on the floor slowly start to rise once again. I began to fill the new pot with water and proceeded to put it on the stove so that I could complete my cup of tea.

I turned and looked at Sam and his colleagues, all in quite bad shape. My own shirt was torn. I pulled it to straighten it as best I could.

"Tell Gambino that I'll go, but understand that when I've completed this job my debt to him is paid!" I focused back on Sam. Sam jumped down off his chair, still quite nervous, as he made his way over to the boys. He hurried them out the door as he himself headed there. As he left, he shook his head in acknowledgement and with that they were gone.

My water came to a boil and I poured myself a much-needed tea. I straightened out the chair and sat down with my cup. As I sipped my tea, I couldn't help but smile.

Chapter 15

I arrived at Penn Station early in the morning, my trip apparently all arranged for me already. I had packed a minimal amount of clothes and such. As I sat on the old wooden benches and waited for one of Gambino's men to arrive, I looked around at the new station. The current building had been substantially remodelled into a lesser version of the original grander structure that was first being built around the time of my first visit when I used to work for the subway company. I had been there once as construction started and I'll tell you, the original Pennsylvania Station was an outstanding masterpiece and one of the architectural jewels of New York City. The above-ground portion of the original structure was demolished by early1963 to make room for the current Pennsylvania Plaza/Madison Square Garden complex. The original structure was a pink-granite building and it combined frank glass-and-steel train sheds and a magnificent concourse with a breath-taking entrance to New York City. The main waiting room was apparently inspired by the Roman Baths and was expressed in a steel framework clad in travertine.

Now when I looked around, I couldn't see any of its original grandeur. Hell, even the floor with its ornate glass bricks were gone. But the thing that was most disturbing was the fact that the grand stone eagles were gone. Apparently though, they were saved and given refuge in other places. As I looked around, all I could think about was all the work had gone into that magnificent station lasted less than fifty years. I shook my head in disgust. What a shame!

To my surprise Sam showed up about ten minutes after I had arrived. Along side him was only one of the men that had been with him in my apartment earlier in the week. His face heavily bandaged. I noticed that the nearer they got to me the more his head began to face the floor as if he was ashamed of the beating he received. I was proud of that moment. Damn proud!

Sam came up to me and sat down beside me. With him he had a large envelope that I would assume held my instructions. He never said a word. He just handed me the envelope, my ticket, and both men turned and walked away.

I looked down at my ticket and proceeded to grab my bag and headed off. I found my train and got on board for the long ride into Boston. I sat there for a few minutes before opening the envelope that Sam had given me. Inside was a hand written note that detailed for me whom I was to meet in Boston and that was all? Upon reflection, I would suppose that they wouldn't write anything down that may cause them grief later. The name written on the note was a Harold Paul Rico. It sounded familiar to me but I couldn't place the name. Maybe Sam had mentioned it sometime? I wasn't sure and it probably didn't matter. It still being early in the morning, I placed my head back and tried to get a little sleep before arriving in Boston.

I had some trouble falling asleep but soon the rumble of the tracks beneath us slowly put me out. I'm not sure for how long I slept. I was awoke a few times, but I always managed to fall back asleep.

"Boston," I thought, as I attempted to fall back asleep. I'd never been there and hadn't thought about it since I visited my old apartment that Diana and I had shared with Jacob.

As I drifted in and out, my thoughts always went back to the two of them. I was happy then, truly happy for once in my life. I smiled as I lay back. I hoped that as I slept I would dream of them a little and somehow find a little comfort. I awoke a moment later. The train had stopped, not in Boston but in New York? I wondered what the hell was going on? We had been riding for quite some time and there was no way we had turned around!

I rose from my seat bewildered. I slipped open the door and poked my head out into the passageway. I turned from side to side looking back and forth but I saw no one. Was I the only one left on the train? How was that possible?

I stepped out into the hall and walked a short distance to the exit. I looked out the window and saw Penn station. But not the Penn Station I left hours before! It was different this time. It resembled the original station that I saw when I worked for the city! The grand station was before me again, in all its glory. In front of me were the platforms of steel and glass. I looked about and smiled at its beauty. People swarmed the platforms, their clothes reminiscent of the old days.

I opened the door and stepped out to find out what was going on. The door swung back and I took a step onto the concourse. I walked down the platform not knowing exactly where I was going, but I continued to head in the direction of the old waiting room. As I walked past the throngs of people, I felt calm and peaceful, as if I was home. I slowly made my way through the concourse, taking in every moment as I walked. Beyond the noise of the crowd, I could hear music playing as I walked towards the waiting room. I seemed to be walking forever, or so it seemed. I enjoyed it; it was as it was before.

A smile came over my face as I continued. The people all moved together as if choreographed in this manner. It was as if they were taking part in some grand ballet. All in unison, no confusion, but orderly in their manner.

After a few moments I noticed a familiar coat and hat way back in the crowd. Diana had the same kind, I remembered. I watched this lady as she walked up the stairs; she was around the same height as Diana as well. God, how I missed her!

She walked up the stairs and when she got to the top she turned around and in that instant I saw that she was carrying an infant in her arms. I stumbled when I saw this! Could it be? It was she! Diana, in front of me! Leaving the station? I stood for a moment, frozen in my tracks not knowing what to do. My eyes! Were they deceiving me? No, I saw what I saw, of that there was little doubt. I began to move again, pushing my way thru the crowd.

Gone was the ballet of unison now. As if they knew where I needed to be and were trying to keep me from my destination! Utter chaos filled the concourse as I pushed and pushed my way to the stairs. I could see her leave the top of the platform and I yelled out her name. Again and again I shouted but to no avail. She couldn't hear me over the roar of the crowd, and then in an instant she disappeared into the sea of people and I lost sight of her.

I ran up the stairs, not caring who I bowled over. When I reached the top of the stairs, I stood looking for her, my neck straining to see above the crowd. "Where? Where did she go?" I looked and looked turning in circles to catch a glimpse of her anywhere. Finally I saw her, about five hundred feet from me. She was walking towards the exit door that would take her to the other train platform. I moved as fast as I could but the crowd kept me at bay! Slowly I moved as I watched her get nearer and nearer to the door, her back to me, I could see the bundle that she carried so gingerly in her arms. I knew that Jacob was with her, swathed in thick blankets to keep him warm. I kept pushing as she kept getting farther and farther away. I pressed on as I saw her enter the door and disappear once again. By the time I reached the door she was gone. I spotted her again as this time she made her way down the platform stairs to where the trains were. I had just come from there and here she is sending me in a circle.

I followed her again as she descended onto the platform from the stairs, Jacob safe in her arm's. It was then when I was at the top of the stairs looking down that I noticed there was a gentleman helping her along. Diana could never have navigated these passages on her own.

I hurried down the stairs again, calling out her name. The sounds of the trains again drowned out any hope I had of getting her attention. I made it to the bottom of the stairs and jumped onto the platform just as she entered the train. Holding the gentleman's hand she carefully navigated the steps onto the train. I ran harder and harder, almost out of breath by this time. I wouldn't lose her again! Never again! I watched as she entered the train and right behind her was the gentleman. I heard the train whistle blow as the conductor held out his lantern, swinging it by calling "All Aboard,

Last train to Boston". My mind raced, I had to make that train. Just a few feet more and I would be with her again.

As I ran I came across a young man begging for money by the side of the train, and without reason he reached out and grabbed hold of my coat. I tried to pull forward but he held tight asking for anything I could provide.

Almost stopped now, I tried to pull the coat from my body. I pulled harder as I heard the coat tear slightly by my outer pocket where he held it. With that he loosed his grip and I was able to continue on. The train moving slowly now was beginning to pull from the station as I ran beside it, looking throughout the windows of the compartments! "Where was she?" Then ahead of me in the third window I saw her coat. I ran harder past her so that I could make it on the train itself. My lungs were about to burst but still I pressed on. The train was moving much quicker now and as I tried to reach for the handrail, I stumbled on a small bag that someone had left there! I tumbled over once before landing on my knees. The train rushed past me, no hope of ever catching it now. The windows rushed past me now. I waited to try to catch a glimpse of Diana! Every window was there for but a moment now as they flew past one by one. Then I saw it coming, Diana's compartment. As it rushed by I saw the blinds being drawn in her car. Not by her, but by the gentleman. I managed to catch a glimpse of his face as he went by.

"NO!" I screamed! I knew his face. I knew in an instant he wore one of his many faces. I had seen it once before as I lay before him on the cold slab of the morgue. It was he that reached over to close my eyes, as I lay still so long ago. I knelt there, crying, screaming, all that I could muster just to remain sane. I watched as the train left. Diana left. I watched it as it disappeared from the station and on to Boston where I would lose them both, forever!

My body jerked violently from its seat. My mind not quite comprehending where I was. I looked about and noticed I was still sitting in the train compartment where I had been all this time. A dream? Yes, a dream. I had dreamt the whole thing. My mind was once again playing tricks on me. So much for having a restful sleep. But yet it seemed so real, not like most dreams. It was as if I could have touched her once again, and the station, its grandeur I had witnessed in such great detail. I had never been there after its completion but yet I saw it! I saw it all, and it baffled my mind. Regardless, I came to realize that it was all part of a dream and I settled back down and relaxed into my seat. I grasped my face as I sat there; both hands covering it as if too hold back reality. Just then I felt the train begin to slow down. I lowered my hands and peered out the window. We were coming into South Station. Boston lay before me."

The train continued to slow, as we got nearer to the station. I heard the compartment door open behind me and as I turned to look I saw one of the train's employees peer his head inside. "South Station," he called, and with that, he pulled his head back and closed the door.

My gaze turned back to the window as I wondered what Boston had in store for me? The train came to a stop and I looked around to see if I had everything. My bag lay above me in the storage compartment. I got up to retrieve it and noticed on my seat that my ticket had obviously fallen out of my pocket and landed there. I reached down to pick it up and then stood up and grabbed my bag.

As I left my tiny compartment on the train I went to the door and momentarily notice that my hands were full, too full to open the door. I put my bag down and with my ticket in the other hand proceeded to put it in my outside pocket. As soon as I had put the ticket there, it fell to the directly to the floor. I stopped for a moment before I looked down at the ticket. I placed my hand in my pocket and realized in a moment that my pocket was ripped. Ripped exactly as it was in my dream!

Was it all a dream? Or did it happen? Did I witness how Diana left for Boston after my 'death'? I had trouble comprehending all that was being put before me, so I did the only thing I could. I picked the ticket off the floor and placed it in my other pocket. I chuckled a nervous laugh and picked up my bag. I opened the door and left the train. Better to forget what had just transpired, rather than dwell on the improbable. With that I left the train to meet my contact in Boston and finish this job as soon as I could!

I got into the station not knowing what to expect. I made my way to the concourse and stopped to look around. South Station seemed to be rather large, a five-story building from what I could see. South Station, from what I remember from my Subway days, was built before Grand Central and the old Penn Station in New York City sometime in the late 1800's. For the next several decades, it was the busiest railroad station in the county. Even busier than Grand Central they say! It used to be a grand old building, but now as I looked around, South Station was dilapidated and virtually unused. Some commuter rails were being used but the building itself seemed to have only one working elevator and one open staircase. The third floor and the fifth floor seemed completely abandoned. The desolate facility seemed to have become a haven for the homeless.

I made my way through the building heading towards the Atlantic Avenue and Summer Street entrance still not knowing whom I was to meet. As I got closer to the entrance I spotted a man near the doors with a sign in his hand. As I approached I saw that the sign had my name written on it. I suppose this was the person that I was to meet. But something didn't fit just right.

I became hesitant as I approached him. From his attire I could tell that this man was not of the clientele that I was expecting. On the contrary, he was the exact opposite! He had on a very tailored black suit covered with a gray overcoat. His hair was neatly trimmed and covered by a hat that had a large black band around it. I could feel it already. This man was a cop! No, not a cop, he was better paid than that. He was a federal agent! Why on earth would I be meeting a fed? Did someone tip them off to my arriving here?

"Shit!" I muttered quietly to myself." "Now what the hell was I to do?"

I continued forward looking for a way out that wouldn't draw attention to myself. But there wasn't anywhere to go at this point except straight for the exit. I kept the same pace and averted my eyes to the ground and tried to make my way past him. There were a couple of people heading in the same direction so I tried to blend in with them as well.

Closer and closer I got to the doors. Passing the man, I looked out the corner of my eye and saw that he was still looking forward, searching for me. I got past him and made it through the doors to the outside. I turned to my right and made my way down Atlantic Avenue. I took a few more steps and then realizing that I had made it past him, I stopped and took a deep breath!

"What the hell happened?" I thought. "Why would a federal agent be after me?" The thoughts were running rampant by now and I decided to continue on. It seemed I would have to find a place to sleep for the night, before heading back to New York in the morning. I took another ten paces when I felt as if someone was watching me. Again I stopped for a moment and looked around. Nothing!

I rounded the corner and turned down Essex Street searching for a place to stay. As I walked, again the feeling came over me as if I was being watched. I kept on moving and tried to ignore the feeling. Then without warning, ahead of me came two men in similar dress, walking directly towards me. I glanced from side to side looking for a way around them. With no visible escape route in sight I turned around as if to head back from where I came. I spun around and before I could take a step I saw another man standing directly in front of me, the same man from the station!

"William McReedy?" he asked. "You must have missed our sign at the station?" he spoke in a sarcastic manner.

With that the other two men were now behind me and I couldn't move in any direction. We stood there for a moment until beside us on the street a black car pulled up. "Your ride is here, Mr. McReedy," the man said as he gestured with his hand towards the door of the car.

With little choice I walked up to the car and opened the back door. Peering in all I could see were a pair of the finest leather shoes that I had ever seen. A voice from the car beckoned me in and I entered the car not knowing what to expect.

The car sped away down the busy street and I looked over at the man sitting beside me. He looked back with a scowl on his face. "Nice bloke!" I thought.

"McReedy," he spoke. "Word from Gambino is that you're the one to help me out?"

I turned my face forward, shrugged my shoulders a bit, and replied, "I suppose."

His eyes were still facing forward as I wondered what the hell was going on.

"Well, you fucking well better be all that Gambino claims you are or as God is my witness…."

I interrupted him, "Who the hell are you?" I asked. "And what the fuck is Gambino needing from you?"

He turned and looked at me, for the first time. "My name," he spoke, "doesn't matter. Just understand this! You're here to do a job for Gambino and me. Do it well and you'll be back on the train going home to your pathetic little life soon enough. Fuck it up and you'll be going home. Permanently!"

I sat there slowly becoming angry at the situation that I was now in. I hate it when people threaten me! Especially when it comes from somebody like this, a dirty cop! At least I know what I am; I make no bones about it!

I looked over at him and smiled. I wasn't about to be intimidated by this piece of shit, and even if I was, I'd be damned if I let him know it! He looked me straight in the eyes I never even flinched, as if we were seeing who would buckle first. Moments went by as in slow motion, neither of us wanting to give in to the other. The sound of a car horn finally broke the silence as he turned to look in the direction of the noise.

He turned back to me and once again started talking.

"Here's the deal! We need you to break into the FBI field office and get back a 'gypsy' on Ed McLaughlin."

"A gypsy?" I asked.

"Yea! A gypsy. It's a wire tap," He answered. "It has Eddy's location on it. We need the transcription of the tap in order to find him."

I shrugged my shoulders kind of bewildered "Sounds easy enough, but don't you have people inside?" I asked.

He turned his head and looked out the car window. "Sure," he answered, "but no one that wants to be connected to this."

The car began to slow down and finally stopped in front of a building that I assumed was where I was to be staying.

"Get out!" the man bellowed. "You're staying on the fourth floor. Room 409. Don't leave. Don't talk with anyone. Your meals will be brought up to you. Here's the key to get you in." He handed me the key. "We'll be in touch as to when and where." And with that the back door of the car opened and I was ushered out.

I stood on the sidewalk for a moment looking about the building when I heard him call me from inside the car. I turned and as he was leaning over he said, "Remember, if you leave, if you talk with anyone...." I cut him off once again and said, "Yea, I get it!". Then I closed the door of the car as so I didn't have to listen to his bullshit anymore. I turned and walked into the building and up the stairs to the fourth floor to find my room.

It was a hole was the best way to describe this place. It was more than likely an FBI safe house. A place where they put people that they didn't want found. I don't think anyone that stayed here would want to be found! But, I'd been in worse places. I made my way to the living area and turned on the television. There was nothing else for me to do but wait now. So I settled in as best I could and sat there as the television played out the day's events on the news.

It started getting late as I watched the sun begin to set. I had stayed there all day watching television. I was getting bored now. There was nothing to watch and I was also starting to get hungry. Finally a knock came at the door. A quiet one but at least the waiting was over! I got up off the sofa and made my way to the door. I opened it and saw a rather large man holding a brown bag in his hand. As soon as I opened the door I could smell the aroma coming from the bag. I stepped aside and he walked into the room. As he headed for the table near the kitchen, I asked him when I was going? He set the bag down on the table and began to speak.

"I dunno." he said, "Ain't my call. I'm just here to bring you some dinner."

From what I could tell he wasn't the brightest bulb in the organization! Still he might be able to give me some information that I wasn't getting as of yet. I like to know what I'm getting into rather than doing something on faith, and these people were definitely lacking that.

"Hope you like onions," he stated as I opened up the bag. Inside the bag was a sandwich, another smaller bag soaked in oil and a coffee. I took them out and began unwrapping them. The sandwich smelled good even with the abundance of onions. In the smaller bag were French fries, obviously left to sit in oil for too long. The coffee itself was already lukewarm at best.

I noticed that the man was beginning to leave, his job obviously done. "Hey," I called out, "you want to help me with these fries?" hoping to entice him to stay for a while. He stopped, looked at me and then the fries and then back at me again. "Listen," I said, "I've been sitting here all day already with nobody to talk to. I was kind of hoping that I could get to talk to someone for a little while?"

He looked back at me and without saying a word sat down at the table and grabbed a handful of fries. It was disgusting watching him eat, never once closing his mouth as he chewed.

"So…what you wanna talk about?" he said. "Not much I can tell you anyways."

I smiled as I grabbed the sandwich and took a bite. "What's your name?" I asked.

He grabbed another handful of the greasy potatoes and replied, "Gerry."

I nodded and continued, "Well, Gerry. I didn't think you could. About the reason I'm here, anyways. But, there was one thing I was wondering. Exactly how bad is the war down here?"

Gerry began telling me how things had gotten so bad in Boston over the last few months that Hoover himself was looking into 'fixing' the problem if things weren't taken care of and soon. He told me basically what I already knew with a couple of extra points that I didn't. Not much of a surprise, that's for sure.

I did learn that Edward "Punchy" McLaughlin's brother Bernie was murdered in 1961, and George his other brother was still imprisoned for a 1964 Roxbury murder. "Punchy" had already survived numerous gangland assassination attempts. Apparently during one, Stevie Flemmi and Frank Salemme dressed up as rabbis to try and hit Edward, and during another, his hand was shot off. Either he was one poor bastard or one lucky bastard, depending on how you looked at it.

I asked Gerry why everyone wanted this guy gone. Gerry told that Eddie was basically the last of the brothers. With him gone, their organization would fold, and Gambino already had someone in the wings to head the new re-structuring. Amazing! Simply amazing how everyone worked together regardless of what they said they represented.

I guess I shouldn't have been surprised. It just seemed to re-enforce what I always thought. Mafia or FBI, both working together while pretending to be at odds with each other. When I asked Gerry who the guy in the car was, he seemed almost to take this personally.

"Oh, that was Rico. He takes on everything personally." Gerry said. It seemed that the more French fries Gerry ate, the more talkative he got!

Apparently, Edward's final error was calling FBI agent Rico a "fag," a term I could see him disliking. Rico had been monitoring the wiretaps when he heard Edward insult him. I suppose Rico was a tad touchy!

The more we talked the more I got to know this Rico character. Rico grew up like any typical Boston youngster. He got a degree in history from Boston College in 1950, which led him on the path to a career in the FBI.

Rico was crooked, of that there was little doubt. Gerry told me that he was legendary among his fellow agents for bringing mobsters in to co-operate with the government. Rumor had it though, his two top informants were given license to extort, peddle heroin, and even kill, so long as they helped bust up the Italian Mafia and helped Rico look good.

I watched as Gerry devoured my French fries and talked at the same time. I quietly listened and ate my sandwich. For the most part Gerry gave me enough information to let me in on a few things that were transpiring. I had the general picture of what they wanted but still lacked all the details. I couldn't understand why Rico just didn't get the transcripts himself? He seemed to be a top man in Boston and it should have been easy for him to acquire the information that he needed. Or maybe he was smarter than I gave him credit for? By distancing himself from this event, maybe he was allowing others to take the fall if they got caught! Yes, that was more than likely it.

As we sat there, a knock came at the door. Gerry spun around really quickly and I could see that he was a little agitated.

"Shit!" he said. I assumed that Gerry wasn't supposed to hang around, just drop off the food and leave. I sat there eating my meal as Gerry got up to answer the door. He opened the door and standing there was Rico. Rico looked at Gerry with his now infamous scowl and Gerry left. No words were said but I could tell from Rico's look that he was not happy with Gerry.

Rico made his way in and walked up to the table where I was eating. He stood there for a moment before throwing down an envelope onto the table. I put my sandwich down and took up the envelope. As I started to open it, Rico began talking. "A car will be here to pick you up in four hours. I suggest in that time you study the plans in front of you. In the envelope were some standard picks that you need in order to get into some doors. I'm assuming that you know how to use them?"

I nodded in agreement as I continued studying the floor plan that was in the envelope.

Rico continued, "If you get caught, you're on your own!"

I looked up and answered, "What else would I expect?" asking the question but not really expecting an answer.

Rico's face was expressionless as he continued. "The transcript is located in room 327. There are three guards on duty at the time you're going to be in there. One guard will be located by the main lobby and entrance. You will not be going in that way! The other guards patrol the inside of the building and the grounds. If any of the guards are alerted to your presence, the building will be crawling with agents within two minutes of the alarm sounding. Once inside the building, take the south stairs up to the third floor. That door will be locked but you should be able to pass it easily. Enter the room and you'll find a bank of filing cabinets all labeled. You're going to be looking for the one labeled 'Source'. Inside look for the file marked 'Case 87'. Grab it and leave. Once you're out, head towards the corner of Dorchester Avenue and Congress Street. There you'll find a car waiting for you. Don't waste any time in there! Get what you need and get out as quick as possible."

I finished my sandwich and took a sip of the now cold coffee. All was laid out for me. All I had to do is what I've done best for the last few decades! I looked up at Rico as he turned and made his way out the apartment. He closed the door behind him and I got up to sit back on the sofa, my coffee in one hand, the floor plan in the other. I had a few hours to kill so I might as well continue familiarizing myself with the building. I was tired of watching television anyways.

I must have fallen asleep for a few minutes because I awoke to a knock at the door. As I got up, I looked at the clock on the wall. It was time! I opened the door and beckoned my driver into the apartment. "I need a couple of minutes," I said, as I made my way to the bathroom to freshen up. He waited while I splashed some cold water on my face. I grabbed a towel of the rack and wiped off the water. Looking in the mirror I saw my face looking back at me. The scar was there again, on my cheek, to remind me of who I was. I pulled my hair back and also looked at the side of my skull, still quite misshapen since shooting myself. Nothing to do now but get this over with, I thought as I put the towel back.

I made my way into the bedroom and got changed for the evening. Dark colors seemed most appropriate as I got my clothes out of my small bag. I got dressed and made my way back to the door where the driver was still waiting.

No words were spoken as we left the small apartment and made our way down to the street and into the awaiting van that was parked there. The drive took only a few minutes and the van came to a stop only a few miles from where I was staying. The driver looked at me and pointed out the building that I was to be going to. It was still a few blocks away and I guess I was to make the rest of the trip on foot.

I got out and continued in the direction of the Field Office building.

I pulled up the collar of my jacket, as it was considerably windy out this night. The cold began to cut through my clothes and I began to curse the weather. Closer and closer I got until I was able to see some lights on in the building.

It was an older building from what I could surmise. The stonework told me that it was built around the turn of the century. I figured then, this shouldn't be that hard to break into! I made my way past the front of the building where I looked inside and saw the one guard sitting at the front desk. He seemed to be reading the paper and was oblivious to anything else around him. I turned the corner and spotted the side door. This was my way in and out of the building. I still hadn't seen the other two guards, but I was sure that they were inside making their rounds.

I got to the door and looked at the lock. Nothing that fancy. It would probably take me about twenty seconds to get in. I pulled out the picks and found the right one for the job. The lock gave way right away and I moved in as quietly as I could. Once inside, I looked around in the dimly-lit building and found the south stairs. Quietly I made my way to the stairs and proceeded to go up them to the third floor.

When I got to the third floor I leaned my ear against the door. I heard some shuffling on the other side! It was distant but I assumed that I had just located the whereabouts of guard number two! I sat there and waited until I couldn't hear him anymore and then proceeded to work on the lock at this door.

This one was a little more complicated than the last one and I found myself working on it for about two minutes before it unlocked. With the door opened, I peered my head into the hallway and had a look around to make sure there was no one there. Confident that I was indeed alone on the floor, I made my way down the hall, looking for room 327. I found it about forty paces from the stairwell exit and tried the doorknob. To my surprise it was unlocked!

I entered the room and saw inside the bank of file cabinets that Rico described to me. The room was dark for the most part. A slight bit of light came from the hallway and it took a few moments for my eyes to adjust. Cabinet by cabinet, I looked for the right one. At about the sixth cabinet I found the one labeled 'Source'! I began to rifle through the drawers looking for the file that I was supposed to take. It appeared before me in the third drawer.

I grabbed the file and made my way over to the door where there was more light. Leaning against another filing cabinet, I opened the folder and began to read it. It seems that the wiretap had the exact whereabouts of Edward laid right out. With this information it would be easy for them to get rid of him and end the war that was raging here in Boston.

I closed the folder and was about to leave when I noticed the label on the cabinet that I was leaning on. For some reason it caught my eye, as if the light struck it just right. The cabinet was labeled 'Surveillance' and I decided while I was there, it may be advantageous for me to snoop around a bit.

I opened the first drawer and started to leaf through the file folders, my fingers slowly passing over the titles. There were some interesting things in here! I knew my ride would be waiting but I figured that it couldn't hurt to grab something of value for myself. I was thinking of Rico. I knew I didn't quite trust him and possibly if I found something here, I would have a bit of a bargaining chip!

I looked quickly through some of the files but nothing in the top drawer held any interest for me. I moved on to the second drawer and repeated in the same fashion. My fingers again graced the top of the folders until I came upon a folder named 'Gambino'. This was it! Exactly what I wanted to find. Exactly what I needed…. Wait! Down farther in the cabinet another folder appeared before me. The name on the file was mine! McReedy, written in pen on the label! Why would the FBI have a file on me? I had always kept to myself and had never been arrested in this country anyway.

Did they know about me? Had they been following me for a while now? I couldn't even fathom it. I tucked the Gambino file back in the drawer and grabbed the other one. Gambino didn't seem as important now. The FBI was onto me and I needed to know what they had. I tucked Edwards's folder under my arm and opened up my own. Just as I opened the file I heard a noise from down the hall.

"Shit", I muttered. It was one of the guards! He was coming back to finish his rounds. I could hear him as he slowly made his way down the hall from the north stairs. There was no way I could get out now without sounding the alarms. It was better to hide and wait out the guard. But, where to hide?

I closed my folder and began to look around. The office was small and hiding places were at a minimum. The room was mostly made up of cabinets and there didn't seem to be any place other than behind the door to try and attempt to conceal myself. I moved up against the door and beside one of the cabinets.

As I waited I noticed a memo holder on top of the cabinet! Nothing fancy, just a six inch sharpened metal rod attached to a square base. I grabbed the holder and held it above the door with my right arm in case it would be needed. If I had to kill the guard, I would need to do it quickly and quietly as to not alert the others!

The footsteps got closer and closer as I waited. In a matter of moments I saw the light of his flashlight enter through the window of the door and encompass most of the room. I waited, holding my breath so that I would be as quiet as possible. The light went back and forth for a few moments and then I saw the handle of the door begin to move.

My arm tensed up as I figured I would not get out as cleanly as I had thought I would. The knob slowly began to turn a half revolution. The door began to open slowly until it was a third of-the-way open. I could see his head through the window as he stood in the doorway. My arm was getting heavy as I prepared myself to bring down the sharpened rod onto his body.

Tense moments passed as I waited for him to fully enter the room. Sweat began to bead on my forehead and my teeth began to clench in anticipation. Then without warning the door slowly closed again and the light was gone! I heard his footsteps go down the hall and I heard him open up the next office door.

My arm relaxed and I put down the memo holder back from where it came. I breathed a sigh of relief and slowly sank down the wall as I waited for him to move from this floor to the next.

After a few minutes I could hear the door close as the guard made his way from the third floor. I got up and quietly opened the door. Peering out I saw that the coast was clear and I proceeded down the hall to the south stairs. At least the door wasn't locked from this side! I quietly made my way down the stairs, both folders in my hand. Step by step I took in stride, always cautious not to alert the guards. I was almost free; I could see the door ahead of me. A few more steps and I was on the exit door. I pushed on the bar and swung the door open! The noise of the door opening made the guard turn around and look!

"Fuck!" I muttered. "What were the chances?" I was so careful all the way down and here I was standing twenty paces from a guard patrolling the grounds! Without hesitation I began to run! The guard was caught completely by surprise and it took him a full moment to realize what was going on! I had run about ten steps before his mind even began to comprehend what was happening. I ran as fast as I could towards the street, never looking back to see if the guard was following. It was just a matter of time until he began chasing after me.

I heard him blowing his whistle behind me. I ran faster, and rounded the corner toward where we were to meet. As I came around the corner, I saw the guard that had been sitting in the front come out the entrance door! My mind raced as I looked for another route of escape. He began to run towards me and then I saw it a slim chance of escape!

To my right was a darkened alleyway just off the main street that I was on. I turned from the guard in front of me and made my way down the alley. I heard three whistles blowing behind me now!

All the guards were pursuing me at this point. I ran harder and harder down the alley slightly gaining the distance between myself and the guards with every step! The whistles began to sound further and further away. I started to smile now as I made my way down the alley! Then without warning I saw the wall before me! I had run into a dead end! I slowed my pace as I got nearer the brick wall. My eyes began frantically searching for a way around. I heard the sound of their footsteps coming up fast behind me! Any advantage that I had gained was slowly disappearing now as I started to see the lights from their flashlights.

I began to scramble up some boxes that were set against the wall, but I was still too short to scale the rest of the way! I turned around and almost hit the fire escape ladder that was behind me! At last something I could reach. I put the folders in my jacket and I jumped as high as I could and with one hand grabbed the ladder that was hanging there! The boxes beneath my feet gave way to my thrust and spilled along the concrete below. With my other hand I pulled myself up till I was able to get a foot on the bottom rung. It was dark and the guards were almost upon me now.

I squatted on the fire escape knowing that if I made a sound they would hear me and I would be caught! I prayed that it was dark enough that they wouldn't see me, and that they would eventually give up the chase. If not, I would have to sprint up the fire escape and find an alternative route. One by one they came up the alley towards the end. I sat quietly!

They had stopped running by now, as they got closer to the wall. Flashlights were aimed at the wall as I heard them talking and looking about to see where I had gone. It seemed like hours that they stood there. I waited and waited and then without warning I overheard one of the guards thinking that maybe I had gone through one of the doors that were located on the other side of the alley. All the guards began to run back and I sat as I watched them start checking all the doors.

Within a few more moments they were far enough back that I figured I could attempt leaving again. I slowly pulled myself up the ladder until I reached the first floor and then stepped onto the grating. I continued up the fire escape hoping that there would be somewhere for me to go. As I continued my ascent I stopped near the roof to look around to see if there were any guards or agents watching me. I stood there looking about and when I turned in the direction of Dorchester, I saw a black car parked. I wondered if that was my ride back or not. I wasn't that far anymore and I figured even though I was late there had to be someone still waiting for me! I saw smoke coming from the cars exhaust as I stood there, so I figured that someone had it running, keeping it warm. The streetlight that was a few feet from it allowed me a perfect vantage point from which to see. I continued up the fire escape until I got to the roof. I had to get to that car before they left me here!

When I got to the roof, I looked back again at the car and noticed that another car was driving past it slowly as if to stop. I watched for a few moments wondering if some agents were looking for anything suspicious. As the car approached I could see the driver of the parked car roll down his window. The other car then also came to a stop and it seemed as if they were talking back and forth. The driver of the parked car got out and crossed over to the passenger side of the other car. I wondered what was this all about?

My answer came quickly as he opened the rear door of the other car and out stepped a child! No! Not a child.

"Could that be?" I wondered to myself. "It looked like Sam!" My eyes straining by now, started to focus more on this character and as they did, I began to realize that it indeed was Sam! Why would Sam be here? Shouldn't he be in New York? I watched as he talked for a few moments then got back into the car and drove away. Something didn't make sense! I wasn't sure what was going on anymore, but what I did know was that the area was now probably swarming with federal agents and I still needed to get out of here.

I scampered across the roof until I got to the other side. Looking down I could see that there was no wall to pen me in as was on the other side. I quickly ran down the fire escape on that side! Floor after floor I went, until I came to the bottom platform. I climbed down the ladder and in the last four feet, I jumped to the ground!

I ran now. My breath was back and I made it down the street as quickly as I could until I came close to the car. I hid behind a bench that was located in a dark area on the street directly across from where the car was parked. I waited a moment and looked around to make sure that no one followed me. I darted towards the car and the rear door opened! Out stepped a rather large man and beckoned into the vehicle. I jumped in not realizing that in the back seat was another man waiting. I slammed into him and was quite surprised. The other man got back in the car and I was sandwiched between the two, my arms pinned between their shoulders. I began to wonder if getting into the car was the smartest thing I had ever done.

The car began to drive away and from the front seat I heard some talking. The voice sounded familiar and I recognized it after a few words were spoken! Rico! It all started to make sense now, Sam, Rico, the goons in the back seat. I wasn't to finish this job and go home at all! I was being double-crossed once again!

Rico turned from the front seat and looked me in the eye. For the first time since I had met the man he was grinning from ear to ear. "Well, Billy, did you get what we needed?" as he extended his hand towards me looking for the folder.

I sat there for a moment not moving, not speaking. I knew at this point if I gave him the folder I was to be done away with! But what choice did I have? There was nowhere to run now. The car was rumbling down the street and even if I wanted to jump out the men beside me prevented that from happening. So I sat, not moving, not knowing what to do at this point. Rico nodded to the two men who each grabbed one of my arms and held me there.

With my arms pulled back the top of my coat opened slightly revealing the corner of the light brown of the file folders! I struggled a bit as Rico reached over and grabbed the folders from the inside of my jacket. Sitting back in his seat he looked at the folders.

"Two? What the hell! You piece of shit, Billy! You were only supposed to get the file on Eddie! What did you figure? While I'm there I might as well do some shopping? You fucked this up Billy! Completely and totally. Fuck!" he said again.

I suppose he was a little miffed at me by this point. Guys like Rico need things to go exactly as they plan it. They like to be in control and when things don't go the way they planned, then they get flustered beyond belief. Rico was indeed upset. You could tell from his body language that he wasn't happy. He kept swearing under his breath as if that would help. Then without warning he lunged to the back and hit me square in the face with his fist. I sat there for a moment, stunned, my head spinning and hurting for but a moment, and then the blackness came, once again.

My body was shivering when I woke. Cold! My whole body was cold, as if I caught a chill that wouldn't go away even with all the heat from the sun! I was lying down, but where? I opened my eyes slowly and saw the moon peering above me. The more conscience I got, the more I could figure out my surroundings. I heard voices but couldn't see where they were coming from. My head still hurt a bit and I attempted to stand but couldn't. My hands were tied! No, not tied but handcuffed behind my back, no less. As I moved a bit more I felt my legs were bound as well! Where was I? I could feel a cold wind blowing on my back and the dampness beneath me and I seemed to be lying on the pavement in a puddle, but nowhere could I see anything around me except the blackness of night cut only slightly by the crescent above.

My head began to hurt again. That's the problem with consciousness it seems. There wasn't much I could do now but lay here, I was bound pretty tight and escape seemed improbable.

I tried rolling back and forth a bit to see if I could get some type of vantage point from where to see something but to no avail! I could only do a half turn, as it seemed that my legs were not only tied together but also tied to something solid that was restricting my movements. As well the rope went up to my hands behind my back.

I lay there for some time before I heard the footsteps come closer. It seemed that I wasn't to wait alone for long. The footsteps came up behind me and then traveled around until I saw a pair of shoes in front of me. Not very large shoes, so I figured that I was now to be discussing the situation with Sam. My neck straining as I looked up, I peered upon his tiny form in the moonlight.

"Billy, Billy, Billy," Sam spoke, while shaking his head back and forth. "It was to be so simple, but you had to throw a wrench into our plans once again, didn't you, Billy?"

I rolled over slightly to get a better view of his face, my movements still restricted. His smug look on his face showed me that he thought he was in charge, possibly for the first time in his life. I suppose the situation was grave but for some reason I couldn't help but laugh! I laughed out loud until the point where I was almost brought too tears.

Sam bent down as if he was wondering if I had truly gone insane. Closer and closer he got till he was a mere two feet from my face. That's when I looked at him once again and proceeded to spit in his smug little face. A direct hit!

I watched as he took a step back and wiped his face with his hand. That sight kept me laughing for a few more moments until the breath left my lungs as Sam kicked me in the stomach! I coughed for a few moments and rolled onto my back. Sam got closer again, as well as three large men.

"Always the rebel, huh, Billy?" Sam said, "What did you think was going to happen? Did you honestly think that you were going home safe and sound? You're pathetic!"

Sam began to circle me as I watched him walk around. "That file you stole. What was the purpose? Did you even read it? Do you know what's on it? No, I don't think you did, did you? You probably just read the name on the top and assumed that it was about you! You silly bastard! Why is it guys like you always seem to think the world revolves around them? What is it Billy? Ego, or something else? Well I suppose it doesn't matter now, does it Billy? In a few minutes everything won't matter for you anyways."

Sam called over the men still standing close. "Pick him up boys!" Sam spoke, "Show him where he is."

The men came closer and two of them grabbed me by my arms and picked me up to my feet. I stood up, my arms nearly wrenched from my sockets! The men turned me around and I faced the water. I was on a dock? I attempted to move my legs to try and stand better but when I did their movement was still restricted. I looked down and saw tied to both my legs a cinder block, like the ones used in constructing a building. I looked back up at Sam and began to laugh once more. Sam looked at me, puzzled.

"Fuck Billy, you are one sick person!" he said.

I had always suspected some type of double cross, but I was never really sure just what they had in mind. Now apparently, it was all too clear. Both men still held me by my arms and it looked as if they were getting ready to toss me into the water when I heard Sam speak once again. "Hold on boys." He paused for a moment as the boys turned me back around to face him. Sam walked closer to me, a folder tucked under his arm. "Before we part company, I just wanted to thank you for all your hard work. Rico has what he needs.

Gambino will be happy that the war will end and I'll get a nice bonus for this." Sam stopped talking and smiled.

I looked back at him and said "You're welcome! But if you could indulge me for a moment before my demise?"

Sam replied, "Sure, Billy, I suppose that would only be the civil thing to do. What is it that you want?"

Looking at Sam, my eyes peered down towards the folder. Sam looked down as well. "This? This is what you're curious about?" he said. I nodded and looked back at him. Sam grabbed the folder from under his arm and opened it up. "I guess I could see why you thought this might be important. It's a FBI file on a McReedy. Not you, of course," he said as I let out a breath of relief as I had assumed it was about me. The last thing I wanted was the FBI monitoring my actions and myself! "That better, Billy? You think now you can go on with a clear conscience?" Sam replied to my obvious feeling of relief.

"Yea, now I can go meet my maker in peace!" I said sarcastically.

Sam who was still looking at the folder looked up and laughed. "Billy", he said, "You got balls! You know that? It's almost a shame that you gotta go for a swim, you know?" He looked down at the folder again and mumbled to himself, as if reading a bit more.

"What?" I asked. Sam kept on reading and then looked up. "I was just wondering…you got any cousins in Boston? I mean how common is the name McReedy?" I shook my head-answering no.

Sam raised his arms to the men and they proceeded to take me closer to the edge of the dock. My thoughts were muddled at this time as I could already feel the cold water against my body. Then a thought hit me. "Wait," I called out, "one last question!"

The men stopped and waited for Sam to give them direction. "What?" Sam said.

"What's the name on the file?" I asked.

Sam looked down and read from the file. As he spoke I waited with anticipation hoping beyond belief that I could be wrong. "The name?" he mumbled again as he looked over the file. "McReedy, Richard McReedy, born July 29th, 1943. Age 22 years." Sam read from the file.

"Again I sighed a breath of relief as my fears were not confirmed. I was almost expecting the worst. As soon as the thought had occurred to me I firmly believed that I'd find my son's name in there. I always felt that there were no coincidences in life and after my last few conversations with 'him' I would have assumed he would partake in the cruelest of jokes. Now it seemed, I was to be spared at least once in my pitiful existence.

I was lifted now to the edge of the dock up the wooden rail that spanned the whole of the dock. Sam still reading out loud, "Apparently this Richard's under surveillance for activities within the organization. Huh? He must be new. I've never heard of him. Probably some kid wanting to get in."

I chuckled for a moment as the men waited for their cue. The water below me now, was dark and surprisingly calm. The moon above shone on the top of the water making it seem as glass! Sam walked over still reading to himself. The moon illuminated everything around us. Sam standing beside me now put the folder down on the rail of the dock. His hand rested on my body as high as he could reach. Apparently he felt a need to help with the task of pushing me in. I glanced back for a moment and then down as I waited for the water's cold embrace. A gust of wind blew by me and for some reason I looked down at the folder that Sam had placed by my feet. The cover blew open and I could make out the information on the opening page. It took a moment for my head to comprehend what I was reading. I read the name that Sam had said before, his birth date and his age. What Sam had forgotten to mention was his lineage was listed as well.

"Lawrence and Janet McReedy, parents" it said. The next line chilled my blood to the bone. Almost oblivious at this point, I felt my body start to move forward towards the icy water. They were pushing me in! And I didn't seem to care as I fell down towards the water. Fate had once again confirmed my place in the world as I hit the water. Cold, I felt the cold, as I sank. Down and down I went, until a few moments later I felt the block touch bottom. The rope stretched taught as my body wanted to ascend to the surface, but to no avail. The block and rope ensured that we were never to reach the surface again! I hung there in the cold liquid, alone with my thoughts. My lungs screaming for air with each passing second. I didn't fight it this time. I opened up my mouth and my lungs filled with water! The feeling of dread only lasted a few moments as I now felt my body slowly fall to the earth beside the block that held me down. I lay there, my eyes closed. No pain, only cold! I didn't want to get up anymore. I'd had enough of life at this point, especially now after what I had read. What a fucking joke, I thought. I suppose he's laughing at me as well? On the file as I went down my eyes were able to focus on one more name, that of Richard's grandparents. "Jacob and Lisa McReedy" was what I had read. My son, my only son! Fate it seems was playing a cruel joke, not just on me but on all my family as well! As I lay there I hoped that this time I would be able to fall asleep, fall asleep for good!

Chapter 16

I lay there for what seemed an eternity, waiting, simply waiting for the end. But once again, it did not come! I thought of Jacob and all that he might have done if not for me and my own stinking existence. I lay there and thought of all the reasons why I should never have had a child to begin with. I knew better! My first son now resides in eternity with pure evil, and my second child now feels the curse of my own mistakes. All I had were my thoughts down here. Nothing I could do now, nothing but wait.

I opened my eyes again hoping to see something but of course the water was black. Blacker than any night I have ever seen! I looked up or at least what I thought was up and wondered if it was day yet? I couldn't tell. I couldn't see the surface. All I could see was darkness. I wondered again about Jacob and his family. Did he have a good life? Did his son have a good life? Did they marry well? Were they happy? All of these thoughts went through my mind. Also why…why would my great grandson be under surveillance by the FBI? Was he already involved? I didn't know. But I found myself desiring to know.

The more I thought about it, the more I realized that I hadn't come to Boston to steal a file. No, I was here because as usual, fate had brought me here to find my family. It was then that I knew that I had to find Jacob! If for any reason other than to see how his life turned out. I had dreaded ever finding him before. But now, here in the murky darkness, it came to reason that I couldn't outrun fate any longer.

And so I sat up from the waters floor and began attempting to pull my hands apart from the ropes and cuffs which bound me! I struggled back and forth hoping each time I would gather a bit of slack. Luck was on my side as the ropes they used were completely saturated with water and had begun moving slightly from the expansion. I sat there for a while wondering how I would loosen my hands from the cuffs.

Then it occurred to me. I still had Rico's lock picks in my pocket! I suppose they wouldn't have thought to take them away as most people would have died before they could take advantage of the situation. With enough slack now in the ropes I was able to swing my arm's enough to reach into my pocket. Carefully I pulled out the picks and felt for the right one. My hand contorted to hold the pick in the lock, fumbling and feeling the tumblers until I felt a click! One cuff now off, I continued.

I struggled and with each passing moment, I felt the bondage of my watery grave give way until I freed one of my hands! With my free hand I felt down towards my ankles and felt the knots, which bound my legs to the block. My other hand still tied to the rope that held my legs was useless.

I began to work on the knot, completely by feel. In a matter of moments my legs were free and I was able to swing my body around and then try to release my other hand. Now with some vantage point to the knot I was able to loosen my last restraint and remove the other cuff. I stood there on the bottom, free of any shackles, rubbing my now sore wrists.

I looked up and pushed as hard as I could towards the surface, and began to kick my legs as I swam closer and closer to my freedom! Farther and farther I got, until at last the blackness began to fade and I began to see light striking the surface of the water. Harder and harder I kicked until finally I broke the surface!

My head just above the water now, I saw the shore and began to swim for it. My lungs still filled with water, not even craving air yet, began to push up the water that had filled them. As I made it to shore I crawled a few feet up and collapsed on the bank. My lungs now fully purged of the seawater began to replace the water with air. I lay there for a few moments until I felt some of my strength returning. The pleasure of breathing no longer holding the same fascination as it once did.

I rolled over, still cold and wet, but I knew beyond any doubt that I had to find that folder! And the person that had it was Sam. Wouldn't he be surprised to see me again? Surely I would scare the poor little man half to death! But, so it was to be, and I didn't have a choice anyway. Fate was deciding my actions now, and maybe instead of fighting it, now would be the time to embrace it!

I made my way past the docks. Still cold and wet, I found an open door in one of the many buildings that littered the port. I welcomed the heat from within and found a bathroom in which I could stay for a while until I had dried off. It gave me some time to think of how to find Sam. And so I sat, under the open metal ductwork, that slowly began to take the chill from my bones, as it blew warm air all around me.

As I sat I began to think of where Sam could be. The only place I seemed to know in Boston was the 'safe house' where I stayed and the bottom of Boston Harbor! I didn't even know where Rico or his cohorts were! Rico was but a pawn anyway. He would eventually get his payback. I wasn't so interested in him as I was in Sam! Sam held the key for me, the key to my past and to my future. Plus, I was pissed at him for trying to kill me, and the little shit needed to be taught a lesson!

After about an hour my clothing was sufficiently dry enough that I could venture outside once again. I headed down the streets back to the only place I knew, the safe house! It still held my bag and maybe someone would be there to answer a question or two as to Sam's whereabouts.

The sun was starting to peer up through the evening sky and I wondered how long I had been away this time.

I stopped on the corner as I heard a truck coming around. The truck stopped a few feet from my location and the back opened up. A man threw out a bundle of papers letting me know that the morning edition had arrived. Then the door closed and the truck moved on. I made my way to the bundle of papers and bent down to see it. The date on the paper told me that I had only been under the water for a day and more than likely Sam would still be here, in town! At least months or years hadn't passed by this time.

I grabbed a paper from the bundle and read the headline. Nothing of interest for me. I flipped the paper over and in the bottom corner a story caught my eye. It appeared that Rico had carried out his mission! Edward was dead. I read through the story wondering if the information I had supplied them had led to his demise. Not that it was my concern; I was more curious than anything.

The story read: *Edward "Punchy" McLaughlin, Charlestown hoodlum, brother of Bernie McLaughlin who had been murdered in 1961, and other brother George McLaughlin, who was imprisoned for a 1964 Roxbury murder. Punchy had survived repeated gangland assassination attempts – during one attempt two men dressed as rabbis tried to shoot Punchy, and during another, in Brooklyn, Punchy's hand had been shot off. Punchy had gone into hiding and for months his whereabouts were not known by authorities or anyone else.*

Edward, was shot and killed as he boarded a bus to go to his brother's murder trial. Witnesses say they saw him with a revolver in a brown paper lunch bag. But before he could get it out, two men shot him to death and left the scene before authorities arrived. The story continued with a few more in-sequential details. From what I could tell, the task had been completed. Gambino, Rico, and Sam had done what they had set out to do. I suppose now the war would be over between the gangs. Life could get back to normal. I put the paper back down on the pile and continued on. Just a few short blocks and I would be at the safe house. The sun was rising faster now and I could already feel its warmth as it came over the horizon.

In a matter of minutes I was at the front door of the apartment. I climbed up the stoop and pulled on the front door. Inside, I made my way back up the stairs to the apartment and came upon the door. A few feet from it, I heared voices coming from inside.

"Rico!" I whispered. Rico was inside the apartment with someone else! I moved up closer to the door and I waited for a few moments and listened. It seemed that everything had gone as planned and that Rico was quite pleased with himself. I chuckled at the thought of what he'd think if he knew I was standing on the other side of the door! The voices moved away a bit, I assumed that they moved from the living area to the kitchen. I reached for the knob on the door and slowly turned it. The door wasn't locked and I opened it as quietly as I could. I entered the room and stayed close to the wall as I moved in closer and closer to the kitchen.

Rico would know how to find Sam and that folder. He just needed to be persuaded in the right manner. I sneaked around the corner and saw three men sitting at the table. I darted my head back and wondered how I would get by all of them? My eyes began to look around the room spying anything that could be used as a weapon. The only thing I could see that I could remotely use was a lamp.

I stepped back to the table on which it rested and pulled the cord from the wall. I picked up the lamp and held it up. It occurred to me to pull the cord from the base of the lamp. Two weapons? "Maybe if timed right!"

I held the lamp in my right hand and the cord in my left. I took a couple of deep breaths and from there I was off! I ran into the kitchen and as I brought the lamp down on the head of one gentleman the others didn't move. I had completely taken them by surprise!

Before the first man had fallen, I was on the next man striking him with what was left of the lamp. Rico sat there stunned, unable to speak or move. I reigned down blow after blow on the second man until blood sprayed up and onto Rico's frozen face. The lamp now broken and splintered was useless. I dropped it to the floor. He knew the devil had come back to pay him his due.

The second man slumped over and I made my way around the table to where Rico was sitting. He still sat there, scared I suppose, as if a ghost had attacked them. I moved up behind him, the cord still in my left hand. He just sat there staring forward as I came up standing directly behind him. I dangled the cord from my hand as I leaned forward to look over his shoulder. With my breath passing against the side of his neck, I could also see the drops of blood that had landed on his cheek and saw the hair on his neck stiffen and rise.

I waited a moment or two then I leaned in closer to his ear and began to talk to him. "Sam!" I muttered quietly, more as a statement than a question. Rico knew that this time I was in charge. He continued to look forward as if frozen in fear. The cord now came up and draped loosely across his neck. Once again I repeated myself, "Sam!" This time his head turned slightly as his eyes focused on the two men slumped over the table.

"Copley Square" he whispered back to me. "Harcourt and Huntington." His eyes were still focused on the two men in front of him. I pulled the cord a little higher towards his Adam's apple, ready to kill this bastard without even a thought.

That's when I looked down and noticed that while sitting there Rico had soiled himself! His pants were soaked and a puddle lay at his feet on the floor. Pissed himself! The poor guy was so scared, he pissed himself! In a way it was almost sad to see him this way, pathetic at the very least. Somehow I felt that killing him would be anti-climatic in a sense.

I dropped the cord from his neck and used it to tie him to the chair. It was better this way, when his cohorts came to they would see him in all his pathetic glory. The embarrassment of the situation was better than killing him! And anyways, fate it seems always took care of things. Rico would get his eventually!

I smiled, patted him on the shoulder and turned towards the door. I took a few steps and stopped by the first man I hit with the lamp. I began to rifle through his pockets, as I figured I needed a cab to make it too the hotel and money was something that I lacked! Luckily he had his wallet on him and inside was a huge wad of cash! I made my way out the door and down the street to hail a cab.

It wasn't a long ride to the hotel, just a few minutes away. I got out of the cab and paid the fare with a twenty that I had liberated from Rico's man. A doorman greeted me upon exiting the cab, something I was not accustomed to. I looked up at the old six-story building and wondered where I might find Sam this early in the morning. I entered the hotel through the front door. Above it was a tremendous awning with the name of the hotel hanging off it's edge in bold white flags, each letter separate from one another. "Quite classy," I thought, as I entered the lobby and began searching for anything that might lead me to Sam's room. I should have asked Rico the room number but the thought had escaped me at that point. Ididnt know his last name, so it was pretty hard to go up to the front desk and ask for his room! Plus, I didn't want to take the chance that someone would warn him of an announced guest!

The lobby was pretty much deserted this early in the morning. A desk clerk and a chambermaid were talking, but that was about it. I looked up at the clock and saw that the time was only

7:30 in the morning. I supposed it was still fairly early in the morning and maybe Sam was still sleeping. I ran my hand over my hair and felt the stiffness of it! All that seawater must have caused it to look hideous. I turned left and headed toward the washroom. Maybe I could clean myself up a bit as to not draw that much attention to myself.

The washroom was nice and clean, four sinks, marbled countertops, and tiled floors! This was one nice hotel, something I never thought Sam would stay in. He seemed more of a seedy-side-of town type of person. No, this place was indeed elegant and with my appearance I didn't belong, at least in this condition!

I ran the water until it was warm and proceeded to stick my head under the tap. There were bars of soap available, so I decided to give my hair a quick wash. A nearby towel helped dry my now soaking head. But I felt a lot better. I washed my face and grabbed a comb, slicking my hair back so that at least I would look presentable when I went back into the hallway. Satisfied that I looked better I turned to head back into the lobby. But before I went out, nature picked the exact right time for me to go relieve myself. With time to kill anyway, I entered the stall and sat down.

I had been there for a number of minutes when I heard the door open. Someone else needed the facilities as well! The stall door beside me opened and shut and I heard a rather large grunt within my neighbors stall. I finished up and got up to leave. As I did I curiously looked between the metal partitions of the stall to the gentleman beside me. My head quickly darted back as I recognized the fellow! This was one of the men that helped push me into the harbor! Luck was with me this morning. I left my stall and proceeded to look around the bathroom for anything that could be of use. What I should have done was grab Rico's gun when I had him tied up. That would have made things much easier. Unfortunately though it would also make things quite a bit noisier and that I couldn't have.

I searched for a moment until I came upon a plumber's helper standing in the corner of the bathroom! It wasn't much I'll admit, but it was better than nothing.

I grabbed the plunger in my right hand and walked up to the stall door. With my left foot I kicked open the door to the stall and came face to face with one of my so-called murderer! The look on his face was priceless, as he sat there! Man is like any animal; the most vulnerable time we all have is when we excrete the waste from our body. Animals circle first to make sure the coast is clear. We lock ourselves in for privacy with no place to escape. Humility will always be our downfall!

I looked down at the plunger for a moment wondering how to use it and then I just shrugged my shoulders and slammed the top of it down on his head. The wooden handle cracked and broke from the strain, and the rubber head flew up and into the next stall. He was bleeding from his forehead now. I'm sure the blow at least cracked the top of his skull! I moved in closer and held the now broken slightly sharper top of the plunger to his neck. I bent down and grabbed him by the collar, the blood now flowing more freely and unto my hands that held him.

Again, I asked the question, "Sam!" He looked up at me, blood all over his face now, quite disorientated from the look of things. His head shaking slightly from side to side he opened his mouth to try and speak. The blood moved into the new opening and he attempted to talk but all he could do was mouth the number 610. I think he was going to pass out at any minute. I stood up knowing that he wasn't a threat anymore and when I stepped back he fell forward onto the floor, his still bare ass sticking up in the air. It was actually quite amusing if you didn't understand the context in which it happened. I dropped what was left of the handle as the floor began to run crimson from his wound. I looked down and quickly sidestepped the blood in order to save my shoes from being covered in it.

I had to move quickly now, surely someone would see this soon and it would just be a matter of time before the police were summoned! I exited the bathroom and made my way back into the lobby. I pulled the collar of my jacket up as I made my way to the stairs, which took me past the desk clerk who luckily was still enthralled with the maid.

Once past them I began to sprint up the stairs, two, and sometimes three steps at a time! I was in a hurry to find that tiny shit! I reached the sixth floor, breathing heavily at this point. Slowly I made my way down the hall looking for the right door. I started to catch my breath again as I came upon room 610.

Standing outside I put my ear to the door to see if I could hear any noise from inside. Nothing! I suppose the little rat was still asleep. Back into my pocket my hand went and pulled out the picks once again.

The lock gave way easily and I entered the darkened suite.

The area was quite large with a kitchenette included and from the looks, a separate bedroom. Perfect! I closed the door behind me as I entered and began to search out the folder that I so desperately needed. On the sofa was a stack of papers including yesterday's paper in disarray. I picked them up and found the folder resting gently underneath. I sat down now oblivious to anything else but finding out some more information about my family. I leaned over and opened the curtain a crack so that I could have a little bit of light from which to read. I read the file from start to finish twice until I finally put it down on the coffee table before me. Then I leaned back into the sofa and put my hand to my forehead and closed my eyes. I sat there trying to comprehend all the knowledge I had just acquired.

My thoughts drifted back to a better time, when Diana and I had learned that she was pregnant with little Jacob. How we prepared for his arrival and how we yearned for his safe birth. I smiled a bit sitting there. It was one of those times that I can honestly say that I was happy. Now as I sat, the thought of finding my son terrified me beyond anything I had ever encountered before. What would I tell him? What could I say? Nothing would ever sound right. My son was old now. How would I explain to him that his dead father had come back and seemed younger than he? I couldn't see how it was possible. But I knew that I needed to see him!

I sat there pondering my options as I heard Sam snoring from within the next room. I opened my eyes and knew that it was time to get back to the task at hand. Quietly, I rose from the sofa and made my way to the bedroom door. I stood there briefly allowing myself a moment to gather my thoughts once again. I looked forward at the front door, and then back at the bedroom door, wondering if it would just be easier to make my way out and forget about Sam. I suppose after reflecting I wasn't as angry as I was before. But then I remembered the gentleman I left downstairs and thought about what might happen and the attention it would bring.

Rico would tell Sam that I was still alive, Sam would tell Gambino, and I would be running forever! Rico, it seemed, didn't have any other connection to Gambino but through Sam. So unfortunately for Sam, I wasn't given much of a choice.

I grasped the knob and slowly turned it to open the door. Inside I saw him sleeping in the middle of a rather large bed. He looked silly in there, as the size of the bed in relation to his tiny frame seemed disproportional. Sam was still snoring and the more I stood there, the more it seemed his noises irritated me. I walked over to the side of the bed and sat down. Sam rolled over and opened his eyes. He looked up at me, and his eyes opened wider and wider. I put my hand over his mouth, as it seemed he was getting ready to scream. I put my index finger to my mouth as to quiet him. He nodded, his eyes as wide as a deer now! No words were spoken now, there didn't have to be. He knew what was to come and there was little he could do about it.

With my free hand I grabbed the extra pillow that lay beside his head and brought it over to his face. I removed my hand from his mouth and grabbed the pillow with both hands as I brought it down over his face. He let out a yelp as the pillow came down over his nose and mouth and I could hear a muffled scream as I continued to put pressure on the pillow!

"Shhh", I kept saying, "it's time to go to sleep." His body began to writhe now. He struggled valiantly as I held the pillow in place. After a few moments his body began to jerk more and more violently until all motion began to stop. I waited about another minute then I removed the pillow from his face and laid it back down beside him. I looked at his face, now slightly contorted, his mouth open as if still screaming! His eyes were wide open and I could see that blood vessels had burst from within the whites.

I reached over and closed his eyes. I had figured that his death would have given me more satisfaction but for some reason I didn't feel it.

I actually felt sorrow this time. Maybe it was my mood this morning thinking about Jacob or maybe I, in some ways, had grown to respect the little man. We weren't much different, he and I. In some ways we had done much of the same things in life, overcome disadvantages, overcome adversity, and such. In a way I now envied him. He was now enjoying his rest, something that I too always longed for and would never have.

I sat there for a few more minutes before getting up and moving back into the main room. Feeling rather meloncholy I grabbed the folder off the coffee table and made my out the door. It was time to get something to eat and then begin the journey of locating my son.

Chapter 17

I spent the night in another hotel across town. Most of the next day I just walked around, deep in thought. Upon my arrival at the hotel I had acquired a map and a telephone directory. Each, I thought would help in my quest to locate Jacob. The FBI folder did not contain his address, only the address of my great-grandson, who apparently was in trouble with the law. I sat down on the bed and begin to rifle through the phone directory looking for a Jacob McReedy. I found the appropriate page and my index finger began to scroll down the page searching until I came across a J. McReedy, the only one in the book. I paused for a moment wondering if this was he? It seemed to be only logical as he was the only J. McReedy in the book.

I felt the nervousness enter my body again as I looked over towards the phone. I hesitated again, not knowing what I was going to say or do. I reached over and picked up the receiver. Hearing the dial tone I looked back at the phone book and began dialing the number. One by one, my finger found the appropriate hole and turned the dial around until I had dialed all the numbers but one! I sat for a moment, again pondering the wisdom of my decision. But enough was enough! I couldn't turn away this time and I knew it, so I rounded up the last of my courage and dialed the last number.

I heard a ring and then another. The time between the rings seemed endless as another ring went by. My heart seemed to be holding its beat waiting until it heard the next ring again. A lump started in my throat as I waited for a voice from the other end. Then after five rings, a voice answered! Not a male voice, but one that was of a woman, elderly I gathered from the tone.

"Hello" the voice answered. A moment passed as I thought of what to say. "Hello?" the voice said again. My thoughts came back to the task at hand.

"Hello" I replied, "may I speak with Jacob McReedy?" I wondered if I had dialed the right number as I asked.

"I'm sorry", the voice said, "Jake's not in right now. May I take a message for him?"

I had the right house! This was Jacob's residence then! Stunned and without thinking I slammed the receiver back into its cradle! I sat there for a few minutes wondering how I would interact with him. It almost seemed my sole purpose now was to see him again, as if some unseen force was pushing me towards this.

Jacob was old now, around 63 years of age. Had he had a good life? Was he still working? I suppose I was to find out. I looked back to the directory and wrote down the address on a piece of paper. I closed the directory and picked up the map and began to search for his residence. Within a few minutes I had found the street where he lived. I would leave in the morning for his place and hopefully by then, I would have a plan in place in which to approach him. I put the map and paper down on the nightstand and tried to fall asleep. Tomorrow would be a big day.

I grabbed a cab the next morning from the hotel. It was still dark out but I wanted to get there before anyone woke up. Plus I hadn't slept well the night before and I got up rather early. Sitting in the cab, I still wondered how I was going to approach him. I hadn't yet come up with a plan, and I was still extremely nervous at the thought of finally meeting him.

I couldn't believe it. My son! I was to see him again after all these years! He was just a babe the last time I saw him, swaddled in his blankets as I held him tightly, trying to keep him safe from harm. All those years, now gone. He had grown up without his father; I hoped that his mother had raised him well. But of course, she would have! Diana always had an inner strength to her that far surpassed anything within myself. I almost envied that about her at times.

The cab began to slow down; we must be coming near now. We circled the street on which he lived and I motioned to the cab driver to stop at the intersection rather than the house itself. I would walk the rest of the way. I didn't want to draw attention to myself.

I paid the fare and made my way down the street toward the address. I walked past the house and continued on. There was a light on in the kitchen it seemed and stopping didn't seem that good an idea. So I continued to the end of the street and made my way across the road to find a better vantage point in which to wait. I found an area a few yards from the front of the house, a nice transit bench on which to sit and wait.

I sat and waited for some movement from the house and within a matter of minutes I saw someone come out the side entrance. It was still dark and I couldn't make out many details, but I believe it was an older gentleman with a dog on a leash! I got up to get a closer look. My heart racing as I moved forward to try and catch up. They had moved down the street already and I began to quicken my pace. A few feet from them I wondered if this was indeed Jacob? My heart felt like it was ready to burst in anticipation.

I walked along side them now directly across the street, watching, looking for any clues. This was Jacob, it had to be! I felt it in my heart to be true. My son was alive and well! We walked a few more feet until his dog it seemed to need to relieve itself. I, too, slowed down my pace.

The dog found a tree and turned to relieve itself, and then it looked up at me and began to bark! The last thing I wanted was to draw undue attention to myself. Damn that dog! Jacob looked over towards me and I was able to make out his face before I turned and walked in the other direction. In that moment, that one fleeting second, I could see Diana's face from within him. It was my son!

I turned quickly and I don't believe he got a good look at me. I walked straight to the end of the street and then I rounded the corner and waited, waited until I could see him return home. He was almost as I had pictured him, thick brown hair, a square jaw, my Roman nose and Diana's eyes! He was beautiful. He was old but to me he would always be my little boy.

I watched him as he went back, slowly wiping the tears from my eyes as he made his way home. All the regrets I ever had hit me again in the moment I saw him. All the things I had missed, most of his life now passed, and I had missed it all. "My boy, my dear sweet boy" I whispered as he went back into the house and disappeared once again.

I waited there that morning, waited for him too come out once again. It was cold but as the day progressed it began to warm up. A few hours later I saw the door open again and out came Jacob. He began to walk again, this time alone. I followed along, a bit farther back this time. We walked a couple of blocks until we came to an intersection where Jacob stopped and sat down at a bench. I looked up and saw the transit sign as I concluded he was waiting for a bus. I stood back a bit and waited for the bus to arrive. A few short minutes later the bus arrived and Jacob got on along with a few other people. I ran towards the bus and almost missed it. The doors were just closing and I had to bang on them to get the driver to open them up.

I climbed up the couple of steps and made my way down the aisle. Jacob sat near the front and as I passed him, I looked down at my boy. My hand, lightly and purposely brushed the arm of his coat. I hadn't touched him since his birth and as I made my way past him to find a seat, the hurt began again. I sat down near the rear as to not attract attention. Then I waited to see where it was we were going.

The bus continued on for about six or seven more miles until I noticed Jacob pull the cord for the next stop. As the bus began to slow up, Jacob slowly got up and made his way to the front of the bus. I waited until he was almost off and made my way to the rear exit. Jacob began walking and I again resumed following him from a distance.

We walked three more blocks until he turned into "Oak Lawn Cemetery", at least that's what the sign stated. I kept back a bit more and started to circle around the cemetery as I kept an eye on Jacob. Jacob moved to an area, which resembled a series of military looking graves. Stark white crosses all in neat rows. He walked through them until he came upon a bench and sat there, just looking at the crosses. I waited a few more minutes then I started to make my way over. Jacob seemed deep in thought and this seemed as good a place as any to attempt meeting with him.

I walked up closer to the bench until I stood beside it. Jacob was looking down at the ground as if in deep thought. Then his head turned up towards me and I knew there was nowhere else to go! His hand rose and he beckoned me to sit. That's when I noticed a tear in his eye. Someone had died and was buried here. A friend? Maybe, I thought as I sat down, and we both looked forward for a few moments. The crosses were all lined up in neat rows, just as if the soldiers were still in formation. I was never one for the military, but I understood it. I looked over at Jacob and saw he was hurting.

"It's never fair. Is it?" I said casually. Jacob looked up and then down again.

"No," he said as he leaned a bit forward, "it never is."

Wiping the tear from his eye, he glanced over at me. "Damn wars!" he angrily stated. He noticed the side of my head when he looked over, "Just got back, huh?" he asked. It was as easy an explanation as I could make up so I nodded in agreement. War was never worthwhile. Something civilization invented based on man's history to expand the 'hunting ground'!

We sat there for several minutes discussing the tragedies of war and slowly we began to discuss other things as well. "My name's Billy," I said, as I put out my hand, "and you are?"

He looked over and stretched out his hand and said, "Jake. My friends call me Jake."

I smiled and we shook hands. He had a strong grip even for his age. His hands were rough and calloused as if he had worked with them most of his life. We continued talking and it seemed we were getting along fairly well. Politics came into the conversation as well as the weather, women and the downfall of society because of television.

Jacob, it seemed, had become quite opinionated during his life and I relished in it. We had very similar ideals, he and I. We sat, talking well into the afternoon, discussing anything that may have even remotely been of interest to more important things such as life in general. We even laughed a few times. It almost seemed as if we had been friends for years.

It took a while to ask him about his family. I wanted to know everything but I didn't want it to seem that I was prying. He told me of his Aunt who helped raise him when he was just a small lad. He told tales of his poor blind mother who worked everyday just so that he could eat properly.

At the mention of Diana, my heart seemed to skip a beat as I thought of her raising this child all by herself. "But, she always made sure that I was happy," Jake stated, almost as if he knew I needed to hear that. "She worked for many people over her lifetime. Mostly taking in laundry and sorts. Being blind it was hard to find steady work. My Aunt's house where we stayed was always busy and noisy. She had three kids as well, all boys, and between my cousins and myself, I'm sure we drove the two of them crazy! But it was always a good place, you know?"

I nodded in agreement.

"My father I'm told, died when I was just a few days old. My mother would talk about him for hours. She wanted to make sure I knew where I came from. He was a good man, she would tell me, a hard working man right up to the day he died. He died on the job, apparently caught in a collapse of some kind. Mom didn't like to talk about it much. But from the other things she told me I made sure that I grew up to be someone he could be proud of!"

I listened to Jacob as he spoke and a tear began to well in my eye. I turned my head slightly to wipe it away as Jacob continued. "Got married, to a wonderful woman. Leni's her name. She's a good woman that has stuck by me through the good times and the bad. I couldn't have asked for someone better. We had a son, Larry who grew up to be a wonderful man. He got married and gave us a grandson." Jacob hesitated for a moment, looking back at the crosses and staring. It was when he looked up that it began to sink in as to why we were here! His son, my grandson was the reason we were here! It hit me now! Lawrence, my grandson, was dead. Jacob had suffered a loss that he never should have. Here in these unmarked graves, Lawrence was represented.

I put my hand on Jacob's shoulder and asked, "How?"

Jacob looked back up at me and as the tears came from his eyes, he began to reply, "Larry was a good boy. Always responsible, even as a child. When the war broke out and his country called, he left his family behind to fight. He went to fight the Japanese in the Pacific. They landed August 7th, 1942 on the island Tulagi and took back the island by the end of the day." Jacob paused for a moment and sighed before continuing, "I was so proud of him! It was a glorious victory for the allies. He fought a good fight. So many boys lost their lives that day. So many parents wept that day, we were among them. Leni cried for months, there was no comfort for her. It's one of the worst feelings in the world, when a mother loses her child and there's nothing you can do to help."

The tears that had started a few moments before now began to fall from my eyes as he told his story. It hurt terribly to listen knowing that my boy had suffered so great a loss. He went on to tell me how Lawrence's wife and child came to live with them, after his death, as they had nowhere else to go. Jacob and Leni took them in and helped raise Richard until he was about fourteen years old. Then Janet re-married and they moved into their own place.

I began to compose myself a bit more as I listened. I didn't want Jacob to see me crying, but apparently he was caught up in the moment as well and failed to notice. He shook his head as he discussed Richard. Seems he was a troubled child right from the start.

"That boy was never quite right!" Jacob claimed as he looked over to me, "As sharp as a tack, but there was something wrong. He always seemed to be getting into trouble for some reason or another. Even before he started school, that boy was always doing things that didn't seem normal. He was four years old and a bird had hit our living room window. Richard, just being a child, called to us and we all went outside to look. When we got up to the bird you could see that it was still alive, just stunned. The three of us sat there discussing that maybe Richard could take care of it until it got better. He seemed to get excited about that and me and the missus left him there to get a box to keep the bird in. When we got back we saw Richard sitting on the grass with the bird in his hands as he was petting the thing. We put the box down and Richard placed it in and that's when we noticed that it was dead! Leni and I looked at each other in disbelief as just a few minutes earlier the bird had been standing, stunned but standing. I picked up the now dead bird and looked over at Richard as if to ask him what had happened. That's when I noticed that its neck was broken. Puzzled, I looked at Leni and then back at Richard who had a smirk on his face. Then he turned around and went back inside the house. It was strange to say the least."

Jacob continued telling stories about Richard, but something in his voice made the tiny hairs on the back of my neck begin to stand up. Somehow this sounded too familiar to me. Jacob told some nice stories of Richard and others that didn't make a lot of sense, as though when he was telling them, he was still trying to figure them out.

I asked how the boy was doing now, knowing full well that he was under surveillance. Jacob told me that when Richards's mother got remarried, he seemed to get into trouble with the law. Even joined a gang from the looks of it. Jacob and Leni had tried their best but it didn't seem that they did enough. I looked at Jacob and tried to console him as best I could. But I had this nagging feeling that seemed to put a knot in my belly every time I thought of Richard. I could see the regret in Jacob's face, as if he felt that he had somehow let down his own son. I assured him that he hadn't, but you could tell that it was very personal to him. Richard may have been his grandson but to Jacob it was as if Lawrence lived through him and Jacob wanted to see Richard live a life that Lawrence didn't have the time to have.

I shook my head knowing full well what he meant. Jacob caught his breath, and then as if to change the subject, asked me if I had any children. I looked at him deeply and said that I had two children. One died in childbirth and the other I hadn't seen in a long time.

"How long?" Jacob asked.

"Years," I said. "Years."

"It couldn't be that long ago," he said, "why you're not that old yet. Not like me anyways."

What was I to tell him, the truth? That my son was sitting before me, looking far more aged than his own father? That would go over well. He would think me insane at the very least.

"It's a long story," I replied. "One that would take many afternoons to tell!"

Upon the mention of time, Jacob looked quickly down at his watch and then stood up. "Shoot, I didn't realize how late it was. I gotta get home. Leni's waiting for me." And with that Jacob turned to me and said, "Sorry friend, it's been nice talking with you and I hope one day we can talk like this again." He stretched out his hand and I took it with both of mine. We shook for a moment and I never wanted to let go, as if I knew if I let go we would never have this time or opportunity again!

Jacob pulled his hand back and began walking away. I sat down again and watched him as he went home. The tears that I had willed away before now appeared again as Jacob disappeared from view. Somehow I knew, in my heart I knew, that I would never see or talk with him again.

I sat alone for about an hour, just thinking about all the things we had talked about. My poor son had suffered quite a bit during his life. But for some reason he never gave up, not like me anyways. Diana raised him well, better than I could have. Maybe it was better that I wasn't there to help him grow. Maybe my influence would have had a negative effect on him. But I knew he was still hurting about Richard, Lawrence was already gone and I gathered from the way he spoke, that he wanted Richard to straighten out and have a good life. But Richard it seemed had his own path to follow. And something bothered me about Richard, almost as if he had outside influences all his life.

Some of the stories Jacob told me about him seemed to mirror my own decisions I made as a youth. I began to wonder if Richard was following the same path as I? As I sat there thinking about everything, I noticed an elderly woman walking through the crosses, stopping occasionally to put her hands on the markers. Another poor soul, I thought as I watched her move slowly about. She methodically went about the rows, line by line and with each pass she came a bit closer to where I was sitting.

Richard still was bothering me as I sat. The more and more I thought about it the more I somehow wanted to help my son have some peace with the time he had left. I didn't feel guilty though. On the contrary, I actually wanted to help what was left of my family! Jacob never had his father and maybe in some strange way I felt the need to make it up to him somehow. He was my son after all, and I felt a longing to do what I could for him.

Oblivious to anything else around me I suddenly felt a hand touch my shoulder. I looked up and the elderly woman that had been moving about the markers before now was standing beside me. I smiled up to her as she moved to sit down on the other side of me. We sat there for a couple of minutes until I heard her cough. I looked over to her to see if she was okay as she pulled out a napkin in which to wipe her mouth.

"Billy", she quietly said. I figured I must have misunderstood as I looked back towards the crosses. "Billy", I heard again! I turned back in shock. How did she know my name? She took the napkin from her mouth and gently put it in her handbag. She closed the clasp and turned towards me. Still not understanding who this woman was, I asked her how she knew my name. She smiled and said, "Billy, I've always known who you were, just as you always know who I am. Has it been that long?" She looked down at the way she was dressed and then looked up and chuckled. "I'm sorry, Billy, I suppose you're not used to me dressed in this fashion. But then you've always had trouble seeing the truth, haven't you?"

It took but a split second and then I realized who I was sitting with!

"There you go," he said. "I sometimes like to alter my appearance from time to time. It kind of helps with blending in, you know?"

My mood began to change as I sat there watching him. "What do you want this time?" I asked.

His gaze turned back towards the crosses and replied, "Billy, why are you so angry? Why do you always think the worst of me? I just figured it was time that we had a little talk. You looked like you could use it."

"Fuck you", I said. I knew no good could come from this visit!

"Why so hostile Billy? I thought you'd be in a good mood after talking with your son? I wasn't even sure if you were going to go through with it at first, but I guess the possibility of a meeting was too attractive to say no."

He turned back to me and I felt the tension building within my body as I wondered what he wanted.

"Billy," he spoke again, "I often wonder how you're doing? Even now I find it hard to figure out what you need. I'm here because I know what you're thinking of doing. I never figured you to be one to get involved! Why Billy? Why would you want to get involved? You've always been one of my favorites. Heck, most of the time I didn't even have to tell you what to do, you just did it!"

I sat there wondering what he meant by that. I never did what he told me to, and I always paid the price. "I know! It's confusing isn't it? You still can't see it, can you? Sometimes Billy, I wish I could explain it to you, help you to understand. But then again what would be the fun in that?" He giggled as he spoke. "You want to help him, don't you? Jacob, that is. But I like Richard, he seems to be a fast learner."

It began to dawn on me that my earlier fears were starting to be confirmed. Was Richard to follow the same path as I? I shook my head as I thought about it. No one should live the life I've had! My family deserved better, Jacob deserved better.

"No!" I said.

He laughed again as if he knew there was nothing I could do. "Billy, this is good news for you! You don't even realize what I've done for you. I thought it would be simple, so simple that even you would understand. But I can see by your look that I'll have to spell it out for you."

What the hell was he talking about now? How could Richard's situation help me? He always spoke in riddles as if he wanted me to figure things out as we went along. Maybe this time I would have at least know what he wanted!

"Atonement, Billy," he began "That's what it's all about isn't it? Are you tired, Billy? Immortality not exactly what you expected was it? Satisfaction for all offences, it's just that simple. The hard part is understanding whom you must satisfy. Mankind has fallen, not once but many times throughout the ages. You remember when you were in the orphanage? The nuns always spoke of this didn't they? Told you how man was saved."

I nodded in agreement. He began to speak again, quoting from the bible that I so resented!

"Whence it came to pass, that the Heavenly Father, the Father of mercies and the God of all comfort, when that blessed fullness of the time was come sent unto man, his own Son who had been, both before the law and during the time of the law, to many of the holy fathers announced and promised, that He might both redeem the Jews, who were under the Law and the Gentiles who followed not after justice might attain to justice and that all men might receive the adoption of sons. Him had proposed as a propitiator, through faith in His blood, for our sins, and not for our sins only, but also for those of the whole world." Simple isn't it? Hell, man doesn't even have to work for his salvation. Embody the will of God into flesh and that's it! So why doesn't it seem right? Maybe, just maybe there's more to it? But I can see again that you're confused and yet, it's not that hard to grasp, Billy. Why is it that you can't see it, even when I show it to you? No matter, I suspect you'll see it eventually. You really have no choice in the matter. Just as I can see there won't be any way of swaying you from what you feel you need to do."

He shook his head and proceeded to rise from the bench. I remained seated, as he got up, as confused as ever as to the reason of his visit. Not completely, mind you. His arrival here told me that I would have to do something about Richard. I was damned already and there was no way that I would allow him to take another of my kin and have them suffer as I have! On that I would thwart him any way I possibly could, no matter what the consequences!

Chapter 18

It was getting dark by the time I made my way back towards the hotel. Along the way I began to think about what he told me. I still didn't understand what he meant for the most part. Atonement? Atonement for what?

It seemed different this time, when he spoke. I thought about all the times we had met before, and upon reflection, it seemed that he was always trying to warn me of the consequences of my actions, as though to steer me in the right direction or the direction he wanted me to go in. Most of the time I did the exact opposite of what he said. Was it time that I listened? But how could I do that knowing my great grandson was in trouble? Not just with the law but also with something so evil that it would make even me cringe at the thought. Could I stand aside? From what I gathered of his speech, I would somehow benefit from it. It wasn't as if my own existence could get any worse. Could it? I didn't know, but maybe it was time I looked into what he meant. Maybe somehow if I took some time and attempted to figure it out, then maybe I could make the right choice! I had too know as it weighed heavily on me. Was I to make a choice? Richard or myself? Either way I knew that somehow I would lose!

I made my way down Clarendon Street, still not quite familiar with the city and down to Coley Square. Here I found the Boston Public Library! An enormous building from the outside, the library presents a façade reminiscent of a sixteenth century Italian architecture that I had seen so much back in England before the turn of the century.

I went inside and looked about. Once inside, I saw Bates Hall, a huge reading room! The form of Bates Hall was grand in style, rectangular in shape butending with a semi-circle on each end, recalling somewhat a Roman basilica. A series of robust double coffers in the ceiling provide a sculptural canopy to the room. The east side had a rhythmic series of arched windows with light buffered by a wide overhanging hood on the exterior. Heavy deep green silk velvet drapery hung from the walls, one would assume to help muffle the sound.

I made my way over to the front desk. A younger woman sat there, reading. I stood there for a moment and then she looked up from her book.

With a smile she asked "How may I help you?"

I began to ask her if she could direct me to the religious section of the library, I was looking for books or research on atonement.

She got up and we walked over to a rather secluded section. She pointed to the books and told me that I should be able to find what I needed in here. I thanked her and waited until she left before looking through the books. I combed through the titles and was able to come across a small section that dealt with theology and atonement. There were about a dozen or so books. I reached for them and took them to one of the old wooden tables that the hall had. I began to read and read. The first three books didn't help, as all they did was recite text from the bible. Most of that I had been taught as a child!

I had been there for about two hours when I started on the fourth book. In it I found something of interest. Instead of reciting text from the Bible, it also attempted to decipher it as well. I riffled past page after page until I began to see what it was that I was searching for.

Atonement! A whole chapter dedicated to this notion of man's quest for immortality through the power of God! Maybe I could get some answer's here? I kept reading, sometimes reading the same page again to make sure I understood it properly.

It seemed that the doctrine of atonement was started mainly by the Catholic church. A speculation on the mystery of atonement and not to controversy with heretics. The central fact of atonement, it seemed, was that mankind had fallen and was raised up and redeemed from all sin by the blood of Christ. Man, it said, had reconciled with God through the life, suffering, and death of Christ. Sin is as a state of bondage or servitude and man who has fallen would be redeemed or bought with a price. It seemed, upon reading, that atonement was a deliverance from captivity by payment of some type of ransom! St. Augustine stated that, "Men were held captive under the devil and served the demons, but they were redeemed from captivity. For they could sell themselves. The redeemer came, and gave the price; he poured forth his blood and bought the whole world."

I continued reading but I couldn't see or yet still understand the meanings. I had pretty much learned this all when I was a child at the orphanage and nothing seemed to bring about any different understanding. I finally closed the books and left the library, frustrated and even more confused than ever,

I walked around the block and came across a church within the same square. I stopped for a moment and smiled. Fate it seems is not without a sense of humour. I suppose this was a coincidence? I stood there for a moment contemplating whether or not I should enter. Religion and churches weren't among my favorite things after all, but I really didn't have a choice. I needed answers and maybe I could find them here.

I ascended the steps to the door and proceeded to make my way in. It was a large church, old, from the looks of it, and quite ornate. The lighting was low as I made my way down the aisle towards the altar. The church was fairly empty except for an older couple who sat near the back. I was feeling quite uncomfortable the more I moved forwards. Churches always centered everything towards the front, altars symbols, and the like. The closer I got, the more I knew I didn't belong here, I was not welcome. But I still had to know, and besides, where else could I turn to?

I sat down in the second row of pews and began to think once again. Jacob was in pain, Richard was in trouble, and I didn't know what to do. The more I sat there and thought about it, the more I started to wonder if maybe I would ever understand the dilemma.

I looked up at the altar and then my eyes drifted back down towards the pew in front of me and I began to wonder what my life would have been like if I wouldn't have excepted his offer all those years ago. Would my life have turned out differently? Would my children's lives have been different? I don't think I'd ever really sat down and asked for answers before.

Ever since I was a young lad, even in the orphanage, I always had taken care of myself, followed the only path I had ever known. If God cared so much for me, then why didn't he help me before? Why did he leave me all the time I was growing up? I sat there thinking about it more and more. I started to take stock in my life, all the things I had done wrong, and all the things that I attempted to do right. Even then, it seemed my life always turned.

No, God didn't need to help me! Just as I never needed him! I was beginning to get angrier as I sat in the church. I looked back up at the cross and mumbled a curse under my breath. Tears had already begun to cross the skin of my cheek as I once again felt foresaken by God. I rose slightly from the pew in order to leave and that's when I heard a voice come from behind.

"Good evening, my son. You seem troubled? Is there something that I can help you with?" the voice said.

I turned and saw the priest standing behind me in the aisle. "No, I don't think you can." I responded.

He took a step towards me and looked me over for a minute. I turned my head and wiped the tears from my cheek, trying to hide them, but he had already seen them. Again he took another step closer and put his hand on my shoulder. "Whatever troubles you, God is by your side to help," he spoke as he looked at me.

I chuckled sarcastically at his comment. I could tell from his expression that he was a little put off by my reaction. I was so angry right now that I just wanted to leave this place. It was a mistake to think that I could ever find any answers here!

"Please," he spoke again, taking his hand from my shoulder and motioning to the pew. "Sit and we'll talk for awhile. Whatever it is, I'm sure God has the answers!"

I sat down, not sure why, but I did. It was as if there was something in his voice that calmed me. I stared at the altar again, as if the answers lay in the cross that adorned it.

The priest began to speak and it took a few minutes for me to even realize that he was speaking to me! I turned and looked at him as he spoke of God and love and such things. I was almost ready to strike him when I looked him square in the face and spoke just one word. "Atonement!" I blurted. He abrubtly stopped talking as if he had been taken by surprise.

"Atonement?" he asked surprisingly. "Atonement for what? For your sins?"

I turned back towards the front again, looking at the cross. "Just atonement," I replied. "What is it? Why does God want it? And how does one achieve it?"

The priest looked as if I were asking him the meaning of life, almost as if he couldn't answer it. "That question, my son, is not that easily answered. Do you want me to tell you that God wants you to repent your sins and accept him as your Lord and Savior, or is there more to it? I suspect you already know the simplest of answers." He spoke and I nodded, as I still stared forward. "Atonement means many things to many people. What exactly is it you would like to know?"

I turned back to him and said "I don't know." I paused for a moment. "I thought it would be easy. But now...I'm not sure anymore."

He put his hand to his cheek and thought for a moment before replying, "I can see that you're upset and that something is weighing heavily on you. God has given you the tools to find your own path, to make a choice, but which choice is the right one? That, only you can answer. It would be easier if I just told people the right choice. Unfortunately it doesn't work that way. The choice can only be yours. You must look to your heart to see what is right and just. If you make the right choice then God will forgive you and you will redeem yourself in his eyes."

"Bullshit!" I thought as I rose from the pew. I turned to leave once again. The priest, startled, that I was leaving, took a moment before rising himself. "My son, what is it that troubles you?" he said, as I pushed my way past him and back into the aisle. I never responded, just left the same way I had entered, though a bit angrier and with my resolve that much more solidified about these places!

I left the church and walked back down the steps toward the street. I made my way over to a corner bar and with what little money I had left, decided to drink myself into a stupor. I entered the smokey hall and took a seat at the old wooden bar. The bartender filled my glass over and over again until I began to feel a numbness throughout my body and more importantly in my mind.

An hour of peace went by and then a man sat down in the seat beside me. I shot back my drink as he said hello. I smiled politely not really wanting to talk.

The bartender came over and asked the man what he wanted to drink. He looked over at my glass and said, "I'll have what he's having. Oh…and get him one too."

A bit stunned at his generosity, I looked over and thanked him. The bartender poured our drinks and the gentleman lifted his glass towards me as if to toast. I raised mine as well and we both drank. He began talking to me and the way I was feeling after the few drinks I had, I wasn't all that annoyed anymore. I suppose the liquor was allowing me to let my guard down. As long as he was buying, I figured it would only be polite to listen. Heck, I was pretty much out of money anyway!

We drank for a while, talking about everything from politics to family. Apparently he and his wife had just had a child and as fate has a devilish mind, he was also drafted to Vietnam! He had one week to get ready, to get all his affairs in order, before he was to be shipped out. It seems that sometimes we are all destined to suffer when we are at our best! As if something in the universe decides to fuck us when we're up. Maybe that's why I tolerated this guy as he spoke. I, too, had suffered the same cruel joke when Jacob was born.

His name was Carey and he was a welder by trade, a blue collar worker who only wanted what was best for his own. In a way he reminded me of what I wanted to be. But that was never to happen. He talked about his family, their dreams and hopes for their child. He pulled out his wallet and showed me a picture of the two of them.

I listened as he spoke, wondering if Jacob had the same dreams? Did his life turn out the way he wanted it to? Probably not. He, as well, had a lot of tragedy in his life, from the death of his son to the trouble with his grandson.

The more we drank and talked, the more I realized that right or wrong, I had to help! I decided that evening that I would take my chances! What else could happen to me? Everything that I had ever loved was gone. He made sure of that. Jacob and his kin were all that I had left and Jacob, I knew, would be safe! That he promised me a long time ago. Lawrence, my grandson was dead so there was no way he could be hurt anymore. Richard it seemed was destined to follow in my footsteps and if that were true then no greater fate could ever befall him. It seemed that my decision was made! There didn't seem to be any disadvantages to helping this time.

Carey and I drank another couple of drinks and then he decided it was time to go home. Half drunk he lifted himself from the stool and slowly made his way to the door. He stumbled once and then made his way to the street. I watched him through the window as he made his way down the street and around the corner out of sight. I turned back to the bar, finished my drink and then left as well.

The next morning I woke and began rifling through the FBI folder. I needed to know where I could find Richard and just what kind of trouble he had gotten himself into. There wasn't much to go on. It seems that he had begun befriending a few gang members in his neighbourhood. The file stated that he was a prospect for the gang and that his name be kept on file if anything occurred. He had gotten into some minor offences when he was younger from the looks of it, petty theft and the like, but nothing involving any substantial crimes. The gang hung out in East Boston near Maverick Square. Petty thieves for the most part, it seemed that their numbers were increasing as well as their hold on the area. Richard lived near here and possibly was being influenced by the gang. Police had caught a few of the members but got nothing substantial that would break the gang. According to the file, the mayor's department was becoming increasingly concerned with the level of violence and crime in the area. The FBI were called in to help curb the gangs activity, but from the looks of it, they hadn't done much so far, except keep the area under survellience.

I left around noon toward Maverick square. I didn't actually have a plan, but I figured something would come to me when the moment was right. For now, I wanted to take a look around. I didn't even know what Richard looked like! No photo in the file, just a description was all I had to go on. The only real clue in the file that I had to go by in locating him was that he worked part-time in a grocery store, stocking shelves. Either he had no real ambition or he was looking for some easy money. Well, I suppose it ran in the family. Jacob, however, seemed to be a hard worker, and his father Lawrence had joined the army at an early age. Maybe Richard was closer to me than even I thought!

I arrived in East Boston and proceeded to look around. East Boston, and specifically the Maverick Square area, was a streetcar suburb. It contained a lot of homes, with commercial buildings on the main roads. It seemed to me that it started out with mainly single-family homes, like most suburbs. These houses looked as if they gradually had changed to multi-family housing.

I suppose at one time it was a beautiful place, only a few blocks from the waterfront. But now all it seemed to be was a transportation hub filled with commercial business and low-income housing. No wonder that Jacob didn't seem to like Richard moving here. It almost reminded me of where I grew up, near the orphanage.

I continued walking around hoping to see something that would lead me to Richard. Most of the afternoon I spent wandering, looking for grocery stores so that I might find him working. Nothing happened though and during the evening the cold forced me back indoors.

A hotel? No, more like a room with a view of a brick and concrete wall to the south, but it was all I needed for now. I wish that I had brought more money with me from New York at this point. I suppose I could always find some cash, but I didn't want to draw attention to myself while I searched for Richard. Besides, I didn't know the area that well, and the risk of getting caught was too great. I could afford one night here and then I had to make a decision of where to find some money.

The rumbling from my stomach woke me up around one in the morning! I was definitely hungry and the decision I suppose had been made. I got dressed and left the hotel. It was still dark out and that was to my advantage. I walked a few blocks, making sure that if I was to rob anybody that it wouldn't be in the area where I was staying. Luckily, it was to be an easy night! Some of the clubs were still open and all I had to do was wait until a drunken patron came out.

A few minutes of waiting at the corner and I spied an older gentleman come out of the bar. He was definitely drunk and stumbled his way down the street. I followed behind and waited until the right opportunity. He rounded the corner of a deserted street and I crept closer. A few more steps and I was right behind him. He didn't hear me until I was right on top of him. He turned and I struck him squarely in the nose! He fell, obviously unconscious, into my arms. I dragged him over to the side and rested his body against the building as I rifled through his pockets. I found a hundred and forty dollars in his wallet! At least I had some cash now to stay and eat while I searched for Richard. I lowered him down to the sidewalk to sleep and then made my way back to the neighborhood where I was staying. Hopefully I would find something still open where I could eat.

After finding some food, I made my way back to the hotel to try and get a little more sleep. The streetlights lit up Maverick Square and when I got closer I could see that there were some people milling about one of the intersections. As I got closer and was able to see better, I saw that it was a bunch of kids hanging out. "Maybe", I thought, "these were gang kids!"

I approached cautiously from the other side of the street, looking to see if Richard was among them. According to the file he was a tall, skinny lad, around six feet tall and one hundred and forty pounds and with shoulder length brown hair. That's all I had to go on. It wasn't much, but maybe my luck would continue this evening.

I stood across the street for a while trying to see if I could pick him out from the crowd of about eight kids. They definitely were a gang. They had the mannerisms of a group of thieves and hooligans. I watched them as they harassed the people that went by. Some crossed the street so as not to pass them directly; others went by not realizing it was too late to change their course. I decided to walk over and hope that I may be able to get some information without too many problems.

I was noticed within a few steps of my approaching them. One of the kids turned and took a few steps towards me, a rather large young man with a scowl that could curdle milk! I suppose he was meant to intimidate me. Fortunately, I don't get intimidated that easily so I continued to walk directly towards the group. I paused for a moment as I walked by the large youth that came toward me. Our eyes met for a brief second. I continued on, into the center of where they were gathered. Nothing but silence when I arrived and stopped in their midst. Apparently they weren't used to having people confront them. Confused, the other youth rejoined the group and closed the circle, trapping me within. We stood there for a few seconds, looking at each other

Then another youth took a step forward into the circle. He slowly looked me over from head to toe, as if he couldn't believe the audacity I had. As his eyes gazed back up to mine, I smiled a little smile.

"Who the fuck do you think you are, man!" he finally said.

"I'm looking for somebody. I was thinking that maybe you fine young gentlemen could help," I replied.

"How about if we just look through your pockets and help ourselves to what you got?" he sarcastically said.

The others began to smile at his suggestion. I didn't think it was going to be easy to get their help, never is. I suppose I had to somehow persuade them into helping me, and even if I did have more money with me, I'm sure they would have just taken it and left me cold. I looked at him and smiled back. "Now, that would be rather simple don't you think? And you boys seem to be a little more intelligent than just common thugs," I said, knowing full well that

their egos would step in to hear me out. "Rather than do that, I
propose a contest of sorts. If you win, I release whatever value I
have to you. If I win, you help me."

They looked back and forth at each other almost confused at
the idea. The young man in front of me turned back to me, and as I
predicted, nodded in agreement. "What's the contest, man?" he said
smiling.

Now at least now I had something, and it was just a simple
matter of enduring a little pain to win. I explained to him that the
contest would be simple. A minor battle of wills that involved one of
them and myself. "Here's the deal," I said. "Pick somebody and we'll
take turns hitting each other! Whoever quits first, loses." I knew that
while this might be painful, I'd endured worse throughout my life.
And, if I couldn't handle a bit of pain, then I had no business even
trying to find Richard!

The boys talked amongst themselves for a few moments.
Then the one who was talking with me looked back at me. "We can
pick anyone?" he asked.

"Anyone," I replied, thinking that they would naturally pick the
large youth who had attempted to block my path prior. I looked over
at him waiting to see him come closer. The youth in front of me
said, "Nah! Not him. He may look tough, but he hits like a girl! We
got someone else in mind."

Then the circle parted a bit as they made room for another
youth that was standing in the back. He stepped up towards me, a
laugh emitting from his mouth. Confident, I would say! A tall boy
with short hair and what looked to be a three-day growth on his

face. Not very heavy, but he was probably adequate for the task. The circle closed again and we stood there, face to face.

"You wanna take the first shot?" the youth asked as he looked back to his buddies. He wasn't even paying attention to me. I suppose he figured he'd win this without too much trouble. So without saying a word I swung at him and connected right in his breadbasket. His attention now focused on me again as he bent over from the shot. Both hands went to his knees as he tried to recapture his breath! I stood there waiting thinking that maybe the contest was over before it began, when he raised up his index finger to me as if too indicate he needed a moment. I waited until he stood upright again, then I saw him as he curled his hand together and swung hard, landing directly on my chin! I went down to the pavement almost as quick as he sent the blow.

I lay there for a moment and then began to lift myself up to the sounds of their laughter. I felt my chin and knew that I was bleeding already. I stood up and focused myself once again on my opponent. He was still smiling as I delivered my next blow to his nose! This time I heard him let out a yelp, that told me I had most likely broken it! I smiled as he turned towards me again! I waited and then once again he hit me with a crushing blow that found my right eye. This time I staggered back but did not fall. I stepped back up and took my next swing directly to his now broken nose again! I knew it would hurt him more this time than even the previous hit had.

He fell down, hurting! His friends helped him to his feet. I had almost believed he was ready to give up, but by now the adrenaline was flowing and he more than likely had to prove something to his friends. Unlucky for me, I guess, that this youth had this type of determination.

We continued on, striking blow after blow, neither of us wanting to give in or quit. I was starting to get tired after a while but I felt his blows starting to lack as much energy as before, so I would venture to say that he also was tiring.

Again we continued on. We hit in the torso, we hit in the face. Both of us by this point had more blood and broken bones than we thought possible. His next blow landed to my side and I could hear the rib breaking as he landed his fist! God that hurt! I stepped back again and tried to straighten out. The pain was intense as I hunched over again. I felt my side with my hand, only too discover that part of the rib had pierced the skin on my side. At this point I wanted to quit. The others could see it as well. The pain was overwhelming. My shirt soaked with blood at the point of exit. You could see the bone protruding as my shirt was raised in that area. I un-tucked my shirt carefully from my pants and lifted it up too see the damage. One of the boys turned and began to gag at the sight! My combatant began too smile as if he knew I could not carry on. His friends patted him on the back as if to congratulate him.

Watching this I began to get angry, more determined if you will, and started to push the pain aside! I reached down to my side once again and as they looked on, I slowly began to push my rib back into my body. The pain was intense but I never uttered a sound! I concentrated my gaze to the surprise faces of the boys and started to grin from ear to ear. I knew I had only one last shot before I would again collapse, but by now they were scared! He was scared! My right arm now held my side together and with only my left ready I managed to take my one last shot connecting right on his chin!

He went down again and so did I! Both of us collapsed on the sidewalk. As I lay there I could hear the others yelling to their friend to get up and continue, even as I felt I was to pass out at any moment. It was so easy just to lie there and not move, but I knew I had to win. Win for Jacob. So, putting my arms forward on the pavement, and hoping they would hold my weight, I attempted to get up. I could still hear them even as I thought I was about to black out! Slowly my arms pushed up my body until I was able to kneel. I held there for a moment, my torso swinging a bit from side to side, as I tried to retrieve some more strength for the rest of the journey. My side, flaming from the pain, made me realize it would give no quarter. I mustered whatever energy I had left and raised myself from the ground! I was standing, not well, but I was standing nonetheless. I stood there, watching, as they egged on their friend, almost berating him as he lay there. Nausea started as I stood there hoping that he wouldn't get up. I was definitely hurting, but I'd had worse! I would recover once again.

The boys kept yelling at their friend until finally it became apparent that he wouldn't get up. He tried to lift himself up but he had nothing left! I will admit for a rather thin lad he had one hell of a punch! The boys finally turned their attention back to me, knowing full well that I had won.

Holding my side I smiled a bit, the others seemed disappointed in the outcome. The lad did his best I thought, but they seemed almost angry at his lacking performance. They all turned from him and left him lying there, which struck me as strange! Even

I would have helped him to his feet. I guess nobody likes a loser! The boy I had earlier spoken with approached me now. I could tell he wasn't very happy. "So," he paused, "seems that you're tougher than you look."

As I raised my head, I spit out the blood that had partially congealed in my mouth. "I suppose I am," I replied. "Now, how about your helping me out?"

The other boys now started to form a circle around me again, indicating that they weren't about to honor the rules of the agreement. I knew that I couldn't do anything but stand there! I had nothing left, no strength, no way I could fight off an attack from these boys. I stood there as he spoke to me, not even listening as I saw him come nearer. It didn't matter what he was telling me anyways, I felt ready to pass out again! I didn't even see him hit me; I felt some pain, but my body just collapsed onto the sidewalk again. I felt the multiple kicks as they all took turns. I didn't feel them anymore, my body had pretty much given up trying to let me know the pain I was feeling. As if I had gone numb already from the abuse. I lay there for another moment, then the blows stopped and I looked up to see the young man rifling through my coat pockets, taking anything of value! "Fucking bastard." I was able to mutter through the blood that flowed from my mouth. As he took the cash from my pocket, he smiled at me and began to stand up.

"By the way…who were you looking for?" he asked.

"Richard, Richard McReedy," I managed to stammer out.

"No shit?" he said as he walked away, I could hear him laughing and then I passed out.

I felt a tug on my arm, as if someone was trying to get my attention. It took a moment or two until I was able to open my eyes and see what was going on. Once opened, I remembered where I was and what had happened! Still on the pavement, I lifted my head up slightly from the stains that had accumulated around where my mouth was. Instantly the pain from my rib reminded me that I was again still alive and awake! I looked over to my side and saw the boy that I had just beaten moments prior tugging at my sleeve as to pull me up! He too was well in pain but was still trying to help me up rather than leave me there. It seemed a bit odd at first, why didn't he leave with his friends? They left him there as well as I. No matter, I thought as I tried to become vertical once again. We both stood there for a moment holding our wounds when I looked at the youth and thanked him for his help. "No problem." He said, "I figured you could use a hand."

Again I thanked him before falling into the light standard beside me. My rib was still inside, but it hurt like hell! Leaning against the light pole I looked over at the boy who by this time was lighting a cigarette between his now swollen lips. I wondered again why this boy was still here? Was there no longer honor among thieves? In my day we would never have left a comrade to fend for himself. At the least we would have ensured his safety if we could.

He looked back at me and began to speak. "What was it you wanted?" he asked, "Seems only fair that you should get something for your trouble. I mean you did win."

Gathering some more of my breath I looked over to him again and said, "Why? Why did they leave you?" I wondered. "Nice friends you have there."

He pulled the cigarette from his mouth and exhaled, "Not my friends. Not yet anyways," he replied.

Very confused I asked him what he meant by that. "I'm not their friend yet. I need to prove to them first that I can be their friend. Fuck, it's a long story and I'm not in the mood to share it right now."

I nodded my head, as I kind of understood. I would surmise that he wasn't in the gang yet. Probably had to pass some type of initiation or test as it were, to be included. I tried to straighten out, pushing myself off the lamppost. The pain was intense and I staggered for a moment again. The youth lunged ahead as catch me if I should fall.

I motioned that I was all right and he went back to assuming a tougher stance, as if I had somehow tricked him into showing me a side that I wasn't supposed to see!

"Come on," I said, "I'll buy you a cup of coffee."

He chuckled and then said, "Asshole! You got no money! You can't buy shit!"

I reached down and took off my shoe. From inside I pulled out a twenty. I always carried some money in my shoe in case of an emergency. I held it up to my young friend and smiled. He smiled at my ingenuity and put out his smoke.

"All right." he said, as we both started walking away from the corner and towards a coffee shop.

"Name's Billy," I said. "What's yours?"

He looked over and said, "Richard, but my friends call me Dick."

I laughed as we continued on. Splitting the silence of the night air with my voice. "Fucking pathetic!" I thought as we made our way down the road to find a place to sit.

I sat at the booth waiting for Richard to return from the washroom where he was washing up. The coffee had arrived and I sat there stirring it while thinking about the chain of events that brought us together. My side was on fire but at least I had found him and I suppose the price I paid was worth it! The FBI file had said that Richard had long hair, that was probably why I didn't think he was the one I searched for. I grabbed a napkin from the container and started to wipe off some of the blood from my mouth. Most of it was dried already and it took some rubbing to get it off. So I had finally found Richard and all I needed to figure out was how to help him.

Atonement, the word still ringing in my ears! What was I to do for Richard? Help him atone, but for what? Something he had already done? Or maybe something he was going to do? I didn't know. Hopefully after talking to him I could get some type of idea that would help focus me in some direction. Jacob was my son, and after the death of his boy, there had to be some joy in his life! I would help him, even if I could never tell him the truth.

My mind wandered again as I thought of the possibilities that were in front of me. How many people get the chance to see their lineage this far? Not many, I would assume. In a way I wished that I could tell him the truth, who I was, where I'd been, tell him the whole story! I've never been able to that with anybody. I've had friends throughout the years but never anyone that truly would understand me. Someone to confide in would have been nice. Even my wives could never know the truth! As much as I loved them, they too would have thought me mad! No, never a friend that would understand. There was one, but I never counted him as a friend.

I took a sip of the coffee and nearly yelped from the pain of the hot liquid on the cut on my mouth. It brought me back to the reality of the situation at hand! Richard finally arrived from the washroom and sat down across from me. He picked up his coffee and took a sip. I sat there looking at him now. I wonder how I could not have seen it? He looked like Jacob, Diana as well. He was my great grandson after all. It did seem quite surreal at the moment and awkward as well. Both of us sat for a moment, not knowing what to say to each other. We had just beaten the hell out of each other and now we were having coffee together? Men are like that though. We can fight and then after we could be best friends! Women aren't like that. They fight and they are mortal enemies for life. But it still seemed quite weird us both sitting there.

Richard was the first to talk, complaining about how his nose hurt. I looked at it and I had definitely broken it. It was misshapen and out of sorts. It would heal but it would take a while. I apologized to him for the injury.

"Don't worry about it," he said, "it ain't the first time it's been broke!"

We both chuckled for a moment and began discussing the evening's events. Richard was curious as to how I was able to withstand that much punishment. I just told him that I had been in a few fights in my lifetime and that I had grown accustomed to it. We talked about other things as well.

I tried to listen for anything that may help me understand what Richard was to atone for, but for the most part it was all very basic stuff, petty crimes and such, nothing that I would assume would warrant such a stringent need to be forgiven! We talked about his friends and why they left him there. It was part of his initiation, apparently! He wanted to join the gang and was hoping that by fighting me he would have passed one of the hurdles.

"They told me that there was something I would have to do in order to gain their trust. I was kinda hoping that this was it. But now I'm not too sure," Richard said. "What was it that you were looking for?" he asked.

My coffee was beginning to get cold as I motioned to the waiter for a re-fill. "Nothing anymore," I replied. "I found out what I needed from them even though they didn't exactly help." I couldn't tell him the truth, no point in that.

The waiter came over with the pot of coffee and poured us some fresh cups. I couldn't help but keep looking at Richard and wondering what it was that I could do to help.

"You look familiar." Richard said, "Have we met before?"

I choked a bit on my coffee as he asked the question. It kind of took me by surprise. "No, I don't think so," I replied, not knowing what else too say.

"Funny," Richard continued, "You look awfully familiar."

I lowered my head a bit not really knowing what to say. Maybe I should tell him the truth? That would go over real well. I look familiar because I'm your great-grandfather come back from the dead to make sure you don't screw your life up the way I did. Yea...that'd go over real well!

"Sorry kid," I said, "I've never met you before in my life. You must have me confused with someone else."

He shook his head and finished his coffee. At least that was over for now. I don't know why I was worried.

Even if he knew the truth, he'd never believe it! Maybe in some strange way I wanted to tell him, wanted him to know that I was family, and that he needed my help.

The more I thought of it the more I figured that was the reason why I was so put- off by his initial question. I always wanted to be a part of something. It always seemed that I was on the outside never really belonging to anything or anyone. After all these years I probably just wanted to call some place home. It was my longing for it that probably made the question uncomfortable to me.

I could see that Richard had let go of it already. The more I thought of it, maybe Richard and I were very similar? His need to belong to this gang could be exactly the same feeling that I have. Maybe that's why he was still sitting here having coffee with a complete stranger? I could understand that! I had been alone for so long now that I had gotten used to what it was like to have nothing or anybody. But I never forgot the feeling, the longing to be accepted by others in either friendship or family! I missed my friends. I missed my family, all those that I'd left behind, doomed to do so again and again.

Even now looking at Richard, I knew I would see him perish in time as well. Even his children and their children would all pass by my eyes if I stayed too long! So many times I pushed this from my mind so that I wouldn't think of it. Eternal life, it's not a blessing!

It was better that I find out what I need to do here and then move on as quickly as possible.

We continued to sit in silence until I was able to appropriately frame my next question. It seemed that trying to find something out through a normal discussion would just not work. I had too snoop a bit more. "Richard," I asked, as he looked up from his cup. "What is it you want?" He stared back at me in confusion. "I mean, what is it you're looking for?"

He paused for a moment. "Oh....Fuck! I just wanna make some money," he answered. "I'm fucking tired of living in this shithole! I figured I wasn't making it on my own and the guys seemed the better bet. I work some dead end job to make my mother happy and what do I get for it? A shitty paycheck and some asshole in a white shirt and tie that wants me to bend over every time he feels the need to talk down to me! Fuck that! I want out of here and to be on my own, make some real money, and maybe get my own place!"

Listening to Richard, I understood his needs and wants. He was an angry young man, the same as I was, or still am, depending on how you look at it. He kept talking about what he wanted for his future, money mostly. He never mentioned family or friends. He was a loner! He didn't seem to give a shit about anybody but himself.

I asked him about his family trying to understand his frame of mind. He mentioned his mother and his stepfather as well as Jacob. He didn't seem to have a lot of respect for his stepfather; his mother on the other hand was a different story. He started telling me how his mother seemed to change after the death of his father. I think in a way he resented her for his father's death. It seemed that in a way he held her responsible, even though he knew that she had no control. He was very young when his father died and over time his mother began to pay less and less attention to him. His grandfather, Jacob, tried to help and fill the void. His grandfather had known what it was like to grow up without a father and tried his best to help him through the rough times.

Funny, as he spoke of it I realized that all three of us had grown up without fathers. At least they had their mothers, something I was also deprived of. As we talked about it, I came to realize that Richard had taken his anger out on his mother and grandfather for most of his life. He did things, bad things during the years, that he could not explain why?

His mother withdrew more and more during his childhood and Jacob became sterner with him as his attitude grew progressively worse. When his mother re-married, it just seemed to compound the anger that he had. His stepfather wasn't a bad man but Richard, I believe anyways, saw him as a symbol of his dead father and attacked him in rebellion to his real father! I began to understand why 'he' wanted Richard now, why Richard made an excellent candidate for 'his' wicked purpose! Richard was weak and selfish, looking for an easy way out, one that he could provide. It sounded all too eerily familiar.

I had to make Richard understand that if he continued on this path that he had chosen, he would end up just like me! If that happened I didn't know how I could live with myself. Jacob, Richard's mother and even Richard, deserved better! But I still needed to figure out what I could do. The word atonement kept ringing in my head. What did 'he' mean? I still didn't know, but I would eventually. Even if I would have to follow Richard for the rest of his life…I would know!

Richard and I left the restaurant about an hour later. He went one way and I made it appear that I was going another way. But I doubled back and followed him from a distance. I followed him as he went home and went to sleep. I waited a few moments until I was sure he was sleeping and made my way looking for the nearest shelter for a warm meal and a cot to catch a bit of sleep. Richard would be out for a while and I, too, needed some rest after the fight! My body needed some time to heal and also a good hot meal. My rib was starting to heal. The pain had lessened a tiny bit over the last couple of hours and hopefully I would be able to fall asleep without too much discomfort.

A few blocks away I found such a place and was able to acquire a spot in which to sleep. As I lay there my thoughts again went to Richard and Jacob. What did I have to do? Slowly I drifted off without an answer; maybe with a rest I would be able to think clearer.

My eyes slowly opened, as the morning sun appeared through the top the windows of the shelter. I had slept but I was still tired. Probably only a couple of hours, I would have thought, not enough to fully replenish myself. I heard moans from the room, the sounds of men who probably would be better off dead than to exist as they did now. Some in pain, some in withdrawal! I closed my eyes again and tried in vain to fall back asleep, but to no avail. The noise was too great for anyone to sleep.

As I became more cognizant, my nose began to catch the smell of baked bread! I got up and made my way past the rows of cot's to the next room. There were tables all over and men in various degrees of stature littered the seats. A line formed at one end where they were serving each of the homeless an approximation of a meal.

As I got closer I could see that they were given a piece of bread and a bowl, which resembled soup. I grabbed a tray and gathered within the line, waiting my turn. The bread was thick and slightly dry, the soup seemed more like hot water with some color with a small piece of potato in it. Not much, but it would be the best I would receive until I could find a suitable donor that could increase my funds. With less than fifteen dollars left I would have to go to work soon.

I sat down among the men and began to dip my bread into the colored water. My side though not as painful as before still continued to annoy me as I sat. My face was still swollen and bruised as well. Eating was almost a chore as I opened my mouth too take a bite. Soaking the bread helped me from attempting to chew.

The men were loud all around me! Some sat there quietly, but some were being loud and boisterous, as if they were happy to be here. "Strange," I thought, as I looked around. Why would anyone be happy to be in a place such as this? Most of these men were poor with no job and no future. "What the hell were they happy about"? I looked around for a minute and then lowered my head and continued to eat, hoping to be on my way soon and hoping that today it wouldn't be as cold out as it was yesterday.

With my last bite of the bread already in my mouth I picked up the bowl to spill whatever was left into my mouth.

As I did this a man, quite violently I'll add, sat down beside me. His elbow leaned into my sore side and I spilled the last of the soup on my shirt from wincing from the pain he just caused! The pain subsided as I put down the bowl and looked over at the man that by now was devouring his soup! "Asshole!" I muttered as I stood up and started to make my way back to the entrance.

Along the way down the passageway past the sleeping room, I passed another room where I heard singing. As I listened I could tell they were the same hymns that the sisters used to have us sing when we were young. I stood there listening to the singing and looking at the men who were in there. Some of them I recognized from the meal room. The ones that were happy and boisterous before! I stepped into the doorway, my head shaking as I watched these fools give thanks to a God that had all but forsaken them.

For years I had wondered why it is that the most pitiful have the most faith! It took a while, but I finally understood that religion is for the poor. I mean, the poor need religion and their belief more because of the situation that they find themselves in. They pray for a better life in the next world because this world has given them nothing! Pray that eternity holds all that you could ever imagine or want. They go through life with this in mind never understanding that life in itself is what we make of it. Praying for something is just hope without substance for the ability one needs to make it happen.

I was about to turn away when I felt a hand on my shoulder. Before me stood a man better dressed than the rest of the riff-raff in here. My eyes went up and down scrutinizing his appearance before I realized that he was one of the people helping dish out the food in the next room. He was either a volunteer or minister, and knowing my luck he was probably the latter!

"Would you like to join in with the rest?" he asked.

I shook my head. The last thing I wanted to do was start singing the praises of a god that had always forsaken me!

"You seem lost. Is there anything I can do to help?" he replied.

Again I shook my head. It was time for me to get back to Richard and find out what it is he was too atone for. I didn't have the luxury of time to have someone try and 'save' me once again.

I turned to leave when the man moved to block my way.

"Please," he said, "I can tell that something is bothering you. Let me try to help."

I looked him in the eyes and said, "Fine. You want to help?" Figuring he wouldn't stop until I gave him something. "Why did you choose to be a minister? Why do God's work? Do you believe in a God that would allow all this to happen? All this misery to continue? Look around you. What kind of God would allow his people to suffer like this?"

I was a tad miffed by this point. I did catch him off guard as he hesitated in replying to me. But of course he would, they all do. I've seen this too many times, these members of the order always attempting to sway the ones that can see clearly! It's always the same, never different as they try to sell you on the 'Word of God'! But they can never really answer the question can they? No, their argument is always about faith. You have to have faith in order to believe the lies they tell you.

I stood there waiting for him to answer, knowing full well that he would have the same answer that I've heard a thousand times before! He turned from me and began to walk away! Under his breath I heard him mutter, "Jeez, What an asshole!" "What?" I thought. I wasn't expecting that for an answer.

"Hold on," I called out. "What kind of minister are you?"

He stopped, turned back and looked at me. "First off, I'm not a minister. Secondly, who the fuck do you think you are? You come here with the expectation that you'll have a warm place to sleep and some food in your belly and then you have the nerve to slap the hand that feed's you? I ask you if I can help and you ask me the dumbest of questions! I deal with a lot of different people that come through this place; guys like you I have no time for. If you want my help then you'd better start learning to have some common courtesy, at the very least. If you want or need some help then ask me. If not, then go fuck yourself, and stop wasting my time!"

I stood there and for the first time, I didn't know what to say. I was shocked! I wasn't angry so much as impressed! I'd never heard anyone who was trying to spread the word ever be at this direct. The only thing that came out of my mouth was, "Sorry?" I think he figured I was going to tell him off, but I couldn't do it. This man was definitely different from the others that did this type of work. He wasn't in to all the bullshit, not like the regular sheep that I would always see.

He took a moment to compose himself again and looked back at me and said, "So what do you need? What are you looking for?" There was still only one question that was plaguing my mind.

"Atonement. I always wondered about atonement," I said, wondering if even he could help me.

"Atonement, huh? Want to know how to save yourself, do ya?" he replied.

I guess if he thought that then it was easier than trying to tell him the truth.

"Yea," I replied, "But I already know all the bullshit, that I'm supposed to do good and repent from all the things I've done wrong in my life."

He began to nod in agreement. "So, then you know all the standard answers then? What exactly about atonement is it that you need to know?" I wasn't sure, I was still confused. It was supposed to be right in front of me but yet I still couldn't figure out the truth. "I'm not sure," I answered, "not really sure of anything anymore."

He grabbed me by the arm and said "Come on. Lets go sit down and have some coffee. Maybe that theology degree I almost got will finally come in handy!"

We sat down and had a coffee and I listened as he spoke of the different theories on atonement, much more detailed than I was ever taught in the orphanage. He started by telling me some of the background that he himself had been taught, that a series of theologians have read the Bible and done their best to reduce atonement down to a single story. But, the problem is that the story is too large to be reduced to a single solitary story. Various stories are needed. They are stories of the one gospel. He went on to mention that one can't describe grace in just one word, and you can't describe the gospel in the same way, and surely we can't reduce the work of God for us to one story. It takes a number of stories to unravel the mystery of atonement.

The early theologians very quickly began to argue the understanding of God and his teachings. The whole Church, everywhere, came to the conclusion that God was a Trinity – Father, Son, and Holy Spirit. This is what written in the Nicene Creed. These creeds were discussed and debated for more than four centuries. The Church never needed to articulate a plain, single explanation for the atonement. Some asked why the Church never "solved" the atonement question. The answer still hasn't been found. But there have been theories! He spoke of a few as we sat there sipping our coffee. Irenaeus had one theory, that Jesus became what we are so that we might become what he is. Simple, I suppose, but it still didn't make sense.

He got up to get us another cup of coffee and continued talking as he did. At least he was able to tell me other things I had never known before. Maybe there would be something in here that would make sense, a way of letting me figure this out, once and for all! He ran through some other theories dealing with atonement, but it was when he got to the theory of ransom that something seemed to click!

"What?"

He looked at me as he sat down with the new coffee. "Ransom? What the hell does that mean?" I asked.

He pushed my coffee over to me and continued, "It's probably the earliest of all the theories and possibly the most confusing. Conquest, captivity, and ransom are familiar facts within our history. Man, who had yielded to the temptations of Satan, was like one overcome in battle. Sin, is like a state of slavery in some respects. And when Christ set man free by the shedding of his precious Blood, this deliverance from sin would naturally recall the redemption of whoever was captive by the payment of a ransom."

I looked at him confused still.

He laughed a bit. "Sorry," he said. "I kind of revert back to my college days when I talk about this stuff. I'll try and make it as simple as I can. It's actually very easy to understand if not revolting in a way. When someone is ransomed, a price is naturally paid to the conqueror, or in this case a being, who holds him or her in bondage. Hence, if you took this theory and interpreted it literally in all its details, it would seem that the price of man's ransom must be paid to Satan!"

Startled by this, I choked on the sip of coffee I was having. In a moment it all seemed to make sense. In order to atone you had to pay the devil his due! We all have to, in order to save our souls. It was becoming clearer as he continued, I listened as he went on,

"Christ spilled his blood for us in order to pay the devil his price of ransom! God sent Christ to us for that purpose."

It seemed all too simple; Richard would have to pay him a price to be free of his bond! His earlier sins put him, as well as it does all of us, into bondage! I smiled as it now made some semblance of sense. And as he told me, it was simple. I guess my mind had always been so clouded from the teachings of the nuns that I never stopped to think about that aspect of it before.

I quickly finished up my coffee. It was time to find Richard and help him to redeem himself!

"I helped then?" he asked as I stood up to leave.

"Sir, more than you will ever know! Thank you."

I shook his hand as I turned and headed for the door. Back out into the cold I went, more determined now than ever to help Richard and Jacob. All I had to do was find out the cost of his soul! Not the simplest of tasks, but what else did I have to do?

Chapter 19

I arrived back at Richard's residence within the hour. I wasn't sure if he was still inside asleep or not. I waited around a bit until the cold of the morning air forced me to move on. I waited close to two hours and by that time. I was uncomfortable enough to start moving. I suspected he was still sleeping or that maybe had gone to work. Either way, I had some time where I wouldn't have to worry about what he was doing.

I made my way down the street, still tired from the previous evening. My rib had begun to hurt in the cold weather and maybe a cup of coffee would help ease the pain. I made my way to the same coffee shop that Richard and I had been the night before, I sat down in a booth by the back of the restaurant and waited for the waitress to come by to take my order. I ordered a coffee as I just had enough money to pay for that. I suppose it was time for me to go to work again. Maybe later tonight, I would go out and acquire some more funds!

The coffee arrived and the warmth of the cup allowed my hands to start regaining some feeling that I had lost to the cold. At least re-fills were free and I could have a few cups before I went out again.

After about an hour, I had decided that it was time to go out and get some money. I waited until it was dark out and then I stood around waiting for a mark. It didn't take long until I was able to follow an older gentleman who arrived on the street. He was well dressed, and from his look, it would seem that he had money. I followed him for about a block until luck came my way and he turned down an alleyway, probably taking a shortcut towards his destination. Lucky for me, unlucky for him, that he would turn just in the direction that made life easy for me.

I followed until he was halfway down the alley and then as quickly as I could, ran towards him! He was oblivious to me as I quickly approached him from the rear. My fist came down on the back of his neck and he fell to the ground unconscious!

I began to search through his pockets and found his wallet stuffed with twenty-dollar bills! I smiled at my luck as I grabbed the cash from his wallet and stuffed it in my pocket. I looked down at him and on his wrist I noticed an expensive looking wristwatch that would probably fetch me a hundred dollars in a pawnshop. I reached down and took the watch. Then I noticed a gold chain around his neck. The end of it was tucked under his shirt but I figured that while I was here, I might as well take that also.

I reached down and grabbed the chain and pulled it up out of his shirt. The chain broke from around his neck and as I ripped it out, I saw that it had a medallion at the end. I held it up to my eyes and that's when I noticed it! The same medallion that 'he' showed me before! The one that 'he' gives out to the select few! A peace medallion!

I knelt there wondering when to my surprise the man lying in front of me suddenly grabbed my wrist that was holding the chain! I pulled my arm back but to no avail. His grip was like a vise! I pulled and pulled as he held fast, but I couldn't escape!

"Billy," the man's voice calmly called out.

I looked at him and I realized who it was!

"Billy, Billy, Billy," he said again as he shook his head and his grip lessened so I was able to take back my hand, "I figured we needed to meet and well, you needed funds so I thought I'd have a little fun."

"What did I do now?" I asked.

"Nothing… yet!" he answered. "I thought we had an understanding, Billy? Apparently you're having trouble figuring things out, so maybe it's time I spell things out for you."

He rose to his feet and began to dust himself off as he spoke. "I thought by now you'd be able to figure this out on your own. I've shown you so many things but still you can't see it, can you? No, I can tell by the look on your face that it's all too much for you to comprehend. I would have figured you smarter than that, you know. After all this time and all the things we've spoken about, it's never enough, is it?"

He straightened his tie and put out his left hand. I looked at his hand and realized he wanted his trinket back. I handed it back to him and he put it around his neck! The chain had been broken, but there, within a blink of an eye, he had it hanging from his neck once again. "Just a parlor trick, Billy," he said, "Something to amuse the ignorant. But we need to talk about more important issues, namely Richard and what you plan to do."

I knew from his tone that he was trying to tell me something more about Richard. But now I was even more confused! I had thought this was about atoning for Richard's past or future transgressions. "What in the hell was he talking about now?"

"I thought it was all so simple, so simple that even you'd see it," he sighed. "Well then, Billy, I guess it's time to tell you the truth because for some reason, you can't see it as plain as the nose on your face. You look tired Billy. Are you tired?" he asked.

"Tired? Yea, I'm tired! Tired of your bullshit!" I angrily shouted back.

"Angry as well? Well, that's to be expected, I guess," He smirked as he spoke back to me. "What I meant, Billy, was, are you tired, yet? You've been around quite a while, seen and done many things during the years. What's the one thing you've always wanted more than anything else? Rest? Isn't it time to go home?"

I focused on what he was saying as if he was finally granting me my deepest wish! But what exactly was he talking about? Was he asking me if I wanted to die? More than anything I've wanted to leave this shitty existence behind, but never thought I could. Why was he fucking with my mind? I can't die, can I? No, he took that luxury away from me a long time ago! He wanted something, wanted me to do something probably. Why else would he come and see me now? Maybe I was close in figuring out things with Richard? Nothing good ever came from his visits; somehow I was screwing up his plans!

"What the fuck do you want?" I demanded, not wanting to answer his question. There was no point in giving him any satisfaction.

He stepped closer to me and, as if we were friends, put his arm around me. "Billy, my boy. I can make it happen for you. Sleep, beautiful, peaceful sleep! That's what you want isn't it? To find the next stage of life. You know there is one, past this flesh. I couldn't be here if there wasn't," he stated.

He was probably right on that note. It had to be true that there was something past this mortal existence, good or bad; at least it would be different. My mind pondered the idea that I could move on. I had pushed it away so many times, but it was always tucked away somewhere in the back of my mind. I thought about how wonderful it would be. To move on, finally after all these years, after all the heartache, all the hardships, the deaths I witnessed, and so forth.

Then my mind came back to reality and I remembered with whom I was dealing! Never had he done anything that benefited me in the past! He wanted something, something important! Otherwise, he would never make such an offer! He didn't owe me anything and, as I thought about it, I wanted to remain cautious as to why? I shrugged my shoulder so to remove his arm from me.

"Why?" I asked. "Why are you offering this to me. Why now?"

He stepped back a bit and chuckled in that way that he does, slightly menacing and mischievous! "You have trust issues, Billy," he answered. "Sure I know in the past things might not have gone your way, but that doesn't mean you can't trust me." A little smirk came over his face. "I've always given you the truth Billy! You're the one who took what I gave you and misconstrued it. How many times do I have to tell you that the truth is there? It's always there! But it's up to you to see it!"

How I wanted to wipe that smirk from his face. "Yeah, I've seen his 'truth'. I've witnessed his honesty for over a hundred years now! I knew there was going to be a catch. There always is, But I couldn't see any advantage that he would gain for offering me a way out.

"Billy!" his voice sounding a bit sterner this time, "I realize that no matter how much I protest my innocence, you'll probably never trust me. So rather than try to convince you of my true intentions any longer, how about I make you a deal? Rather, how about I reverse the deal we had originally made? You can do with it whatever you like. But I feel that you should realize the stakes involved here. I offer you the peace that you've been longing for all these years. A way out, a chance to pass your flesh back to the earth from where it came, and all it requires is very little effort from you."

I heard him; at least I think I heard him correctly! In a split second the thought ran through my mind! All these years I'd wanted nothing more! But at what cost? What did I have to give him in order for this to happen? I looked back at him and wondered again, "why?"

I spoke finally to ask him, afraid of the answer he would give me. "What do I have to do?"

He looked out to the street and then back at me as if he knew he had me once again. "Nothing, Billy, simply nothing. Reach into your pocket and feel the money I have just given you. Can you feel it, Billy?" I nodded in agreement. It was a large sum of money.

He continued, "Take the money and buy yourself a train ticket back. Go home Billy. Forget about Richard and go on with your life. You can live or die, no longer immortal. The choice is yours. Just turn away and go. It's that simple."

That was all? I had to abandon Richard and go on? I thought about it for a while but I still had to know why Richard was so important to him. Obviously I knew that he was important and that somehow I could hurt his plans in some way. But how? I still needed to know so I pressed him for an answer. "Why do you need Richard?" I asked.

He paused and pulled out a cigar from his jacket and lit it up.

As I awaited my answer he took a long breath from it and as if by magic in one draw turned a quarter of the cigar into ash. He looked back at me with a serious look on his face and spoke, "I love a good cigar! Don't you?, nothing like the smell of the fresh burning leaves rolling in your mouth." He was hesitating again. Was he going to answer me or just talk in riddles again? He took another draw on the cigar and blew the smoke out into the alley. "Again you can't see it, can you? Well, then, for the sake of relieving you of some of the burden you obviously feel, I'll explain it to you. Richard, you see, has been groomed from birth. I watched you all these years, Billy, watched you grow, watched you love, watched you kill! I suppose I'm getting soft in my old age. I've watched you suffer Billy, and I suppose for lack of a better word, feel pity for you. Richard is here for you Billy. I've been watching him as well."

Again his words rang within my head but I still couldn't understand what he meant. "Really Billy," he continued, "do I have to spell it out for you?" He took another breath from the cigar before stamping it out on the pavement. "Fine then!" he shouted, "Richard is being groomed to be your replacement! It's a simple trade. Your soul for his!"

I took a step back finally understanding what he meant. I was shocked! I never saw it coming! I shook my head in disbelief as I continued my journey backwards. I didn't stop until my back hit the wall behind me. Then I felt as if my legs were unable to hold up my body weight and I slid to the ground, still in shock.

He walked up to me and knelt down beside me. He brushed the hair back from my brow and as he did this, I stared at nothing. If he was attempting to comfort me, I still was not able to focus by this point. He leaned in and whispered to me.

"Go home Billy. Enjoy whatever time you have left. Richard is almost ready anyways. He's been slower than you in his education, but he only has a little left to learn. Understand that I'll only ever offer you this choice but once. Take it! You and I both know this is what you want. What you've wanted for a long time. Think about it! You could be with your wives again, your friends. You can be happy, Billy. For once you could be truly happy."

He rose from his knees and stood up again. My mind was all over the place. He turned and left the alley. I could hear him whistle as he walked away. I sat there for a while not moving, not knowing what to do. And as if it had its own mind, my hand reached down into my pocket and took out the money he had given me. My head slowly tilted down and I sat there, staring at the wad of bills, staring at my salvation!

Chapter 20

I had wandered around for a few days, drifting around. The first night, I don't even remember sleeping. I ate when I had to, but that was about it. I had seen Richard by the second day and even spoken with him at his job while I bought a few apples. He was an angry man, like me I suppose.

He left work that night with his jacket that bore the colors of his gang, still missing the patch that would make him a full member. He had told me in the store while he was stocking the shelves that he was almost there, almost a full member. They just had one more thing that he had to do. I asked him what he had to do, but he didn't know himself and I was in my own world at that time anyways, so I was having trouble paying attention.

The brief visit, I guess, wasn't as accidental, as I probably would like to think. I was in turmoil of what to do, and speaking with Richard didn't help anyway. I wanted to help him, truly I did. But how?

Maybe that's why the wooden bench that I was sitting on felt uncomfortably cold and hard. I looked up and wondered when these stations would have better seats for those waiting to board! I had purchased my ticket early in the morning but due to a series of events, the train would not be leaving until late in the evening. I had made my decision, and hopefully I wouldn't live long enough to regret it. As I sat and waited I thought about all those I would see again, how it would end, and an eternity of bliss. My friends, the few I had made, Diana and Mary, would once again be with me. I longed to be able to hold them again, kiss them and love them. Thinking of them, I was finally able to drift off for a moment or two.

It took my mind a few moments to comprehend the voices I heard behind me. Still half asleep I awoke to the argument of two young men accosting a middle aged woman by the corner near the train entrance. My eyes still half closed, I tilted my head over and began to focus on the situation at hand. It took another moment before I recognized the jackets that they were wearing. The same as Richard!

I hadn't seen these two before; they weren't around the first night that I had met the rest of them along with my great-grandson. The woman was holding her purse as the two circled around her, taunting her and berating her! Probably a mugging gone wrong, I figured. Rather than run they decided to have a little sport with her.

I turned back to try and fall asleep again and think about the future, but as usual I was not to have any peace as they escalated their taunting to the point where the woman was becoming more distraught. I looked back and forth and it seemed no one around wanted to interfere. "Human nature at its best once again!"

"Fine!" I said out loud as I stood up and made my way past the benches to the corner where the ruckus was continuing. I surveyed the situation until I was able to ascertain that the boys seemed to have more of a goal in mind than I had originally thought. As I made my way down it seemed that the boys were determined to get this woman's purse regardless of the witnesses. Not that they had much of a concern as most people just looked for a moment or two and then turned and continued on with their pathetic lives. Too many times had I witnessed the apathy of my fellow man. As if nothing else but their own little problems were all that mattered. Even I had some empathy for this woman, and I really never cared about most things. But I suppose I was also getting soft within the last few years. Or maybe it was as simple as I was looking for a fight.

Regardless of the reason I still made my way over to the woman and managed to step between her and the boys.

"What you doing, Man!" one of the youths said. I looked at the two of them acting tough, thinking that they were in charge.

"Just trying to get a little sleep, friend!" was my response. "Seems all the commotion up here woke me up, so I thought I'd see what all the fuss was about."

I motioned to the woman to leave. She grabbed my forearm as she moved behind me, I think in some way to thank me. The boys watched her as she walked towards the front door and disappeared into the crowd.

Well, at least that was done. Now I had to focus my attention back to the boys as I could tell they weren't exactly happy. They moved in closer, their attention changing to me. They got right up to me as if to try and intimidate me. The problem was that I didn't intimidate easily these days. I'd had to deal with assholes like this most of my life and I was getting sick of it! The closer they got the angrier I began to get.

The larger one began to speak.

"Fuck you, man. Why you sticking your nose in where it ain't wanted?" he said as he stuck his index finger in my face.

"Who the hell did this kid think he was? I've gone face to face with the devil and he thinks that he'll scare me?" I smiled as he pushed his finger closer and closer. I believe he was getting angry at my lack of response to his scare tactics.

The other one got in behind his friend and whispered to him that they should go. It seems he was the smarter one between the two. I think he realized that I might be more trouble than it was worth!

"Get the fuck off me, man! You think I'm gonna let this piece of shit fuck with us?" he said to his partner. His friend stepped aside and covered his back, looking around to see if there were any police nearby.

"Why don't you boys go get a soda or something and I'll go back to sleep." I said, "Otherwise this might end badly."

I did want to go back to my seat, I didn't need the attention as there were a few people milling about and watching. Maybe I shouldn't have gotten involved, but now it was too late anyway.

"Fuck you, man! Don't fucking tell us what to do!" he shouted. "You fucking get in here and fuck everything up for us and then you want us to relax and go? Fuck you!"

Apparently I didn't seem to be getting through to this young gentleman. I thought that maybe he would shout a few harsh words and then that would be the end of it. But alas, it seemed he had something to prove. More than likely I insulted his self-esteem or something of that nature.

Regardless, I turned to walk away. Enough of this already! I just wanted to go back and forget Boston all together! As I turned to go back to my seat, I heard the other man shout, "Shit!"

I felt a piercing burning come from my side just underneath my ribs! I felt with my hand and noticed it was wet with blood!

I turned back and saw the young man holding what appeared to be a small knife and that's when I realized that he had stabbed me in the back! It hurt like hell and the blood was already falling to the floor! The pain diminished, as I grew more and more angry by the second! I didn't care that there were several people around, I grabbed the boy's hand that held the knife and we struggled for a few seconds until I heard the knife fall to the floor!

I grabbed the boy closer to me and our faces were within an inch of each other as I smiled at him and began to laugh. The other boy backed up more and more as if they had just seen the devil himself!

As the blood left my body it was replaced with an overwhelming need to do harm to this boy! I let go of his jacket and grabbed his face, one hand on either cheek. I smiled again, and by now I could see the expression on the young lad change as he finally realized that he should have walked away! My arms twisted and I heard the crack as his body went limp and his eyes rolled back into his skull exposing nothing but the white! I let go and he fell hard.

I heard screams from the people around me but I no longer cared. The other boy stood a few steps away from me but was also too frightened to move. I took a step closer, the rage all but consuming me now. As I did he finally was able to gather his wits and turned to run. He made it to the exit door and down the street.

I was right behind him, my side no longer hurting as I ran as fast as I could! He ran faster and faster, every once in a while turning his head to see if I was in pursuit! I managed to catch him within a couple of blocks and tackled him into a newsstand that was on the corner!

Papers flew about as I turned him over and straddled his chest! I grabbed him by the collar and began bringing my fist down on his face.

"Wait! Wait!" he pleaded, his face already covered in blood, "Please, mister."

My hands came to a stop as I looked about. People were standing about and I began to hear the calls for police. I looked down to see the boy covering his face with his hands, whimpering as he lay there. I was breathing hard trying to catch my breath when I looked down and noticed that with all the mess of the papers my train ticket lay on his chest. It somehow had slipped out of my pocket when I tackled him. I grabbed it and stood up.

I heard the sounds of the police sirens approaching and gathered that I'd best leave the area as soon as possible. Getting arrested didn't seem like the best of ideas right now! With my ticket in hand I took off down the street until I couldn't hear the sirens anymore. I ran for blocks until I felt it was safe to stop. I rested in a familiar place to me, an alleyway. I sat down on the cold pavement and caught my breath as I rested.

My side hurt a bit and blood was still coming out of the wound! It seemed that I had by this time lost a bit of blood as I looked down at my hands to see that they had already turned color. My skin was pale and I was becoming increasingly cold! My breathing had also changed as my breaths became smaller and smaller in length! I knew I had to stop the blood from leaving my side and here in this alley there didn't seem to be anything that could help me!

I scoured through the trashcans, looking for a towel or anything that may benefit me. I eventually found an old oily rag from the can of a restaurant! I slowly lifted up my cloak, and with little else around, I grabbed the dirty cloth and held it tight against my side. The pressure caused the wound to flame up once again and I nearly fainted from the pain. My face contorted as I held fast and kept the pressure on hoping that the feeling would subside in another moment or two! I began to drool as well as I held the cloth close to the opening. Every time this happens I always wonder when it would end. If this would be the last time I would have to endure the pain! I slowly sank down to the ground as my legs had started to become numb already. I sat there panting like a dog, hiding in a darkened corner like a rat, wondering how I would get out of here now. It was obvious that the police would be looking for me. There had been too many witnesses. So I knew my train ticket was now useless. How would I leave now? I wondered over and over until finally my head began to spin from the loss of blood and I slumped to the ground losing consciousness once again.

The moon was high when I came to once again. I lifted my head and cursed the stars that I still lived! All that would change soon, once I went home. I put my hand down onto the concrete and slowly raised myself until I sat upright. There was still pain but not as bad as before. I winced a bit as I straightened out, my breathing seemed to be a bit fuller now and my skin seemed to start retaining some color once again. I thought that I had started generating new fluids once again.

I felt down at my side and noticed that the cloth had clotted itself to the wound and was stuck to my side. Upon closer examination I could see that there was still a small point of the wound that was releasing blood. I suppose the cloth had helped but being as unsanitary as it was, probably could not help contain the entire wound. I would have to take it easy, lest I re-open my wound again. Now it was time to figure out how to get back home.

Home! That was the plan wasn't it? Go home and forget about this cursed city! But now, with all that happened earlier in the day, everything had changed. There were too many witnesses that saw me at the station and I'm sure a description of me was being handed out to every police officer in the city. I started thinking over my options and the only thing that came to mind was that I should find a place to lay low for a while and try and leave the city by bus or something in the morning. The train station was obviously too hot to even consider entering now. Police were more than likely all over the place searching for clues or evidence to the killing! No, it was best to wait until the early morning and hope that the bus stations would have slower business, not as many people as the train station, and with one or two switches, I could be back in New York within a few days! But for now all I wanted was to get out of this cursed cold and have something warm to eat.

I slowly stood up as to not tear open the wound again and proceeded to turn to the street. The moonlight glinted off the pavement from where I lay and I could see the stain of all the blood that had left me while I slept. It was dry now and dark in color, as if someone had butchered a pig or two. I shook my head and made my way too the street, I pulled up my collar and began to search for somewhere to get a bowl of soup, something to take the sting of the night's chill from my bones.

I kept a low profile as I walked the streets in search of food and shelter. I stayed near the shadows and only crossed the streets when I knew that it was absolutely safe. I found a seedy looking bar on the East side that I hoped would also serve a bit of food. I entered and made my way to the back where it was darker and quiet. I ordered a scotch and a bowl of soup and then I sat and waited for both to arrive.

Still cold, I rubbed my hands together to help keep them warm. I noticed that they were covered in dried blood and I probably should clean myself up before anyone noticed. I got up, grabbed the cloth napkin that the waitress had put on the table, and slowly made my way to the bathroom in order to clean up. The cloth stuck to my side could probably be changed and the napkin would do nicely!

I made my way over to the sink and turned on the water. The hot wasn't that hot but at least it would help. I rinsed my hand under the tap for a few minutes trying to get all the stains from my hands. The white porcelain sink turned pinkish in color as the water swirled down the drain. There was no soap so all I could do was keep rubbing until most of it was off.

With my hands somewhat clean, I stood up and pulled back my coat to see if I could change the cloth without rupturing the wound once again! It was still bleeding and as I looked back to the door of the bathroom, I could see tiny drops of blood that were still escaping! I looked in the mirror and slowly pulled the dry cloth away from my skin and clothes, being very careful not to agitate it further. It took a few moments of slow pulling but it eventually came off. I lifted up my stained shirt and attempted to wash a little of the dry blood away. The area was both wet and dry as I was still bleeding near the bottom of the wound. The tear ran a good inch or two and was jagged in nature. Stitches would probably have done me well, but that was not to be! I threw the old cloth into the garbage can and held the clean napkin against my side. I pulled my shirt down and stuffed it into my pants hoping to hold the new napkin in place. I turned and made my way back too my seat, hoping that the soup had arrived.

When I arrived back at my seat I saw the steaming bowl of soup waiting for me along with my drink! Hoping the alcohol would take some of the sting away, I picked up the glass and drank it all in one swig. It helped! At the very least I felt a bit warmer for the moment.

I dove into the soup with a bit of aggression. It tasted fine, better than I'd had had in a while. They had also brought a piece of bread that I dipped into the broth. I was about halfway through the soup when I decided to take a break. I didn't want to eat everything in a hurry. I had time to kill before I would try to leave in the morning and the soup was a nice distraction.

I ordered another scotch and sank back a little into my seat. I began to close my eyes a bit in order to relax. But as usual, the two gentlemen sitting in the next booth were drunk and talking loud enough to wake the dead. I opened my eyes and straightened myself out; I figured I wouldn't get any rest until they were gone!

I put my hand to my side and felt to make sure the napkin was still in place. Still there! It was holding. I pulled my hand back up to have some more soup and slightly brushed my pocket. I felt something in there. I reached in and pulled out a piece of paper. It was slightly covered in blood. I had forgotten that I had grabbed my train ticket from the chest of the young lad earlier that day. It must have been when I was running away that I put it in my pocket.

"Useless now," I thought, as I threw it down on the seat beside me. I picked up the spoon and took another sip of soup before I realized that maybe leaving that ticket here wouldn't be the best of ideas. Why leave any evidence that could say I was here? Covered in blood it would raise some suspicion as to the owner and then it wouldn't take much for the police to put two and two together.

I picked it up again and that's when I noticed there was another piece of paper stuck to the underside. The blood had permeated both pieces of paper and I suppose that when I took it off his chest, I had inadvertently grabbed a piece from him as well. No matter, I thought as I examined it. It only had an address on it anyway, nothing important.

I put it back in my pocket and continued to devour the soup. The bread was all but gone by now, but the soup itself was still warm enough to be enjoyed. I sat there and ate as I listened to these two idiots behind me keep talking up a storm. I turned my head slightly over the booth seat as if to give them a hint that they were too loud. That's when I noticed they were wearing the same colors as that of the two gentlemen from this morning and that of Richard. The same gang!

I turned slowly and began to listen, as I was able to make out that they were drinking to their friend who had died this morning! I chuckled as I wondered what they would do if they knew that the man who killed their friend was sitting right behind them? They were posturing and talking that if they ever found the guy how they would go about killing him. Same mentality with gangs, they all seem to share one brain, as if they couldn't have just one coherent thought on their own!

I smiled and went back to my soup as they continued. Drunk as they were, I suppose they had some loyalty to their fallen comrade. If anything I could respect that. My soup nearly gone now, and the only entertainment being these two behind me, I decided to take my leave and slowly slid over to the end of the booth.

That's when I heard them start discussing something else. Almost out of the booth, I slid back in and began to listen a little more intently! I overheard them as they were discussing the evening's activities. I thought I heard Richard's name mentioned! It was enough to pique my interest and wonder if it wouldn't be prudent of me to listen a bit longer before leaving. It was hard to make out what exactly they were saying in between the noise from the other patrons and the television set that was at the bar, but I think I got most of it!

It seemed there was a job happening that night, one in which Richard was going to finally prove himself worthy to the gang. They never mentioned where though, and I wondered what exactly the job entailed. It seemed to involve another rival gang member and money, of course. But what was it? A robbery, a mugging, what I wondered? The voices started to fade and I turned to notice the men leaving! I quickly shuffled out of the booth and followed them. I still wondered what part Richard played in all this.

They exited the bar and I wasn't far behind them. Close enough to hear their conversation, but far enough so that I wouldn't draw attention to myself. As they walked down the street I began to decipher what they were actually discussing. It seemed the job consisted of a couple of them, Richard and another lad, breaking in to the home of this individual and stealing what they could. Sounded simple enough! Something I was rather good at! It was the next thing I heard that chilled my bones. Entrance into the gang it seems, involves killing!

Now it all started to make sense! Why I was to leave before the night was through. He said Richard wasn't ready yet! This would have been the one thing that could push Richards immortal soul beyond reach! I knew it; I knew there was some reason that he wanted me to leave! Richard was to commit murder and for some reason he wanted me long gone. I stopped cold on the sidewalk and watched the other two gentlemen stagger off.

I stood there for a moment wondering why I had followed them in the first place! What was I thinking? Why didn't I just sit there and eat my soup in peace? Wasn't it enough that I had suffered so much already? Now it seemed I would suffer again, even with my end coming soon. I would never rest in peace it seemed, after everything and his promise to me. He would make me suffer until the end. I couldn't take it anymore and right there on the sidewalk I began to sob!

What about Jacob? How would he survive this? He had already lost his son and with this latest turn of events he would also lose his grandson, but in a more turbulent manner! Dealing with death was easy in comparison to what he had planned for Richard. Eternity in his service, like me, Richard would suffer!

As I stood there on the sidewalk crying, I thought of how it would affect Jacob and the rest of his family to know that his grandson was a cold-blooded killer. It killed me to think about it. I stood there for a few moments and then I heard the sirens of the police cruiser come up the street behind me. It was enough to snap me out of it and to start moving back into the shadows. I didn't think they were looking for me, but also I didn't want to be out in the open, just in case. I walked towards the corner and ducked into a darkened yard waiting for the cruiser to pass. Once it did I made my way onto the street and turned in the direction of the bus depot. I needed to go home now. Home to die!

I made it down to the bus depot and waited in the dark rather than inside. I looked down at my clothes and noticed that my attire might raise some concerns with the locals! My coat was stained with dry darkened blood and was gashed in the side from the knife. In the dark it was passable but in the light of the terminal it could cause me problems.

I continued to wait outside until I was able to procure another coat! At least one thing was going right this night as I spied a gentleman, obviously homeless, searching for food in a dumpster. We seemed to be about the same size and his coat, while not nearly as nice as mine, would afford me the luxury of passing through with little fanfare.

I approached the man and presented in my hand a twenty-dollar bill! It wouldn't do me much good to rid him of his pain, here and now. The last thing I wanted to do was draw attention to this area as well! After a few moments of talking the man traded his coat for mine, though it cost me another twenty! A small price to pay if I was able to make it out of here without incident.

I left the man as he continued to search the garbage cans. I put on the jacket, which smelled a bit foul and made my way into the terminal and up to the wicket to purchase a ticket to take me home. There were two people in line and no police seemed to be present as I looked around.

I waited as the first woman paid for her ticket and left the line. We moved up a couple of feet and again I waited for the gentleman in front of me to finish his transaction. As I waited I started to relax a bit, as it was clear the end of this hellish trip was almost over. A few more minutes and I would have my ticket and hopefully I could leave as soon as possible.

I began to think of Diana and Mary, my first-born, and even my friend, Jack. How wonderful it would be to be re-united with them once again. Once I went home I would be mortal and I assumed it would be up to me when to make the decision to end my wretched life! A chance to finally be at peace, only one chance!

I stepped up to the wicket as soon as the gentleman before me was finished and I began to purchase my ticket to New York when I heard a noise behind me and a tug at my jacket. It turned to see the man that I had traded my jacket with earlier standing behind me clutching something in his hand.

" 'scuse me Sir, I found this in the pocket and figured you may need it."

His hand extended to pass me the bloody ticket and the piece of paper! Instinctively I grabbed it and looked down. The ticket still visible through the darkened dry blood that had soaked it earlier. Still attached was the other piece of paper with the address on it! Looking about, as I was sure that we were starting to draw attention, I stuffed both in the pocket of my new coat.

"Thanks, man," I said as I turned back to the wicket.

He tugged again at my coat and began to ask for a reward for bringing it back. I tried to ignore him as I continued to purchase my ticket, but he kept getting louder and louder. His actions caused people to stop and start staring at us. Again I looked about and figured it would be in my best interest to pay him something.

I turned and handed him a five and when I did so in the corner of my eye I noticed that he had already garnered the attention of a police officer that by this time was walking over towards us!

"Shit!" I said as I hurriedly handed him the money and made my way out towards the crowd so that hopefully I could get lost within its folds. I watched as I moved outwards that the officer had stopped at the homeless man and was asking him questions. Within a minute he looked at the coat and grabbed the fabric. The next thing I knew he was grabbing the man and blowing his whistle for backup!

I kept moving, faster now, toward the exit door and back out to the street! Apparently the bus was out now as well! It would only be a matter of time till the police questioned the man and would figure out that he wasn't the killer, but had gotten the jacket from the real killer.

"Fuck!" I blurted out into the night air. "What the hell was going on? All I wanted to do was leave but for some reason it began to seem impossible to do this one simple task!" I walked down the street and put my hands in my pockets, as it was chilly. Of course I once again touched the ticket. I pulled it out and threw it to the ground! I took another four or five steps and then stopped. "Why?" I began to think. "Why was it so hard?"

I turned and looked back at the ticket that lay on the ground. It was as if fate had a hand in this all along. The guilt had been eating away at me since I had made the decision to abandon my family. I had been nauseous all day and that damn ticket kept showing up to remind me of my failings! Then the wind blew it over and stuck to the other side was the piece of paper. No…upon closer examination I realized it wasn't the ticket, but the other piece of paper that accompanied it! Maybe there was a reason I couldn't seem to leave.

I stood there and thought about how he wanted so much for me to leave that night. I had to trade Richards's soul for mine. But yet he made it seem that I had no choice! "Was he scared that I could screw with his plan?" Maybe, maybe not! But it seemed possible the more I thought about it.

In the back of my mind, I think I always knew I had a choice. Maybe this was my chance to pay him back for all the years of agony I had suffered. I wanted death more than anything else, but maybe it would be worth it to finally thwart his plans! I hated him more than anything else in my life, so it might be worth an eternity here knowing that at least once I was able to do something that he couldn't control! Jacob would be happy as well and Richard wouldn't have to suffer as I had!

I kept looking at the piece of paper on the ground now fully knowing that I wasn't going home! I would give up all I wanted in order to help save Richards soul. The die had been cast! My eyes focused now rather than staring into space. I walked up and grabbed up the paper. On it was an address. If I was correct and fate was playing me, this would be the address to where Richard was going tonight! Somehow I knew that I could change his fate though it would condemn me to an eternity of hell! It was worth it! I turned and hailed a cab, hoping that I would still be able to make it in time!

Chapter 21

I stopped a few blocks from the address and I figured I'd walk the rest of the way. I wondered if the cab driver had noticed me or not. He looked at me a few times in the rear view mirror. I hoped that the police hadn't issued a sketch yet! It could very well be, as I hadn't seen the news that day. Walking though, would draw less attention to the house and myself.

It was late by now, possibly around one thirty in the morning, and apparent that no one was here yet and that whoever was in the house was fast asleep. I walked around the block and waited for anything out of the ordinary. It was about thirty minutes later when in the still of the night I heard the distinctive sound of a dog barking. I was at the other end of the block and I had a feeling that the boys were in the process of sneaking into the house! I hurried back but it took me a couple of minutes to arrive at the house.

"I knew it, I was right! I knew that this was the place that Richard was going to be tonight," I thought as I ran back towards the house.

By the time I got there, no one was around. There were some footprints in the snow that led around to the side window of the house. I looked at the window and noticed that it had been pried open! The locks on these windows have very little strength and a large screwdriver is all that's needed to open them!

I slowly raised the window a bit more and jumped onto the sill. My side burned a bit as my stomach balanced on the sill, half of my body in the warmth of the house and the other half still dangling outside.

Quietly I pulled myself inside and silently fell to the floor. I touched my side and realized that my wound had re-opened once again and I was bleeding more rapidly now. The pain returned once again and I held my side as I held back the pain and the blood and moved towards the hallway. All was quiet in the house but I was able to make out a squeak or two from the floorboards as Richard and his accomplice moved about. I guess stealth didn't run in the family.

I heard them upstairs by now and I made my way down the hall and to the bottom of the stairs. Still quiet, I made my way up the stairs, one step at a time! I still didn't have a plan but I knew somehow I would have to stop Richard from doing what he thought he needed to do.

About three steps from the top I stopped as I saw the glint of light from a flashlight make its way back! The erratic behavior of the light told me that I was dealing with amateurs.

"Damn!" I thought. "Flashlights? Why not rent a sign or hire a news crew to tell what they were doing? "My sarcasm started to come through again as I thought about it." But they'll wake up the whole house like this.

I needed to get him out of here and in a hurry! I knew they were looking for someone in here, a gang member. Killing is never easy at first and maybe their inexperience would assist me by giving me some more time. I would have been out of here by now, but these two had no idea what they were doing.

In the distance I heard the dog still barking and I heard the wind as it blew against the house. The light now had turned away and again I made my way up the rest of the stairs. When I got to the top I had seen them finally switch the light off. They were both standing by a bedroom door getting ready to enter. I figured they had found their prey and were mere seconds away from doing the one thing that would never allow them to turn back!

I panicked! I ran, no longer caring about the noise. The first boy opened the door as I made my way down the hall! Richard right behind him turned my way when my hip accidentally hit the table in the hall and caused the lamp to fall to the floor with a crash! He raised his weapon my way. He probably didn't know who it was in the dark! Then I heard a shot scream out and break the silence of the night! For a moment I thought that Richard had shot me!

Richard stood there transfixed, as I saw the first boy come flying back out the room. The shot had come from inside the room, the noise I made had awoken their intended target and now it seemed the tables were being turned.

Richard turned as his friend pushed back into him. Richard caught him in his arms as the force of the gunshot carried them both back into the hallway. In the moonlight I could see the young boy was obviously dead! The bullet had taken half his face away and he lay slumped and bloody in Richards's arms. Richard staggered back and fell to the floor holding his hands up that were now covered in blood and his eyes as wide as a deer.

I heard movement come from the bedroom as I figured the man inside had now gotten out of bed to finish the job. I ran faster towards Richard. "He couldn't die! I couldn't be responsible for his death, could I?" No! I ran harder, "he" wouldn't win! Not like this, not this time!

Richard was still staring at his blood soaked friend, his revolver now on the floor beside him. My heart was pumping harder now as I raced to pick it up! My side was hurting more and more as I knew that the wound had opened more!

I dove for the gun and picked it up with my left hand. I saw the other man as he stood in the doorway. I was right handed and I had too sit up in order to get a clear shot! I sat between Richard and the man and as quick as I could, changed the position of the gun to my other hand. That's when I heard the second shot ring out. I took my shot as well and saw the man stagger back into the room before falling to the floor!

I lowered the gun and that's when I felt the pain in my chest! I looked down and watched as the blood escaped from my chest! I had trouble breathing and as I watched the blood ebb its way out, I noticed bubbles come from it. My lung had been hit. It must have lodged somewhere in there and it felt as if my lung was collapsing! I sat there for a moment and then I heard the sounds of police sirens in the distance.

It was time to leave and in a hurry. I turned to Richard who was still sitting there, his eyes still focused on his dead friend. He had begun to cry, as I'm sure that he was terrified. I picked up his chin and looked him straight in the eye.

"Richard! Pay attention!" I screamed, trying to focus his attention on the situation at hand. There was no reaction, as I called him again. Finally, with my other hand, I slapped him across the cheek and he looked up at me. It was in that moment when he recognized me and said in his confused state, "You? Why are you here?"

I didn't have time to explain. The sirens were getting closer and closer and we needed to move! "We need to go!" I shouted. "Now!" Richard's eyes began to focus again as he began to realize the situation. He stood up and gave me his hand as I was having a little bit of trouble on my own. He looked down and against the moonlight saw the crimson covered shirt I was now wearing. Again confused he looked back up at me.

"It's not that bad" I said as I closed my coat, "Let's get the hell out of here!" I pushed him towards the stairwell.

We both ran down as quickly as we could. Richard took the stairs two at a time and I was barely able to catch up from the pain. I made it to the window and I saw that Richard was already outside. He waited for me and I climbed up the sill but the pain was too great! I looked back at him and smiled. He was nervous, jumping slightly as he kept telling me to come. The sirens were closing fast and I looked at Richard and put my hand on his cheek. My son, my great-grandson could still be safe. I knew that in my condition I would only hold him back.

"Go!" I screamed. "Go home and forget this night ever happened!"

He looked at me and in an instant he knew that I wouldn't make it. He hesitated as if he wanted to stay, but then he stopped shaking and looked at me almost calmly and said, "Thank you." Then he turned and ran.

I watched him as he scurried through the back yard. He was almost out of sight when I saw him take off his jacket and throw it to the ground! I laughed and smiled knowing that I had finally beaten 'him'. At least my efforts had naught been in vain!

The sirens were closing around the house and lights were being turned on from the surrounding houses in every direction as I figured the police were finally here. I turned back when Richard was gone from view and slumped against the wall. A revolver in my hand with only five shots left. The police had me surrounded and for the first time in my life I knew there was no escape! I would be captured and then what? Spend eternity in jail? What would happen after fifty or so years? Would they be able to explain or even understand who I was? I wouldn't age and they would see that! Would I become an oddity or something even worse for their amusement? I gathered my thoughts once again and decided that I would have to at least try to escape.

"Push the pain down!" I told myself. "Push it and find a way out of here."

I stood straight again and looked to the front door. The lights from the squad cars filtered through the windows and filled the main floor. I knew I wouldn't make it that way. I turned towards the stairs to climb back up and as I did, I heard the rattling from the front door as the police were trying to enter the house. I fired a shot at the door and the noises ceased as they withdrew back to a safe distance. I turned back to the stairs and made my way up still trying in vain to push the pain away.

By the time I made it back up, I could tell that I had lost a lot of blood by now. My chest almost entirely collapsed on my left side as the breathing became more and more difficult. I staggered down the hallway and into the bedroom of the dead man. I needed to see what I was up against.

I looked over to the bedroom window and slid up against the side. I lifted back the curtains and moved to see the situation outside. There were police cars everywhere! It seemed like utter confusion as some were trying to hold back the neighbors that had come out of their houses to see what was happening, while others were focused on the front of the house, guns drawn by now. I could see that it would be next to impossible to make my way out of here! Only four shots left and thirty or so policemen! I lowered the curtain and then my right leg gave way and I tripped slightly.

Then I heard the shot! I had stumbled right into the front of the window. I turned and I saw a policeman sitting on the roof of the house next door. The bullet seemed to travel in slow motion as it came towards me. I could see it as it traveled the short distance from his gun towards the window. I could never move in time! The bullet hit the glass of the window and then I heard the most awful sound as it hit my stomach and exited through my back. The force of it twirled me around and I heard the crunch as if someone had broken a stick between his knees!

I fell hard this time. My body limp as I hit the wall and landed on my ass! I was sitting underneath the window now. The pain seemed less excruciating as I sat there and tried to catch my breath. I held the revolver up over my head and attempted to aim it across the street. I took two or three wild shots and then slumped back down. At least they would know that I was still alive and still dangerous. It would buy me a little time in order to find an escape route!

I looked down and my legs were covered in blood. I tried to stand or at least move away from the window but I couldn't! I tried to move my legs but they were limp now almost dead. I laughed at the irony. It seems the officer who shot me had hit me in the one place that would prevent me from going anywhere. The sound I had heard when he shot me was the sound of my spine shattering! The bullet had passed through my backbone and now I was paralyzed from the waist down. There would be no escaping unless I could crawl very fast!

I sat there and laughed harder and harder, knowing full well that I would be captured now. I looked over to the man slumped on the floor in front of me and cursed his luck that he was already dead! One bullet left as I looked down at my hand that held the revolver, not even good enough to help me now. I sat there chuckling as I stared straight ahead awaiting my fate. It would be a matter of moments before the police would enter and take me away. At least I knew Richard was to be safe. Jacob wouldn't have to suffer. There was some consolation in that. I would live with my fate; eternity wouldn't be so lonely now!

I sat there waiting when I noticed that the noises had stopped! The sirens, the yelling had all stopped. I listened closer and I heard nothing! Even the sound of the traffic in the distance had stopped. It was dead calm. I looked back and forth and wondered what was happening. I turned my head back and that's when I noticed the dead man in front of me was sitting up! "What the fuck??" I thought.

His eyes began to open and he looked over at me, grinning from ear to ear. I knew that smile, I recognized it instantly! The man in front of me was dead, but he wasn't. He had come to gloat once again. I watched him as he stood up and made his way over too me. He leaned down and kissed me on the forehead?

"Evening, Billy," he said, "How are things going?"

I looked up not even acknowledging his sarcasm.

"Well, you really did it this time, didn't you?" he asked.

I smiled back at him knowing full well that he wouldn't have Richard.

"It was so easy Billy, all you had to do was go home and you would have been free." he stated, "Why Billy, why did you do this?"

Again I smiled as I looked upon him! He put his hand on my head and smiled back at me. He looked towards the door and I turned to follow his eyes.

We waited as if he was expecting something to happen and then I heard the scurrying of tiny footsteps just beyond the door. The next thing I knew a small dog came into the room and ran directly towards me and lay in my lap. He looked down and I wondered what the hell was going on. I looked down at the little puppy that lay in my lap and as I did, it started to dawn on me that I had seen this dog before! No, it couldn't be! I looked back up at him and he nodded his head in agreement. I looked down again and I knew that the dog sleeping in my lap was the same one I had found all those years before! I looked back up to him and asked,

"Why?" He took a moment as he watched the puppy sleep in my lap and then sat down in front of me.

"Look at me, Billy," he said.

I looked, wondering what he wanted.

"No, Billy. Really look. For so long I've wanted you too see the truth but you never have until today."

What was he talking about? I looked closer. I stared at his face then I began to stare into his eyes. Bloodshot and red they were, as if looking into hell itself!

"Keep looking, Billy" he muttered and I continued to look. I stared harder and harder until I began too notice a change! His eyes! His eyes were changing! They began to clear from the blood and I felt the evil started too disappear as I peered into them. Was this another of his tricks?

"No, William, this is no trick," he said as if he could read my thoughts.

I kept staring as I began too see beyond his eyes. The red all gone now was replaced by the deepest hue of blue I had ever seen! It was as if I could see past his eyes and into something much deeper. I couldn't explain but I began to feel at peace, as if everything would be all right. I blinked for a second as if my eyes were playing tricks on me and I was then able to look at his face.

His face was different. It was still the same man that I had shot before, but now it seemed different! As if there was no evil left in him! As if he had transformed.

"There William, now do you see?" he asked.

I shook my head; I still didn't understand what was going on.

"The truth William, you can finally see the truth. After all these years you have finally done it." he stated.

Again confused, I wondered what he meant.

"The truth, William. It was always in front of you but you never took the time to figure it out. I have always been there for you, but it was you who needed to see. So much hatred has always clouded your judgment." he said.

Nothing made sense anymore; the feeling of peace I felt, the pain in my body was gone. What was going on? Who was he? I wondered. Then it hit me!

"Lord?" I asked almost hesitant not knowing or even wanting to know.

He smiled, "The truth, William. For once you have seen the truth!" he answered. He spoke and I heard him. Was this just some more cruel taunting? Was I in shock, maybe in denial? He leaned over and kissed me on my forehead once again. When he did so, I relaxed even more. The revelation hit me like a ton of bricks! He was God! I didn't understand.

He began to speak, and as he did, he started to answer all my questions, "William, my son. I know you're having trouble understanding. But it had to be this way. All your pain, all your suffering served me well. It's difficult to explain but I'll do my best." he said comfortingly.

He put his hand on my head and I began to see, see throughout the ages in my mind. Pictures flashed before me at a mind-numbing rate. Image after image began to tell me what I wanted to know. He never spoke as he bestowed his wisdom upon me. I understood! I understood why. Finally after all this time I knew the truth, the whole truth! It made sense now; all the doubts I'd ever had were gone! He showed me heaven in all its glory! I now understood that there were seven of them, all different in some way, all in the care of angels.

First was Shamayim, governed by Archangel Gabriel, the closest of heavenly realms to the Earth. Second came Raquia, then Shehaqim, the third Heaven, under the leadership of Anahel, which serves as the home of the Garden of Eden and the Tree of Life. Then there was Machonon, Machon and Zebul! Araboth was the final heaven under the leadership of Cassiel, the holiest of the seven Heavens in that it houses the Throne of Glory attended by the Seven Archangels and serves as the realm in which God dwells.

Shehaqim, the third Heaven was the one that answered all my questions. The northern region of this heaven has a river of flame that flows through the land of cold and ice. Here the wicked are punished by the angels. The southern lands are a bountiful paradise, where the souls of the righteous will come after death. Two rivers, the river of milk and honey and the river of wine and oil flow here. This heaven is where the "Tree of Life" can be found.

The beautiful celestial garden is where all perfect souls go after death and is guarded by three hundred angels of light. It was also recorded that the entrance to this Heaven is a gate of gold. Heaven and hell both reside here! It made sense to me now. Both heaven and Hell, God and Satan! Each was unique but still were one! Two sides of the same coin! I looked back to him and asked him, "why, why" he would let us suffer like this when he had the choice.

He looked down on me and said, "You were given a choice, a choice to see what you wanted to see. All man has been given a choice, a path to follow. We are one and in a way different. Man must always choose his own path to help maintain the balance."

"Balance?" I asked.

"Yes, William. There is a balance that must be followed. We both live in the same realm from time to time. If the balance is upset then the end is close at hand," he answered.

I nodded, as it seemed clear to me now, except that is for one thing. "Why me? Why have I suffered for so long?" I asked. Tears began to well in my eyes.

He stroked my cheek, wiping the tear as it fell and answered, "William, you have been the balance!"

I was confused at his statement but he continued.

"Man has the opportunity to choose his own path, to decide his fate. But, in order to maintain some stability I have to choose one every two thousand years. You were chosen, William, chosen to preserve the balance."

The tears streamed down my cheek as I still wondered.

"I've told you many times William, every soul has a role to play. You were chosen from all the souls to help in allowing mankind to grow! Every thought, every action was by your choice. I led you to the roads but it was you that decided which path to take. Now it seems you have finally taken the right path!" he said.

Even though I understood some of it now, I began to wonder if I knew the whole truth.

"Am I…" I started to ask.

He smiled and nodded. "You suffered, William, so that mankind didn't have to," he answered. "You always knew you were different, didn't you? You were always searching for something, wondering why you were more special than the rest. I expected you to figure it out long ago. The clues have always been there, but you never opened your eyes long enough to see. All your pain, all your heartache was needed. Mankind needs to save it from itself from time to time. You are my second... my son."

A tear flowed from my eye, as I finally understood all the suffering in my life. I looked down at my dead legs, the puppy still in my lap. I wondered what was next. The noise from the sirens had now started to fade back and I looked towards him once again as he began to stand up. He started to walk back to the doorway where he had originally risen. He turned and said, "The choice is now yours again, William. I give that to you as a final gift, a final gesture! Saving Richard was the one thing you did right. When you made that decision you gave yourself the right! The right to do whatever it is you need. Live William, or not. Either way the choice is once again yours! I will love you either way."

He lay down again and rested his head back onto the floor. I called out but I knew he had gone! I looked down and the puppy was gone! I heard the sounds of footsteps as the police entered the house. I raised my hand. I looked at the revolver, which still held one bullet. The footsteps came closer and closer! I raised the gun to the side of my head.

The first officer entered the room just as I pulled the trigger! I heard the shot but it seems I was to be fooled again. The officer looked at me and began to throw up! I suppose it wasn't that pleasant a sight! He ran from the room and I sat there still looking forward. I chuckled, as I knew it seemed too easy.

That's when I heard more footsteps coming. My eyes focused on the shadow in the door. It was hard to see but it seemed to be the figure of a woman. I looked harder as the woman made her way into the room. Then I saw her! The moonlight hit her just right and I saw her! Dear lord she was beautiful! As beautiful as the day I had married her. She beckoned me to come with her and it was then that I realized that he had not lied! He had given me the choice I so desperately wanted. My legs, no longer dead, lifted me from the floor. I took two steps forward and then turned back to see myself lying still on the floor!

I smiled and turned back to Diana and made my way over to her. Her arms outstretched welcomed me back home. I ran to her and hugged her with all my might. The pain was gone, the resentment, everything left behind in the vessel that lay on the floor. I looked at Diana and said to her, "Come. Let's go home." She smiled, kissed me on the cheek and we both turned. It was time to go home!

Made in the USA
Charleston, SC
16 May 2011